T0375019

OVID

III

LCL 42

OVID

METAMORPHOSES
BOOKS 1–8

WITH AN ENGLISH TRANSLATION BY

FRANK JUSTUS MILLER

REVISED BY G. P. GOOLD

HARVARD UNIVERSITY PRESS
CAMBRIDGE, MASSACHUSETTS
LONDON, ENGLAND

First published 1916
Second Edition 1921
Third Edition 1977

LOEB CLASSICAL LIBRARY® is a registered trademark
of the President and Fellows of Harvard College

ISBN 978-0-674-99046-3

Printed on acid-free paper and bound by
The Maple-Vail Book Manufacturing Group

CONTENTS

PREFACE TO THE THIRD EDITION   vii
INTRODUCTION   ix
BIBLIOGRAPHY   xv

METAMORPHOSES

   Book I   1
   Book II   59
   Book III   123
   Book IV   177
   Book V   237
   Book VI   287
   Book VII   341
   Book VIII   405

PREFACE TO THE THIRD EDITION

THIS volume of the Loeb Ovid originally appeared in 1916, and a second edition (so styled, though without change) was issued in 1921. The work was reprinted many times and reset in 1960, some (though not all) of the errors then imported being corrected in the impression of 1971, when a few items were added to the bibliography. Although the time is not yet ripe for a complete revision (critical editions by William S. Anderson for the Bibliotheca Teubneriana and R. J. Tarrant for the Oxford Classical Texts having been announced), there was much which in the light of recent scholarship called for amendment. This edition, therefore, follows the principles of my revision of the Loeb *Heroides and Amores*: I have everywhere sought to present the best Latin text and accommodated the English translation to it, but I have otherwise disturbed the original edition as little as possible.

A few details call for comment. Considerations of economy have enforced adherence to the old pagination and consequently not permitted the introduction of critical notes; I have for the same reason refrained from switching to a fuller system of punctuation and from standardizing orthography,

PREFACE

particularly desirable in the case of non-assimilated compounds and the accusative plurals of *i*-stems (incorrect spellings, however, like *cygnus* and *Erechtheus*, have been banished). One major textual problem requires notice. Here and there in the *Metamorphoses* the manuscripts present alternative versions, and many scholars interpret this as evidence of two editions by Ovid himself. The crucial passages are: 1.544f, 547 (*al.* 546, 547a); 8.595f, 601f, 609f (*al.* 595–600, 600b, 601a, 602–608); 8.651, 655f (*al.* 651–654, 655a, 656a); and 8.693–699 (*al.* 693a, 693b, 697a, 698a). This notion of a revised edition by Ovid needs to be scouted, for the alternative passages are slight, inferior, and utterly insignificant; and at a number of other places (*e.g.* 6.282 and 8.286) interpolated lines have arisen as a result of textual difficulty. The fact is that the manuscript tradition is not good: we have no 9th-century manuscript like *P* for the *Heroides*, and nothing forbids the natural presumption that the *Metamorphoses* descends to us from a medieval archetype.

The original bibliography wore an old-fashioned look by its inclusion of many old and abstruse items: these I have now omitted and listed in their place the chief modern works bearing on our text.

Lastly, an innovation. To enable the reader to find his bearings I have prefixed to each book a brief table of contents.

UNIVERSITY COLLEGE LONDON   G. P. GOOLD
February 1977

viii

INTRODUCTION

PROBABLY no Roman writer has revealed himself more frankly in his works than has Publius Ovidius Naso. Indeed, the greater part of our knowledge of him is gained from his own writings. References to his parentage, his early education, his friends, his work, his manner of life, his reverses—all lie scattered freely through his pages. Especially is this true of the *Amores*, and of the two groups of poems written from his exile. The *Metamorphoses* are naturally free from biographical material. Not content with occasional references, the poet has taken care to leave to posterity a somewhat extended and formal account of his life.

From this (*Tristia*, IV. 10) we learn that he was born at Sulmo in the Pelignian country, 43 B.C., of well-to-do parents of equestrian rank, and that he had one brother, exactly one year older than himself. His own bent, from early childhood, was towards poetry; but in this he was opposed by his practical father, who desired that both his sons should prepare for the profession of the law, a desire with which both the brothers complied, but the younger with only half-hearted and temporary devotion.

Having reached the age of manhood, young Ovid found public life utterly distasteful to him, and now that he was his own master, he gave loose rein to his poetic fancy and abandoned himself to the enjoyment of the gay social life of Rome. He soon gained admission to the choice circle of the poets of his day, paying unlimited devotion to the masters of his art, and quickly becoming himself the object of no small admiration on the part of younger poets. His youthful poems soon gained fame among the people also, and his love poems became the popular lyrics of the town.

Though extremely susceptible to the influences of love, he proudly boasts that his private life was above reproach. He contracted two unhappy marriages in his youth, but his third marriage was a lasting joy to him.

And now his father and his mother died. The poet, while deeply mourning their loss with true filial devotion, still cannot but rejoice that they died before that disgrace came upon him which was to darken his own life and the lives of all whom he loved. For now, as the early frosts of age were beginning to whiten his locks, in the year 8 of our era, a sudden calamity fell upon him, no less than an imperial decree against him of perpetual banishment to the far-off shores of the Euxine Sea. The cause of this decree he only hints at; but he gives us to understand that it was an error of his judgment and not of his heart.[1]

Exiled to savage Tomi, far from home and friends and the delights of his beloved Rome, he was forced to live in a rigorous climate, an unlovely land, midst a society of uncultured semi-savages. His chief solace was the cultivation of his art, and in this he spent the tiresome days. He ends his autobiography

---

[1] Augustus, indeed, gave as his reason the immorality of Ovid's love poems, but this is generally supposed to be only a cloak for a more personal and private reason.

INTRODUCTION

with a strain of thanksgiving to his muse, and a prophecy of his world-wide fame and literary immortality.

Though Ovid says that he strove to bear his misfortunes with a manly fortitude, the poems of his exile abound in plaintive lamentations at his hard lot, petitions to his friends in Rome, and unmanly subserviency to Augustus, and later to Tiberius, in the hope of gaining his recall. These, however, were all in vain, and he died at Tomi in A.D. 18, after a banishment of nearly ten years.

Ovid's greatest work, the fruit of the best years of the prime of his life, when his imagination had ripened and his poetic vigour was at its height, was the *Metamorphoses*, finished in A.D. 7, just before his banishment.

In the poet's own judgment, however, the poem was not finished, and, in his despair on learning of his impending exile, his burned his manuscript. He himself tells us of his motive for this rash act (*Tristia*, I. 7): " On departing from Rome, I burned this poem as well as many others of my works, either because I was disgusted with poetry which had proved my bane, or because this poem was still rough and unfinished." But fortunately copies of this great work still survived in the hands of friends ; and in this letter he begs his friends now to publish it, and at the same time he begs his readers to remember that the poem has never received its author's finishing touches and so to be lenient in their judgment of it.

In the *Metamorphoses* Ovid attempts no less a task than the linking together into one artistically harmonious whole all the stories of classical mythology. And this he does, until the whole range of wonders

INTRODUCTION

(miraculous changes, hence the name, *Metamorphoses*) is passed in review, from the dawn of creation, when chaos was changed by divine fiat into the orderly universe, down to the very age of the poet himself, when the soul of Julius Caesar was changed to a star and set in the heavens among the immortals. Every important myth is at least touched upon, and though the stories differ widely in place and time, there is no break in the sequence of narration. The poet has seized upon every possible thread of connexion as he passes on from cycle to cycle of story; and where this connexion is lacking, by various ingenious and artistic devices a connecting-link is found.

The poem thus forms a manual of classical mythology, and is the most important source of mythical lore for all writers since Ovid's time. This is the real, tangible service which he has done the literary world. Many of these stories could now be obtained from the sources whence Ovid himself drew them—from Homer, Hesiod, the Greek tragedians, the Alexandrine poets, and many others. And yet many stories, but for him, would have been lost to us; and all of them he has so vivified by his strong poetic imagination that they have come down to us with added freshness and life.

The classic myths have always had a strong fascination for later writers, and so numerous are both passing and extended references to these in English literature, and especially in the poets, that he who reads without a classical background reads with many lapses of his understanding and appreciation. While the English poets have, of course, drawn from all classic sources, they are indebted for their mythology largely to Ovid. The poet would have been accessible after 1567 even to writers not versed in Latin, for in that year Golding's translation of Ovid appeared.

An admirable study of the influence of classic myth on the writings of Shakespeare has been made,[1] in which the author finds that Shakespeare was thoroughly familiar with the myths, and makes very free use of them. We read: "Though the number of definite allusions in Shakespeare is smaller than that of the vague ones, they are yet sufficiently numerous to admit of satisfactory conclusions. Of these allusions, for which a definite source can be assigned, it will be found that an overwhelming majority are directly due to Ovid, while the remainder, with few exceptions, are from Vergil. . . . Throughout, the influence of Ovid is at least four times as great as that of Vergil; the whole character of Shakespeare's mythology is essentially Ovidian."

What is true of Shakespeare is still more true of numerous other English poets in respect to their use of classical mythology. They do not always, indeed, use the myths in Ovid's manner, which is that of one whose sole attention is on the story, which he tells with eager interest, simply for the sake of telling; and yet such earlier classicists as Spenser and Milton [2] have so thoroughly imbibed the spirit of the classics that they deal with the classic stories quite as subjectively as Ovid himself. But among later English poets we find a tendency to objectify the myths, to rationalize them, to philosophize upon them, draw

[1] *Classical Mythology in Shakespeare.* By Robert Kilburn Root. New York: Henry Holt and Co., 1903.
[2] See *The Classical Mythology of Milton's English Poems.* By Charles Grosvenor Osgood. New York: Henry Holt and Co., 1900.

INTRODUCTION

lessons from them, and even to burlesque them.
Perhaps the most interesting development of all is
found in our own time, a decided tendency to revamp
the classical stories, though not always in the classical
spirit—a kind of Pre-Raphaelite movement in poetry.
Prominently in this class of poets should be named
Walter Savage Landor, Edmund Gosse, Lewis and
William Morris, and Frederick Tennyson; while
many others have caught the same spirit and written
in the same form.

The Latin text of this edition is based on that of
Ehwald, published by Messrs. Weidmann, of Berlin,
who have generously given permission to use it.
All deviations of any importance from Ehwald's text
have been noted, and Ehwald's readings given with
their sources.

CHICAGO, *March* 1915.

SHORT BIBLIOGRAPHY

Editions and Editorial

PUTEOLANUS, Franciscus: The Editio Princeps. Bologna, 1471.

BURMANNUS, P.: *Opera*, vol. 2—*Metamorphoses*. Variorum edition including notes of Heinsius. Amsterdam, 1727.

MAGNUS, Hugo: *Metamorphoses*, including *Narrationes* of Lactantius. Berlin, 1914.

EHWALD, R.: The Teubner edition, vol. 2—*Metamorphoses*. Leipzig, 1915.

SLATER, D. A.: *Towards a Text of the Metamorphosis of Ovid* (an apparatus criticus based on Riese[2] 1889). Oxford, 1927.

LENZ, F. W.: *Ovid's Metamorphoses*, Prolegomena to a revision of Hugo Magnus's edition. Weidmann, 1967.

Editions with commentary

HAUPT, Moritz and KORN, Otto: 1–7, Weidmann, 1969[11]; 8–15, 1970[6].

BÖMER, Franz (*commentary only*): 1–3, Heidelberg, 1969; 4–5, 1976.

Book 1, ed. A. G. Lee. Cambridge, 1953.

SHORT BIBLIOGRAPHY

Books 6–10, ed. William S. Anderson. Oklahoma, 1972.

Book 8, ed. A. S. Hollis. Oxford, 1970.

Literary

FRÄNKEL, Hermann: *Ovid, A Poet between Two Worlds* (Sather Classical Lectures 18). Univ. of California, 1945.

WILKINSON, L. P.: *Ovid Recalled*. Cambridge, 1955.

OTIS, Brooks: *Ovid as an Epic Poet*. Cambridge, 1970[2].

GALINSKY, G. Karl: *Ovid's Metamorphoses*. Oxford, 1975.

Concordance

DEFERRARI, R. J., BARRY, M. I. and McGUIRE, M. R. P.: *A Concordance of Ovid*. Washington, 1939.

Translations

GOLDING, A. (=Shakespeare's Ovid). London, 1567.

INNES, Mary M. (prose): Penguin Classics, 1955.

HUMPHRIES, Rolfe (verse): Indiana Univ., 1955.

METAMORPHOSES

.

BOOK I

1– 4	*Prologue*
5– 88	*The Creation*
89–150	*The Four Ages*
151–162	*The Giants*
163–252	*Lycaon*
253–312	*The Flood*
313–415	*Deucalion and Pyrrha*
416–451	*Python*
452–567	*Daphne*
568–746	*Io, Argus*
689–712	*Pan and Syrinx*
747–779	*Phaethon—i*

METAMORPHOSEON

LIBER I

In nova fert animus mutatas dicere formas
corpora; di, coeptis (nam vos mutastis et illas)
adspirate meis primaque ab origine mundi
ad mea perpetuum deducite tempora carmen!
    Ante mare et terras et quod tegit omnia caelum   5
unus erat toto naturae vultus in orbe,
quem dixere chaos: rudis indigestaque moles
nec quicquam nisi pondus iners congestaque eodem
non bene iunctarum discordia semina rerum.
nullus adhuc mundo praebebat lumina Titan,   10
nec nova crescendo reparabat cornua Phoebe,
nec circumfuso pendebat in aere tellus
ponderibus librata suis, nec bracchia longo
margine terrarum porrexerat Amphitrite;
utque erat et tellus illic et pontus et aer,   15
sic erat instabilis tellus, innabilis unda,
lucis egens aer; nulli sua forma manebat,
obstabatque aliis aliud, quia corpore in uno
frigida pugnabant calidis, umentia siccis,
mollia cum duris, sine pondere, habentia pondus.   20
    Hanc deus et melior litem natura diremit.
nam caelo terras et terris abscidit undas

2

METAMORPHOSES

BOOK I

My mind is bent to tell of bodies changed into new forms. Ye gods, for you yourselves have wrought the changes, breathe on these my undertakings, and bring down my song in unbroken strains from the world's very beginning even unto the present time.

Before the sea was, and the lands, and the sky that hangs over all, the face of Nature showed alike in her whole round, which state have men called chaos : a rough, unordered mass of things, nothing at all save lifeless bulk and warring seeds of ill-matched elements heaped in one. No sun as yet shone forth upon the world, nor did the waxing moon renew her slender horns ; not yet did the earth hang poised by her own weight in the circumambient air, nor had the ocean stretched her arms along the far reaches of the lands. And, though there was both land and sea and air, no one could tread that land, or swim that sea ; and the air was dark. No form of things remained the same ; all objects were at odds, for within one body cold things strove with hot, and moist with dry, soft things with hard, things having weight with weightless things.

God—or kindlier Nature—composed this strife ; for he rent asunder land from sky, and sea from land,

et liquidum spisso secrevit ab aere caelum.
quae postquam evolvit caecoque exemit acervo,
dissociata locis concordi pace ligavit: 25
ignea convexi vis et sine pondere caeli
emicuit summaque locum sibi fecit in arce;
proximus est aer illi levitate locoque;
densior his tellus elementaque grandia traxit
et pressa est gravitate sua; circumfluus umor   30
ultima possedit solidumque coercuit orbem.

Sic ubi dispositam quisquis fuit ille deorum
congeriem secuit sectamque in membra coegit,
principio terram, ne non aequalis ab omni
parte foret, magni speciem glomeravit in orbis.   35
tum freta diffundi rapidisque tumescere ventis
iussit et ambitae circumdare litora terrae;
addidit et fontes et stagna inmensa lacusque
fluminaque obliquis cinxit declivia ripis,
quae, diversa locis, partim sorbentur ab ipsa,   40
in mare perveniunt partim campoque recepta
liberioris aquae pro ripis litora pulsant.
iussit et extendi campos, subsidere valles,
fronde tegi silvas, lapidosos surgere montes,
utque duae dextra caelum totidemque sinistra   45
parte secant zonae, quinta est ardentior illis,
sic onus inclusum numero distinxit eodem
cura dei, totidemque plagae tellure premuntur.
quarum quae media est, non est habitabilis aestu;
4

and separated the ethereal heavens from the dense
atmosphere. When thus he had released these ele-
ments and freed them from the blind heap of things,
he set them each in its own place and bound them
fast in harmony. The fiery weightless element that
forms heaven's vault leaped up and made place for
itself upon the topmost height. Next came the air
in lightness and in place. The earth was heavier
than these, and, drawing with it the grosser ele-
ments, sank to the bottom by its own weight. The
streaming water took the last place of all, and held
the solid land confined in its embrace.

When he, whoever of the gods it was, had thus
arranged in order and resolved that chaotic mass,
and reduced it, thus resolved, to cosmic parts, he
first moulded the earth into the form of a mighty
ball so that it might be of like form on every side.
Then he bade the waters to spread abroad, to rise in
waves beneath the rushing winds, and fling them-
selves around the shores of the encircled earth.
Springs, too, and huge, stagnant pools and lakes he
made, and hemmed down-flowing rivers within their
shelving banks, whose waters, each far remote from
each, are partly swallowed by the earth itself, and
partly flow down to the sea; and being thus received
into the expanse of a freer flood, beat now on shores
instead of banks. Then did he bid plains to stretch
out, valleys to sink down, woods to be clothed in
leafage, and the rock-ribbed mountains to arise. And
as the celestial vault is cut by two zones on the right
and two on the left, and there is a fifth zone between,
hotter than these, so did the providence of God mark
off the enclosed mass with the same number of zones,
and the same tracts were stamped upon the earth.
The central zone of these may not be dwelt in by

5

OVID

nix tegit alta duas; totidem inter utramque locavit 50
temperiemque dedit mixta cum frigore flamma.

Inminet his aer, qui, quanto est pondere terrae
pondus aquae levius, tanto est onerosior igni.
illic et nebulas, illic consistere nubes
iussit et humanas motura tonitrua mentes 55
et cum fulminibus facientes fulgura ventos.

His quoque non passim mundi fabricator habendum
aera permisit; vix nunc obsistitur illis,
cum sua quisque regat diverso flamina tractu,
quin lanient mundum; tanta est discordia fratrum.
Eurus ad Auroram Nabataeaque regna recessit 61
Persidaque et radiis iuga subdita matutinis;
vesper et occiduo quae litora sole tepescunt,
proxima sunt Zephyro; Scythiam septemque triones
horrifer invasit Boreas; contraria tellus 65
nubibus adsiduis pluviaque madescit ab Austro.
haec super inposuit liquidum et gravitate carentem
aethera nec quicquam terrenae faecis habentem.

Vix ita limitibus dissaepserat omnia certis,
cum, quae pressa diu fuerant caligine caeca, 70
sidera coeperunt toto effervescere caelo;
neu regio foret ulla suis animalibus orba,
astra tenent caeleste solum formaeque deorum,
cesserunt nitidis habitandae piscibus undae,
terra feras cepit, volucres agitabilis aer. 75

Sanctius his animal mentisque capacius altae
deerat adhuc et quod dominari in cetera posset:
6

reason of the heat ; deep snow covers two, two he placed between and gave them temperate climate, mingling heat with cold.

The air hung over all, which is as much heavier than fire as the weight of water is lighter than the weight of earth. There did the creator bid the mists and clouds to take their place, and thunder, that should shake the hearts of men, and winds which produce lightning and thunderbolts. To these also the world's creator did not allot the air that they might hold it everywhere. Even as it is, they can scarce be prevented, though they control their blasts, each in his separate tract, from tearing the world to pieces. So fiercely do these brothers strive together. But Eurus drew off to the land of the dawn and the realms of Araby, and where the Persian hills flush beneath the morning light. The western shores which glow with the setting sun are the place of Zephyrus : while bristling Boreas betook himself to Scythia and the farthest north. The land far opposite is wet with constant fog and rain, the home of Auster, the South-wind. Above these all he placed the liquid, weightless ether, which has naught of earthy dregs.

Scarce had he thus parted off all things within their determined bounds, when the stars, which had long been lying hid crushed down beneath the darkness, began to gleam throughout the sky. And, that no region might be without its own forms of animate life, the stars and divine forms occupied the floor of heaven, the sea fell to the shining fishes for their home, earth received the beasts, and the mobile air the birds.

A living creature of finer stuff than these, more capable of lofty thought, one who could have dominion over all the rest, was lacking yet. Then man was born :

7

natus homo est, sive hunc divino semine fecit
ille opifex rerum, mundi melioris origo,
sive recens tellus seductaque nuper ab alto   80
aethere cognati retinebat semina caeli.
quam satus Iapeto, mixtam pluvialibus undis,
finxit in effigiem moderantum cuncta deorum,
pronaque cum spectent animalia cetera terram,
os homini sublime dedit caelumque videre   85
iussit et erectos ad sidera tollere vultus:
sic, modo quae fuerat rudis et sine imagine, tellus
induit ignotas hominum conversa figuras.

  Aurea prima sata est aetas, quae vindice nullo,
sponte sua, sine lege fidem rectumque colebat.   90
poena metusque aberant, nec verba minantia fixo
aere legebantur, nec supplex turba timebat
iudicis ora sui, sed erant sine vindice tuti.
nondum caesa suis, peregrinum ut viseret orbem,
montibus in liquidas pinus descenderat undas,   95
nullaque mortales praeter sua litora norant;
nondum praecipites cingebant oppida fossae;
non tuba derecti, non aeris cornua flexi,
non galeae, non ensis erat: sine militis usu
mollia securae peragebant otia gentes.   100
ipsa quoque inmunis rastroque intacta nec ullis
saucia vomeribus per se dabat omnia tellus,
contentique cibis nullo cogente creatis
arbuteos fetus montanaque fraga legebant
cornaque et in duris haerentia mora rubetis   105
et quae deciderant patula Iovis arbore glandes.

8

whether the god who made all else, designing a more perfect world, made man of his own divine substance, or whether the new earth, but lately drawn away from heavenly ether, retained still some elements of its kindred sky—that earth which the son of Iapetus mixed with fresh, running water, and moulded into the form of the all-controlling gods. And, though all other animals are prone, and fix their gaze upon the earth, he gave to man an up-lifted face and bade him stand erect and turn his eyes to heaven. So, then, the earth, which had but lately been a rough and formless thing, was changed and clothed itself with forms of men before unknown.

Golden was that first age, which, with no one to compel, without a law, of its own will, kept faith and did the right. There was no fear of punishment, no threatening words were to be read on brazen tablets; no suppliant throng gazed fearfully upon its judge's face; but without defenders lived secure. Not yet had the pine-tree, felled on its native mountains, descended thence into the watery plain to visit other lands; men knew no shores except their own. Not yet were cities begirt with steep moats; there were no trumpets of straight, no horns of curving brass, no swords or helmets. There was no need at all of armed men, for nations, secure from war's alarms, passed the years in gentle ease. The earth herself, without compulsion, untouched by hoe or plowshare, of herself gave all things needful. And men, content with food which came with no one's seeking, gathered the arbute fruit, strawberries from the mountain-sides, cornel-cherries, berries hanging thick upon the prickly bramble, and acorns fallen from the spreading tree of Jove. Then spring was everlasting, and

ver erat aeternum, placidique tepentibus auris
mulcebant zephyri natos sine semine flores;
mox etiam fruges tellus inarata ferebat,
nec renovatus ager gravidis canebat aristis;   110
flumina iam lactis, iam flumina nectaris ibant,
flavaque de viridi stillabant ilice mella.

  Postquam Saturno tenebrosa in Tartara misso
sub Iove mundus erat, subiit argentea proles,
auro deterior, fulvo pretiosior aere.   115
Iuppiter antiqui contraxit tempora veris
perque hiemes aestusque et inaequalis autumnos
et breve ver spatiis exegit quattuor annum.
tum primum siccis aer fervoribus ustus
canduit, et ventis glacies adstricta pependit;   120
tum primum subiere domos; domus antra fuerunt
et densi frutices et vinctae cortice virgae.
semina tum primum longis Cerealia sulcis
obruta sunt, pressique iugo gemuere iuvenci.

  Tertia post illam successit aenea proles,   125
saevior ingeniis et ad horrida promptior arma,
non scelerata tamen; de duro est ultima ferro.
protinus inrupit venae peioris in aevum
omne nefas: fugere pudor verumque fidesque;
in quorum subiere locum fraudesque dolusque   130
insidiaeque et vis et amor sceleratus habendi.
vela dabant ventis nec adhuc bene noverat illos
navita, quaeque prius steterant in montibus altis,
fluctibus ignotis insultavere carinae,
communemque prius ceu lumina solis et auras   135

gentle zephyrs with warm breath played with the flowers that sprang unplanted. Anon the earth, untilled, brought forth her stores of grain, and the fields, though unfallowed, grew white with the heavy, bearded wheat. Streams of milk and streams of sweet nectar flowed, and yellow honey was distilled from the verdant oak.

After Saturn had been banished to the dark land of death, and the world was under the sway of Jove, the silver race came in, lower in the scale than gold, but of greater worth than yellow brass. Jove now shortened the bounds of the old-time spring, and through winter, summer, variable autumn, and brief spring completed the year in four seasons. Then first the parched air glared white with burning heat, and icicles hung down congealed by freezing winds. In that age men first sought the shelter of houses. Their homes had heretofore been caves, dense thickets, and branches bound together with bark. Then first the seeds of grain were planted in long furrows, and bullocks groaned beneath the heavy yoke.

Next after this and third in order came the brazen race, of sterner disposition, and more ready to fly to arms savage, but not yet impious. The age of hard iron came last. Straightway all evil burst forth into this age of baser vein : modesty and truth and faith fled the earth, and in their place came tricks and plots and snares, violence and cursed love of gain. Men now spread sails to the winds, though the sailor as yet scarce knew them ; and keels of pine which long had stood upon high mountain-sides, now leaped insolently over unknown waves. And the ground, which had hitherto been a common possession like the sunlight and the air, the careful surveyor now

cautus humum longo signavit limite mensor.
nec tantum segetes alimentaque debita dives
poscebatur humus, sed itum est in viscera terrae,
quasque recondiderat Stygiisque admoverat umbris,
effodiuntur opes, inritamenta malorum.   140
iamque nocens ferrum ferroque nocentius aurum
prodierat, prodit bellum, quod pugnat utroque,
sanguineaque manu crepitantia concutit arma.
vivitur ex rapto: non hospes ab hospite tutus,
non socer a genero, fratrum quoque gratia rara est;
inminet exitio vir coniugis, illa mariti,   146
lurida terribiles miscent aconita novercae,
filius ante diem patrios inquirit in annos:
victa iacet pietas, et virgo caede madentis
ultima caelestum terras Astraea reliquit.   150

    Neve foret terris securior arduus aether,
adfectasse ferunt regnum caeleste gigantas
altaque congestos struxisse ad sidera montis.
tum pater omnipotens misso perfregit Olympum
fulmine et excussit subiecto Pelion Ossae.   155
obruta mole sua cum corpora dira iacerent,
perfusam multo natorum sanguine Terram
immaduisse ferunt calidumque animasse cruorem
et, ne nulla suae stirpis monimenta manerent,
in faciem vertisse hominum; sed et illa propago 160
contemptrix superum saevaeque avidissima caedis
et violenta fuit: scires e sanguine natos.

    Quae pater ut summa vidit Saturnius arce,
ingemit et facto nondum vulgata recenti

marked out with long-drawn boundary-line. Not only did men demand of the bounteous fields the crops and sustenance they owed, but they delved as well into the very bowels of the earth; and the wealth which the creator had hidden away and buried deep amidst the very Stygian shades, was brought to light, wealth that pricks men on to crime. And now baneful iron had come, and gold more baneful than iron; war came, which fights with both, and brandished in its bloody hands the clashing arms. Men lived on plunder. Guest was not safe from host, nor father-in-law from son-in-law; even among brothers 'twas rare to find affection. The husband longed for the death of his wife, she of her husband; murderous stepmothers brewed deadly poisons, and sons inquired into their fathers' years before the time. Piety lay vanquished, and the maiden Astraea, last of the immortals, abandoned the blood-soaked earth.

And, that high heaven might be no safer than the earth, they say that the Giants essayed the very throne of heaven, piling huge mountains, one on another, clear up to the stars. Then the Almighty Father hurled his thunderbolts, shattered Olympus, and dashed Pelion down from underlying Ossa. When those dread bodies lay o'erwhelmed by their own bulk, they say that Mother Earth, drenched with their streaming blood, informed that warm gore anew with life, and, that some trace of her former offspring might remain, she gave it human form. But this new stock, too, proved contemptuous of the gods, very greedy for slaughter, and passionate. You might know that they were sons of blood.

When Saturn's son from his high throne saw this he groaned, and, recalling the infamous revels of

foeda Lycaoniae referens convivia mensae   165
ingentes animo et dignas Iove concipit iras
conciliumque vocat: tenuit mora nulla vocatos.
   Est via sublimis, caelo manifesta sereno;
lactea nomen habet, candore notabilis ipso.
hac iter est superis ad magni tecta Tonantis   170
regalemque domum: dextra laevaque deorum
atria nobilium valvis celebrantur apertis.
plebs habitat diversa locis: hac parte potentes
caelicolae clarique suos posuere penates;
hic locus est, quem, si verbis audacia detur,   175
haud timeam magni dixisse Palatia caeli.
   Ergo ubi marmoreo superi sedere recessu,
celsior ipse loco sceptroque innixus eburno
terrificam capitis concussit terque quaterque
caesariem, cum qua terram, mare, sidera movit.   180
talibus inde modis ora indignantia solvit:
" non ego pro mundi regno magis anxius illa
tempestate fui, qua centum quisque parabat
inicere anguipedum captivo bracchia caelo.
nam quamquam ferus hostis erat, tamen illud ab uno
corpore et ex una pendebat origine bellum;   186
nunc mihi qua totum Nereus circumsonat orbem,
perdendum est mortale genus: per flumina iuro
infera sub terras Stygio labentia luco!
cuncta prius temptanda, sed inmedicabile curae   190
ense recidendum, ne pars sincera trahatur.
sunt mihi semidei, sunt rustica numina, nymphae
faunique satyrique et monticolae silvani;
quos quoniam caeli nondum dignamur honore,

14

Lycaon's table—a story still unknown because the deed was new—he conceived a mighty wrath worthy of the soul of Jove, and summoned a council of the gods. Naught delayed their answer to the summons.

There is a high way, easily seen when the sky is clear. 'Tis called the Milky Way, famed for its shining whiteness. By this way the gods fare to the halls and royal dwelling of the mighty Thunderer. On either side the palaces of the gods of higher rank are thronged with guests through folding-doors flung wide. The lesser gods dwell apart from these. In this neighbourhood the illustrious and strong heaven-dwellers have placed their household gods. This is the place which, if I may make bold to say it, I would not fear to call the Palatine of high heaven.

So, when the gods had taken their seats within the marble council chamber, the king himself, seated high above the rest and leaning on his ivory sceptre, shook thrice and again his awful locks, wherewith he moved the land and sea and sky. Then he opened his indignant lips, and thus spoke he : " I was not more troubled than now for the sovereignty of the world when each one of the serpent-footed giants was in act to lay his hundred hands upon the captive sky. For, although that was a savage enemy, their whole attack sprung from one body and one source. But now, wherever old Ocean roars around the earth, I must destroy the race of men: I swear it by the infernal streams that glide beneath the earth through Stygian groves. All means should first be tried, but what responds not to treatment must be cut away with the knife, lest the untainted part also draw infection. I have demigods, rustic divinities, nymphs, fauns and satyrs, and sylvan deities upon the mountain-slopes. Since we do not yet esteem them

quas dedimus, certe terras habitare sinamus.   195
an satis, o superi, tutos fore creditis illos,
cum mihi, qui fulmen, qui vos habeoque regoque,
struxerit insidias notus feritate Lycaon? "
  Confremuere omnes studiisque ardentibus ausum
talia deposcunt: sic, cum manus inpia saevit   200
sanguine Caesareo Romanum exstinguere nomen,
attonitum tantae subito terrore ruinae
humanum genus est totusque perhorruit orbis;
nec tibi grata minus pietas, Auguste, tuorum
quam fuit illa Iovi. qui postquam voce manuque   205
murmura conpressit, tenuere silentia cuncti.
substitit ut clamor pressus gravitate regentis,
Iuppiter hoc iterum sermone silentia rupit:
" ille quidem poenas (curam hanc dimittite!) solvit;
quod tamen admissum, quae sit vindicta, docebo.   210
contigerat nostras infamia temporis aures;
quam cupiens falsam summo delabor Olympo
et deus humana lustro sub imagine terras.
longa mora est, quantum noxae sit ubique repertum,
enumerare: minor fuit ipsa infamia vero.   215
Maenala transieram latebris horrenda ferarum
et cum Cyllene gelidi pineta Lycaei:
Arcadis hinc sedes et inhospita tecta tyranni
ingredior, traherent cum sera crepuscula noctem.
signa dedi venisse deum, vulgusque precari   220
coeperat: inridet primo pia vota Lycaon,
mox ait ' experiar deus hic discrimine aperto
an sit mortalis: nec erit dubitabile verum.'

16

worthy the honour of a place in heaven, let us at least allow them to dwell in safety in the lands allotted them. Or do you think that they will be safe, when against me, who wield the thunderbolt, who have and rule you as my subjects, Lycaon, well known for savagery, has laid his snares?"

All clamoured, and with eager zeal demanded him who had been guilty of such bold infamy. So, when an impious band was mad to blot out the name of Rome with Caesar's blood, the human race was dazed with a sudden fear of mighty ruin, and the whole world shuddered in horror. Nor is the loyalty of thy subjects, Augustus, less pleasing to thee than that was to Jove. After he, by word and gesture, had checked their outcry, all held their peace. When now the clamour had subsided, checked by his royal authority, Jove once more broke the silence with these words: "He has indeed been punished; have no care for that. But what he did and what his punishment I will relate. An infamous report of the age had reached my ears. Eager to prove this false, I descended from high Olympus, and as a god disguised in human form travelled up and down the land. It would take too long to recount how great impiety was found on every hand. The infamous report was far less than the truth. I had crossed Maenala, bristling with the lairs of beasts, Cyllene, and the pine-groves of chill Lycaeus. Thence I approached the seat and inhospitable abode of the Arcadian king, just as the late evening shades were ushering in the night. I gave a sign that a god had come, and the common folk began to worship me. Lycaon at first mocked at their pious prayers; and then he said: 'I will soon find out, and that by a plain test, whether this fellow be god or mortal. Nor

17

nocte gravem somno necopina perdere morte
comparat: haec illi placet experientia veri;   225
nec contentus eo, missi de gente Molossa
obsidis unius iugulum mucrone resolvit
atque ita seminecis partim ferventibus artus
mollit aquis, partim subiecto torruit igni.
quod simul inposuit mensis, ego vindice flamma   230
in domino dignos everti tecta penates;
territus ipse fugit nactusque silentia ruris
exululat frustraque loqui conatur: ab ipso
colligit os rabiem solitaeque cupidine caedis
vertitur in pecudes et nunc quoque sanguine gaudet.
in villos abeunt vestes, in crura lacerti: 236
fit lupus et veteris servat vestigia formae;
canities eadem est, eadem violentia vultus,
idem oculi lucent, eadem feritatis imago est.
occidit una domus, sed non domus una perire   240
digna fuit: qua terra patet, fera regnat Erinys.
in facinus iurasse putes! dent ocius omnes,
quas meruere pati, (sic stat sententia) poenas."

    Dicta Iovis pars voce probant stimulosque frementi
adiciunt, alii partes adsensibus inplent.   245
est tamen humani generis iactura dolori
omnibus, et quae sit terrae mortalibus orbae
forma futura rogant, quis sit laturus in aras
tura, ferisne paret populandas tradere terras.
talia quaerentes (sibi enim fore cetera curae)   250

18

shall the truth be at all in doubt.' He planned that night while I was heavy with sleep to kill me by an unexpected murderous attack. Such was the experiment he adopted to test the truth. And not content with that, he took a hostage who had been sent by the Molossian race, cut his throat, and some parts of him still warm with life, he boiled, and others he roasted over the fire. But no sooner had he placed these before me on the table than I, with my avenging bolt, brought the house down upon its household gods, gods worthy of such a master. The king himself flies in terror and, gaining the silent fields, howls aloud, attempting in vain to speak. His mouth of itself gathers foam, and with his accustomed greed for blood he turns against the sheep, delighting still in slaughter. His garments change to shaggy hair, his arms to legs. He turns into a wolf, and yet retains some traces of his former shape. There is the same grey hair, the same fierce face, the same gleaming eyes, the same picture of beastly savagery. One house has fallen; but not one house alone has deserved to perish. Wherever the plains of earth extend, wild fury reigns supreme. You would deem it a conspiracy of crime. Let them all pay, and quickly too, the penalties which they have deserved. So stands my purpose."

When he had done, some proclaimed their approval of his words, and added fuel to his wrath, while others played their parts by giving silent consent. And yet they all grieved over the threatened loss of the human race, and asked what would be the state of the world bereft of mortals. Who would bring incense to their altars? Was he planning to give over the world to the wild beasts to despoil? As they thus questioned, their king bade them be of good cheer (for the rest should be his care), for

rex superum trepidare vetat subolemque priori
dissimilem populo promittit origine mira.

Iamque erat in totas sparsurus fulmina terras;
sed timuit, ne forte sacer tot ab ignibus aether
conciperet flammas longusque ardesceret axis: 255
esse quoque in fatis reminiscitur, adfore tempus,
quo mare, quo tellus correptaque regia caeli
ardeat et mundi moles obsessa laboret.
tela reponuntur manibus fabricata cyclopum;
poena placet diversa, genus mortale sub undis   260
perdere et ex omni nimbos demittere caelo.

Protinus Aeoliis Aquilonem claudit in antris
et quaecumque fugant inductas flamina nubes
emittitque Notum.   madidis Notus evolat alis,
terribilem picea tectus caligine vultum;   265
barba gravis nimbis, canis fluit unda capillis;
fronte sedent nebulae, rorant pennaeque sinusque.
utque manu lata pendentia nubila pressit,
fit fragor: hinc densi funduntur ab aethere nimbi;
nuntia Iunonis varios induta colores   270
concipit Iris aquas alimentaque nubibus adfert.
sternuntur segetes et deplorata coloni
vota iacent, longique perit labor inritus anni.

Nec caelo contenta suo est Iovis ira, sed illum
caeruleus frater iuvat auxiliaribus undis.   275
convocat hic amnes: qui postquam tecta tyranni
intravere sui, " non est hortamine longo

he would give them another race of wondrous origin far different from the first.

And now he was in act to hurl his thunderbolts 'gainst the whole world; but he stayed his hand in fear lest perchance the sacred heavens should take fire from so huge a conflagration, and burn from pole to pole. He remembered also that 'twas in the fates that a time would come when sea and land, the enkindled palace of the sky and the beleaguered structure of the universe should be destroyed by fire. And so he laid aside the bolts which Cyclopean hands had forged. He preferred a different punishment, to destroy the human race beneath the waves and to send down rain from every quarter of the sky.

Straightway he shuts the North-wind up in the cave of Aeolus, and all blasts soever that put the clouds to flight; but he lets the South-wind loose. Forth flies the South-wind with dripping wings, his awful face shrouded in pitchy darkness. His beard is heavy with rain; water flows in streams down his hoary locks; dark clouds rest upon his brow; while his wings and garments drip with dew. And, when he presses the low-hanging clouds with his broad hands, a crashing sound goes forth; and next the dense clouds pour forth their rain. Iris, the messenger of Juno, clad in robes of many hues, draws up water and feeds it to the clouds. The standing grain is overthrown; the crops which have been the object of the farmers' prayers lie ruined; and the hard labour of the tedious year has come to naught.

The wrath of Jove is not content with the waters from his own sky; his sea-god brother aids him with auxiliary waves. He summons his rivers to council. When these have assembled at the palace of their king, he says: " Now is no time to employ a long

nunc " ait " utendum ; vires effundite vestras :
sic opus est ! aperite domos ac mole remota
fluminibus vestris totas inmittite habenas ! "   280
iusserat ; hi redeunt ac fontibus ora relaxant
et defrenato volvuntur in aequora cursu.

  Ipse tridente suo terram percussit, at illa
intremuit motuque vias patefecit aquarum.
exspatiata ruunt per apertos flumina campos   285
cumque satis arbusta simul pecudesque virosque
tectaque cumque suis rapiunt penetralia sacris.
si qua domus mansit potuitque resistere tanto
indeiecta malo, culmen tamen altior huius
unda tegit, pressaeque latent sub gurgite turres. 290
iamque mare et tellus nullum discrimen habebant :
omnia pontus erat, derant quoque litora ponto.

  Occupat hic collem, cumba sedet alter adunca
et ducit remos illic, ubi nuper arabat :
ille supra segetes aut mersae culmina villae   295
navigat, hic summa piscem deprendit in ulmo.
figitur in viridi, si fors tulit, ancora prato,
aut subiecta terunt curvae vineta carinae ;
et, modo qua graciles gramen carpsere capellae,
nunc ibi deformes ponunt sua corpora phocae. 300
mirantur sub aqua lucos urbesque domosque
Nereides, silvasque tenent delphines et altis
incursant ramis agitataque robora pulsant.
nat lupus inter oves, fulvos vehit unda leones,
unda vehit tigres ; nec vires fulminis apro,   305
crura nec ablato prosunt velocia cervo,

harangue. Put forth all your strength, for there is need. Open wide your doors, away with all restraining dykes, and give full rein to all your river steeds." So he commands, and the rivers return, uncurb their fountains' mouths, and in unbridled course go racing to the sea.

Neptune himself smites the earth with his trident. She trembles, and at the stroke flings open wide a way for the waters. The rivers overleap all bounds and flood the open plains. And not alone orchards, crops and herds, men and dwellings, but shrines as well and their sacred contents do they sweep away. If any house has stood firm, and has been able to resist that huge misfortune undestroyed, still do the overtopping waves cover its roof, and its towers lie hid beneath the flood. And now the sea and land have no distinction. All is sea, and a sea without a shore.

Here one man seeks a hill-top in his flight; another sits in his curved skiff, plying the oars where lately he has plowed; one sails over his fields of grain or the roof of his buried farmhouse, and one takes fish caught in the elm-tree's top. And sometimes it chanced that an anchor was embedded in a grassy meadow, or the curving keels brushed over the vineyard tops. And where but now the slender goats had browsed, the ugly sea-calves rested. The Nereids are amazed to see beneath the waters groves and cities and the haunts of men. The dolphins invade the woods, brushing against the high branches, and shake the oak-trees as they knock against them in their course. The wolf swims among the sheep, while tawny lions and tigers are borne along by the waves. Neither does the power of his lightning stroke avail the boar, nor his swift limbs the stag, since both are alike swept away by the flood; and

23

quaesitisque diu terris, ubi sistere possit,
in mare lassatis volucris vaga decidit alis.
obruerat tumulos inmensa licentia ponti,
pulsabantque novi montana cacumina fluctus.   310
maxima pars unda rapitur; quibus unda pepercit,
illos longa domant inopi ieiunia victu.

   Separat Aonios Oetaeis Phocis ab arvis,
terra ferax, dum terra fuit, sed tempore in illo
pars maris et latus subitarum campus aquarum.   315
mons ibi verticibus petit arduus astra duobus,
nomine Parnasos, superantque cacumina nubes.
hic ubi Deucalion (nam cetera texerat aequor)
cum consorte tori parva rate vectus adhaesit,
Corycidas nymphas et numina montis adorant   320
fatidicamque Themin, quae tunc oracla tenebat:
non illo melior quisquam nec amantior aequi
vir fuit aut illa metuentior ulla deorum.
Iuppiter ut liquidis stagnare paludibus orbem
et superesse virum de tot modo milibus unum,   325
et superesse vidit de tot modo milibus unam,
innocuos ambo, cultores numinis ambo,
nubila disiecit nimbisque aquilone remotis
et caelo terras ostendit et aethera terris.
nec maris ira manet, positoque tricuspide telo   330
mulcet aquas rector pelagi supraque profundum
24

the wandering bird, after long searching for a place to alight, falls with weary wings into the sea. The sea in unchecked liberty has now buried all the hills, and strange waves now beat upon the mountain-peaks. Most living things are drowned outright. Those who have escaped the water slow starvation at last o'ercomes through lack of food.

The land of Phocis separates the Boeotian from the Oetean fields, a fertile land, while still it was a land. But at that time it was but a part of the sea, a broad expanse of sudden waters. There Mount Parnasus lifts its two peaks skyward, high and steep, piercing the clouds. When here Deucalion and his wife, borne in a little skiff, had come to land—for the sea had covered all things else—they first worshipped the Corycian nymphs and the mountain deities, and the goddess, fate-revealing Themis, who in those days kept the oracles. There was no better man than he, none more scrupulous of right, nor than she was any woman more reverent of the gods. When now Jove saw that the world was all one stagnant pool, and that only one man was left from those who were but now so many thousands, and that but one woman too was left, both innocent and both worshippers of God, he rent the clouds asunder, and when these had been swept away by the North-wind he showed the land once more to the sky, and the heavens to the land. Then too the anger of the sea subsides, when the sea's great ruler lays by his three-pronged spear and calms the waves; and, calling sea-hued Triton, showing forth above the deep, his shoulders thick o'ergrown with shell-fish, he bids him blow into his loud-resounding conch, and by that signal to recall the floods and streams. He lifts his hollow shell, which twisting from the bottom of a

exstantem atque umeros innato murice tectum
caeruleum Tritona vocat conchaeque sonanti
inspirare iubet fluctusque et flumina signo
iam revocare dato: cava bucina sumitur illi,　335
tortilis in latum quae turbine crescit ab imo,
bucina, quae medio concepit ubi aera ponto,
litora voce replet sub utroque iacentia Phoebo;
tum quoque, ut ora dei madida rorantia barba
contigit et cecinit iussos inflata receptus,　340
omnibus audita est telluris et aequoris undis,
et quibus est undis audita, coercuit omnes.
iam mare litus habet, plenos capit alveus amnes,
flumina subsidunt collesque exire videntur;
surgit humus, crescunt sola decrescentibus undis, 345
postque diem longam nudata cacumina silvae
ostendunt limumque tenent in fronde relictum.

　Redditus orbis erat; quem postquam vidit inanem
et desolatas agere alta silentia terras,
Deucalion lacrimis ita Pyrrham adfatur obortis:　350
" o soror, o coniunx, o femina sola superstes,
quam commune mihi genus et patruelis origo,
deinde torus iunxit, nunc ipsa pericula iungunt,
terrarum, quascumque vident occasus et ortus,
nos duo turba sumus; possedit cetera pontus.　355
haec quoque adhuc vitae non est fiducia nostrae
certa satis; terrent etiamnum nubila mentem.
quis tibi, si sine me fatis erepta fuisses,
nunc animus, miseranda, foret? quo sola timorem
ferre modo posses? quo consolante doleres!　360
namque ego (crede mihi), si te quoque pontus haberet,
te sequerer, coniunx, et me quoque pontus haberet.

spiral expands into a broad whorl—the shell which, when in mid-sea it has received the Triton's breath, fills with its notes the shores that lie beneath the rising and the setting sun. So then, when it had touched the sea-god's lips wet with his dripping beard, and sounded forth the retreat which had been ordered, 'twas heard by all the waters both of land and sea; and all the waters by which 'twas heard it held in check. Now the sea has shores, the rivers, bank full, keep within their channels; the floods subside, and hill-tops spring into view; land rises up, the ground increasing as the waves decrease; and now at length, after long burial, the trees show their uncovered tops, whose leaves still hold the slime which the flood has left.

The world was indeed restored. But when Deucalion saw that it was an empty world, and that deep silence filled the desolated lands, he burst into tears and thus addressed his wife: " O sister, O my wife, O only woman left on earth, you whom the ties of common race and family,[1] whom the marriage couch has joined to me, and whom now our very perils join: of all the lands which the rising and the setting sun behold, we two are the throng. The sea holds all the rest. And even this hold which we have upon our life is not as yet sufficiently secure. Even yet the clouds strike terror to my heart. What would be your feelings, now, poor soul, if the fates had willed that you be rescued all alone? How would you bear your fear, alone? who would console your grief? For be assured that if the sea held you also, I would follow you, my wife, and the sea should hold me also.

[1] *patruelis origo.* See line 390. Deucalion and Pyrrha were cousins, a relationship which on the part of the woman is sometimes expressed by *soror.*

o utinam possim populos reparare paternis
artibus atque animas formatae infundere terrae!
nunc genus in nobis restat mortale duobus.   365
sic visum superis: hominumque exempla manemus."
dixerat, et flebant: placuit caeleste precari
numen et auxilium per sacras quaerere sortes.
nulla mora est: adeunt pariter Cephesidas undas,
ut nondum liquidas, sic iam vada nota secantes.   370
inde ubi libatos inroravere liquores
vestibus et capiti, flectunt vestigia sanctae
ad delubra deae, quorum fastigia turpi
pallebant musco stabantque sine ignibus arae.
ut templi tetigere gradus, procumbit uterque   375
pronus humi gelidoque pavens dedit oscula saxo
atque ita " si precibus " dixerunt " numina iustis
victa remollescunt, si flectitur ira deorum,
dic, Themi, qua generis damnum reparabile nostri
arte sit, et mersis fer opem, mitissima, rebus! " 380
  Mota dea est sortemque dedit: " discedite templo
et velate caput cinctasque resolvite vestes
ossaque post tergum magnae iactate parentis! "
obstupuere diu: rumpitque silentia voce
Pyrrha prior iussisque deae parere recusat,   385
detque sibi veniam pavido rogat ore pavetque
laedere iactatis maternas ossibus umbras.
interea repetunt caecis obscura latebris
verba datae sortis secum inter seque volutant.
inde Promethides placidis Epimethida dictis   390
mulcet et " aut fallax " ait " est sollertia nobis,
28

Oh, would that by my father's arts I might restore
the nations, and breathe, as did he, the breath of life
into the moulded clay. But as it is, on us two only
depends the human race. Such is the will of Heaven:
and we remain sole samples of mankind." He
spoke; and when they had wept awhile they resolved
to appeal to the heavenly power and seek his aid
through sacred oracles. Without delay side by side
they went to the waters of Cephisus' stream, which,
while not yet clear, still flowed within their familiar
banks. From this they took some drops and sprinkled
them on head and clothing. So having done, they
bent their steps to the goddess's sacred shrine, whose
gables were still discoloured with foul moss, and upon
whose altars the fires were dead. When they had
reached the temple steps they both fell prone upon
the ground, and with trembling lips kissed the chill
stone and said: " If deities are appeased by the
prayers of the righteous, if the wrath of the gods is
thus turned aside, O Themis, tell us by what means
our race may be restored, and bring aid, O most
merciful, to a world o'erwhelmed."

The goddess was moved and gave this oracle:
" Depart hence, and with veiled heads and loosened
robes throw behind you as you go the bones of your
great mother." Long they stand in dumb amaze;
and first Pyrrha breaks the silence and refuses to
obey the bidding of the goddess. With trembling
lips she prays for pardon, but dares not outrage her
mother's ghost by treating her bones as she is bid.
Meanwhile they go over again the words of the
oracle, which had been given so full of dark per-
plexities, and turn them over and over in their minds.
At last Prometheus' son comforts the daughter of
Epimetheus with reassuring words: " Either my wit

29

aut (pia sunt nullumque nefas oracula suadent!)
magna parens terra est: lapides in corpore terrae
ossa reor dici; iacere hos post terga iubemur."

  Coniugis augurio quamquam Titania mota est, 395
spes tamen in dubio est: adeo caelestibus ambo
diffidunt monitis; sed quid temptare nocebit?
descendunt: velantque caput tunicasque recingunt
et iussos lapides sua post vestigia mittunt.
saxa (quis hoc credat, nisi sit pro teste vetustas?) 400
ponere duritiem coepere suumque rigorem
mollirique mora mollitaque ducere formam.
mox ubi creverunt naturaque mitior illis
contigit, ut quaedam, sic non manifesta videri
forma potest hominis, sed uti de marmore coepta
non exacta satis rudibusque simillima signis,   406
quae tamen ex illis aliquo pars umida suco
et terrena fuit, versa est in corporis usum;
quod solidum est flectique nequit, mutatur in ossa,
quae modo vena fuit, sub eodem nomine mansit, 410
inque brevi spatio superorum numine saxa
missa viri manibus faciem traxere virorum
et de femineo reparata est femina iactu.
inde genus durum sumus experiensque laborum
et documenta damus qua simus origine nati.   415

  Cetera diversis tellus animalia formis
sponte sua peperit, postquam vetus umor ab igne
percaluit solis, caenumque udaeque paludes
intumuere aestu, fecundaque semina rerum

is at fault, or else (oracles are holy and never counsel guilt!) our great mother is the earth, and I think that the bones which the goddess speaks of are the stones in the earth's body. 'Tis these that we are bidden to throw behind us.''

Although Pyrrha is moved by her husband's surmise, yet hope still wavers; so distrustful are they both as to the heavenly command. But what harm will it do to try? They go down, veil their heads, ungird their robes, and throw stones behind them just as the goddess had bidden. And the stones— who would believe it unless ancient tradition vouched for it?—began at once to lose their hardness and stiffness, to grow soft slowly, and softened to take on form. Then, when they had grown in size and become milder in their nature, a certain likeness to the human form, indeed, could be seen, still not very clear, but such as statues just begun out of marble have, not sharply defined, and very like roughly blocked-out images. That part of them, however, which was earthy and damp with slight moisture, was changed to flesh; but what was solid and incapable of bending became bone; that which was but now veins remained under the same name. And in a short time, through the operation of the divine will, the stones thrown by the man's hand took on the form of men, and women were made from the stones the woman threw. Hence come the hardness of our race and our endurance of toil; and we give proof from what origin we are sprung.

As to the other forms of animal life, the earth spontaneously produced these of divers kinds; after that old moisture remaining from the flood had grown warm from the rays of the sun, the slime of the wet marshes swelled with heat, and the fertile

vivaci nutrita solo ceu matris in alvo   420
creverunt faciemque aliquam cepere morando.
sic ubi deseruit madidos septemfluus agros
Nilus et antiquo sua flumina reddidit alveo
aetherioque recens exarsit sidere limus,
plurima cultores versis animalia glaebis   425
inveniunt et in his quaedam modo coepta per ipsum
nascendi spatium, quaedam inperfecta suisque
trunca vident numeris, et eodem in corpore saepe
altera pars vivit, rudis est pars altera tellus.
quippe ubi temperiem sumpsere umorque calorque,
concipiunt, et ab his oriuntur cuncta duobus,   431
cumque sit ignis aquae pugnax, vapor umidus omnes
res creat, et discors concordia fetibus apta est.
ergo ubi diluvio tellus lutulenta recenti
solibus aetheriis altoque recanduit aestu,   435
edidit innumeras species; partimque figuras
rettulit antiquas, partim nova monstra creavit.

    Illa quidem nollet, sed te quoque, maxime Python,
tum genuit, populisque novis, incognita serpens,
terror eras: tantum spatii de monte tenebas.   440
hunc deus arcitenens, numquam letalibus armis
ante nisi in dammis capreisque fugacibus usus,
mille gravem telis exhausta paene pharetra
perdidit effuso per vulnera nigra veneno.
neve operis famam posset delere vetustas,   445
instituit sacros celebri certamine ludos,
Pythia de domitae serpentis nomine dictos.
hic iuvenum quicumque manu pedibusve rotave

seeds of life, nourished in that life-giving soil, as in a mother's womb, grew and in time took on some special form. So when the seven-mouthed Nile has receded from the drenched fields and has returned again to its former bed, and the fresh slime has been heated by the sun's rays, farmers as they turn over the lumps of earth find many animate things; and among these some, but now begun, are upon the very verge of life, some are unfinished and lacking in their proper parts, and oft-times in the same body one part is alive and the other still nothing but raw earth. For when moisture and heat unite, life is conceived, and from these two sources all living things spring. And, though fire and water are naturally at enmity, still heat and moisture produce all things, and this inharmonious harmony is fitted to the growth of life. When, therefore, the earth, covered with mud from the recent flood, became heated up by the hot ethereal rays of the sun, she brought forth innumerable forms of life; in part she restored the ancient shapes, and in part she created creatures new and strange.

She, indeed, would have wished not so to do, but thee also she then bore, thou huge Python, thou snake unknown before, who wast a terror to new-created men; so huge a space of mountain-side didst thou fill. This monster the god of the bow destroyed with lethal arms never before used except against does and wild she-goats, crushing him with countless darts, well-nigh emptying his quiver, till the creature's poisonous blood flowed from the black wounds. And, that the fame of his deed might not perish through lapse of time, he instituted sacred games whose contests throngs beheld, called Pythian from the name of the serpent he had overthrown. At these games,

vicerat, aesculeae capiebat frondis honorem.
nondum laurus erat, longoque decentia crine   450
tempora cingebat de qualibet arbore Phoebus.
    Primus amor Phoebi Daphne Peneia, quem non
fors ignara dedit, sed saeva Cupidinis ira,
Delius hunc nuper, victa serpente superbus,
viderat adducto flectentem cornua nervo   455
" quid " que " tibi, lascive puer, cum fortibus
        armis ? "
dixerat : " ista decent umeros gestamina nostros,
qui dare certa ferae, dare vulnera possumus hosti,
qui modo pestifero tot iugera ventre prementem
stravimus innumeris tumidum Pythona sagittis.   460
tu face nescio quos esto contentus amores
inritare tua, nec laudes adsere nostras ! "
filius huic Veneris " figat tuus omnia, Phoebe,
te meus arcus " ait; " quantoque animalia cedunt
cuncta deo, tanto minor est tua gloria nostra."   465
dixit et eliso percussis aere pennis
inpiger umbrosa Parnasi constitit arce
eque sagittifera prompsit duo tela pharetra
diversorum operum : fugat hoc, facit illud amorem;
quod facit, auratum est et cuspide fulget acuta,   470
quod fugat, obtusum est et habet sub harundine
        plumbum.
hoc deus in nympha Peneide fixit, at illo
laesit Apollineas traiecta per ossa medullas;
protinus alter amat, fugit altera nomen amantis
silvarum latebris captivarumque ferarum   475

34

every youth who had been victorious in boxing, running, or the chariot race received the honour of an oaken garland. For as yet the laurel-tree was not, and Phoebus was wont to wreathe his temples, comely with flowing locks, with a garland from any tree.

Now the first love of Phoebus was Daphne, daughter of Peneus, the river-god. It was no blind chance that gave this love, but the malicious wrath of Cupid. Delian Apollo, while still exulting over his conquest of the serpent, had seen him bending his bow with tight-drawn string, and had said: " What hast thou to do with the arms of men, thou wanton boy? That weapon befits my shoulders; for I have strength to give unerring wounds to the wild beasts, my foes, and have but now laid low the Python swollen with countless darts, covering whole acres with plague-engendering form. Do thou be content with thy torch to light the hidden fires of love, and lay not claim to my honours." And to him Venus' son replied: " Thy dart may pierce all things else, Apollo, but mine shall pierce thee; and by as much as all living things are less than deity, by so much less is thy glory than mine." So saying he shook his wings and, dashing upward through the air, quickly alighted on the shady peak of Parnasus. There he took from his quiver two darts of opposite effect: one puts to flight, the other kindles the flame of love. The one which kindles love is of gold and has a sharp, gleaming point; the other is blunt and tipped with lead. This last the god fixed in the heart of Peneus' daughter, but with the other he smote Apollo, piercing even unto the bones and marrow. Straightway he burned with love; but she fled the very name of love, rejoicing in the deep fastnesses of the woods, and in the spoils of beasts

exuviis gaudens innuptaeque aemula Phoebes:
vitta coercebat positos sine lege capillos.
multi illam petiere, illa aversata petentes
inpatiens expersque viri nemora avia lustrat
nec, quid Hymen, quid Amor, quid sint conubia curat.
saepe pater dixit: " generum mihi, filia, debes,"   481
saepe pater dixit: " debes mihi, nata, nepotes ";
illa velut crimen taedas exosa iugales
pulchra verecundo suffuderat ora rubore
inque patris blandis haerens cervice lacertis   485
" da mihi perpetua, genitor carissime," dixit
" virginitate frui! dedit hoc pater ante Dianae."
ille quidem obsequitur, sed te decor iste quod optas
esse vetat, votoque tuo tua forma repugnat:
Phoebus amat visaeque cupit conubia Daphnes,   490
quodque cupit, sperat, suaque illum oracula fallunt,
utque leves stipulae demptis adolentur aristis,
ut facibus saepes ardent, quas forte viator
vel nimis admovit vel iam sub luce reliquit,
sic deus in flammas abiit, sic pectore toto   495
uritur et sterilem sperando nutrit amorem.
spectat inornatos collo pendere capillos
et " quid, si comantur? " ait.   videt igne micantes
sideribus similes oculos, videt oscula, quae non
est vidisse satis; laudat digitosque manusque   500
bracchiaque et nudos media plus parte lacertos;
si qua latent, meliora putat. fugit ocior aura
illa levi neque ad haec revocantis verba resistit:
" nympha, precor, Penei, mane! non insequor hostis;
nympha, mane! sic agna lupum, sic cerva leonem, 505

which she had snared, vying with the virgin Phoebe.
A single fillet bound her locks all unarranged. Many
sought her; but she, averse to all suitors, impatient
of control and without thought for man, roamed the
pathless woods, nor cared at all that Hymen, love, or
wedlock might be. Often her father said: " Daughter,
you owe me a son-in-law "; and often: " Daughter,
you owe me grandsons." But she, hating the wed-
ding torch as if it were a thing of evil, would blush
rosy red over her fair face, and, clinging around her
father's neck with coaxing arms, would say: " O
father, dearest, grant me to enjoy perpetual virginity.
Her father has already granted this to Diana." He,
indeed, yielded to her request. But that beauty of
thine, Daphne, forbade the fulfilment of thy desire,
and thy form fitted not with thy prayer. Phoebus
loves Daphne at sight, and longs to wed her; and
what he longs for, that he hopes; and his own gifts
of prophecy deceive him. And as the stubble of
the harvested grain is kindled, as hedges burn with
the torches which some traveller has chanced to
put too near, or has gone off and left at break of
day, so was the god consumed with flames, so did he
burn in all his heart, and feed his fruitless love on
hope. He looks at her hair hanging down her neck
in disarray, and says: " What if it were arrayed? "
He gazes at her eyes gleaming like stars, he gazes
upon her lips, which but to gaze on does not satisfy.
He marvels at her fingers, hands, and wrists, and her
arms, bare to the shoulder; and what is hid he deems
still lovelier. But she flees him swifter than the fleet-
ing breeze, nor does she stop when he calls after her:
" O nymph, O Peneus' daughter, stay! I who pursue
thee am no enemy. Oh stay! So does the lamb flee
from the wolf; the deer from the lion; so do doves
on fluttering wing flee from the eagle; so every

37

sic aquilam penna fugiunt trepidante columbae,
hostes quaeque suos: amor est mihi causa sequendi!
me miserum! ne prona cadas indignave laedi
crura notent sentes et sim tibi causa doloris!
aspera, qua properas, loca sunt: moderatius, oro, 510
curre fugamque inhibe, moderatius insequar ipse.
cui placeas, inquire tamen: non incola montis,
non ego sum pastor, non hic armenta gregesque
horridus observo. nescis, temeraria, nescis,
quem fugias, ideoque fugis: mihi Delphica tellus 515
et Claros et Tenedos Patareaque regia servit;
Iuppiter est genitor; per me, quod eritque fuitque
estque, patet; per me concordant carmina nervis.
certa quidem nostra est, nostra tamen una sagitta
certior, in vacuo quae vulnera pectore fecit! 520
inventum medicina meum est, opiferque per orbem
dicor, et herbarum subiecta potentia nobis.
ei mihi, quod nullis amor est sanabilis herbis
nec prosunt domino, quae prosunt omnibus, artes!"
  Plura locuturum timido Peneia cursu 525
fugit cumque ipso verba inperfecta reliquit,
tum quoque visa decens; nudabant corpora venti,
obviaque adversas vibrabant flamina vestes,
et levis inpulsos retro dabat aura capillos,
auctaque forma fuga est. sed enim non sustinet ultra
perdere blanditias iuvenis deus, utque monebat 531
ipse Amor, admisso sequitur vestigia passu.
ut canis in vacuo leporem cum Gallicus arvo
vidit, et hic praedam pedibus petit, ille salutem;
alter inhaesuro similis iam iamque tenere 535

creature flees its foes. But love is the cause of my pursuit. Ah me! I fear that thou wilt fall, or brambles mar thy innocent limbs, and I be cause of pain to thee. The region here is rough through which thou hastenest. Run with less speed, I pray, and hold thy flight. I, too, will follow with less speed. Nay, stop and ask who thy lover is. I am no mountain-dweller, no shepherd I, no unkempt guardian here of flocks and herds. Thou knowest not, rash one, thou knowest not whom thou fleest, and for that reason dost thou flee. Mine is the Delphian land, and Claros, Tenedos, and the realm of Patara acknowledge me as lord. Jove is my father. By me what shall be, has been, and what is are all revealed; by me the lyre responds in harmony to song. My arrow is sure of aim, but oh, one arrow, surer than my own, has wounded my heart but now so fancy free. The art of medicine is my discovery. I am called Help-Bringer throughout the world, and all the potency of herbs is given unto me. Alas, that love is curable by no herbs, and the arts which heal all others cannot heal their lord! "

He would have said more, but the maiden pursued her frightened way and left him with his words unfinished, even in her desertion seeming fair. The winds bared her limbs, the opposing breezes set her garments a-flutter as she ran, and a light air flung her locks streaming behind her. Her beauty was enhanced by flight. But the chase drew to an end, for the youthful god would not longer waste his time in coaxing words, and urged on by love, he pursued at utmost speed. Just as when a Gallic hound has seen a hare in an open plain, and seeks his prey on flying feet, but the hare, safety; he, just about to fasten on her, now, even now thinks he has her, and

sperat et extento stringit vestigia rostro,
alter in ambiguo est, an sit conprensus, et ipsis
morsibus eripitur tangentiaque ora relinquit:
sic deus et virgo est hic spe celer, illa timore.
qui tamen insequitur pennis adiutus Amoris,   540
ocior est requiemque negat tergoque fugacis
inminet et crinem sparsum cervicibus adflat.
viribus absumptis expalluit illa citaeque
victa labore fugae spectans Peneidas undas [1]   544
"fer, pater," inquit "opem! si flumina numen habetis,
qua nimium placui, mutando perde figuram! "   547
vix prece finita torpor gravis occupat artus,
mollia cinguntur tenui praecordia libro,
in frondem crines, in ramos bracchia crescunt,   550
pes modo tam velox pigris radicibus haeret,
ora cacumen habet: remanet nitor unus in illa.
     Hanc quoque Phoebus amat positaque in stipite
          dextra
sentit adhuc trepidare novo sub cortice pectus
conplexusque suis ramos ut membra lacertis   555
oscula dat ligno; refugit tamen oscula lignum.
cui deus " at, quoniam coniunx mea non potes esse,
arbor eris certe " dixit " mea! semper habebunt
te coma, te citharae, te nostrae, laure, pharetrae;
tu ducibus Latiis aderis, cum laeta Triumphum   560
vox canet et visent longas Capitolia pompas;
postibus Augustis eadem fidissima custos
ante fores stabis mediamque tuebere quercum,

---

[1] *Most MSS. have two verses for 547:*

> qua nimium placui, tellus, ait, hisce, vel istam
> quae facit ut laedar mutando perde figuram.

Probably quae facit ut laedar *was first written as a gloss to* qua
nimium placui, *and the line completed by an emendation.*

grazes her very heels with his outstretched muzzle; but she knows not whether she be not already caught, and barely escapes from those sharp fangs and leaves behind the jaws just closing on her: so ran the god and maid, he sped by hope and she by fear. But he ran the more swiftly, borne on the wings of love, gave her no time to rest, hung over her fleeing shoulders and breathed on the hair that streamed over her neck. Now was her strength all gone, and, pale with fear and utterly overcome by the toil of her swift flight, seeing her father's waters near, she cried: "O father, help! if your waters hold divinity; change and destroy this beauty by which I pleased o'er well." Scarce had she thus prayed when a down-dragging numbness seized her limbs, and her soft sides were begirt with thin bark. Her hair was changed to leaves, her arms to branches. Her feet, but now so swift, grew fast in sluggish roots, and her head was now but a tree's top. Her gleaming beauty alone remained.

But even now in this new form Apollo loved her; and placing his hand upon the trunk, he felt the heart still fluttering beneath the bark. He embraced the branches as if human limbs, and pressed his lips upon the wood. But even the wood shrank from his kisses. And the god cried out to this: "Since thou canst not be my bride, thou shalt at least be my tree. My hair, my lyre, my quiver shall always be entwined with thee, O laurel. With thee shall Roman generals wreathe their heads, when shouts of joy shall acclaim their triumph, and long processions climb the Capitol. Thou at Augustus' portals shalt stand a trusty guardian, and keep watch over the civic crown of

utque meum intonsis caput est iuvenale capillis,
tu quoque perpetuos semper gere frondis honores ! "
finierat Paean : factis modo laurea ramis   566
adnuit utque caput visa est agitasse cacumen.
    Est nemus Haemoniae, praerupta quod undique claudit
silva : vocant Tempe ; per quae Peneos ab imo
effusus Pindo spumosis volvitur undis   570
deiectuque gravi tenues agitantia fumos
nubila conducit summisque adspergine silvis
inpluit et sonitu plus quam vicina fatigat :
haec domus, haec sedes, haec sunt penetralia magni
amnis, in his residens facto de cautibus antro,   575
undis iura dabat nymphisque colentibus undas.
conveniunt illuc popularia flumina primum,
nescia, gratentur consolenturne parentem,
populifer Sperchios et inrequietus Enipeus
Apidanosque senex lenisque Amphrysos et Aeas, 580
moxque amnes alii, qui, qua tulit inpetus illos,
in mare deducunt fessas erroribus undas.
Inachus unus abest imoque reconditus antro
fletibus auget aquas natamque miserrimus Io
luget ut amissam : nescit, vitane fruatur   585
an sit apud manes ; sed quam non invenit usquam,
esse putat nusquam atque animo peiora veretur.
    Viderat a patrio redeuntem Iuppiter illam
flumine et " o virgo Iove digna tuoque beatum
nescio quem factura toro, pete " dixerat "umbras 590
altorum nemorum " (et nemorum monstraverat
    umbras)

oak which hangs between. And as my head is ever young and my locks unshorn, so do thou keep the beauty of thy leaves perpetual." Paean was done. The laurel waved her new-made branches, and seemed to move her head-like top in full consent.

There is a vale in Thessaly which steep-wooded slopes surround on every side. Men call it Tempe. Through this the River Peneus flows from the foot of Pindus with foam-flecked waters, and by its heavy fall forms clouds which drive along fine, smoke-like mist, sprinkles the tops of the trees with spray, and deafens even remoter regions by its roar. Here is the home, the seat, the inmost haunt of the mighty stream. Here, seated in a cave of overhanging rock, he was giving laws to his waters, and to his water-nymphs. Hither came, first, the rivers of his own country, not knowing whether to congratulate or console the father of Daphne: the poplar-fringed Sperchios, the restless Enipeus, hoary Apidanus, gentle Amphrysos and Aeas; and later all the rivers which, by whatsoever way their current carries them, lead down their waters, weary with wandering, into the sea. Inachus only does not come; but, hidden away in his deepest cave, he augments his waters with his tears, and in utmost wretchedness laments his daughter, Io, as lost. He knows not whether she still lives or is among the shades. But, since he cannot find her anywhere, he thinks she must be nowhere, and his anxious soul forbodes things worse than death.

Now Jove had seen her returning from her father's stream, and said: " O maiden, worthy of the love of Jove, and destined to make some husband happy, seek now the shade of these deep woods "—and he pointed to the shady woods—" while the sun at his

43

dum calet, et medio sol est altissimus orbe!
quodsi sola times latebras intrare ferarum,
praeside tuta deo nemorum secreta subibis,
nec de plebe deo, sed qui caelestia magna   595
sceptra manu teneo, sed qui vaga fulmina mitto.
ne fuge me! " fugiebat enim. iam pascua Lernae
consitaque arboribus Lyrcea reliquerat arva,
cum deus inducta latas caligine terras
occuluit tenuitque fugam rapuitque pudorem.   600
    Interea medios Iuno despexit in Argos[1]
et noctis faciem nebulas fecisse volucres
sub nitido mirata die, non fluminis illas
esse, nec umenti sensit tellure remitti;
atque suus coniunx ubi sit circumspicit, ut quae 605
deprensi totiens iam nosset furta mariti.
quem postquam caelo non repperit, " aut ego fallor
aut ego laedor " ait delapsaque ab aethere summo
constitit in terris nebulasque recedere iussit.
coniugis adventum praesenserat inque nitentem   610
Inachidos vultus mutaverat ille iuvencam;
bos quoque formosa est. speciem Saturnia vaccae,
quamquam invita, probat nec non, et cuius et
        unde
quove sit armento, veri quasi nescia quaerit.
Iuppiter e terra genitam mentitur, ut auctor   615
desinat inquiri : petit hanc Saturnia munus.
quid faciat? crudele suos addicere amores,
non dare suspectum est : Pudor est, qui suadeat illinc,

----

[1] Argos *Merkel and Müller:* agros *MSS.*

zenith's height is overwarm. But if thou fearest to go alone amongst the haunts of wild beasts, under a god's protection shalt thou tread in safety even the inmost woods. Nor am I of the common gods, but I am he who holds high heaven's sceptre in his mighty hand, and hurls the roaming thunderbolts. Oh, do not flee from me!"—for she was already in flight. Now had she left behind the pasture-fields of Lerna, and the Lyrcean plains thick-set with trees, when the god hid the wide land in a thick, dark cloud, caught the fleeing maid and ravished her.

Meanwhile Juno chanced to look down upon the midst of Argos, and marvelled that quick-rising clouds had wrought the aspect of night in the clear light of day. She knew that they were not river mists nor fogs exhaled from the damp earth; and forthwith she glanced around to see where her lord might be, as one who knew well his oft-discovered wiles. When she could not find him in the sky she said: "Either I am mistaken or I am being wronged"; and gliding down from the top of heaven, she stood upon the earth and bade the clouds disperse. But Jove had felt beforehand his spouse's coming and had changed the daughter of Inachus into a white heifer. Even in this form she still was beautiful. Saturnia looked awhile upon the heifer in grudging admiration; then asked whose she was and whence she came or from what herd, as if she did not know full well. Jove lyingly declared that she had sprung from the earth, that so he might forestall all further question as to her origin. Thereupon Saturnia asked for the heifer as a gift. What should he do? 'Twere a cruel task to surrender his love, but not to do so would arouse suspicion. Shame on one side prompts to give her

OVID

hinc dissuadet Amor.   victus Pudor esset Amore,
sed leve si munus sociae generisque torique   620
vacca negaretur, poterat non vacca videri!
   Paelice donata non protinus exuit omnem
diva metum timuitque Iovem et fuit anxia furti,
donec Arestoridae servandam tradidit Argo.
centum luminibus cinctum caput Argus habebat 625
inde suis vicibus capiebant bina quietem,
cetera servabant atque in statione manebant.
constiterat quocumque modo, spectabat ad Io,
ante oculos Io, quamvis aversus, habebat.
luce sinit pasci; cum sol tellure sub alta est,   630
claudit et indigno circumdat vincula collo.
frondibus arboreis et amara pascitur herba.
proque toro terrae non semper gramen habenti
incubat infelix limosaque flumina potat.
illa etiam supplex Argo cum bracchia vellet   635
tendere, non habuit, quae bracchia tenderet Argo,
conatoque queri mugitus edidit ore
pertimuitque sonos propriaque exterrita voce est.
venit et ad ripas, ubi ludere saepe solebat,
Inachidas: rictus[1] novaque ut conspexit in unda 640
cornua, pertimuit seque exsternata refugit.
naides ignorant, ignorat et Inachus ipse,
quae sit; at illa patrem sequitur sequiturque sorores
et patitur tangi seque admirantibus offert.
decerptas senior porrexerat Inachus herbas: 645
illa manus lambit patriisque dat oscula palmis
nec retinet lacrimas et, si modo verba sequantur,

---

[1] Inachidas: rictus *Merkel:* Inachidas ripas *MSS.*

46

up, but love on the other urges not. Shame by love
would have been o'ercome; but if so poor a gift as a
heifer were refused to her who was both his sister
and his wife, perchance she had seemed to be no
heifer.

Though her rival was at last given up, the goddess
did not at once put off all suspicion, for she feared
Jove and further treachery, until she had given her
over to Argus, the son of Arestor, to keep for her.
Now Argus' head was set about with a hundred eyes,
which took their rest in sleep two at a time in turn,
while the others watched and remained on guard.
In whatsoever way he stood he looked at Io; even
when his back was turned he had Io before his eyes.
In the daytime he allowed her to graze; but when
the sun had set beneath the earth he shut her up
and tied an ignominious halter round her neck. She
fed on leaves of trees and bitter herbs, and instead
of a couch the poor thing lay upon the ground,
which was not always grassy, and drank water from
the muddy streams. When she strove to stretch out
suppliant arms to Argus, she had no arms to stretch;
and when she attempted to voice her complaints, she
only mooed. She would start with fear at the sound,
and was filled with terror at her own voice. She
came also to the bank of her father's stream, where
she used to play; but when she saw, reflected in the
water, her gaping jaws and sprouting horns, she fled
in very terror of herself. Her Naiad sisters knew
not who she was, nor yet her father, Inachus himself.
But she followed him and her sisters, and offered
herself to be petted and admired. Old Inachus had
plucked some grass and held it out to her; she
licked her father's hand and tried to kiss it. She
could not restrain her tears, and, if only she could

oret opem nomenque suum casusque loquatur;
littera pro verbis, quam pes in pulvere duxit,
corporis indicium mutati triste peregit.   650
" me miserum! " exclamat pater Inachus inque
    gementis
cornibus et nivea pendens cervice iuvencae
" me miserum! " ingeminat; " tune es quaesita
    per omnes
nata mihi terras? tu non inventa reperta
luctus eras levior! retices nec mutua nostris   655
dicta refers, alto tantum suspiria ducis
pectore, quodque unum potes, ad mea verba
    remugis!
at tibi ego ignarus thalamos taedasque parabam,
spesque fuit generi mihi prima, secunda nepotum.
de grege nunc tibi vir, nunc de grege natus
    habendus.   660
nec finire licet tantos mihi morte dolores;
sed nocet esse deum, praeclusaque ianua leti
aeternum nostros luctus extendit in aevum."
talia maerenti stellatus submovet Argus
ereptamque patri diversa in pascua natam   665
abstrahit. ipse procul montis sublime cacumen
occupat, unde sedens partes speculatur in omnes.
   Nec superum rector mala tanta Phoronidos
    ultra
ferre potest natumque vocat, quem lucida partu
Pleias enixa est letoque det imperat Argum.   670
parva mora est alas pedibus virgamque potenti
somniferam sumpsisse manu tegumenque capillis.
haec ubi disposuit, patria Iove natus ab arce
desilit in terras; illic tegumenque removit
et posuit pennas, tantummodo virga retenta est: 675
hac agit, ut pastor, per devia rura capellas

speak, she would tell her name and sad misfortune, and beg for aid. But instead of words, she did tell the sad story of her changed form with letters which she traced in the dust with her hoof. "Ah, woe is me!" exclaimed her father, Inachus; and, clinging to the weeping heifer's horns and snow-white neck: "Ah, woe is me! art thou indeed my daughter whom I have sought o'er all the earth? Unfound, a lighter grief wast thou than found. Thou art silent, and givest me back no answer to my words; thou only heavest deep sighs, and, what alone thou canst, thou dost moo in reply. I, in blissful ignorance, was preparing marriage rites for thee, and had hopes, first of a son-in-law, and then of grandchildren. But now from the herd must I find thee a husband, and from the herd must I look for grandchildren. And even by death I may not end my crushing woes. It is a dreadful thing to be a god, for the door of death is shut to me, and my grief must go on without end." As he thus made lament star-eyed Argus moved his daughter away and drove her, torn from her father's arms, to more distant pastures. There he perched himself apart upon a high mountain-top, where at his ease he could keep watch on every side.

But now the ruler of the heavenly ones can no longer bear these great sufferings of Io, and he calls his son whom the shining Pleiad bore, and bids him do Argus to death. Without delay Mercury puts on his winged sandals, takes in his potent hand his sleep-producing wand, and dons his magic cap. Thus arrayed, the son of Jove leaps down from sky to earth, where he removes his cap and lays aside his wings. Only his wand he keeps. With this, in the character of a shepherd, through the sequestered

dum venit abductas, et structis cantat avenis.
voce nova captus custos Iunonius " at tu,
quisquis es, hoc poteras mecum considere saxo "
Argus ait; " neque enim pecori fecundior ullo   680
herba loco est, aptamque vides pastoribus umbram."

Sedit Atlantiades et euntem multa loquendo
detinuit sermone diem iunctisque canendo
vincere harundinibus servantia lumina temptat.
ille tamen pugnat molles evincere somnos   685
et, quamvis sopor est oculorum parte receptus,
parte tamen vigilat. quaerit quoque (namque reperta
fistula nuper erat), qua sit ratione reperta.

Tum deus "Arcadiae gelidis sub montibus" inquit
" inter hamadryadas celeberrima Nonacrinas   690
naias una fuit: nymphae Syringa vocabant.
non semel et satyros eluserat illa sequentes
et quoscumque deos umbrosaque silva feraxque
rus habet. Ortygiam studiis ipsaque colebat
virginitate deam; ritu quoque cincta Dianae   695
falleret et posset credi Latonia, si non
corneus huic arcus, si non foret aureus illi;
sic quoque fallebat.
                    Redeuntem colle Lycaeo
Pan videt hanc pinuque caput praecinctus acuta
talia verba refert "—restabat verba referre   700
et precibus spretis fugisse per avia nympham,

country paths he drives a flock of goats which he has rustled as he came along, and plays upon his reed pipe as he goes. Juno's guardsman is greatly taken with the strange sound. " You, there," he calls, " whoever you are, you might as well sit beside me on this rock; for nowhere is there richer grass for the flock, and you see that there is shade convenient for shepherds."

So Atlas' grandson takes his seat, and fills the passing hours with talk of many things; and by making music on his pipe of reeds he tries to overcome those watchful eyes. But Argus strives valiantly against his slumberous languor, and though he allows some of his eyes to sleep, still he continues to watch with the others. He asks also how the reed pipe came to be invented; for at that time it had but recently been invented.

Then said the god: " On Arcadia's cool mountain-slopes, among the wood nymphs who dwelt on Nonacris, there was one much sought by suitors. Her sister nymphs called her Syrinx. More than once she had eluded the pursuit of satyrs and all the gods who dwell either in the bosky woods or fertile fields. But she patterned after the Delian goddess in her pursuits and above all in her life of maidenhood. When girt after the manner of Diana, she would deceive the beholder, and could be mistaken for Latona's daughter, were not her bow of horn, were not Diana's of gold. But even so she was mistaken for the goddess.

" One day Pan saw her as she was coming back from Mount Lycaeus, his head wreathed with a crown of sharp pine-needles, and thus addressed her. . . ." It remained still to tell what he said and to relate how the nymph, spurning his prayers, fled

donec harenosi placidum Ladonis ad amnem
venerit; hic illam cursum inpedientibus undis
ut se mutarent liquidas orasse sorores,
Panaque cum prensam sibi iam Syringa putaret, 705
corpore pro nymphae calamos tenuisse palustres,
dumque ibi suspirat, motos in harundine ventos
effecisse sonum tenuem similemque querenti.
arte nova vocisque deum dulcedine captum
"hoc mihi colloquium tecum" dixisse "manebit," 710
atque ita disparibus calamis conpagine cerae
inter se iunctis nomen tenuisse puellae.
talia dicturus vidit Cyllenius omnes
subcubuisse oculos adopertaque lumina somno;
supprimit extemplo vocem firmatque soporem 715
languida permulcens medicata lumina virga.
nec mora, falcato nutantem vulnerat ense,
qua collo est confine caput, saxoque cruentum
deicit et maculat praeruptam sanguine rupem. 719
Arge, iaces, quodque in tot lumina lumen habebas,
exstinctum est, centumque oculos nox occupat una.

Excipit hos volucrisque suae Saturnia pennis
collocat et gemmis caudam stellantibus inplet.
protinus exarsit nec tempora distulit irae
horriferamque oculis animoque obiecit Erinyn 725
paelicis Argolicae stimulosque in pectore caecos
condidit et profugam per totum exercuit orbem.
ultimus inmenso restabas, Nile, labori;
quem simulac tetigit, positisque in margine ripae
procubuit genibus resupinoque ardua collo, 730

through the pathless wastes until she came to Ladon's stream flowing peacefully along his sandy banks; how here, when the water checked her further flight, she besought her sisters of the stream to change her form; and how Pan, when now he thought he had caught Syrinx, instead of her held naught but marsh reeds in his arms; and while he sighed in disappointment, the soft air stirring in the reeds gave forth a low and complaining sound. Touched by this wonder and charmed by the sweet tones, the god exclaimed: " This converse, at least, shall I have with thee." And so the pipes, made of unequal reeds fitted together by a joining of wax, took and kept the name of the maiden. When Mercury was going on to tell this story, he saw that all those eyes had yielded and were closed in sleep. Straightway he checks his words, and deepens Argus' slumber by passing his magic wand over those sleep-faint eyes. And forthwith he smites with his hooked sword the nodding head just where it joins the neck, and sends it bleeding down the rocks, defiling the rugged cliff with blood. Argus, thou liest low; the light which thou hadst within thy many fires is all put out; and one darkness fills thy hundred eyes.

Saturnia took these eyes and set them on the feathers of her bird, filling his tail with star-like jewels. Straightway she flamed with anger, nor did she delay the fulfilment of her wrath. She set a terror-bearing fury to work before the eyes and heart of her Grecian rival, planted deep within her breast a goading fear, and hounded her in flight through all the world. Thou, O Nile, alone didst close her boundless toil. When she reached the stream, she flung herself down on her knees upon the river bank; with head thrown back she raised her face,

quos potuit solos, tollens ad sidera vultus
et gemitu et lacrimis et luctisono mugitu
cum Iove visa queri finemque orare malorum.
coniugis ille suae conplexus colla lacertis,   734
finiat ut poenas tandem, rogat " in " que " futurum
pone metus " inquit : " numquam tibi causa doloris
haec erit," et Stygias iubet hoc audire paludes.

Ut lenita dea est, vultus capit illa priores
fitque, quod ante fuit : fugiunt e corpore saetae,
cornua decrescunt, fit luminis artior orbis,   740
contrahitur rictus, redeunt umerique manusque,
ungulaque in quinos dilapsa absumitur ungues :
de bove nil superest formae nisi candor in illa.
officioque pedum nymphe contenta duorum
erigitur metuitque loqui, ne more iuvencae   745
mugiat, et timide verba intermissa retemptat.

Nunc dea linigera colitur celeberrima turba.
huic [1] Epaphus magni genitus de semine tandem
creditur esse Iovis perque urbes iuncta parenti
templa tenet. fuit huic animis aequalis et annis   750
Sole satus Phaethon, quem quondam magna
      loquentem
nec sibi cedentem Phoeboque parente superbum
non tulit Inachides " matri " que ait " omnia demens
credis et es tumidus genitoris imagine falsi."
erubuit Phaethon iramque pudore repressit   755
et tulit ad Clymenen Epaphi convicia matrem
"quo" que "magis doleas, genetrix" ait, "ille ego liber,

      [1] huic *Heinsius:* nunc *MSS.*

54

which alone she could raise, to the high stars, and with groans and tears and agonized mooings she seemed to voice her griefs to Jove and to beg him to end her woes. Thereupon Jove threw his arms about his spouse's neck, and begged her at last to end her vengeance, saying: " Lay aside all fear for the future; she shall never be source of grief to you again "; and he called upon the Stygian pools to witness his oath.

The goddess's wrath is soothed; Io gains back her former looks, and becomes what she was before. The rough hair falls away from her body, her horns disappear, her great round eyes grow smaller, her gaping mouth is narrowed, her shoulders and her hands come back, and the hoofs are gone, being changed each into five nails. No trace of the heifer is left in her save only the fair whiteness of her body. And now the nymph, able at last to stand upon two feet, stands erect; yet fears to speak, lest she moo in the heifer's way, and with fear and trembling she resumes her long-abandoned speech.

Now, with fullest service, she is worshipped as a goddess by the linen-robed throng. A son, Epaphus, was born to her, thought to have sprung at length from the seed of mighty Jove, and throughout the cities dwelt in temples with his mother. He had a companion of like mind and age named Phaëthon, child of the Sun. When this Phaëthon was once speaking proudly, and refused to give way to him, boasting that Phoebus was his father, the grandson of Inachus rebelled and said: " You are a fool to believe all your mother tells you, and are swelled up with false notions about your father." Phaëthon grew red with rage, but repressed his anger through very shame and carried Epaphus' insulting taunt straight to his mother, Clymene. " And that you

ille ferox tacui! pudet haec opprobria nobis
et dici potuisse et non potuisse refelli.
at tu, si modo sum caelesti stirpe creatus,   760
ede notam tanti generis meque adsere caelo! "
dixit et inplicuit materno bracchia collo
perque suum Meropisque caput taedasque sororum
traderet oravit veri sibi signa parentis.
ambiguum Clymene precibus Phaethontis an ira 765
mota magis dicti sibi criminis utraque caelo
bracchia porrexit spectansque ad lumina solis
" per iubar hoc " inquit " radiis insigne coruscis,
nate, tibi iuro, quod nos auditque videtque,   769
hoc te, quem spectas, hoc te, qui temperat orbem,
Sole satum; si ficta loquor, neget ipse videndum
se mihi, sitque oculis lux ista novissima nostris!
nec longus labor est patrios tibi nosse penates.
unde oritur, domus est terrae contermina nostrae:
si modo fert animus, gradere et scitabere ab ipso! "
emicat extemplo laetus post talia matris   776
dicta suae Phaethon et concipit aethera mente
Aethiopasque suos positosque sub ignibus Indos
sidereis transit patriosque adit inpiger ortus.

may grieve the more, mother," he said, " I, the high-spirited, the bold of tongue, had no word to say. Ashamed am I that such an insult could have been uttered and yet could not be answered. But do you, if I am indeed sprung from heavenly seed, give me a proof of my high birth, and justify my claims to divine origin." So spoke the lad, and threw his arms around his mother's neck, begging her, by his own and Merops' life, by his sisters' nuptial torches, to give him some sure token of his birth. Clymene, moved (it is uncertain whether by the prayers of Phaëthon, or more by anger at the insult to herself), stretched out both arms to heaven, and, turning her eyes on the bright sun, exclaimed: " By the splendour of that radiant orb which both hears and sees me now, I swear to you, my boy, that you are sprung from the Sun, that being whom you behold, that being who sways the world. If I speak not the truth, may I never see him more, and may this be the last time my eyes shall look upon the light of day. But it is not difficult for you yourself to find your father's house. The place where he rises is not far from our own land. If you are so minded, go there and ask your question of the sun himself." Phaëthon leaps up in joy at his mother's words, already grasping the heavens in imagination; and after crossing his own Ethiopia and the land of Ind lying close beneath the sun, he quickly comes to his father's rising-place.

BOOK II

1–400	*Phaethon—ii*
401–530	*Callisto*
531–632	*Corvus, Coronis, Cornix*
633–675	*Ocyroe*
676–707	*Battus*
708–832	*Aglauros and Envy*
833–875	*Europa*

LIBER II

Regia Solis erat sublimibus alta columnis,
clara micante auro flammasque imitante pyropo,
cuius ebur nitidum fastigia summa tegebat,
argenti bifores radiabant lumine valvae.
materiam superabat opus: nam Mulciber illic   5
aequora caelarat medias cingentia terras
terrarumque orbem caelumque, quod imminet orbi.
caeruleos habet unda deos, Tritona canorum
Proteaque ambiguum ballaenarumque prementem
Aegaeona suis inmania terga lacertis   10
Doridaque et natas, quarum pars nare videtur,
pars in mole sedens viridis siccare capillos,
pisce vehi quaedam: facies non omnibus una,
non diversa tamen, qualem decet esse sororum.
terra viros urbesque gerit silvasque ferasque   15
fluminaque et nymphas et cetera numina ruris.
haec super inposita est caeli fulgentis imago,
signaque sex foribus dextris totidemque sinistris.
    Quo simul adclivi Clymeneia limite proles
venit et intravit dubitati tecta parentis,   20
protinus ad patrios sua fert vestigia vultus
consistitque procul; neque enim propiora ferebat
lumina: purpurea velatus veste sedebat

BOOK II

THE palace of the Sun stood high on lofty columns,
bright with glittering gold and bronze that shone
like fire. Gleaming ivory crowned the gables above;
the double folding doors were radiant with burnished
silver. And the workmanship was more beautiful
than the material. For upon the doors Mulciber had
carved in relief the waters that enfold the central
earth, the circle of the lands and the sky that over-
hangs the lands. The sea holds the dark-hued gods:
tuneful Triton, changeful Proteus, and Aegaeon,
whose strong arms can overpower huge whales;
Doris and her daughters, some of whom are shown
swimming through the water, some sitting on a rock
drying their green hair, and some riding on fishes.
They have not all the same appearance, and yet not
altogether different; as it should be with sisters.
The land has men and cities, woods and beasts,
rivers, nymphs and other rural deities. Above these
scenes was placed a representation of the shining
sky, six signs of the zodiac on the right-hand doors,
and six signs on the left.

Now when Clymene's son had climbed the steep
path which leads thither, and had come beneath the
roof of his sire whose fatherhood had been ques-
tioned, straightway he turned him to his father's
face, but halted some little space away; for he could
not bear the radiance at a nearer view. Clad in a

in solio Phoebus claris lucente smaragdis.
a dextra laevaque Dies et Mensis et Annus   25
Saeculaque et positae spatiis aequalibus Horae
Verque novum stabat cinctum florente corona,
stabat nuda Aestas et spicea serta gerebat,
stabat et Autumnus calcatis sordidus uvis
et glacialis Hiems canos hirsuta capillos.   30
    Ipse loco medius rerum novitate paventem
Sol oculis iuvenem, quibus adspicit omnia, vidit
" quae " que " viae tibi causa? quid hac " ait " arce
    petisti,
progenies, Phaethon, haud infitianda parenti? "
ille refert: " o lux inmensi publica mundi,   35
Phoebe pater, si das usum mihi nominis huius,
nec falsa Clymene culpam sub imagine celat,
pignora da, genitor, per quae tua vera propago
credar, et hunc animis errorem detrahe nostris! "
dixerat, at genitor circum caput omne micantes   40
deposuit radios propiusque accedere iussit
amplexuque dato " nec tu meus esse negari
dignus es, et Clymene veros " ait " edidit ortus,
quoque minus dubites, quodvis pete munus, ut illud
me tribuente feras!   promissi testis adesto   45
dis iuranda palus, oculis incognita nostris! "
vix bene desierat, currus rogat ille paternos
inque diem alipedum ius et moderamen equorum.
    Paenituit iurasse patrem: qui terque quaterque
concutiens inlustre caput " temeraria " dixit   50
" vox mea facta tua est; utinam promissa liceret
62

purple robe, Phoebus sat on his throne gleaming with brilliant emeralds. To right and left stood Day and Month and Year and Century, and the Hours set at equal distances. Young Spring was there, wreathed with a floral crown; Summer, all unclad with garland of ripe grain; Autumn was there, stained with the trodden grape, and icy Winter with white and bristly locks.

Seated in the midst of these, the Sun, with the eyes which behold all things, looked on the youth filled with terror at the strange new sights, and said: " Why hast thou come? What seekest thou in this high dwelling, Phaëthon—a son no father need deny?" The lad replied: " O common light of this vast universe, Phoebus, my father, if thou grantest me the right to use that name, if Clymene is not hiding her shame beneath an unreal pretence, grant me a proof, my father, by which all may know me for thy true son, and take away this uncertainty from my mind." He spoke; and his father put off his glittering crown of light, and bade the boy draw nearer. Embracing him, he said: " Thou art both worthy to be called my son, and Clymene has told thee thy true origin. And, that thou mayst not doubt my word, ask what boon thou wilt, that thou mayst receive it from my hand. And may that Stygian pool whereby gods swear, but which mine eyes have never seen, be witness of my promise." Scarce had he ceased when the boy asked for his father's chariot, and the right to drive his winged horses for a day.

The father repented him of his oath. Thrice and again he shook his bright head and said: " Thy words have proved mine to have been rashly said. Would that I might retract my promise! For I confess, my

63

non dare! confiteor, solum hoc tibi, nate, negarem.
dissuadere licet: non est tua tuta voluntas!
magna petis, Phaethon, et quae nec viribus istis
munera conveniant nec tam puerilibus annis: 55
sors tua mortalis, non est mortale, quod optas.
plus etiam, quam quod superis contingere possit,
nescius adfectas; placeat sibi quisque licebit,
non tamen ignifero quisquam consistere in axe
me valet excepto; vasti quoque rector Olympi,   60
qui fera terribili iaculatur fulmina dextra,
non agat hos currus: et quid Iove maius habemus?
ardua prima via est et qua vix mane recentes
enituntur equi; medio est altissima caelo,
unde mare et terras ipsi mihi saepe videre   65
fit timor et pavida trepidat formidine pectus;
ultima prona via est et eget moderamine certo:
tunc etiam quae me subiectis excipit undis,
ne ferar in praeceps, Tethys solet ipsa vereri.
adde, quod adsidua rapitur vertigine caelum,   70
sideraque alta trahit celerique volumine torquet.
nitor in adversum, nec me, qui cetera, vincit
inpetus, et rapido contrarius evehor orbi.
finge datos currus: quid ages? poterisne rotatis
obvius ire polis, ne te citus auferat axis?   75
forsitan et lucos illic urbesque deorum
concipias animo delubraque ditia donis
esse: per insidias iter est formasque ferarum!
utque viam teneas nulloque errore traharis,
per tamen adversi gradieris cornua tauri   80

son, that this alone would I refuse thee. But I may
at least strive to dissuade thee. What thou desirest
is not safe. Thou askest too great a boon, Phaëthon,
and one which does not befit thy strength and those
so boyish years. Thy lot is mortal: not for mortals
is that thou askest. In thy simple ignorance thou
dost claim more than can be granted to the gods
themselves. Though each of them may do as he
will, yet none, save myself, has power to take his
place in my chariot of fire. Nay, even the lord of
great Olympus, who hurls dread thunderbolts with
his awful hand, could not drive this chariot; and what
have we greater than Jove? The first part of the
road is steep, up which my steeds in all their morning
freshness can scarce make their way. In mid-heaven
it is exceeding high, whence to look down on sea and
land oft-times causes even me to tremble, and my
heart to quake with throbbing fear. The last part
of the journey is precipitous, and needs an assured
control. Then even Tethys, who receives me in her
underlying waters, is wont to fear lest I fall head-
long. Furthermore, the vault of heaven spins round
in constant motion, drawing along the lofty stars
which it whirls at dizzy speed. I make my way
against this, nor does the swift motion which over-
comes all else overcome me; but I drive clear con-
trary to the swift circuit of the universe. Suppose
thou hast my chariot. What wilt thou do? Wilt
thou be able to make thy way against the whirling
poles that their swift axis sweep thee not away?
Perhaps, too, thou deemest there are groves there,
and cities of the gods, and temples full of rich gifts?
Nay, the course lies amid lurking dangers and fierce
beasts of prey. And though thou shouldst hold the
way, and not go straying from the course, still shalt

65

OVID

Haemoniosque arcus violentique ora Leonis
saevaque circuitu curvantem bracchia longo
Scorpion atque aliter curvantem bracchia Cancrum.
nec tibi quadripedes animosos ignibus illis,
quos in pectore habent, quos ore et naribus efflant, 85
in promptu regere est: vix me patiuntur, ubi acres
incaluere animi cervixque repugnat habenis.—
at tu, funesti ne sim tibi muneris auctor,
nate, cave, dum resque sinit tua corrige vota!
scilicet ut nostro genitum te sanguine credas,   90
pignora certa petis: do pignora certa timendo
et patrio pater esse metu probor.   adspice vultus
ecce meos; utinamque oculos in pectora posses
inserere et patrias intus deprendere curas!
denique quidquid habet dives, circumspice, mundus 95
eque tot ac tantis caeli terraeque marisque
posce bonis aliquid; nullam patiere repulsam.
deprecor hoc unum, quod vero nomine poena,
non honor est: poenam, Phaethon, pro munere
      poscis!
quid mea colla tenes blandis, ignare, lacertis?   100
ne dubita! dabitur (Stygias iuravimus undas),
quodcumque optaris; sed tu sapientius opta!"
   Finierat monitus; dictis tamen ille repugnat
propositumque premit flagratque cupidine currus.
ergo, qua licuit, genitor cunctatus ad altos   105
deducit iuvenem, Vulcania munera, currus.
aureus axis erat, temo aureus, aurea summae
curvatura rotae, radiorum argenteus ordo;
66

thou pass the horned Bull full in thy path, the Haemonian Archer, the maw of the raging Lion, the Scorpion, curving his savage arms in long sweeps, and the Crab, reaching out in the opposite direction. Nor is it an easy thing for thee to control the steeds, hot with those strong fires which they have within their breasts, which they breathe out from mouth and nostrils. Scarce do they suffer my control, when their fierce spirits have become heated, and their necks rebel against the reins. But do thou, O son, beware lest I be the giver of a fatal gift to thee, and while still there is time amend thy prayer. Dost thou in sooth seek sure pledges that thou art son of mine? Behold, I give sure pledges by my very fear; I show myself thy father by my fatherly anxiety. See! look upon my face. And oh, that thou couldst look into my heart as well, and understand a father's cares therein! Then look around, see all that the rich world holds, and from those great and boundless goods of land and sea and sky ask anything. Nothing will I deny thee. But this one thing I beg thee not to ask, which, if rightly understood, is a bane instead of blessing. A bane, my Phaëthon, dost thou seek as boon. Why dost thou throw thy coaxing arms about my neck, thou foolish boy? Nay, doubt it not, it shall be given—we have sworn it by the Styx—whatever thou dost choose. But, oh, make wiser choice!"

The father's warning ended; yet he fought against the words, and urged his first request, burning with desire to drive the chariot. So then the father, delaying as far as might be, led forth the youth to that high chariot, the work of Vulcan. Its axle was of gold, the pole of gold; its wheels had golden tyres and a ring of silver spokes. Along the yoke

per iuga chrysolithi positaeque ex ordine gemmae
clara repercusso reddebant lumina Phoebo.   110
   Dumque ea magnanimus Phaethon miratur opusque
perspicit, ecce vigil nitido patefecit ab ortu
purpureas Aurora fores et plena rosarum
atria: diffugiunt stellae, quarum agmina cogit
Lucifer et caeli statione novissimus exit.   115
   Quem petere ut terras mundumque rubescere vidit
cornuaque extremae velut evanescere lunae,
iungere equos Titan velocibus imperat Horis.
iussa deae celeres peragunt ignemque vomentes,
ambrosiae suco saturos, praesepibus altis   120
quadripedes ducunt adduntque sonantia frena.
tum pater ora sui sacro medicamine nati
contigit et rapidae fecit patientia flammae
inposuitque comae radios praesagaque luctus
pectore sollicito repetens suspiria dixit: 125
" si potes his saltem monitis parere parentis
parce, puer, stimulis et fortius utere loris!
sponte sua properant, labor est inhibere volentes.
nec tibi derectos placeat via quinque per arcus!
sectus in obliquum est lato curvamine limes,   130
zonarumque trium contentus fine polumque
effugit australem iunctamque aquilonibus arcton:
hac sit iter—manifesta rotae vestigia cernes—
utque ferant aequos et caelum et terra calores,
nec preme nec summum molire per aethera currum!
altius egressus caelestia tecta cremabis,   136
inferius terras; medio tutissimus ibis.
neu te dexterior tortum declinet ad Anguem,

chrysolites and jewels set in fair array gave back their bright glow to the reflected rays of Phoebus.

Now while the ambitious Phaëthon is gazing in wonder at the workmanship, behold, Aurora, who keeps watch in the gleaming dawn, has opened wide her purple gates, and her courts glowing with rosy light. The stars all flee away, and the morning star closes their ranks as, last of all, he departs from his watch-tower in the sky.

When Titan saw him setting and the world grow red, and the slender horns of the waning moon fading from sight, he bade the swift Hours to yoke his steeds. The goddesses quickly did his bidding, and led the horses from the lofty stalls, breathing forth fire and filled with ambrosial food, and they put upon them the clanking bridles. Then the father anointed his son's face with a sacred ointment, and made it proof against the devouring flames; and he placed upon his head the radiant crown, heaving deep sighs the while, presaging woe, and said: " If thou canst at least obey these thy father's warnings, spare the lash, my boy, and more strongly use the reins. The horses hasten of their own accord; the hard task is to check their eager feet. And take not thy way straight through the five zones of heaven: the true path runs slantwise, with a wide curve, and, confined within the limits of three zones, avoids the southern heavens and the far north as well. This be thy route for the tracks of my wheels thou wilt clearly see, and, that the sky and earth may have equal heat, go not too low, nor yet direct thy chariot along the top of heaven; for if thou goest too high thou wilt burn up the skies, if too low the earth. In the middle is the safest path. And turn not off too far to the right towards the writhing Serpent;

neve sinisterior pressam rota ducat ad Aram,
inter utrumque tene!   Fortunae cetera mando,   140
quae iuvet et melius quam tu tibi consulat opto.
dum loquor, Hesperio positas in litore metas
umida nox tetigit; non est mora libera nobis!
poscimur: effulget tenebris Aurora fugatis.
corripe lora manu, vel, si mutabile pectus   145
est tibi, consiliis, non curribus utere nostris!
dum potes et solidis etiamnum sedibus adstas,
dumque male optatos nondum premis inscius axes,
quae tutus spectes, sine me dare lumina terris! "

Occupat ille levem iuvenali corpore currum   150
statque super manibusque leves contingere habenas
gaudet et invito grates agit inde parenti.

Interea volucres Pyrois et Eous et Aethon,
Solis equi, quartusque Phlegon hinnitibus auras
flammiferis inplent pedibusque repagula pulsant. 155
quae postquam Tethys, fatorum ignara nepotis,
reppulit, et facta est inmensi copia caeli,
corripuere viam pedibusque per aera motis
obstantes scindunt nebulas pennisque levati
praetereunt ortos isdem de partibus Euros.   160
sed leve pondus erat nec quod cognoscere possent
Solis equi, solitaque iugum gravitate carebat;
utque labant curvae iusto sine pondere naves
perque mare instabiles nimia levitate feruntur,
sic onere adsueto vacuus dat in aera saltus   165
succutiturque alte similisque est currus inani.

nor on the left, where the Altar lies low in the heavens, guide thy wheel. Hold on between the two. I commit all else to Fortune, and may she aid thee, and guide thee better than thou dost thyself. While I am speaking dewy night has reached her goal on the far western shore. We may no longer delay. We are summoned: the dawn is glowing, and the shadows all have fled. Here, grasp the reins, or, if thy purpose still may be amended, take my counsel, not my chariot. While still thou canst, while still thou dost stand on solid ground, before thou hast mounted to the car which thou hast in ignorance foolishly desired, allow me to give light to the world, which thou mayst see in safety."

But the lad has already mounted the light chariot, and, standing proudly, takes the light reins with joy into his hands, and thanks his unwilling father for the gift.

Meanwhile the sun's swift horses, Pyroïs, Eoüs, Aethon, and the fourth, Phlegon, fill all the air with their fiery whinnying, and paw impatiently against their bars. When Tethys, ignorant of her grandson's fate, dropped these and gave free course through the boundless skies, the horses dashed forth, and with swift-flying feet rent the clouds in their path, and, borne aloft upon their wings, they passed the east winds that have their rising in the same quarter. But the weight was light, not such as the horses of the sun could feel, and the yoke lacked its accustomed burden. And, as curved ships, without their proper ballast, roll in the waves, and, unstable because too light, are borne out of their course, so the chariot, without its accustomed burden, gives leaps into the air, is tossed aloft and is like a riderless car.

Quod simulac sensere, ruunt tritumque relinquunt
quadriiugi spatium nec quo prius ordine currunt.
ipse pavet nec qua commissas flectat habenas
nec scit qua sit iter, nec, si sciat, imperet illis.   170
tum primum radiis gelidi caluere Triones
et vetito frustra temptarunt aequore tingui,
quaeque polo posita est glaciali proxima Serpens,
frigore pigra prius nec formidabilis ulli,
incaluit sumpsitque novas fervoribus iras;   175
te quoque turbatum memorant fugisse, Boote,
quamvis tardus eras et te tua plaustra tenebant.

Ut vero summo despexit ab aethere terras
infelix Phaethon penitus penitusque iacentes,
palluit et subito genua intremuere timore   180
suntque oculis tenebrae per tantum lumen obortae,
et iam mallet equos numquam tetigisse paternos,
iam cognosse genus piget et valuisse rogando,
iam Meropis dici cupiens ita fertur, ut acta
praecipiti pinus borea, cui victa remisit   185
frena suus rector, quam dis votisque reliquit.
quid faciat? multum caeli post terga relictum,
ante oculos plus est: animo metitur utrumque
et modo, quos illi fatum contingere non est,
prospicit occasus, interdum respicit ortus,   190
quidque agat ignarus stupet et nec frena remittit
nec retinere valet nec nomina novit equorum.
sparsa quoque in vario passim miracula caelo
vastarumque videt trepidus simulacra ferarum.
est locus, in geminos ubi bracchia concavat arcus   195

When they feel this, the team run wild and leave the well-beaten track, and fare no longer in the same course as before. The driver is panic-stricken. He knows not how to handle the reins entrusted to him, nor where the road is; nor, if he did know, would he be able to control the steeds. Then for the first time the cold oxen grew hot with the rays of the sun, and tried, though all in vain, to plunge into the forbidden sea. And the Serpent, which lies nearest the icy pole, ever before harmless because sluggish with the cold, now grew hot, and conceived great frenzy from that fire. They say that you also, Boötes, fled in terror, slow though you were, and held back by your clumsy ox-cart.

But when the unhappy Phaëthon looked down from the top of heaven, and saw the lands lying far, far below, he grew pale, his knees trembled with sudden fear, and over his eyes came darkness through excess of light. And now he would prefer never to have touched his father's horses, and repents that he has discovered his true origin and prevailed in his prayer. Now, eager to be called the son of Merops, he is borne along just as a ship driven before the headlong blast, whose pilot has let the useless rudder go and abandoned the ship to the gods and prayers. What shall he do? Much of the sky is now behind him, but more is still in front! His thought measures both. And now he looks forward to the west, which he is destined never to reach, and at times back to the east. Dazed, he knows not what to do; he neither lets go the reins nor can he hold them, and he does not even know the horses' names. To add to his panic fear, he sees scattered everywhere in the sky strange figures of huge and savage beasts. There is one place where the Scorpion bends out his arms into

Scorpius et cauda flexisque utrimque lacertis
porrigit in spatium signorum membra duorum:
hunc puer ut nigri madidum sudore veneni
vulnera curvata minitantem cuspide vidit,
mentis inops gelida formidine lora remisit.   200
   Quae postquam summum tetigere iacentia tergum,
exspatiantur equi nulloque inhibente per auras
ignotae regionis eunt, quaque inpetus egit,
hac sine lege ruunt altoque sub aethere fixis
incursant stellis rapiuntque per avia currum   205
et modo summa petunt, modo per declive viasque
praecipites spatio terrae propiore feruntur,
inferiusque suis fraternos currere Luna
admiratur equos, ambustaque nubila fumant.
corripitur flammis, ut quaeque altissima, tellus   210
fissaque agit rimas et sucis aret ademptis;
pabula canescunt, cum frondibus uritur arbor,
materiamque suo praebet seges arida damno.
parva queror: magnae pereunt cum moenibus
          urbes,
cumque suis totas populis incendia gentis   215
in cinerem vertunt; silvae cum montibus ardent;
ardet Athos Taurusque Cilix et Tmolus et Oete
et tum sicca, prius creberrima fontibus, Ide
virgineusque Helicon et nondum Oeagrius Haemus:
ardet in inmensum geminatis ignibus Aetne   220
Parnasosque biceps et Eryx et Cynthus et Othrys
et tandem nivibus Rhodope caritura Mimasque
Dindymaque et Mycale natusque ad sacra Cithaeron.

two bows; and with tail and arms stretching out on both sides, he spreads over the space of two signs. When the boy sees this creature reeking with black poisonous sweat, and threatening to sting him with his curving tail, bereft of wits from chilling fear, down he dropped the reins.

When the horses feel these lying on their backs, they break loose from their course, and, with none to check them, they roam through unknown regions of the air. Wherever their impulse leads them, there they rush aimlessly, knocking against the stars set deep in the sky and snatching the chariot along through uncharted ways. Now they climb up to the top of heaven, and now, plunging headlong down, they course along nearer the earth. The Moon in amazement sees her brother's horses running below her own, and the scorched clouds smoke. The earth bursts into flame, the highest parts first, and splits into deep cracks, and its moisture is all dried up. The meadows are burned to white ashes; the trees are consumed, green leaves and all, and the ripe grain furnishes fuel for its own destruction. But these are small losses which I am lamenting. Great cities perish with their walls, and the vast conflagration reduces whole nations to ashes. The woods are ablaze with the mountains; Athos is ablaze, Cilician Taurus, and Tmolus, and Oete, and Ida, dry at last, but hitherto covered with springs, and Helicon, haunt of the Muses, and Haemus, not yet linked with the name of Oeagrus. Aetna is blazing boundlessly with flames now doubled, and twin-peaked Parnasus and Eryx, Cynthus and Othrys, and Rhodope, at last destined to lose its snows, Mimas and Dindyma, Mycale and Cithaeron, famed for sacred rites. Nor does its chilling clime save

OVID

nec prosunt Scythiae sua frigora: Caucasus ardet
Ossaque cum Pindo maiorque ambobus Olympus 225
aeriaeque Alpes et nubifer Appenninus.
    Tum vero Phaethon cunctis e partibus orbem
adspicit accensum nec tantos sustinet aestus
ferventisque auras velut e fornace profunda
ore trahit currusque suos candescere sentit;   230
et neque iam cineres eiectatamque favillam
ferre potest calidoque involvitur undique fumo,
quoque eat aut ubi sit, picea caligine tectus
nescit et arbitrio volucrum raptatur equorum.
    Sanguine tum credunt in corpora summa vocato
Aethiopum populos nigrum traxisse colorem;   236
tum facta est Libye raptis umoribus aestu
arida, tum nymphae passis fontesque lacusque
deflevere comis; quaerit Boeotia Dircen,
Argos Amymonen, Ephyre Pirenidas undas;   240
nec sortita loco distantes flumina ripas
tuta manent: mediis Tanais fumavit in undis
Peneosque senex Teuthranteusque Caicus
et celer Ismenos cum Phegiaco Erymantho
arsurusque iterum Xanthos flavusque Lycormas, 245
quique recurvatis ludit Maeandros in undis,
Mygdoniusque Melas et Taenarius Eurotas.
arsit et Euphrates Babylonius, arsit Orontes
Thermodonque citus Gangesque et Phasis et
       Hister;
aestuat Alpheos, ripae Spercheides ardent,   250
quodque suo Tagus amne vehit, fluit ignibus
       aurum,
et, quae Maeonias celebrabant carmine ripas
flumineae volucres, medio caluere Caystro;
Nilus in extremum fugit perterritus orbem
occuluitque caput, quod adhuc latet: ostia septem
pulverulenta vacant, septem sine flumine valles. 256

76

Scythia; Caucasus burns, and Ossa with Pindus, and Olympus, greater than both; and the heaven-piercing Alps and cloud-capped Apennines.

Then indeed does Phaëthon see the earth aflame on every hand; he cannot endure the mighty heat, and the air he breathes is like the hot breath of a deep furnace. The chariot he feels growing white-hot beneath his feet. He can no longer bear the ashes and whirling sparks, and is completely shrouded in the dense, hot smoke. In this pitchy darkness he cannot tell where he is or whither he is going, and is swept along at the will of his flying steeds.

It was then, as men think, that the peoples of Aethiopia became black-skinned, since the blood was drawn to the surface of their bodies by the heat. Then also Libya became a desert, for the heat dried up her moisture. Then the nymphs with dishevelled hair bewailed their fountains and their pools. Boeotia mourns the loss of Dirce; Argos, Amymone; Corinth, her Pirenian spring. Nor do rivers, whose lot had given them more spacious channels, remain unscathed. The Don's waters steam; old Peneus, too, Mysian Caïcus, and swift Ismenus; and Arcadian Erymanthus, Xanthus, destined once again to burn; tawny Lycormas, and Maeander, playing along upon its winding way; Thracian Melas and Laconian Eurotas. Babylonian Euphrates burns; Orontes burns, and swift Thermodon; the Ganges, Phasis, Danube; Alpheus boils; Spercheos' banks are aflame. The golden sands of Tagus melt in the intense heat, and the swans, which had been wont to throng the Maeonian streams in tuneful company, are scorched in mid Caÿster. The Nile fled in terror to the ends of the earth, and hid its head, and it is hidden yet. The seven mouths lie empty, filled with dust; seven

fors eadem Ismarios Hebrum cum Strymone siccat
Hesperiosque amnes, Rhenum Rhodanumque
    Padumque
cuique fuit rerum promissa potentia, Thybrin.
dissilit omne solum, penetratque in Tartara rimis 260
lumen et infernum terret cum coniuge regem;
et mare contrahitur siccaeque est campus harenae,
quod modo pontus erat, quosque altum texerat
    aequor,
exsistunt montes et sparsas Cycladas augent.
ima petunt pisces, nec se super aequora curvi   265
tollere consuetas audent delphines in auras;
corpora phocarum summo resupina profundo
exanimata natant: ipsum quoque Nerea fama est
Doridaque et natas tepidis latuisse sub antris.
ter Neptunus aquis cum torvo bracchia vultu   270
exserere ausus erat, ter non tulit aeris ignes.
    Alma tamen Tellus, ut erat circumdata ponto,
inter aquas pelagi contractosque undique fontes,
qui se condiderant in opacae viscera matris,
sustulit oppressos collo tenus arida vultus   275
opposuitque manum fronti magnoque tremore
omnia concutiens paulum subsedit et infra,
quam solet esse, fuit fractaque ita voce locuta est:
" si placet hoc meruique, quid o tua fulmina cessant,
summe deum? liceat periturae viribus ignis   280
igne perire tuo clademque auctore levare!
vix equidem fauces haec ipsa in verba resolvo ";
(presserat ora vapor) " tostos en adspice crines

broad channels, all without a stream. The same mis-
chance dries up the Thracian rivers, Hebrus and
Strymon; also the rivers of the west, the Rhine,
Rhone, Po, and the Tiber, to whom had been pro-
mised the mastery of the world. Great cracks yawn
everywhere, and the light, penetrating to the lower
world, strikes terror into the infernal king and his
consort. Even the sea shrinks up, and what was but
now a great, watery expanse is a dry plain of sand.
The mountains, which the deep sea had covered be-
fore, spring forth, and increase the numbers of the
scattered Cyclades. The fish dive to the lowest
depths, and the dolphins no longer dare to leap curv-
ing above the surface of the sea into their wonted air.
The dead bodies of sea-calves float, with upturned
belly, on the water's top. They say that Nereus him-
self and Doris and her daughters were hot as they lay
hid in their caves. Thrice Neptune essayed to lift his
arms and august face from out the water; thrice did
he desist, unable to bear the fiery atmosphere.

Not so all-fostering Earth, who, encircled as
she was by sea, amid the waters of the deep, amid
her fast-contracting streams which had crowded
into her dark bowels and hidden there, though
parched by heat, heaved up her smothered face as
far as the neck. Raising her shielding hand to her
brow and causing all things to shake with her
mighty trembling, she sank back a little lower than
her wonted place, and then in broken tones she
spoke: "If this is thy will, and I have deserved all
this, why, O king of all the gods, are thy lightnings
idle ? If I must die by fire, oh, let me perish by thy
fire and lighten my suffering by thought of him who
sent it. I scarce can open my lips to speak these
words"—the hot smoke was choking her—"See my

inque oculis tantum, tantum super ora favillae!
hosne mihi fructus, hunc fertilitatis honorem   285
officiique refers, quod adunci vulnera aratri
rastrorumque fero totoque exerceor anno,
quod pecori frondes alimentaque mitia, fruges
humano generi, vobis quoque tura ministro?
sed tamen exitium fac me meruisse: quid undae,
quid meruit frater? cur illi tradita sorte   291
aequora decrescunt et ab aethere longius absunt?
quodsi nec fratris nec te mea gratia tangit,
at caeli miserere tui! circumspice utrumque:
fumat uterque polus! quos si vitiaverit ignis,   295
atria vestra ruent! Atlas en ipse laborat
vixque suis umeris candentem sustinet axem!
si freta, si terrae pereunt, si regia caeli,
in chaos antiquum confundimur! eripe flammis,   299
si quid adhuc superest, et rerum consule summae!"
    Dixerat haec Tellus: neque enim tolerare vaporem
ulterius potuit nec dicere plura suumque
rettulit os in se propioraque manibus antra;
at pater omnipotens, superos testatus et ipsum,
qui dederat currus, nisi opem ferat, omnia fato   305
interitura gravi, summam petit arduus arcem,
unde solet nubes latis inducere terris,
unde movet tonitrus vibrataque fulmina iactat;
sed neque quas posset terris inducere nubes
tunc habuit, nec quos caelo demitteret imbres: 310
intonat et dextra libratum fulmen ab aure
misit in aurigam pariterque animaque rotisque

singed hair and all ashes in my eyes, all ashes over my face. Is this the return, this the reward thou payest of my fertility and dutifulness? that I bear the wounds of the crooked plow and mattock, tormented year in, year out? that I provide kindly pasturage for the flocks, grain for mankind, incense for the altars of the gods? But, grant that I have deserved destruction, what has the sea, what has thy brother done? Why are the waters which fell to him by the third lot so shrunken, and so much further from thy sky? But if no consideration for thy brother nor yet for me has weight with thee, at least have pity on thy own heavens. Look around: the heavens are smoking from pole to pole. If the fire shall weaken these, the homes of the gods will fall in ruins. See, Atlas himself is troubled and can scarce bear up the white-hot vault upon his shoulders. If the sea perish and the land and the realms of the sky, then are we hurled back to primeval chaos. Save from the flames whatever yet remains and take thought for the safety of the universe."

So spoke the Earth and ceased, for she could no longer endure the heat; and she retreated into herself and into the depths nearer the land of shades. But the Almighty Father, calling on the gods to witness and him above all who had given the chariot, that unless he bring aid all things will perish by a grievous doom, mounts on high to the top of heaven, whence it is his wont to spread the clouds over the broad lands, whence he stirs his thunders and flings his hurtling bolts. But now he has no clouds wherewith to overspread the earth, nor any rains to send down from the sky. He thundered, and, balancing in his right hand a bolt, flung it from beside the ear at the charioteer and hurled him from the car and from

expulit et saevis conpescuit ignibus ignes.
consternantur equi et saltu in contraria facto
colla iugo eripiunt abruptaque lora relinquunt: 315
illic frena iacent, illic temone revulsus
axis, in hac radii fractarum parte rotarum
sparsaque sunt late laceri vestigia currus.

  At Phaethon rutilos flamma populante capillos
volvitur in praeceps longoque per aera tractu 320
fertur, ut interdum de caelo stella sereno
etsi non cecidit, potuit cecidisse videri.
quem procul a patria diverso maximus orbe
excipit Eridanus fumantiaque abluit ora.
Naides Hesperiae trifida fumantia flamma 325
corpora dant tumulo, signant quoque carmine saxum:

HIC · SITVS · EST · PHAETHON · CVRRVS · AVRIGA · PATERNI
QVEM · SI · NON · TENVIT · MAGNIS · TAMEN · EXCIDIT · AVSIS

  Nam pater obductos luctu miserabilis aegro
condiderat vultus, et, si modo credimus, unum 330
isse diem sine sole ferunt: incendia lumen
praebebant aliquisque malo fuit usus in illo.
at Clymene postquam dixit, quaecumque fuerunt
in tantis dicenda malis, lugubris et amens
et laniata sinus totum percensuit orbem 335
exanimesque artus primo, mox ossa requirens
repperit ossa tamen peregrina condita ripa
incubuitque loco nomenque in marmore lectum
perfudit lacrimis et aperto pectore fovit.
nec minus Heliades fletus et, inania morti 340

life as well, and thus quenched fire with blasting
fire. The maddened horses leap apart, wrench their
necks from the yoke, and break away from the parted
reins. Here lie the reins, there the axle torn from
the pole; in another place the spokes of the broken
wheels, and fragments of the wrecked chariot are
scattered far and wide.

But Phaëthon, fire ravaging his ruddy hair, is hurled
headlong and falls with a long trail through the air;
as sometimes a star from the clear heavens, although
it does not fall, still seems to fall. Him far from his
native land, in another quarter of the globe, Eridanus
receives and bathes his steaming face. The Naiads in
that western land consign his body, still smoking with
the flames of that forked bolt, to the tomb and carve
this epitaph upon his stone:

HERE PHAËTHON LIES: IN PHOEBUS' CAR HE FARED,
AND THOUGH HE GREATLY FAILED, MORE GREATLY DARED.

The wretched father, sick with grief, hid his face;
and, if we are to believe report, one whole day went
without the sun. But the burning world gave light,
and so even in that disaster was there some service.
But Clymene, after she had spoken whatever could
be spoken in such woe, melancholy and distraught and
tearing her breast, wandered over the whole earth,
seeking first his lifeless limbs, then his bones; his
bones at last she found, but buried on a river-bank
in a foreign land. Here she prostrates herself upon
the tomb, drenches the dear name carved in the
marble with her tears, and fondles it against her
breast. The Heliades, her daughters, join in her
lamentation, and pour out their tears in useless
tribute to the dead. With bruising hands beating

OVID

munera, dant lacrimas, et caesae pectora palmis
non auditurum miseras Phaethonta querellas
nocte dieque vocant adsternunturque sepulcro.
luna quater iunctis inplerat cornibus orbem;
illae more suo (nam morem fecerat usus)   345
plangorem dederant: e quis Phaethusa, sororum
maxima, cum vellet terra procumbere, questa est
deriguisse pedes; ad quam conata venire
candida Lampetie subita radice retenta est;
tertia, cum crinem manibus laniare pararet,   350
avellit frondes; haec stipite crura teneri,
illa dolet fieri longos sua bracchia ramos,
dumque ea mirantur, conplectitur inguina cortex
perque gradus uterum pectusque umerosque manusque
ambit, et exstabant tantum ora vocantia matrem.   355
quid faciat mater, nisi, quo trahat inpetus illam,
huc eat atque illuc et, dum licet, oscula iungat?
non satis est: truncis avellere corpora temptat
et teneros manibus ramos abrumpit, at inde
sanguineae manant tamquam de vulnere guttae.   360
"parce, precor, mater," quaecumque est saucia, clamat,
"parce, precor: nostrum laceratur in arbore corpus
iamque vale"—cortex in verba novissima venit.
inde fluunt lacrimae, stillataque sole rigescunt
de ramis electra novis, quae lucidus amnis   365
excipit et nuribus mittit gestanda Latinis.

    Adfuit huic monstro proles Stheneleia Cycnus,
qui tibi materno quamvis a sanguine iunctus,
mente tamen, Phaethon, propior fuit. ille relicto

84

their naked breasts, they call night and day upon
their brother, who nevermore will hear their sad
laments, and prostrate themselves upon his sepulchre.
Four times had the moon with waxing crescents
reached her full orb; but they, as was their habit (for
use had established habit), were mourning still. Then
one day the eldest, Phaëthusa, when she would
throw herself upon the grave, complained that her
feet had grown cold and stark; and when the fair
Lampetia tried to come to her, she was held fast as
by sudden roots. A third, making to tear her hair,
found her hands plucking at foliage. One com-
plained that her ankles were encased in wood,
another that her arms were changing to long
branches. And while they look on those things in
amazement bark closes round their loins, and, by
degrees, their waists, breasts, shoulders, hands; and
all that was free were their lips calling upon their
mother. What can the frantic mother do but run,
as impulse carries her, now here, now there, and
print kisses on their lips? That is not enough:
she tries to tear away the bark from their bodies and
breaks off slender twigs with her hands. But as she
does this bloody drops trickle forth as from a wound.
And each one, as she is wounded, cries out: " Oh,
spare me, mother; spare, I beg you. 'Tis my body
that you are tearing in the tree. And now fare-
well "—the bark closed over her latest words. Still
their tears flow on, and these tears, hardened into
amber by the sun, drop down from the new-made
trees. The clear river receives them and bears them
onward, one day to be worn by the brides of Rome.

Cycnus, the son of Sthenelus, was a witness of this
miracle. Though he was kin to you, O Phaëthon,
by his mother's blood, he was more closely joined in

(nam Ligurum populos et magnas rexerat urbes)   370
imperio ripas virides amnemque querellis
Eridanum inplerat silvamque sororibus auctam,
cum vox est tenuata viro canaeque capillos
dissimulant plumae collumque a pectore longe
porrigitur digitosque ligat iunctura rubentis,   375
penna latus velat, tenet os sine acumine rostrum.
fit nova Cycnus avis nec se caeloque Iovique
credit, ut iniuste missi memor ignis ab illo;
stagna petit patulosque lacus ignemque perosus
quae colat elegit contraria flumina flammis.   380
   Squalidus interea genitor Phaethontis et expers
ipse sui decoris, qualis, cum deficit orbem,
esse solet, lucemque odit seque ipse diemque
datque animum in luctus et luctibus adicit iram
officiumque negat mundo. "satis"inquit" ab aevi   385
sors mea principiis fuit inrequieta, pigetque
actorum sine fine mihi, sine honore laborum!
quilibet alter agat portantes lumina currus!
si nemo est omnesque dei non posse fatentur,
ipse agat ut saltem,dum nostras temptat habenas,   390
orbatura patres aliquando fulmina ponat!
tum sciet ignipedum vires expertus equorum
non meruisse necem, qui non bene rexerit illos."
   Talia dicentem circumstant omnia Solem
numina, neve velit tenebras inducere rebus,   395
supplice voce rogant; missos quoque Iuppiter
      ignes
excusat precibusque minas regaliter addit.

affection. He, abandoning his kingdom—for he ruled over the peoples and great cities of Liguria—went weeping and lamenting along the green banks of the Eridanus, and through the woods which the sisters had increased. And as he went his voice became thin and shrill; white plumage hid his hair and his neck stretched far out from his breast. A web-like membrane joined his reddened fingers, wings clothed his sides, and a blunt beak his mouth. So Cycnus became a strange new bird—the swan. But he did not trust himself to the upper air and Jove, since he remembered the fiery bolt which the god had unjustly hurled. His favourite haunts were the still pools and spreading lakes; and, hating fire, he chose the water for his home, as the opposite of flame.

Meanwhile Phoebus sits in gloomy mourning garb, shorn of his brightness, just as when he is darkened by eclipse. He hates himself and the light of day, gives over his soul to grief, to grief adds rage, and refuses to do service to the world. "Enough," he says; " from time's beginning has my lot been unrestful; I am weary of my endless and unrequited toils. Let any else who chooses drive the chariot of light. If no one will, and all the gods confess that it is beyond their power, let Jove himself do it, that, sometime at least, while he essays to grasp my reins, he may lay aside the bolts that are destined to rob fathers of their boys. Then will he know, when he has himself tried the strength of those fiery-footed steeds, that he who failed to guide them well did not deserve death."

As he thus speaks all the gods stand around him, and beg him humbly not to plunge the world in darkness. Jove himself seeks to excuse the bolt he hurled, and to his prayers adds threats in royal style.

colligit amentes et adhuc terrore paventes
Phoebus equos stimuloque dolens et verbere saevit
(saevit enim) natumque obiectat et inputat illis. 400
  At pater omnipotens ingentia moenia caeli
circuit et, ne quid labefactum viribus ignis
corruat, explorat.   quae postquam firma suique
roboris esse videt, terras hominumque labores
perspicit.   Arcadiae tamen est inpensior illi 405
cura suae: fontesque et nondum audentia labi
flumina restituit, dat terrae gramina, frondes
arboribus, laesasque iubet revirescere silvas.
dum redit itque frequens, in virgine Nonacrina
haesit, et accepti caluere sub ossibus ignes. 410
non erat huius opus lanam mollire trahendo
nec positu variare comas; ubi fibula vestem,
vitta coercuerat neglectos alba capillos;
et modo leve manu iaculum, modo sumpserat
    arcum,
miles erat Phoebes: nec Maenalon attigit ulla 415
gratior hac Triviae; sed nulla potentia longa est.
  Ulterius medio spatium sol altus habebat,
cum subit illa nemus, quod nulla ceciderat aetas;
exuit hic umero pharetram lentosque retendit
arcus inque solo, quod texerat herba, iacebat 420
et pictam posita pharetram cervice premebat.
Iuppiter ut vidit fessam et custode vacantem,
" hoc certe furtum coniunx mea nesciet " inquit,
" aut si rescierit, sunt, o sunt iurgia tanti! "

Then Phoebus yokes his team again, wild and trembling still with fear; and, in his grief, fiercely plies them with lash and goad (yes, fiercely plies them), reproaching and taxing them with the death of his son.

But now the Almighty Father makes a round of the great battlements of heaven and examines to see if anything has been loosened by the might of fire. When he sees that these are firm with their immortal strength, he inspects the earth and the affairs of men. Yet Arcadia, above all, is his more earnest care. He restores her springs and rivers, which hardly dare as yet to flow; he gives grass again to the ground, leaves to the trees, and bids the damaged forests grow green again. And as he came and went upon his tasks he chanced to see a certain Arcadian nymph, and straightway the fire he caught grew hot to his very marrow. She had no need to spin soft wools nor to arrange her hair in studied elegance. A simple brooch fastened her gown and a white fillet held her loose-flowing hair. And in this garb, now with a spear, and now a bow in her hand, was she arrayed as one of Phoebe's warriors. Nor was any nymph who roamed over the slopes of Maenalus in higher favour with her goddess than was she. But no favour is of long duration.

The sun was high o'erhead, just beyond his zenith, when the nymph entered the forest that all years had left unfelled. Here she took her quiver from her shoulder, unstrung her tough bow, and lay down upon the grassy ground, with her head pillowed on her painted quiver. When Jove saw her there, tired out and unprotected: " Here, surely," he said, " my consort will know nothing of my guile; or if she learn it, well bought are taunts at such a price."

protinus induitur faciem cultumque Dianae   425
atque ait: " o comitum, virgo, pars una mearum,
in quibus es venata iugis? " de caespite virgo
se levat et " salve numen, me iudice " dixit,
" audiat ipse licet, maius Iove." ridet et audit
et sibi praeferri se gaudet et oscula iungit,   430
nec moderata satis nec sic a virgine danda.
qua venata foret silva, narrare parantem
inpedit amplexu nec se sine crimine prodit.
illa quidem contra, quantum modo femina posset
(adspiceres utinam, Saturnia, mitior esses),   435
illa quidem pugnat, sed quem superare puella,
quisve Iovem poterat? superum petit aethera victor
Iuppiter: huic odio nemus est et conscia silva;
unde pedem referens paene est oblita pharetram
tollere cum telis et quem suspenderat arcum.   440
   Ecce, suo comitata choro Dictynna per altum
Maenalon ingrediens et caede superba ferarum
adspicit hanc visamque vocat: clamata refugit
et timuit primo, ne Iuppiter esset in illa;
sed postquam pariter nymphas incedere vidit,   445
sensit abesse dolos numerumque accessit ad harum.
heu! quam difficile est crimen non prodere vultu!
vix oculos attollit humo nec, ut ante solebat,
iuncta deae lateri nec toto est agmine prima,
sed silet et laesi dat signa rubore pudoris;   450
et, nisi quod virgo est, poterat sentire Diana
mille notis culpam: nymphae sensisse feruntur.
orbe resurgebant lunaria cornua nono,

Straightway he put on the features and dress of Diana and said: " Dear maid, best loved of all my followers, where hast thou been hunting to-day?" The maiden arose from her grassy couch and said: " Hail thou, my goddess, greater far than Jove, I say, though he himself should hear." Jove laughed to hear her, rejoicing to be prized more highly than himself; and he kissed her lips, not modestly, nor as a maiden kisses. When she began to tell him in what woods her hunt had been, he broke in upon her story with an embrace, and by this outrage betrayed himself. She, in truth, struggled against him with all her girlish might—hadst thou been there to see, Saturnia, thy judgment were more kind!—but whom could a girl o'ercome, or who could prevail against Jove? Jupiter won the day, and went back to the sky; she loathed the forest and the woods that knew her secret. As she retraced her path she almost forgot to take up the quiver with its arrows, and the bow she had hung up.

But see, Diana, with her train of nymphs, approaches along the slopes of Maenalus, proud of her trophies of the chase. She sees our maiden and calls to her. At first she flees in fear, lest this should be Jove in disguise again. But when she sees the other nymphs coming too, she is reassured and joins the band. Alas, how hard it is not to betray a guilty conscience in the face! She walks with downcast eyes, not, as was her wont, close to her goddess, and leading all the rest. Her silence and her blushes give clear tokens of her plight; and, were not Diana herself a maid, she could know her guilt by a thousand signs; it is said that the nymphs knew it. Nine times since then the crescent moon had grown full orbed, when the goddess, quitting the chase and over-

cum de venatu fraternis languida flammis,
nacta nemus gelidum dea, quo cum murmure labens
ibat et attritas versabat rivus harenas.   456
ut loca laudavit, summas pede contigit undas;
his quoque laudatis "procul est" ait "arbiter omnis:
nuda superfusis tinguamus corpora lymphis!"
Parrhasis erubuit; cunctae velamina ponunt;   460
una moras quaerit: dubitanti vestis adempta est,
qua posita nudo patuit cum corpore crimen.
attonitae manibusque uterum celare volenti
" i procul hinc "·dixit " nec sacros pollue fontis! "
Cynthia deque suo iussit secedere coetu.   465
   Senserat hoc olim magni matrona Tonantis
distuleratque graves in idonea tempora poenas.
causa morae nulla est, et iam puer Arcas (id ipsum
indoluit Iuno) fuerat de paelice natus.
quo simul obvertit saevam cum lumine mentem,   470
" scilicet hoc etiam restabat, adultera " dixit,
" ut fecunda fores, fieretque iniuria partu
nota, Iovisque mei testatum dedecus esset.
haud inpune feres: adimam tibi namque figuram,
qua tibi, quaque places nostro, inportuna, marito."
dixit et adversam prensis a fronte capillis   476
stravit humi pronam.   tendebat bracchia supplex:
bracchia coeperunt nigris horrescere villis
curvarique manus et aduncos crescere in unguis
officioque pedum fungi laudataque quondam   480
ora Iovi lato fieri deformia rictu.
neve preces animos et verba precantia flectant,
posse loqui eripitur: vox iracunda minaxque
plenaque terroris rauco de gutture fertur;

vercome by the hot sun's rays, came to a cool grove
hrough which a gently murmuring stream flowed
ver its smooth sands. The place delighted her and
he dipped her feet into the water. Delighted too
vith this, she said to her companions: "Come, no
ne is near to see; let us disrobe and bathe us in
he brook." The Arcadian blushed, and, while all
he rest obeyed, she only sought excuses for delay.
But her companions forced her to comply, and there
her shame was openly confessed. As she stood terror-
stricken, vainly striving to hide her state, Diana cried:
" Begone! and pollute not our sacred pool "; and so
expelled her from her company.

The great Thunderer's wife had known all this
long since; but she had put off her vengeance until
a fitting time. And now that time was come; for,
to add a sting to Juno's hate, a boy, Arcas, had
been born of her rival. Whereto when she turned
her angry mind and her angry eyes, "See there! "
she cried, "nothing was left, adulteress, than to
breed a son, and publish my wrong by his birth, a
living witness to my lord's shame. But thou shalt
suffer for it. Yea, for I will take away thy beauty
wherewith thou dost delight thyself, forward girl, and
him who is my husband." So saying, she caught her
by the hair full in front and flung her face-foremost to
the ground. And when the girl stretched out her arms
in prayer for mercy, her arms began to grow rough
with black shaggy hair; her hands changed into feet
tipped with sharp claws; and her lips, which but now
Jove had praised, were changed to broad, ugly jaws;
and, that she might not move him with entreating
prayers, her power of speech was taken from her, and
only a harsh, terrifying growl came hoarsely from her
throat. Still her human feelings remained, though

93

OVID

mens antiqua tamen facta quoque mansit in ursa,
adsiduoque suos gemitu testata dolores   480
qualescumque manus ad caelum et sidera tollit
ingratumque Iovem, nequeat cum dicere, sentit.
a! quotiens, sola non ausa quiescere silva,
ante domum quondamque suis erravit in agris!   490
a! quotiens per saxa canum latratibus acta est
venatrixque metu venantum territa fugit!
saepe feris latuit visis, oblita quid esset,
ursaque conspectos in montibus horruit ursos
pertimuitque lupos, quamvis pater esset in illis.   495

    Ecce Lycaoniae proles ignara parentis,
Arcas adest ter quinque fere natalibus actis;
dumque feras sequitur, dum saltus eligit aptos
nexilibusque plagis silvas Erymanthidas ambit,
incidit in matrem, quae restitit Arcade viso   500
et cognoscenti similis fuit: ille refugit
inmotosque oculos in se sine fine tenentem
nescius extimuit propiusque accedere aventi
vulnifico fuerat fixurus pectora telo:
arcuit omnipotens pariterque ipsosque nefasque   505
sustulit et pariter raptos per inania vento
inposuit caelo vicinaque sidera fecit.

    Intumuit Iuno, postquam inter sidera paelex
fulsit, et ad canam descendit in aequora Tethyn
Oceanumque senem, quorum reverentia movit   510
saepe deos, causamque viae scitantibus infit:
" quaeritis, aetheriis quare regina deorum
94

she was now a bear; with constant moanings she shows her grief, stretches up such hands as are left her to the heavens, and, though she cannot speak, still feels the ingratitude of Jove. Ah, how often, not daring to lie down in the lonely woods, she wandered before her home and in the fields that had once been hers! How often was she driven over the rocky ways by the baying of hounds and, huntress though she was, fled in affright before the hunters! Often she hid at sight of the wild beasts, forgetting what she was; and, though herself a bear, shuddered at sight of other bears which she saw on the mountain-slopes. She even feared the wolves, although her own father, Lycaon, ran with the pack.

And now Arcas, Lycaon's grandson, had reached his fifteenth year, ignorant of his mother's plight. While he was hunting the wild beasts, seeking out their favourite haunts, hemming the Arcadian woods with his close-wrought nets, he chanced upon his mother, who stopped still at sight of Arcas, and seemed like one that recognized him. He shrank back at those unmoving eyes that were fixed for ever upon him, and feared he knew not what; and when she tried to come nearer, he was just in the act of piercing her breast with his wound-dealing spear. But the Omnipotent stayed his hand, and together he removed both themselves and the crime, and together caught up through the void in a whirlwind, he set them in the heavens and made them neighbouring stars.

Then indeed did Juno's wrath wax hotter still when she saw her rival shining in the sky, and straight went down to Tethys, venerable goddess of the sea, and to old Ocean, whom oft the gods hold in reverence. When they asked her the cause of her coming, she began: " Do you ask me why I, the

95

sedibus huc adsim? pro me tenet altera caelum!
mentior, obscurum nisi nox cum fecerit orbem,
nuper honoratas summo, mea vulnera, caelo   515
videritis stellas illic, ubi circulus axem
ultimus extremum spatioque brevissimus ambit.
et vero quisquam Iunonem laedere nolit
offensamque tremat, quae prosum sola nocendo? 519
o ego quantum egi! quam vasta potentia nostra est!
esse hominem vetui: facta est dea! sic ego poenas
sontibus inpono, sic est mea magna potestas!
vindicet antiquam faciem vultusque ferinos
detrahat, Argolica quod in ante Phoronide fecit
cur non et pulsa ducit Iunone meoque   525
collocat in thalamo socerumque Lycaona sumit?
at vos si laesae tangit contemptus alumnae,
gurgite caeruleo septem prohibete triones
sideraque in caelo stupri mercede recepta
pellite, ne puro tinguatur in aequore paelex!" 530
  Di maris adnuerant: habili Saturnia curru
ingreditur liquidum pavonibus aethera pictis,
tam nuper pictis caeso pavonibus Argo,
quam tu nuper eras, cum candidus ante fuisses,
corve loquax, subito nigrantis versus in alas.   535
nam fuit haec quondam niveis argentea pennis
ales, ut aequaret totas sine labe columbas,
nec servaturis vigili Capitolia voce
cederet anseribus nec amanti flumina cycno.
lingua fuit damno: lingua faciente loquaci   540
qui color albus erat, nunc est contrarius albo.

queen of heaven, am here? Another queen has
usurped my heaven. Count my word false if to-
night, when darkness has obscured the sky, you see
not new constellations fresh set, to outrage me, in
the place of honour in highest heaven, where the
last and shortest circle encompasses the utmost pole.
And is there any reason now why anyone should
hesitate to insult Juno and should fear my wrath,
who do but help where I would harm? Oh, what
great things have I accomplished! What unbounded
power is mine! She whom I drove out of human
form has now become a goddess. So do I punish
those who wrong me! Such is my vaunted might!
It only remains for him to release her from her
bestial form and restore her former features, as he
did once before in Argive Io's case. Why, now that
I am deposed, should he not wed and set her in my
chamber, and become Lycaon's son-in-law? But do
you, if the insult to your foster-child moves you,
debar these bears from your green pools, disown stars
which have gained heaven at the price of shame, and
let not that harlot bathe in your pure stream."

The gods of the sea granted her prayer, and
Saturnia, mounting her swift chariot, was borne back
through the yielding air by her gaily decked pea-
cocks, peacocks but lately decked with the slain
Argus' eyes, at the same time that thy plumage,
talking raven, though white before, had been suddenly
changed to black. For he had once been a bird of
silvery-white plumage, so that he rivalled the spotless
doves, nor yielded to the geese which one day were
to save the Capitol with their watchful cries, nor to the
river-loving swan. But his tongue was his undoing.
Through his tongue's fault the talking bird, which
once was white, was now the opposite of white.

OVID

Pulchrior in tota quam Larisaea Coronis
non fuit Haemonia: placuit tibi, Delphice, certe,
dum vel casta fuit vel inobservata, sed ales
sensit adulterium Phoebeius, utque latentem   545
detegeret culpam, non exorabilis index,
ad dominum tendebat iter.   quem garrula motis
consequitur pennis, scitetur ut omnia, cornix
auditaque viae causa " non utile carpis "
inquit "iter: ne sperne meae praesagia linguae! 550
quid fuerim quid simque vide meritumque require:
invenies nocuisse fidem.   nam tempore quodam
Pallas Ericthonium, prolem sine matre creatam,
clauserat Actaeo texta de vimine cista
virginibusque tribus gemino de Cecrope natis   555
et legem dederat, sua ne secreta viderent.
abdita fronde levi densa speculabar ab ulmo,
quid facerent: commissa duae sine fraude tuentur,
Pandrosos atque Herse; timidas vocat una sorores
Aglauros nodosque manu diducit, et intus   560
infantemque vident adporrectumque draconem.
acta deae refero.   pro quo mihi gratia talis
redditur, ut dicar tutela pulsa Minervae
et ponar post noctis avem!   mea poena volucres
admonuisse potest, ne voce pericula quaerant.   565
at, puto, non ultro nequiquam tale rogantem
me petiit!—ipsa licet hoc a Pallade quaeras:
quamvis irata est, non hoc irata negabit.

METAMORPHOSES BOOK II

In all Thessaly there was no fairer maid than
Coronis of Larissa. She surely found favour in thy
eyes, O Delphic god, so long as she was chaste—or
undetected. But the bird of Phoebus discovered her
unchastity, and was posting with all speed, hard-
hearted tell-tale, to his master to disclose the sin he
had spied out. The gossiping crow followed him on
flapping wings and asked the news. But when he
heard the real object of the trip he said: " 'Tis
no profitable journey you are taking, my friend.
Scorn not the forewarning of my tongue. See
what I used to be and what I am now, and then
ask the reason for it. You will find that good faith
was my undoing. Once upon a time a child was
born, named Erichthonius, a child without a mother.
Him Pallas hid in a box woven of Actaean osiers,
and gave this to the three daughters of double-shaped
Cecrops, with the strict command not to look upon her
secret. Hidden in the light leaves that grew thick
over an elm, I set myself to watch what they would
do. Two of the girls, Pandrosos and Herse, watched
the box in good faith, but the third, Aglauros, called
her sisters cowards, and with her hand undid the
fastenings. And within they saw a baby-boy and
a snake stretched out beside him. I went and be-
trayed them to the goddess, and for my pains I was
turned out of my place as Minerva's attendant and
put after the bird of night! My punishment ought
to be a warning to all birds not to invite trouble by
talking too much. But perhaps (do you say?) she
did not seek me out of her own accord, when I asked
no such thing? Well, you may ask Pallas herself.
Though she be angry with me now, she will not deny
that, for all her anger. It is a well-known story.
I once was a king's daughter, child of the famous

nam me Phocaica clarus tellure Coroneus
(nota loquor) genuit, fueramque ego regia virgo   570
divitibusque procis (ne me contemne) petebar :
forma mihi nocuit.   nam cum per litora lentis
passibus, ut soleo, summa spatiarer harena,
vidit et incaluit pelagi deus, utque precando
tempora cum blandis absumpsit inania verbis,   575
vim parat et sequitur.   fugio densumque relinquo
litus et in molli nequiquam lassor harena.
inde deos hominesque voco ; nec contigit ullum
vox mea mortalem : mota est pro virgine virgo
auxiliumque tulit.   tendebam bracchia caelo :   580
bracchia coeperunt levibus nigrescere pennis ;
reicere ex umeris vestem molibar, at illa
pluma erat inque cutem radices egerat imas ;
plangere nuda meis conabar pectora palmis,
sed neque iam palmas nec pectora nuda gerebam ;
currebam, nec, ut ante, pedes retinebat harena,   586
sed summa tollebar humo ; mox alta per auras
evehor et data sum comes inculpata Minervae.
quid tamen hoc prodest, si diro facta volucris
crimine Nyctimene nostro successit honori ?   590
an quae per totam res est notissima Lesbon,
non audita tibi est, patrium temerasse cubile
Nyctimenen ? avis illa quidem, sed conscia culpae
conspectum lucemque fugit tenebrisque pudorem
celat et a cunctis expellitur aethere toto."   595
    Talia dicenti " tibi " ait " revocamina " corvus
"sint, precor, ista malo : nos vanum spernimus omen."

Coroneus in the land of Phocis, and—nay, scorn me
not—rich suitors sought me in marriage. But my
beauty proved my bane. For once, while I paced,
as is my wont, along the shore with slow steps over
the sand's top, the god of the ocean saw me and
grew hot. And when his prayers and coaxing words
proved but waste of time, he offered force and
pursued. I ran from him, leaving the hard-packed
beach, and was quickly worn out, but all to no
purpose, in the soft sand beyond. Then I cried out
for help to gods and men, but my cries reached no
mortal ear. But the virgin goddess heard a virgin's
prayer and came to my aid. I was stretching my
arms to heaven, when my arms began to darken with
light feathers. I strove to cast my mantle from my
shoulders, but it was feathers, too, which had already
struck their roots deep into my skin. I tried to beat
my bare breasts with my hands, but I found I had
now neither breasts nor hands. I would run; and
now the sand did not retard my feet as before, but I
skimmed lightly along the top of the ground, and
soon I floated on the air, soaring high; and so I was
given to Minerva to be her blameless comrade. But
of what use was that to me, if, after all, Nyctimene,
who was changed into a bird because of her vile sins,
has been put in my place? Or have you not heard
the tale all Lesbos knows too well, how Nyctimene
outraged the sanctity of her father's bed? And, bird
though she now is, still, conscious of her guilt, she
flees the sight of men and light of day, and tries to
hide her shame in darkness, outcast by all from the
whole radiant sky."

In reply to all this the raven said: "On your own
head, I pray, be the evil that warning portends; I
scorn the idle presage," continued on his way to his

nec coeptum dimittit iter dominoque iacentem
cum iuvene Haemonio vidisse Coronida narrat.
laurea delapsa est audito crimine amantis,   600
et pariter vultusque deo plectrumque colorque
excidit, utque animus tumida fervebat ab ira,
arma adsueta capit flexumque a cornibus arcum
tendit et illa suo totiens cum pectore iuncta
indevitato traiecit pectora telo.   605
icta dedit gemitum tractoque a corpore ferro
candida puniceo perfudit membra cruore
et dixit: " potui poenas tibi, Phoebe, dedisse,
sed peperisse prius; duo nunc moriemur in una."
hactenus, et pariter vitam cum sanguine fudit;   610
corpus inane animae frigus letale secutum est.

    Paenitet heu! sero poenae crudelis amantem,
seque, quod audierit, quod sic exarserit, odit;
odit avem, per quam crimen causamque dolendi
scire coactus erat, nec non arcumque manumque 615
odit cumque manu temeraria tela sagittas
conlapsamque fovet seraque ope vincere fata
nititur et medicas exercet inaniter artes.
quae postquam frustra temptata rogumque parari
vidit et arsuros supremis ignibus artus,   620
tum vero gemitus (neque enim caelestia tingui
ora licet lacrimis) alto de corde petitos
edidit, haud aliter quam cum spectante iuvenca
lactentis vituli dextra libratus ab aure
tempora discussit claro cava malleus ictu.   625

master, and then told him that he had seen Coronis lying beside the youth of Thessaly. When that charge was heard the laurel glided from the lover's head; together countenance and colour changed, and the quill dropped from the hand of the god. And as his heart became hot with swelling anger he seized his accustomed arms, strung his bent bow from the horns, and transfixed with unerring shaft the bosom which had been so often pressed to his own. The smitten maid groaned in agony, and, as the arrow was drawn out, her white limbs were drenched with her red blood. " 'Twas right, O Phoebus," she said, " that I should suffer thus from you, but first I should have borne my child. But now two of us shall die in one." And while she spoke her life ebbed out with her streaming blood, and soon her body, its life all spent, lay cold in death.

The lover, alas! too late repents his cruel act; he hates himself because he listened to the tale and was so quick to break out in wrath. He hates the bird by which he has been compelled to know the offence that brought his grief; bow and hand he hates, and with that hand the hasty arrows too. He fondles the fallen girl, and too late tries to bring help and to conquer fate; but his healing arts are exercised in vain. When his efforts were of no avail, and he saw the pyre made ready with the funeral fires which were to consume her limbs, then indeed—for the cheeks of the heavenly gods may not be wet with tears—from his deep heart he uttered piteous groans; such groans as the young cow utters when before her eyes the hammer high poised from beside the right ear crashes with its resounding blow through the hollow temples of her suckling calf. The god pours fragrant incense on her unconscious breast, gives her

ut tamen ingratos in pectora fudit odores
et dedit amplexus iniustaque iusta peregit,
non tulit in cineres labi sua Phoebus eosdem
semina, sed natum flammis uteroque parentis
eripuit geminique tulit Chironis in antrum,   630
sperantemque sibi non falsae praemia linguae
inter aves albas vetuit consistere corvum.
    Semifer interea divinae stirpis alumno
laetus erat mixtoque oneri gaudebat honore;
ecce venit rutilis umeros protecta capillis   635
filia centauri, quam quondam nympha Chariclo
fluminis in rapidi ripis enixa vocavit
Ocyroen: non haec artes contenta paternas
edidicisse fuit, fatorum arcana canebat.
ergo ubi vaticinos concepit mente furores   640
incaluitque deo, quem clausum pectore habebat,
adspicit infantem " toto " que " salutifer orbi
cresce, puer! " dixit; " tibi se mortalia saepe
corpora debebunt, animas tibi reddere ademptas
fas erit, idque semel dis indignantibus ausus   645
posse dare hoc iterum flamma prohibebere avita,
eque deo corpus fies exsangue deusque,
qui modo corpus eras, et bis tua fata novabis.
tu quoque, care pater, nunc inmortalis et aevis
omnibus ut maneas nascendi lege creatus,   650
posse mori cupies, tum cum cruciabere dirae
sanguine serpentis per saucia membra recepto;
teque ex aeterno patientem numina mortis

the last embrace, and performs all the fit offices unfitly for the dead. But that his own son should perish in the same funeral fires he cannot brook. He snatched the unborn child from his mother's womb and from the devouring flames, and bore him for safe keeping to the cave of two-formed Chiron. But the raven, which had hoped only for reward from his truth-telling, he forbad to take their place among white birds.

Meantime the Centaur was rejoicing in his foster-child of heavenly stock, glad at the honour which the task brought with it, when lo! there comes his daughter, her shoulders overmantled with red-gold locks, whom once the nymph, Chariclo, bearing her to him upon the banks of the swift stream, had called thereafter Ocyrhoë. She was not satisfied to have learnt her father's art, but she sang prophecy. So when she felt in her soul the prophetic madness, and was warmed by the divine fire prisoned in her breast, she looked upon the child and cried: "O child, health-bringer to the whole world, speed thy growth. Often shall mortal bodies owe their lives to thee, and to thee shall it be counted right to restore the spirits of the departed. But having dared this once in scorn of the gods, from power to give life a second time thou shalt be stayed by thy grandsire's lightning. So, from a god shalt thou become but a lifeless corpse; but from this corpse shalt thou again become a god and twice renew thy fates. Thou also, dear father, who art now im-mortal and destined by the law of thy birth to last through all the ages, shalt some day long for power to die, when thou shalt be in agony with all thy limbs burning with the fatal Hydra's blood. But at last, from immortal the gods shall make thee capable

efficient, triplicesque deae tua fila resolvent."
restabat fatis aliquid: suspirat ab imis   655
pectoribus, lacrimaeque genis labuntur obortae,
atque ita " praevertunt " inquit " me fata, vetorque
plura loqui, vocisque meae praecluditur usus.
non fuerant artes tanti, quae numinis iram
contraxere mihi: mallem nescisse futura!   660
iam mihi subduci facies humana videtur,
iam cibus herba placet, iam latis currere campis
impetus est: in equam cognataque corpora vertor.
tota tamen quare? pater est mihi nempe biformis."
talia dicenti pars est extrema querellae   665
intellecta parum confusaque verba fuerunt;
mox nec verba quidem nec equae sonus ille videtur
sed simulantis equam, parvoque in tempore certos
edidit hinnitus et bracchia movit in herbas.
tum digiti coeunt et quinos alligat ungues   670
perpetuo cornu levis ungula, crescit et oris
et colli spatium, longae pars maxima pallae
cauda fit, utque vagi crines per colla iacebant,
in dextras abiere iubas, pariterque novata est
et vox et facies; nomen quoque monstra dedere. 675

   Flebat opemque tuam frustra Philyreius heros,
Delphice, poscebat.   nam nec rescindere magni
iussa Iovis poteras, nec, si rescindere posses,
tunc aderas: Elin Messeniaque arva colebas.
illud erat tempus, quo te pastoria pellis   680
texit, onusque fuit baculum silvestre sinistrae,
alterius dispar septenis fistula cannis.

of death, and the three goddesses shall loose thy thread." Still other fates remained to tell; but suddenly she sighed deeply, and with flowing tears said: "The fates forestall me and forbid me to speak more. My power of speech fails me. Not worth the cost were those arts which have brought down the wrath of heaven upon me. I would that I had never known the future. Now my human shape seems to be passing. Now grass pleases as food; now I am eager to race around the broad pastures. I am turning into a mare, my kindred shape. But why completely? Surely my father is half human." Even while she spoke, the last part of her complaint became scarce understood and her words were all confused. Soon they seemed neither words nor yet the sound of a horse, but as of one trying to imitate a horse. At last she clearly whinnied and her arms became legs and moved along the ground. Her fingers drew together and one continuous light hoof of horn bound together the five nails of her hand. Her mouth enlarged, her neck was extended, the train of her gown became a tail; and her locks as they lay roaming over her neck were become a mane on the right side. Now was she changed alike in voice and feature; and this new wonder gave her a new name as well.

The half-divine son of Philyra wept and vainly called on thee for aid, O lord of Delphi. For thou couldst not revoke the edict of mighty Jove, nor, if thou couldst, wast thou then at hand. In those days thou wast dwelling in Elis and the Messenian fields. Thy garment was a shepherd's cloak, thy staff a stout stick from the wood, and a pipe made of seven unequal reeds was in thy hand. And while thy thoughts were all of love, and while thou didst

dumque amor est curae, dum te tua fistula mulcet,
incustoditae Pylios memorantur in agros
processisse boves: videt has Atlantide Maia   685
natus et arte sua silvis occultat abactas.
senserat hoc furtum nemo nisi notus in illo
rure senex; Battum vicinia tota vocabat.
divitis hic saltus herbosaque pascua Nelei
nobiliumque greges custos servabat equarum.   690
hunc tenuit blandaque manu seduxit et illi
" quisquis es, hospes " ait, " si forte armenta requiret
haec aliquis, vidisse nega neu gratia facto
nulla rependatur, nitidam cape praemia vaccam! "
et dedit.   accepta voces has reddidit hospes: 695
" tutus eas! lapis iste prius tua furta loquetur,"
et lapidem ostendit.   simulat Iove natus abire;
mox redit et versa pariter cum voce figura
" rustice, vidisti si quas hoc limite " dixit
" ire boves, fer opem furtoque silentia deme!   700
iuncta suo pretium dabitur tibi femina tauro."
at senior, postquam est merces geminata, " sub illis
.montibus" inquit "erunt," et erant sub montibus illis.
risit Atlantiades et " me mihi, perfide, prodis?
me mihi prodis? " ait periuraque pectora vertit   705
in durum silicem, qui nunc quoque dicitur index,
inque nihil merito vetus est infamia saxo.

discourse sweetly on the pipe, the cattle thou wast
keeping strayed, 'tis said, all unguarded into the
Pylian fields. There Maia's son spied them, and by
his native craft drove them into the woods and
hid them there. Nobody saw the theft except one
old man well known in that neighbourhood, called
Battus by all the countryside. He, as a hired
servant of the wealthy Neleus, was watching a herd
of blooded mares in the glades and rich pasture-
fields thereabouts. Mercury accosted him and,
drawing him aside with cajoling hand, said: " Who-
ever you are, my man, if anyone should chance to
ask you if you have seen any cattle going by here,
say that you have not; and, that your kindness may
not go unrewarded, you may choose out a sleek heifer
for your pay "; and he gave him the heifer forth-
with. The old man took it and replied: " Go on,
stranger, and feel safe. That stone will tell of your
thefts sooner than I "; and he pointed out a stone.
The son of Jove pretended to go away, but soon
came back with changed voice and form, and said:
" My good fellow, if you have seen any cattle
going along this way, help me out, and don't
refuse to tell about it, for they were stolen. I'll
give you a cow and a bull into the bargain if
you'll tell." The old man, tempted by the
double reward, said: " You'll find them over there
at the foot of that mountain." And there, true
enough, they were. Mercury laughed him to scorn
and said: " Would you betray me to myself, you
rogue? me to my very face? " So saying, he
turned the faithless fellow into a flinty stone,
which even to this day is called touch-stone; and
the old reproach still rests upon the undeserving
flint.

OVID

Hinc se sustulerat paribus caducifer alis,
Munychiosque volans agros gratamque Minervae
despectabat humum cultique arbusta Lycei.   710
illa forte die castae de more puellae
vertice supposito festas in Palladis arces
pura coronatis portabant sacra canistris.
inde revertentes deus adspicit ales iterque
non agit in rectum, sed in orbem curvat eundem : 715
ut volucris visis rapidissima miluus extis,
dum timet et densi circumstant sacra ministri,
flectitur in gyrum nec longius audet abire
spemque suam motis avidus circumvolat alis,
sic super Actaeas agilis Cyllenius arces   720
inclinat cursus et easdem circinat auras.
quanto splendidior quam cetera sidera fulget
Lucifer, et quanto quam Lucifer aurea Phoebe,
tanto virginibus praestantior omnibus Herse
ibat eratque decus pompae comitumque suarum. 725
obstipuit forma Iove natus et aethere pendens
non secus exarsit, quam cum Balearica plumbum
funda iacit : volat illud et incandescit eundo
et, quos non habuit, sub nubibus invenit ignes.
vertit iter caeloque petit terrena relicto   730
nec se dissimulat : tanta est fiducia formae:
quae quamquam iusta est, cura tamen adiuvat illam
permulcetque comas chlamydemque, ut pendeat apte,
collocat, ut limbus totumque adpareat aurum,
ut teres in dextra, qua somnos ducit et arcet, 735
virga sit, ut tersis niteant talaria plantis.

The god of the caduceus had taken himself hence on level wings and now as he flew he was looking down upon the Munychian fields, the land that Minerva loves, and the groves of the learned Lyceum. That day chanced to be a festival of Pallas when young maidens bore to their goddess' temple mystic gifts in flower-wreathed baskets on their heads. The winged god saw them as they were returning home and directed his way towards them, not straight down but sweeping in such a curve as when the swift kite has spied the fresh-slain sacrifice, afraid to come down while the priests are crowded around the victim, and yet not venturing to go quite away, he circles around in air and on flapping wings greedily hovers over his hoped-for prey; so did the nimble Mercury fly round the Athenian hill, sweeping in circles through the same spaces of air. As Lucifer shines more brightly than all the other stars and as the golden moon outshines Lucifer, so much was Herse more lovely than all the maidens round her, the choice ornament in the solemn procession of her comrades. The son of Jove was astounded at her beauty, and hanging in mid-air he caught the flames of love; as when a leaden bullet is thrown by a Balearic sling, it flies along, is heated by its motion, and finds heat in the clouds which it had not before. Mercury now turns his course, leaves the air and flies to earth, nor seeks to disguise himself; such is the confidence of beauty. Yet though that trust be lawful, he assists it none the less with pains; he smooths his hair, arranges his robe so that it may hang neatly and so that all the golden border will show. He takes care to have in his right hand his smooth wand with which he brings on sleep or drives it away, and to have his winged sandals glittering on his trim feet.

Pars secreta domus ebore et testudine cultos
tres habuit thalamos, quorum tu, Pandrose, dextrum,
Aglauros laevum, medium possederat Herse.
quae tenuit laevum, venientem prima notavit 740
Mercurium nomenque dei scitarier ausa est
et causam adventus ; cui sic respondit Atlantis
Pleïonesque nepos " ego sum, qui iussa per auras
verba patris porto ; pater est mihi Iuppiter ipse.
nec fingam causas, tu tantum fida sorori 745
esse velis prolisque meae matertera dici :
Herse causa viae ; faveas oramus amanti."
adspicit hunc oculis isdem, quibus abdita nuper
viderat Aglauros flavae secreta Minervae,
proque ministerio magni sibi ponderis aurum 750
postulat : interea tectis excedere cogit.
Vertit ad hanc torvi dea bellica luminis orbem
et tanto penitus traxit suspiria motu,
ut pariter pectus positamque in pectore forti
aegida concuteret : subit, hanc arcana profana 755
detexisse manu, tum cum sine matre creatam
Lemnicolae stirpem contra data foedera vidit,
et gratamque deo fore iam gratamque sorori
et ditem sumpto, quod avara poposcerat, auro.
protinus Invidiae nigro squalentia tabo 760
tecta petit : domus est imis in vallibus huius
abdita, sole carens, non ulli pervia vento,
tristis et ignavi plenissima frigoris et quae
igne vacet semper, caligine semper abundet.
huc ubi pervenit belli metuenda virago, 765

In a retired part of the house were three chambers, richly adorned with ivory and tortoise-shell. The right-hand room of these Pandrosos occupied, Aglauros the left, and Herse the room between. Aglauros first saw the approaching god and made so bold as to ask his name and the cause of his visit. He, grandson of Atlas and Pleione, replied: " I am he who carry my father's messages through the air. My father is Jove himself. Nor will I conceal why I am here. Only do you consent to be true to your sister, and to be called the aunt of my off-spring. I have come here for Herse's sake. I pray you favour a lover's suit." Aglauros looked at him with the same covetous eyes with which she had lately peeped at the secret of the golden-haired Minerva, and demanded a mighty weight of gold as the price of her service; meantime, she compelled him to leave the palace.

The warrior goddess now turned her angry eyes upon her, and breathed sighs so deep and perturbed that her breast and the aegis that lay upon her breast shook with her emotion. She remembered that this was the girl who had with profaning hands uncovered the secret at the time when, contrary to her com-mand, she looked upon the son of the Lemnian, without mother born. And now she would be in favour with the god and with her sister, and rich, besides, with the gold which in her greed she had demanded. Straightway Minerva sought out the cave of Envy, filthy with black gore. Her home was hidden away in a deep valley, where no sun shines and no breeze blows; a gruesome place and full of a numbing chill. No cheerful fire burns there, and the place is wrapped in thick, black fog. When the warlike maiden goddess came to the cave, she

constitit ante domum (neque enim succedere tectis
fas habet) et postes extrema cuspide pulsat.
concussae patuere fores.   videt intus edentem
vipereas carnes, vitiorum alimenta suorum,
Invidiam visaque oculos avertit; at illa   770
surgit humo pigre semesarumque relinquit
corpora serpentum passuque incedit inerti.
utque deam vidit formaque armisque decoram,
ingemuit vultumque una ac suspiria duxit.
pallor in ore sedet, macies in corpore toto.   775
nusquam recta acies, livent robigine dentes,
pectora felle virent, lingua est suffusa veneno;
risus abest, nisi quem visi movere dolores;
nec fruitur somno, vigilantibus excita curis,
sed videt ingratos intabescitque videndo   780
successus hominum carpitque et carpitur una
suppliciumque suum est. quamvis tamen oderat illam,
talibus adfata est breviter Tritonia dictis:
" infice tabe tua natarum Cecropis unam:
sic opus est. Aglauros ea est." haud plura locuta 785
fugit et inpressa tellurem reppulit hasta.
    Illa deam obliquo fugientem lumine cernens
murmura parva dedit successurumque Minervae
indoluit baculumque capit, quod spinea totum
vincula cingebant, adopertaque nubibus atris,   790
quacumque ingreditur, florentia proterit arva
exuritque herbas et summa cacumina carpit
adflatuque suo populos urbesque domosque
polluit et tandem Tritonida conspicit arcem

stood without, for she might not enter that foul
abode, and beat upon the door with end of spear.
The battered doors flew open; and there, sitting
within, was Envy, eating snakes' flesh, the proper
food of her venom. At the horrid sight the goddess
turned away her eyes. But that other rose heavily
from the ground, leaving the snakes' carcasses half
consumed, and came forward with sluggish step.
When she saw the goddess, glorious in form and
armour, she groaned aloud and pulled a face and
therewith heaved a sigh. Pallor o'erspreads her
face and her whole body seems to shrivel up. Her
eyes are all awry, her teeth are foul with mould;
green, poisonous gall o'erflows her breast, and venom
drips down from her tongue. She never smiles,
save at the sight of another's troubles; she never
sleeps, disturbed with wakeful cares; unwelcome
to her is the sight of men's success, and with the
sight she pines away; she gnaws and is gnawed,
herself her own punishment. Although she de-
tested the loathsome thing, yet in curt speech
Tritonia spoke to her: " Infect with your venom one
of Cecrops' daughters. Such the task I set. I mean
Aglauros." Without more words she fled the crea-
ture's presence and, pushing her spear against the
ground, sprang lightly back to heaven.

The hag, eyeing her askance as she flees, mutters
awhile, grieving to think on the goddess' joy of
triumph. Then she takes her staff, thick-set with
thorns, and, wrapped in a mantle of dark cloud, sets
forth. Wherever she goes, she tramples down the
flowers, causes the grass to wither, blasts the high
waving trees, and taints with the foul pollution of
her breath whole peoples, cities, homes. At last she
spies Tritonia's city, splendid with art and wealth

ingeniis opibusque et festa pace virentem   795
vixque tenet lacrimas, quia nil lacrimabile cernit.
sed postquam thalamos intravit Cecrope natae,
iussa facit pectusque manu ferrugine tincta
tangit et hamatis praecordia sentibus inplet
inspiratque nocens virus piceumque per ossa   800
dissipat et medio spargit pulmone venenum,
neve mali causae spatium per latius errent,
germanam ante oculos fortunatumque sororis
coniugium pulchraque deum sub imagine ponit
cunctaque magna facit; quibus inritata dolore   805
Cecropis occulto mordetur et anxia nocte
anxia luce gemit lentaque miserrima tabe
liquitur, ut glacies incerto saucia sole,
felicisque bonis non lenius uritur Herses,
quam cum spinosis ignis supponitur herbis,   810
quae neque dant flammas lentoque vapore cremantur.
saepe mori voluit, ne quicquam tale videret,
saepe velut crimen rigido narrare parenti;
denique in adverso venientem limine sedit
exclusura deum.   cui blandimenta precesque   815
verbaque iactanti mitissima " desine! " dixit,
" hinc ego me non sum nisi te motura repulso."
" stemus " ait " pacto " velox Cyllenius " isto! "
caelestique fores virga patefecit: at illi
surgere conanti partes, quascumque sedendo   820
flectimur, ignava nequeunt gravitate moveri:
illa quidem pugnat recto se attollere trunco,
sed genuum iunctura riget, frigusque per ungues
labitur, et pallent amisso sanguine venae;

and peaceful joy; and she can scarce restrain her
tears at the sight, because she sees no cause for
others' tears. But, having entered the chamber of
Cecrops' daughter, she performed the goddess' bid-
ding, touched the girl's breast with her festering
hand and filled her heart with pricking thorns.
Then she breathed pestilential, poisonous breath into
her nostrils and spread black venom through her
very heart and bones. And, to fix a cause for her
grief, Envy pictured to her imagination her sister,
her sister's blest marriage and the god in all his
beauty, magnifying the excellence of everything.
Maddened by this, Aglauros eats her heart out in
secret misery; careworn by day, careworn by night,
she groans and wastes away most wretchedly with
slow decay, like ice touched by the fitful sunshine.
She is consumed by envy of Herse's happiness; just
as when a fire is set under a pile of weeds, which
give out no flames and burn with smouldering
heat. She often longed to die that she might not
behold such happiness; often to tell it, as 'twere a
crime, to her stern father. At last she sat down at
her sister's threshold, to prevent the god's entrance
when he should come. And when he coaxed and
prayed with his most honeyed words, "Have done,"
she said, "for I shall never stir from here till I have
foiled your purpose." "We'll stand by that bargain,"
Mercury quickly replied, and with a touch of his
heavenly wand he opened the door. At this the girl
struggled to get up, but found the limbs one bends in
sitting made motionless with dull heaviness; she
strove to stand, but her knees had stiffened; a chill
stole through her fingers and toes, and her flesh was
pale and bloodless. And, as an incurable cancer
spreads its evil roots ever more widely and involves

utque malum late solet inmedicabile cancer   825
serpere et inlaesas vitiatis addere partes,
sic letalis hiems paulatim in pectora venit
vitalesque vias et respiramina clausit,
nec conata loqui est nec, si conata fuisset,
vocis habebat iter: saxum iam colla tenebat,   830
oraque duruerant, signumque exsangue sedebat;
nec lapis albus erat: sua mens infecerat illam.

    Has ubi verborum poenas mentisque profanae
cepit Atlantiades, dictas a Pallade terras
linquit et ingreditur iactatis aethera pennis.   835
sevocat hunc genitor nec causam fassus amoris
" fide minister " ait " iussorum, nate, meorum,
pelle moram solitoque celer delabere cursu,
quaeque tuam matrem tellus a parte sinistra
suspicit (indigenae Sidonida nomine dicunt),   840
hanc pete, quodque procul montano gramine pasci
armentum regale vides, ad litora verte! "
dixit, et expulsi iamdudum monte iuvenci
litora iussa petunt, ubi magni filia regis
ludere virginibus Tyriis comitata solebat.   845
non bene conveniunt nec in una sede morantur
maiestas et amor; sceptri gravitate relicta
ille pater rectorque deum, cui dextra trisulcis
ignibus armata est, qui nutu concutit orbem,
induitur faciem tauri mixtusque iuvencis   850
mugit et in teneris formosus obambulat herbis.
quippe color nivis est, quam nec vestigia duri
calcavere pedis nec solvit aquaticus auster.

sound with infected parts, so did a deadly chill little by little creep to her breast, stopping all vital functions and choking off her breath. She no longer tried to speak, and, if she had tried, her voice would have found no way of utterance. Her neck was changed to stone, her features had hardened— there she sat, a lifeless statue. Nor was the stone white in colour; her soul had stained it black.

When Mercury had inflicted this punishment on the girl for her impious words and spirit, he left the land of Pallas behind him, and flew to heaven on outflung pinions. Here his father calls him aside; and not revealing his love affair as the real reason, he says: " My son, always faithful to perform my bidding, delay not, but swiftly in accustomed flight glide down to earth and seek out the land that looks up at your mother's star from the left. The natives call it the land of Sidon. There you are to drive down to the sea-shore the herd of the king's cattle which you will see grazing at some distance on the mountain-side." He spoke, and quickly the cattle were driven from the mountain and headed for the shore, as Jove had directed, to a spot where the great king's daughter was accustomed to play in company with her Tyrian maidens. Majesty and love do not go well together, nor tarry long in the same dwelling-place. And so the father and ruler of the gods, who wields in his right hand the three-forked lightning, whose nod shakes the world, laid aside his royal majesty along with his sceptre, and took upon him the form of a bull. In this form he mingled with the cattle, lowed like the rest, and wandered around, beautiful to behold, on the young grass. His colour was white as the untrodden snow, which has not yet been melted by the rainy south-wind. The muscles stood rounded

colla toris exstant, armis palearia pendent,
cornua vara quidem, sed quae contendere possis 855
facta manu, puraque magis perlucida gemma.
nullae in fronte minae, nec formidabile lumen:
pacem vultus habet.   miratur Agenore nata,
quod tam formosus, quod proelia nulla minetur;
sed quamvis mitem metuit contingere primo, 860
mox adit et flores ad candida porrigit ora.
gaudet amans et, dum veniat sperata voluptas,
oscula dat manibus; vix iam, vix cetera differt;
et nunc adludit viridique exsultat in herba,
nunc latus in fulvis niveum deponit harenis; 865
paulatimque metu dempto modo pectora praebet
virginea plaudenda [1] manu, modo cornua sertis
inpedienda novis; ausa est quoque regia virgo
nescia, quem premeret, tergo considere tauri,
cum deus a terra siccoque a litore sensim 870
falsa pedum primis vestigia ponit in undis;
inde abit ulterius mediique per aequora ponti
fert praedam: pavet haec litusque ablata relictum
respicit et dextra cornum tenet, altera dorso
inposita est; tremulae sinuantur flamine vestes. 875

[1] *Some MSS. read* palpanda.

upon his neck, a long dewlap hung down in front; his horns were twisted, but perfect in shape as if carved by an artist's hand, cleaner and more clear than pearls. His brow and eyes would inspire no fear, and his whole expression was peaceful. Agenor's daughter looked at him in wondering admiration, because he was so beautiful and friendly. But, although he seemed so gentle, she was afraid at first to touch him. Presently she drew near, and held out flowers to his snow-white lips. The disguised lover rejoiced and, as a foretaste of future joy, kissed her hands. Hardly any longer could he restrain his passion. And now he jumps sportively about on the grass, now lays his snowy body down on the yellow sands; and, when her fear has little by little been allayed, he yields his breast for her maiden hands to pat and his horns to entwine with garlands of fresh flowers. The princess even dares to sit upon his back, little knowing upon whom she rests. The god little by little edges away from the dry land, and sets his borrowed hoofs in the shallow water; then he goes further out and soon is in full flight with his prize on the open ocean. She trembles with fear and looks back at the receding shore, holding fast a horn with one hand and resting the other on the creature's back. And her fluttering garments stream behind her in the wind.

BOOK III

1–137	*Cadmus*
138–252	*Actaeon*
253–315	*Semele*
316–338	*Tiresias*
339–510	*Narcissus and Echo*
511–733	*Pentheus*
572–700	*Acoetes and the Lydian Sailors*

LIBER III

IAMQVE deus posita fallacis imagine tauri
se confessus erat Dictaeaque rura tenebat,
cum pater ignarus Cadmo perquirere raptam
imperat et poenam, si non invenerit, addit
exilium, facto pius et sceleratus eodem.   5
orbe pererrato (quis enim deprendere possit
furta Iovis?) profugus patriamque iramque parentis
vitat Agenorides Phoebique oracula supplex
consulit et, quae sit tellus habitanda, requirit.
" bos tibi " Phoebus ait " solis occurret in arvis,   10
nullum passa iugum curvique inmunis aratri
hac duce carpe vias et, qua requieverit herba,
moenia fac condas Boeotiaque illa vocato."
vix bene Castalio Cadmus descenderat antro,
incustoditam lente videt ire iuvencam   15
nullum servitii signum cervice gerentem.
subsequitur pressoque legit vestigia gressu
auctoremque viae Phoebum taciturnus adorat.
iam vada Cephisi Panopesque evaserat arva:
bos stetit et tollens speciosam cornibus altis   20

BOOK III

AND now the god, having put off disguise of the bull, owned himself for what he was, and reached the fields of Crete. But the maiden's father, ignorant of what had happened, bids his son, Cadmus, go and search for the lost girl, and threatens exile as a punishment if he does not find her—pious and guilty by the same act. After roaming over all the world in vain (for who could search out the secret loves of Jove?) Agenor's son becomes an exile, shunning his father's country and his father's wrath. Then in suppliant wise he consults the oracle of Phoebus, seeking thus to learn in what land he is to settle. Phoebus replies: "A heifer will meet you in the wilderness, one who has never worn the yoke or drawn the crooked plough. Follow where she leads, and where she lies down to rest upon the grass there see that you build your city's walls and call the land Boeotia."[1] Hardly had Cadmus left the Castalian grotto when he saw a heifer moving slowly along, all unguarded and wearing on her neck no mark of service. He follows in her track with deliberate steps, silently giving thanks the while to Phoebus for showing him the way. And now the heifer had passed the fords of Cephisus and the fields of Panope, when she halted and, lifting towards the heavens her beautiful head

[1] *i.e.* "the land of the heifer."

ad caelum frontem mugitibus inpulit auras
atque ita respiciens comites sua terga sequentis
procubuit teneraque latus submisit in herba.
Cadmus agit grates peregrinaeque oscula terrae
figit et ignotos montes agrosque salutat. 25

Sacra Iovi facturus erat: iubet ire ministros
et petere e vivis libandas fontibus undas.
silva vetus stabat nulla violata securi,
et specus in media virgis ac vimine densus
efficiens humilem lapidum conpagibus arcum 30
uberibus fecundus aquis; ubi conditus antro
Martius anguis erat, cristis praesignis et auro;
igne micant oculi, corpus tumet omne venenis,
tresque vibrant linguae, triplici stant ordine dentes.
quem postquam Tyria lucum de gente profecti 35
infausto tetigere gradu, demissaque in undas
urna dedit sonitum, longo caput extulit antro
caeruleus serpens horrendaque sibila misit.
effluxere urnae manibus sanguisque reliquit
corpus et attonitos subitus tremor occupat artus. 40
ille volubilibus squamosos nexibus orbes
torquet et inmensos saltu sinuatur in arcus
ac media plus parte leves erectus in auras
despicit omne nemus tantoque est corpore, quanto,
si totum spectes, geminas qui separat arctos. 45
nec mora, Phoenicas, sive illi tela parabant
sive fugam, sive ipse timor prohibebat utrumque,
126

with its spreading horns, she filled the air with her lowings; and then, looking back upon those who were following close behind, she kneeled and let her flank sink down upon the fresh young grass. Cadmus gave thanks, reverently pressed his lips upon this stranger land, and greeted the unknown mountains and the plains.

With intent to make sacrifice to Jove, he bade his attendants hunt out a spring of living water for libation. There was a primeval forest there, scarred by no axe; and in its midst a cave thick set about with shrubs and pliant twigs. With well-fitted stones it fashioned a low arch, whence poured a full-welling spring, and deep within dwelt a serpent sacred to Mars. The creature had a wondrous golden crest; fire flashed from his eyes; his body was all swollen with venom; his triple tongue flickered out and in and his teeth were ranged in triple row. When with luckless steps the wayfarers of the Tyrian race had reached this grove, they let down their vessels into the spring, breaking the silence of the place. At this the dark serpent thrust forth his head out of the deep cave, hissing horribly. The urns fell from the men's hands, their blood ran cold, and, horror-struck, they were seized with a sudden trembling. The serpent twines his scaly coils in rolling knots and with a spring curves himself into a huge bow; and, lifted high by more than half his length into the unsubstantial air, he looks down upon the whole wood, as huge, could you see him all, as is that serpent in the sky that lies outstretched between the twin bears. He makes no tarrying, but seizes on the Phoenicians, whether they are preparing for fighting or for flight or whether very fear holds both in check. Some he slays with his fangs, some

127

occupat: hos morsu, longis conplexibus illos,
hos necat adflati funesta tabe veneni.
  Fecerat exiguas iam sol altissimus umbras: 50
quae mora sit sociis, miratur Agenore natus
vestigatque viros. tegumen derepta leoni
pellis erat, telum splendenti lancea ferro
et iaculum teloque animus praestantior omni.
ut nemus intravit letataque corpora vidit   55
victoremque supra spatiosi tergoris hostem
tristia sanguinea lambentem vulnera lingua,
" aut ultor vestrae, fidissima pectora, mortis,
aut comes " inquit " ero." dixit dextraque molarem
sustulit et magnum magno conamine misit.   60
illius inpulsu cum turribus ardua celsis
moenia mota forent, serpens sine vulnere mansit
loricaeque modo squamis defensus et atrae
duritia pellis validos cute reppulit ictus;
at non duritia iaculum quoque vicit eadem,   65
quod medio lentae spinae curvamine fixum
constitit et totum descendit in ilia ferrum.
ille dolore ferox caput in sua terga retorsit
vulneraque adspexit fixumque hastile momordit,
idque ubi vi multa partem labefecit in omnem,   70
vix tergo eripuit; ferrum tamen ossibus haesit.
tum vero postquam solitas accessit ad iras
causa recens, plenis tumuerunt guttura venis,
spumaque pestiferos circumfluit albida rictus,
terraque rasa sonat squamis, quique halitus exit 75
ore niger Stygio, vitiatas inficit auras.
ipse modo inmensum spiris facientibus orbem

he crushes in his constricting folds, and some he stifles with the deadly corruption of his poisoned breath.

The sun had reached the middle heavens and drawn close the shadows. And now Cadmus, wondering what has delayed his companions, starts out to trace them. For shield, he has a lion's skin; for weapon, a spear with glittering iron point and a javelin; and, better than all weapons, a courageous soul. When he enters the wood and sees the corpses of his friends all slain, and victorious above them their huge-bodied foe licking their piteous wounds with bloody tongue, he cries: " O ye poor forms, most faithful friends, either I shall avenge your death or be your comrade in it." So saying, he heaved up a massive stone with his right hand and with mighty effort hurled its mighty bulk. Under such a blow, high ramparts would have fallen, towers and all; but the serpent went unscathed, protected against that strong stroke by his scales as by an iron doublet and by his hard, dark skin. But that hard skin cannot withstand the javelin too, which now is fixed in the middle fold of his tough back and penetrates with its iron head deep into his flank. The creature, mad with pain, twists back his head, views well his wound, and bites at the spear-shaft fixed therein. Then, when by violent efforts he had loosened this all round, with difficulty he tore it out; but the iron head remained fixed in the backbone. Then indeed fresh fuel was added to his native wrath; his throat swells with full veins, and white foam flecks his horrid jaws. The earth resounds with his scraping scales, and such rank breath as exhales from the Stygian cave befouls the tainted air. Now he coils in huge spiral folds; now shoots up, straight

cingitur, interdum longa trabe rectior adstat,
inpete nunc vasto ceu concitus imbribus amnis
fertur et obstantis proturbat pectore silvas.   80
cedit Agenorides paulum spolioque leonis
sustinet incursus instantiaque ora retardat
cuspide praetenta : furit ille et inania duro
vulnera dat ferro figitque in acumine dentes.
iamque venenifero sanguis manare palato   85
coeperat et virides adspergine tinxerat herbas;
sed leve vulnus erat, quia se retrahebat ab ictu
laesaque colla dabat retro plagamque sedere
cedendo arcebat nec longius ire sinebat,
donec Agenorides coniectum in guttura ferrum   90
usque sequens pressit, dum retro quercus eunti
obstitit et fixa est pariter cum robore cervix.
pondere serpentis curvata est arbor et ima
parte flagellari gemuit sua robora caudae.

    Dum spatium victor victi considerat hostis,   95
vox subito audita est; neque erat cognoscere
      promptum,
unde, sed audita est: " quid, Agenore nate,
      peremptum
serpentem spectas ? et tu spectabere serpens."
ille diu pavidus pariter cum mente colorem
perdiderat, gelidoque comae terrore rigebant: 100
ecce viri fautrix superas delapsa per auras
Pallas adest motaeque iubet supponere terrae
vipereos dentes, populi incrementa futuri.
paret et, ut presso sulcum patefecit aratro,
spargit humi iussos, mortalia semina, dentes.   105
inde (fide maius) glaebae coepere moveri,

and tall as a tree; now he moves on with huge rush, like a stream in flood, sweeping down with his breast the trees in his path. Cadmus gives way a little, receiving his foe's rushes on the lion's skin, and holds in check the ravening jaws with his spear-point thrust well forward. The serpent is furious, bites vainly at the hard iron and catches the sharp spear-head between his teeth. And now from his venomous throat the blood begins to trickle and stains the green grass with spattered gore. But the wound is slight, because the serpent keeps backing from the thrust, drawing away his wounded neck, and by yielding keeps the stroke from being driven home nor allows it to go deeper. But Cadmus follows him up and presses the planted point into his throat; until at last an oak-tree stays his backward course and neck and tree are pierced together. The oak bends beneath the serpent's weight and the stout trunk groans beneath the lashings of his tail.

While the conqueror stands gazing on the huge bulk of his conquered foe, suddenly a voice sounds in his ears. He cannot tell whence it comes, but he hears it saying: " Why, O son of Agenor, dost thou gaze on the serpent thou hast slain? Thou too shalt be a serpent for men to gaze on." Long he stands there, with quaking heart and pallid cheeks, and his hair rises up on end with chilling fear. But behold, the hero's helper, Pallas, gliding down through the high air, stands beside him, and she bids him plow the earth and plant therein the dragon's teeth, destined to grow into a nation. He obeys and, having opened up the furrows with his deep-sunk plow, he sows in the ground the teeth as he is bid, a man-producing seed. Then, a thing beyond belief, the plowed ground begins to stir; and first there

primaque de sulcis acies adparuit hastae,
tegmina mox capitum picto nutantia cono,
mox umeri pectusque onerataque bracchia telis
exsistunt, crescitque seges clipeata virorum: 110
sic, ubi tolluntur festis aulaea theatris,
surgere signa solent primumque ostendere vultus,
cetera paulatim, placidoque educta tenore
tota patent imoque pedes in margine ponunt.
    Territus hoste novo Cadmus capere arma
        parabat: 115
" ne cape! " de populo, quem terra creaverat, unus
exclamat " nec te civilibus insere bellis! "
atque ita terrigenis rigido de fratribus unum
comminus ense ferit, iaculo cadit eminus ipse;
hunc quoque qui leto dederat, non longius illo   120
vivit et exspirat, modo quas acceperat auras,
exemploque pari furit omnis turba, suoque
Marte cadunt subiti per mutua vulnera fratres.
iamque brevis vitae spatium sortita iuventus
sanguineam tepido plangebat pectore matrem,   125
quinque superstitibus, quorum fuit unus Echion.
is sua iecit humo monitu Tritonidis arma
fraternaeque fidem pacis petiitque deditque:
hos operis comites habuit Sidonius hospes,
cum posuit iussus Phoebeis sortibus urbem.   130
    Iam stabant Thebae, poteras iam, Cadme, videri
exilio felix: soceri tibi Marsque Venusque
contigerant; huc adde genus de coniuge tanta,
tot natos natasque et, pignora cara, nepotes,

spring up from the furrows the points of spears, then helmets with coloured plumes waving; next shoulders of men and breasts and arms laden with weapons come up, and the crop grows with the shields of warriors. So when on festal days the curtain in the theatre is raised, figures of men rise up, showing first their faces, then little by little all the rest; until at last, drawn up with steady motion, the entire forms stand revealed, and plant their feet upon the curtain's edge.

Frightened by this new foe, Cadmus was preparing to take his arms. "Take not your arms," one of the earth-sprung brood cried out, "and take no part in our fratricidal strife." So saying, with his hard sword he clave one of his earth-born brothers, fighting hand to hand; and instantly he himself was felled by a javelin thrown from far. But he also who had slain this last had no longer to live than his victim, and breathed forth the spirit which he had but now received. The same dire madness raged in them all, and in mutual strife by mutual wounds these brothers of an hour perished. And now the youths, who had enjoyed so brief a span of life, were beating the breast of their mother earth warm with their blood—all save five. One of these five was Echion, who, at Pallas' bidding, dropped his weapons to the ground and sought and made peace with his surviving brothers. These the Sidonian wanderer had as comrades in his task when he founded the city granted him by Phoebus' oracle.

And now Thebes stood complete; now thou couldst seem, O Cadmus, even in exile, a happy man. Thou hast obtained Mars and Venus, too, as parents of thy bride; add to this blessing children worthy of so noble a wife, so many sons and daughters, the pledges of thy love, and grandsons, too, now grown to budding

OVID

hos quoque iam iuvenes; sed scilicet ultima semper
exspectanda dies hominis, dicique beatus   136
ante obitum nemo supremaque funera debet.

Prima nepos inter tot res tibi, Cadme, secundas
causa fuit luctus, alienaque cornua fronti
addita, vosque, canes satiatae sanguine erili.   140
at bene si quaeras, Fortunae crimen in illo,
non scelus invenies; quod enim scelus error
    habebat?

Mons erat infectus variarum caede ferarum,
iamque dies medius rerum contraxerat umbras
et sol ex aequo meta distabat utraque,   145
cum iuvenis placido per devia lustra vagantes
participes operum conpellat Hyantius ore:
" lina madent, comites, ferrumque cruore ferarum,
fortunaeque dies habuit satis; altera lucem
cum croceis invecta rotis Aurora reducet,   150
propositum repetemus opus: nunc Phoebus utraque
distat idem meta finditque vaporibus arva.
sistite opus praesens nodosaque tollite lina! "
iussa viri faciunt intermittuntque laborem.

Vallis erat piceis et acuta densa cupressu,   155
nomine Gargaphie succinctae sacra Dianae,
cuius in extremo est antrum nemorale recessu
arte laboratum nulla: simulaverat artem
ingenio natura suo; nam pumice vivo
et levibus tofis nativum duxerat arcum;   160
fons sonat a dextra tenui perlucidus unda,
margine gramineo patulos incinctus hiatus.

134

manhood. But of a surety man's last day must ever
be awaited, and none be counted happy till his death,
till his last funeral rites are paid.

One grandson of thine, Actaeon, midst all thy
happiness first brought thee cause of grief, upon whose
brow strange horns appeared, and whose dogs greedily
lapped their master's blood. But if you seek the
truth, you will find the cause of this in fortune's
fault and not in any crime of his. For what crime
had mere mischance?

'Twas on a mountain stained with the blood of many
slaughtered beasts; midday had shortened every
object's shade, and the sun was at equal distance
from either goal. Then young Actaeon with friendly
speech thus addressed his comrades of the chase as
they fared through the trackless wastes: " Both
nets and spears, my friends, are dripping with our
quarry's blood, and the day has given us good luck
enough. When once more Aurora, borne on her
saffron car, shall bring back the day, we will resume
our proposed task. Now Phoebus is midway in his
course and cleaves the very fields with his burning
rays. Cease then your present task and bear home
the well-wrought nets." The men performed his
bidding and ceased their toil.

There was a vale in that region, thick grown with
pine and cypress with their sharp needles. 'Twas
called Gargaphie, the sacred haunt of high-girt Diana.
In its most secret nook there was a well-shaded grotto,
wrought by no artist's hand. But Nature by her own
cunning had imitated art; for she had shaped a native
arch of the living rock and soft tufa. A sparkling
spring with its slender stream babbled on one side
and widened into a pool girt with grassy banks.
Here the goddess of the wild woods, when weary with

OVID

hic dea silvarum venatu fessa solebat
virgineos artus liquido perfundere rore.
quo postquam subiit, nympharum tradidit uni   165
armigerae iaculum pharetramque arcusque retentos,
altera depositae subiecit bracchia pallae,
vincla duae pedibus demunt; nam doctior illis
Ismenis Crocale sparsos per colla capillos
colligit in nodum, quamvis erat ipsa solutis.   170
excipiunt laticem Nepheleque Hyaleque Rhanisque
et Psecas et Phiale funduntque capacibus urnis.
dumque ibi perluitur solita Titania lympha,
ecce nepos Cadmi dilata parte laborum
per nemus ignotum non certis passibus errans   175
pervenit in lucum: sic illum fata ferebant.
qui simul intravit rorantia fontibus antra,
sicut erant, nudae viso sua pectora nymphae
percussere viro subitisque ululatibus omne
inplevere nemus circumfusaeque Dianam   180
corporibus texere suis; tamen altior illis
ipsa dea est colloque tenus supereminet omnis.
qui color infectis adversi solis ab ictu
nubibus esse solet aut purpureae Aurorae,
is fuit in vultu visae sine veste Dianae.   185
quae, quamquam comitum turba est stipata suarum,
in latus obliquum tamen adstitit oraque retro
flexit et, ut vellet promptas habuisse sagittas,
quas habuit sic hausit aquas vultumque virilem
perfudit spargensque comas ultricibus undis   190
addidit haec cladis praenuntia verba futurae:
" nunc tibi me posito visam velamine narres,
sit poteris narrare, licet! " nec plura minata

the chase, was wont to bathe her maiden limbs in the
crystal water. On this day, having come to the grotto,
she gives to the keeping of her armour-bearer among
her nymphs her hunting spear, her quiver, and her
unstrung bow; another takes on her arm the robe she
has laid by; two unbind her sandals from her feet.
But Theban Crocale, defter than the rest, binds into a
knot the locks which have fallen down her mistress'
neck, her own locks streaming free the while. Others
bring water, Nephele, Hyale and Rhanis, Psecas and
Phiale, and pour it out from their capacious urns.
And while Titania is bathing there in her accustomed
pool, lo! Cadmus' grandson, his day's toil deferred,
comes wandering through the unfamiliar woods with
unsure footsteps, and enters Diana's grove; for so
fate would have it. As soon as he entered the grotto
bedewed with fountain spray, the naked nymphs
smote upon their breasts at sight of the man, and
filled all the grove with their shrill, sudden cries.
Then they thronged around Diana, seeking to hide
her body with their own; but the goddess stood head
and shoulders over all the rest. And red as the clouds
which flush beneath the sun's slant rays, red as the
rosy dawn, were the cheeks of Diana as she stood
there in view without her robes. Then, though the
band of nymphs pressed close about her, she stood
turning aside a little and cast back her gaze; and
though she would fain have had her arrows ready,
what she had she took up, the water, and flung it
into the young man's face. And as she poured the
avenging drops upon his hair, she spoke these words
foreboding his coming doom: " Now you are free to
tell that you have seen me all unrobed—if you can
tell." No more than this she spoke; but on the head
which she had sprinkled she caused to grow the

dat sparso capiti vivacis cornua cervi,
dat spatium collo summasque cacuminat aures   195
cum pedibusque manus, cum longis bracchia mutat
cruribus et velat maculoso vellere corpus;
additus et pavor est: fugit Autonoeius heros
et se tam celerem cursu miratur in ipso.
ut vero vultus et cornua vidit in unda,   200
" me miserum! " dicturus erat: vox nulla secuta est!
ingemuit: vox illa fuit, lacrimaeque per ora
non sua fluxerunt; mens tantum pristina mansit.
quid faciat? repetatne domum et regalia tecta
an lateat silvis? pudor hoc, timor inpedit illud.   205
  Dum dubitat, videre canes, primique Melampus
Ichnobatesque sagax latratu signa dedere,
Cnosius Ichnobates, Spartana gente Melampus.
inde ruunt alii rapida velocius aura,   209
Pamphagos et Dorceus et Oribasos, Arcades omnes,
Nebrophonosque valens et trux cum Laelape Theron
et pedibus Pterelas et naribus utilis Agre
Hylaeusque ferox nuper percussus ab apro
deque lupo concepta Nape pecudesque secuta
Poemenis et natis comitata Harpyia duobus   215
et substricta gerens Sicyonius ilia Ladon
et Dromas et Canache Sticteque et Tigris et Alce
et niveis Leucon et villis Asbolos atris
praevalidusque Lacon et cursu fortis Aello
et Thoos et Cyprio velox cum fratre Lycisce   220
et nigram medio frontem distinctus ab albo
Harpalos et Melaneus hirsutaque corpore Lachne
et patre Dictaeo, sed matre Laconide nati
Labros et Argiodus et acutae vocis Hylactor

---

¹ The English names of these hounds in their order would
be: *Black-foot, Trail-follower, Voracious, Gazelle, Mountain-
ranger, Faun-killer, Hurricane, Hunter, Winged, Hunter,
Sylvan, Glen, Shepherd, Seizer, Catcher, Runner, Gnasher, Spot,*

horns of the long-lived stag, stretched out his neck, sharpened his ear-tips, gave feet in place of hands, changed his arms into long legs, and clothed his body with a spotted hide. And last of all she planted fear within his heart. Away in flight goes Autonoë's heroic son, marvelling to find himself so swift of foot. But when he sees his features and his horns in a clear pool, " Oh, woe is me! " he tries to say; but no words come. He groans—the only speech he has— and tears course down his changeling cheeks. Only his mind remains unchanged. What is he to do? Shall he go home to the royal palace, or shall he stay skulking in the woods? Shame blocks one course and fear the other.

But while he stands perplexed he sees his hounds.[1] And first come Melampus and keen-scented Ichnobates, baying loud on the trail—Ichnobates a Cretan dog, Melampus a Spartan; then others come rushing on swifter than the wind: Pamphagus, Dorceus, and Oribasos, Arcadians all; staunch Nebrophonos, fierce Theron and Laelaps; Pterelas, the swift of foot, and keen-scented Agre; savage Hylaeus, but lately ripped up by a boar; the wolf-dog Nape and the trusty shepherd Poemenis; Harpyia with her two pups; Sicyonian Ladon, thin in the flanks; Dromas, Canache, Sticte, Tigris, Alce; white-haired Leucon, black Asbolos; Lacon, renowned for strength, and fleet Aëllo; Thoos and swift Lycisce with her brother Cyprius; Harpalos, with a white spot in the middle of his black forehead; Melaneus and shaggy Lachne; two dogs from a Cretan father and a Spartan mother, Labros and Argiodus; shrill-tongued Hylactor, and others

Tigress, Might, White, Soot, Spartan, Whirlwind, Swift, Cyprian, Wolf, Grasper, Black, Shag, Fury, White-tooth, Barker, Black-hair, Beast-killer, Mountaineer.

quosque referre mora est: ea turba cupidine praedae
per rupes scopulosque adituque carentia saxa,   226
quaque est difficilis quaque est via nulla, sequuntur.
ille fugit per quae fuerat loca saepe secutus,
heu! famulos fugit ipse suos. clamare libebat:
"Actaeon ego sum: dominum cognoscite vestrum!"
verba animo desunt; resonat latratibus aether. 231
prima Melanchaetes in tergo vulnera fecit,
proxima Theridamas, Oresitrophos haesit in armo:
tardius exierant, sed per conpendia montis
anticipata via est; dominum retinentibus illis, 235
cetera turba coit confertque in corpore dentes.
iam loca vulneribus desunt; gemit ille sonumque,
etsi non hominis, quem non tamen edere possit
cervus, habet maestisque replet iuga nota querellis
et genibus pronis supplex similisque roganti 240
circumfert tacitos tamquam sua bracchia vultus.
at comites rapidum solitis hortatibus agmen
ignari instigant oculisque Actaeona quaerunt
et velut absentem certatim Actaeona clamant
(ad nomen caput ille refert) et abesse queruntur 245
nec capere oblatae segnem spectacula praedae.
vellet abesse quidem, sed adest; velletque videre,
non etiam sentire canum fera facta suorum.
undique circumstant, mersisque in corpore rostris
dilacerant falsi dominum sub imagine cervi, 250

whom it were too long to name. The whole pack,
keen with the lust of blood, over crags, over cliffs,
over trackless rocks, where the way is hard, where
there is no way at all, follow on. He flees over the
very ground where he has oft-times pursued; he flees
(the pity of it!) his own faithful hounds. He longs
to cry out: "I am Actaeon! Recognize your own
master!" But words fail his desire. All the air
resounds with their baying. And first Melanchaetes
fixes his fangs in his back, Theridamas next;
Oresitrophos has fastened on his shoulder. They had
set out later than the rest, but by a short-cut across
the mountain had outstripped their course. While
they hold back their master's flight, the whole pack
collects, and all together bury their fangs in his
body till there is no place left for further wounds.
He groans and makes a sound which, though not
human, is still one no deer could utter, and fills the
heights he knows so well with mournful cries. And
now, down on his knees in suppliant attitude, just
like one in prayer, he turns his face in silence towards
them, as if stretching out beseeching arms. But his
companions, ignorant of his plight, urge on the fierce
pack with their accustomed shouts, looking all around
for Actaeon, and call, each louder than the rest, for
Actaeon, as if he were far away—he turns his head
at the sound of his name—and complain that he is
absent and is missing through sloth the sight of the
quarry brought to bay. Well, indeed, might he wish
to be absent, but he is here; and well might he wish
to see, not to feel, the fierce doings of his own
hounds. They throng him on every side and, plung-
ing their muzzles in his flesh, mangle their master
under the deceiving form of the deer. Nor, as
they say, till he had been done to death by many

nec nisi finita per plurima vulnera vita
ira pharetratae fertur satiata Dianae,

Rumor in ambiguo est; aliis violentior aequo
visa dea est, alii laudant dignamque severa
virginitate vocant: pars invenit utraque causas. 255
sola Iovis coniunx non tam, culpetne probetne,
eloquitur, quam clade domus ab Agenore ductae
gaudet et a Tyria collectum paelice transfert
in generis socios odium; subit ecce priori   259
causa recens, gravidamque dolet de semine magni
esse Iovis Semelen; dum linguam ad iurgia solvit,
" profeci quid enim totiens per iurgia? " dixit,
" ipsa petenda mihi est; ipsam, si maxima Iuno
rite vocor, perdam, si me gemmantia dextra
sceptra tenere decet, si sum regina Iovisque   265
et soror et coniunx, certe soror. at, puto, furto est
contenta, et thalami brevis est iniuria nostri.
concipit—id derat—manifestaque crimina pleno
fert utero et mater, quod vix mihi contigit, uno
de Iove vult fieri: tanta est fiducia formae.   270
fallat eam faxo; nec sum Saturnia, si non
ab Iove mersa suo Stygias penetrabit in undas."

Surgit ab his solio fulvaque recondita nube
limen adit Semeles nec nubes ante removit
quam simulavit anum posuitque ad tempora canos
sulcavitque cutem rugis et curva trementi   276

wounds, was the wrath of the quiver-bearing goddess appeased.

Common talk wavered this way and that: to some the goddess seemed more cruel than was just; others called her act worthy of her austere virginity; both sides found good reasons for their judgment. Jove's wife alone spake no word either in blame or praise, but rejoiced in the disaster which had come to Agenor's house; for she had now transferred her anger from her Tyrian rival[1] to those who shared her blood. And lo! a fresh pang was added to her former grievance and she was smarting with the knowledge that Semele was pregnant with the seed of mighty Jove. Words of reproach were rising to her lips, but " What," she cried, " have I ever gained by reproaches? 'Tis she must feel my wrath. Herself, if I am duly called most mighty Juno, must I attack if I am fit to wield in my hand the jewelled sceptre, if I am queen of heaven, the sister and the wife of Jove—at least his sister. And yet, methinks, she is content with this stolen love, and the insult to my bed is but for a moment. But she has conceived— that still was lacking—and bears plain proof of her guilt in her full womb, and seeks—a fortune that has scarce been mine—to be made a mother from Jove. So great is her trust in beauty! But I will cause that trust to mock her: I am no daughter of Saturn if she go not down to the Stygian pool plunged thither by her Jupiter himself."

On this she rose from her seat, and, wrapped in a saffron cloud, she came to the home of Semele. But before she put aside her concealing cloud she feigned herself an old woman, whitening her hair at the temples, furrowing her skin with wrinkles, and

[1] *i.e.* Europa, whose story has already been told.

OVID

membra tulit passu; vocem quoque fecit anilem,
ipsaque erat Beroe, Semeles Epidauria nutrix.
ergo ubi captato sermone diuque loquendo
ad nomen venere Iovis, suspirat et " opto,   280
Iuppiter ut sit " ait; " metuo tamen omnia: multi
nomine divorum thalamos iniere pudicos.
nec tamen esse Iovem satis est: det pignus amoris,
si modo verus is est; quantusque et qualis ab alta
Iunone excipitur, tantus talisque, rogato,   285
det tibi conplexus suaque ante insignia sumat! "
    Talibus ignaram Iuno Cadmeida dictis
formarat: rogat illa Iovem sine nomine munus.
cui deus " elige! " ait " nullam patiere repulsam,
quoque magis credas, Stygii quoque conscia sunto
numina torrentis: timor et deus ille deorum est." 291
laeta malo nimiumque potens perituraque amantis
obsequio Semele " qualem Saturnia " dixit
" te solet amplecti, Veneris cum foedus initis,
da mihi te talem! " voluit deus ora loquentis   295
opprimere: exierat iam vox properata sub auras.
ingemuit; neque enim non haec optasse, neque ille
non iurasse potest.   ergo maestissimus altum
aethera conscendit vultuque sequentia traxit
nubila, quis nimbos inmixtaque fulgura ventis   300
addidit et tonitrus et inevitabile fulmen;
qua tamen usque potest, vires sibi demere temptat
nec, quo centimanum deiecerat igne Typhoea,

144

walking with bowed form and tottering steps. She spoke also in the voice of age and became even as Beroë, the Epidaurian nurse of Semele. When, after gossiping about many things, they came to mention of Jove's name, the old woman sighed and said: " I pray that it be Jupiter; but I am afraid of all such doings. Many, pretending to be gods, have found entrance into modest chambers. But to be Jove is not enough; make him prove his love if he is true Jove; as great and glorious as he is when welcomed by heavenly Juno, so great and glorious, pray him grant thee his embrace, and first don all his splendours."

In such wise did Juno instruct the guileless daughter of Cadmus. She in her turn asked Jove for a boon, unnamed. The god replied: " Choose what thou wilt, and thou shalt suffer no refusal. And that thou mayst be more assured, I swear it by the divinity of the seething Styx, whose godhead is the fear of all the gods." Rejoicing in her evil fortune, too much prevailing and doomed to perish through her lover's compliance, Semele said: " In such guise as Saturnia beholds thee when thou seekest her arms in love, so show thyself to me." The god would have checked her even as she spoke; but already her words had sped forth into uttered speech. He groans; for neither can she recall her wish, nor he his oath. And so in deepest distress he ascends the steeps of heaven, and with his beck drew on the mists that followed, then mingling clouds and lightnings and blasts of wind, he took last the thunder and that fire that none can escape. And yet whatever way he can he essays to lessen his own might, nor arms himself now with that bolt with which he had hurled down from heaven Typhoeus

nunc armatur eo : nimium feritatis in illo est.
est aliud levius fulmen, cui dextra cyclopum   305
saevitiae flammaeque minus, minus addidit irae :
tela secunda vocant superi ; capit illa domumque
intrat Agenoream.   corpus mortale tumultus
non tulit aetherios donisque iugalibus arsit.
inperfectus adhuc infans genetricis ab alvo   310
eripitur patrioque tener (si credere dignum est)
insuitur femori maternaque tempora conplet.
furtim illum primis Ino matertera cunis
educat, inde datum nymphae Nyseides antris
occuluere suis lactisque alimenta dedere.   315
　　Dumque ea per terras fatali lege geruntur
tutaque bis geniti sunt incunabula Bacchi,
forte Iovem memorant diffusum nectare curas
seposuisse graves vacuaque agitasse remissos
cum Iunone iocos et " maior vestra profecto est, 320
quam quae contingit maribus " dixisse " voluptas."
illa negat.   placuit quae sit sententia docti
quaerere Tiresiae : Venus huic erat utraque nota.
nam duo magnorum viridi coeuntia silva
corpora serpentum baculi violaverat ictu   325
deque viro factus (mirabile) femina septem
egerat autumnos ; octavo rursus eosdem
vidit, et " est vestrae si tanta potentia plagae "
dixit, " ut auctoris sortem in contraria mutet,
nunc quoque vos feriam." percussis anguibus isdem
forma prior rediit, genetivaque venit imago.   331
arbiter hic igitur sumptus de lite iocosa

of the hundred hands, for that weapon were too
deadly; but there is a lighter bolt, to which the
Cyclops' hands had given a less devouring flame, a
wrath less threatening. The gods call them his
"Second Armoury." With these in hand he enters
the palace of Agenor's son, the home of Semele. Her
mortal body bore not the onrush of heavenly power,
and by that gift of wedlock she was consumed. The
babe still not wholly fashioned is snatched from the
mother's womb and (if report may be believed) sewed
up in his father's thigh, there to await its full time of
birth. In secret his mother's sister, Ino, watched
over his infancy; thence he was confided to the
nymphs of Nysa, who hid him in their cave and
nurtured him with milk.

Now while these things were happening on the
earth by the decrees of fate, when the cradle of
Bacchus, twice born, was safe, it chanced that Jove
(as the story goes), while warmed with wine, put care
aside and bandied good-humoured jests with Juno in
an idle hour. " I maintain," said he, " that your
pleasure in love is greater than that which we enjoy."
She held the opposite view. And so they decided
to ask the judgment of wise Tiresias. He knew
both sides of love. For once, with a blow of his staff
he had outraged two huge serpents mating in the
green forest; and, wonderful to relate, from man he
was changed into a woman, and in that form spent
seven years. In the eighth year he saw the same
serpents again and said: " Since in striking you there
is such magic power as to change the nature of the
giver of the blow, now will I strike you once again." So
saying, he struck the serpents and his former state was
restored and he became as he had been born. He there-
fore, being asked to arbitrate the playful dispute of

OVID

dicta Iovis firmat: gravius Saturnia iusto
nec pro materia fertur doluisse suique
iudicis aeterna damnavit lumina nocte;   335
at pater omnipotens (neque enim licet inrita cuiquam
facta dei fecisse deo) pro lumine adempto
scire futura dedit poenamque levavit honore.
  Ille per Aonias fama celeberrimus urbes
inreprehensa dabat populo responsa petenti;   340
prima fide vocisque ratae temptamina sumpsit
caerula Liriope, quam quondam flumine curvo
inplicuit clausaeque suis Cephisos in undis
vim tulit: enixa est utero pulcherrima pleno
infantem nymphe, iam tunc qui posset amari,   345
Narcissumque vocat. de quo consultus, an esset
tempora maturae visurus longa senectae,
fatidicus vates " si se non noverit " inquit.
vana diu visa est vox auguris: exitus illam
resque probat letique genus novitasque furoris.   350
namque ter ad quinos unum Cephisius annum
addiderat poteratque puer iuvenisque videri:
multi illum iuvenes, multae cupiere puellae;
sed fuit in tenera tam dura superbia forma,
nulli illum iuvenes, nullae tetigere puellae.   355
adspicit hunc trepidos agitantem in retia cervos
vocalis nymphe, quae nec reticere loquenti
nec prior ipsa loqui didicit, resonabilis Echo.
  Corpus adhuc Echo, non vox erat et tamen usum
garrula non alium, quam nunc habet, oris habebat,
reddere de multis ut verba novissima posset.   361
fecerat hoc Iuno, quia, cum deprendere posset

the gods, took sides with Jove. Saturnia, they say, grieved more deeply than she should and than the issue warranted, and condemned the arbitrator to perpetual blindness. But the Almighty Father (for no god may undo what another god has done) in return for his loss of sight gave Tiresias the power to know the future, lightening the penalty by the honour.

He, famed far and near through all the Boeotian towns, gave answers that none could censure to those who sought his aid. The first to make trial of his truth and assured utterances was the nymph, Liriope, whom once the river-god, Cephisus, embraced in his winding stream and ravished, while imprisoned in his waters. When her time came the beauteous nymph brought forth a child, whom a nymph might love even as a child, and named him Narcissus. When asked whether this child would live to reach well-ripened age, the seer replied: " If he ne'er know himself." Long did the saying of the prophet seem but empty words. But what befell proved its truth— the event, the manner of his death, the strangeness of his infatuation. For Narcissus had reached his sixteenth year and might seem either boy or man. Many youths and many maidens sought his love ; but in that slender form was pride so cold that no youth, no maiden touched his heart. Once as he was driving the frightened deer into his nets, a certain nymph of strange speech beheld him, resounding Echo, who could neither hold her peace when others spoke, nor yet begin to speak till others had addressed her.

Up to this time Echo had form and was not a voice alone ; and yet, though talkative, she had no other use of speech than now—only the power out of many words to repeat the last she heard. Juno had made her thus ; for often when she might have

OVID

sub Iove saepe suo nymphas in monte iacentis,
illa deam longo prudens sermone tenebat,
dum fugerent nymphae. postquam hoc Saturnia
    sensit,   365
" huius " ait " linguae, qua sum delusa, potestas
parva tibi dabitur vocisque brevissimus usus,"
reque minas firmat. tantum haec in fine loquendi
ingeminat voces auditaque verba reportat.
ergo ubi Narcissum per devia rura vagantem   370
vidit et incaluit, sequitur vestigia furtim,
quoque magis sequitur, flamma propiore calescit,
non aliter quam cum summis circumlita taedis
admotas rapiunt vivacia sulphura flammas.
o quotiens voluit blandis accedere dictis   375
et mollis adhibere preces! natura repugnat
nec sinit, incipiat, sed, quod sinit, illa parata est
exspectare sonos, ad quos sua verba remittat.
forte puer comitum seductus ab agmine fido
dixerat: " ecquis adest? " et " adest " responderat
    Echo.   380
hic stupet, utque aciem partes dimittit in omnis,
voce " veni! " magna clamat: vocat illa vocantem.
respicit et rursus nullo veniente " quid " inquit
" me fugis? " et totidem, quot dixit, verba recepit.
perstat et alternae deceptus imagine vocis   385
" huc coeamus " ait, nullique libentius umquam
responsura sono " coeamus " rettulit Echo
et verbis favet ipsa suis egressaque silva
ibat, ut iniceret sperato bracchia collo;
ille fugit fugiensque " manus conplexibus aufer!   390
ante " ait " emoriar, quam sit tibi copia nostri ";

150

surprised the nymphs in company with her lord
upon the mountain-sides, Echo would cunningly
hold the goddess in long talk until the nymphs were
fled. When Saturnia realized this, she said to her:
". That tongue of thine, by which I have been tricked,
shall have its power curtailed and enjoy the briefest
use of speech." The event confirmed her threat.
She merely repeats the concluding phrases of a
speech and returns the words she hears. Now when
she saw Narcissus wandering through the fields, she
was inflamed with love and followed him by stealth;
and the more she followed, the more she burned by
a nearer flame; as when quick-burning sulphur,
smeared round the tops of torches, catches fire from
another fire brought near. Oh, how often does she
long to approach him with alluring words and make
soft prayers to him! But her nature forbids this,
nor does it permit her to begin; but as it allows,
she is ready to await the sounds to which she may
give back her own words. By chance the boy,
separated from his faithful companions, had cried:
" Is anyone here? " and " Here! " cried Echo back.
Amazed, he looks around in all directions and with
loud voice cries " Come! "; and " Come! " she calls
him calling. He looks behind him and, seeing no
one coming, calls again: " Why do you run from
me? " and hears in answer his own words again.
He stands still, deceived by the answering voice,
and " Here let us meet," he cries. Echo, never to
answer other sound more gladly, cries: " Let us
meet "; and to help her own words she comes forth
from the woods that she may throw her arms around
the neck she longs to clasp. But he flees at her
approach and, fleeing, says: " Hands off! embrace
me not! May I die before I give you power o'er

rettulit illa nihil nisi " sit tibi copia nostri ! "
spreta latet silvis pudibundaque frondibus ora
protegit et solis ex illo vivit in antris;
sed tamen haeret amor crescitque dolore repulsae;
extenuant vigiles corpus miserabile curae   396
adducitque cutem macies et in aera sucus
corporis omnis abit; vox tantum atque ossa super-
    sunt:
vox manet, ossa ferunt lapidis traxisse figuram.
inde latet silvis nulloque in monte videtur,   400
omnibus auditur: sonus est, qui vivit in illa.
   Sic hanc, sic alias undis aut montibus ortas
luserat hic nymphas, sic coetus ante viriles;
inde manus aliquis despectus ad aethera tollens
" sic amet ipse licet, sic non potiatur amato ! "   405
dixerat: adsensit precibus Rhamnusia iustis.
fons erat inlimis, nitidis argenteus undis,
quem neque pastores neque pastae monte capellae
contigerant aliudve pecus, quem nulla volucris
nec fera turbarat nec lapsus ab arbore ramus;   410
gramen erat circa, quod proximus umor alebat,
silvaque sole locum passura tepescere nullo.
hic puer et studio venandi lassus et aestu
procubuit faciemque loci fontemque secutus,
dumque sitim sedare cupit, sitis altera crevit,   415
dumque bibit, visae correptus imagine formae
spem sine corpore amat, corpus putat esse, quod
    umbra est.
adstupet ipse sibi vultuque inmotus eodem

152

me!" "I give you power o'er me!" she says, and
nothing more. Thus spurned, she lurks in the woods,
hides her shamed face among the foliage, and lives
from that time on in lonely caves. But still, though
spurned, her love remains and grows on grief; her
sleepless cares waste away her wretched form; she
becomes gaunt and wrinkled and all moisture fades
from her body into the air. Only her voice and her
bones remain: then, only voice; for they say that
her bones were turned to stone. She hides in woods
and is seen no more upon the mountain-sides; but all
may hear her, for voice, and voice alone, still lives in
her.

Thus had Narcissus mocked her, thus had he
mocked other nymphs of the waves or mountains;
thus had he mocked the companies of men. At last
one of these scorned youth, lifting up his hands to
heaven, prayed: "So may he himself love, and not
gain the thing he loves!" The goddess, Nemesis,
heard his righteous prayer. There was a clear pool
with silvery bright water, to which no shepherds
ever came, or she-goats feeding on the mountain-
side, or any other cattle; whose smooth surface
neither bird nor beast nor falling bough ever ruffled.
Grass grew all around its edge, fed by the water near,
and a coppice that would never suffer the sun to
warm the spot. Here the youth, worn by the chase
and the heat, lies down, attracted thither by the
appearance of the place and by the spring. While
he seeks to slake his thirst another thirst springs
up, and while he drinks he is smitten by the sight
of the beautiful form he sees. He loves an unsub-
stantial hope and thinks that substance which is only
shadow. He looks in speechless wonder at himself
and hangs there motionless in the same expression,

haeret, ut e Pario formatum marmore signum;
spectat humi positus geminum, sua lumina, sidus   420
et dignos Baccho, dignos et Apolline crines
inpubesque genas et eburnea colla decusque
oris et in niveo mixtum candore ruborem,
cunctaque miratur, quibus est mirabilis ipse:
se cupit inprudens et, qui probat, ipse probatur,   425
dumque petit, petitur, pariterque accendit et ardet.
inrita fallaci quotiens dedit oscula fonti,
in mediis quotiens visum captantia collum
bracchia mersit aquis nec se deprendit in illis!
quid videat, nescit; sed quod videt, uritur illo,   430
atque oculos idem, qui decipit, incitat error.
credule, quid frustra simulacra fugacia captas?
quod petis, est nusquam; quod amas, avertere, perdes!
ista repercussae, quam cernis, imaginis umbra est:
nil habet ista sui; tecum venitque manetque;   435
tecum discedet, si tu discedere possis!
    Non illum Cereris, non illum cura quietis
abstrahere inde potest, sed opaca fusus in herba
spectat inexpleto mendacem lumine formam
perque oculos perit ipse suos; paulumque levatus
ad circumstantes tendens sua bracchia silvas   441
" ecquis, io silvae, crudelius " inquit " amavit?
scitis enim et multis latebra opportuna fuistis.
ecquem, cum vestrae tot agantur saecula vitae,
qui sic tabuerit, longo meministis in aevo?   445
et placet et video; sed quod videoque placetque,
non tamen invenio "—tantus tenet error amantem—
" quoque magis doleam, nec nos mare separat ingens

like a statue carved from Parian marble. Prone on the ground, he gazes at his eyes, twin stars, and his locks, worthy of Bacchus, worthy of Apollo; on his smooth cheeks, his ivory neck, the glorious beauty of his face, the blush mingled with snowy white: all things, in short, he admires for which he is himself admired. Unwittingly he desires himself; he praises, and is himself what he praises; and while he seeks, is sought; equally he kindles love and burns with love. How often did he offer vain kisses on the elusive pool? How often did he plunge his arms into the water seeking to clasp the neck he sees there, but did not clasp himself in them! What he sees he knows not; but that which he sees he burns for, and the same delusion mocks and allures his eyes. O fondly foolish boy, why vainly seek to clasp a fleeting image? What you seek is nowhere; but turn yourself away, and the object of your love will be no more. That which you behold is but the shadow of a reflected form and has no substance of its own. With you it comes, with you it stays, and it will go with you—if you can go.

No thought of food or rest can draw him from the spot; but, stretched on the shaded grass, he gazes on that false image with eyes that cannot look their fill and through his own eyes perishes. Raising himself a little, and stretching his arms to the trees, he cries: " Did anyone, O ye woods, ever love more cruelly than I? You know, for you have been the convenient haunts of many lovers. Do you in the ages past, for your life is one of centuries, remember anyone who has pined away like this? I am charmed, and I see; but what I see and what charms me I cannot find "— so serious is the lover's delusion—" and, to make me grieve the more, no mighty ocean separates us, no

OVID

nec via nec montes nec clausis moenia portis;
exigua prohibemur aqua! cupit ipse teneri: 450
nam quotiens liquidis porreximus oscula lymphis,
hic totiens ad me resupino nititur ore.
posse putes tangi: minimum est, quod amantibus
 obstat.
quisquis es, huc exi! quid me, puer unice, fallis
quove petitus abis? certe nec forma nec aetas 455
est mea, quam fugias, et amarunt me quoque
 nymphae!
spem mihi nescio quam vultu promittis amico,
cumque ego porrexi tibi bracchia, porrigis ultro,
cum risi, adrides; lacrimas quoque saepe notavi
me lacrimante tuas; nutu quoque signa remittis 460
et, quantum motu formosi suspicor oris,
verba refers aures non pervenientia nostras!
iste ego sum: sensi, nec me mea fallit imago;
uror amore mei: flammas moveoque feroque.
quid faciam? roger anne rogem? quid deinde rogabo?
quod cupio mecum est: inopem me copia fecit. 466
o utinam a nostro secedere corpore possem!
votum in amante novum, vellem, quod amamus, abesset.
iamque dolor vires adimit, nec tempora vitae
longa meae superant, primoque exstinguor in aevo.
nec mihi mors gravis est posituro morte dolores, 471
hic, qui diligitur, vellem diuturnior esset;
nunc duo concordes anima moriemur in una."

   Dixit et ad faciem rediit male sanus eandem
et lacrimis turbavit aquas, obscuraque moto 475
156

long road, no mountain ranges, no city walls with
close-shut gates; by a thin barrier of water we are
kept apart. He himself is eager to be embraced.
For, often as I stretch my lips towards the lucent
wave, so often with upturned face he strives to lift
his lips to mine. You would think he could be
touched—so small a thing it is that separates our
loving hearts. Whoever you are, come forth hither!
Why, O peerless youth, do you elude me? or whither
do you go when I strive to reach you? Surely my
form and age are not such that you should shun them,
and me too the nymphs have loved. Some ground
for hope you offer with your friendly looks, and when
I have stretched out my arms to you, you stretch
yours too. When I have smiled, you smile back; and
I have often seen tears, when I weep, on your cheeks.
My becks you answer with your nod; and, as I sus-
pect from the movement of your sweet lips, you
answer my words as well, but words which do not
reach my ears.—Oh, I am he! I have felt it, I know
now my own image. I burn with love of my own
self; I both kindle the flames and suffer them. What
shall I do? Shall I be wooed or woo? Why woo at
all? What I desire, I have; the very abundance of
my riches beggars me. Oh, that I might be parted
from my own body! and, strange prayer for a lover,
I would that what I love were absent from me! And
now grief is sapping my strength; but a brief space
of life remains to me and I am cut off in my life's
prime. Death is nothing to me, for in death I shall
leave my troubles; I would he that is loved might live
longer; but as it is, we two shall die together in one
breath."

He spoke and, half distraught, turned again to the
same image. His tears ruffled the water, and dimly

reddita forma lacu est; quam cum vidisset abire,
" quo refugis? remane nec me, crudelis, amantem
desere! " clamavit; " liceat, quod tangere non est,
adspicere et misero praebere alimenta furori! "
dumque dolet, summa vestem deduxit ab ora   480
nudaque marmoreis percussit pectora palmis.
pectora traxerunt roseum percussa ruborem,
non aliter quam poma solent, quae candida parte,
parte rubent, aut ut variis solet uva racemis
ducere purpureum nondum matura colorem.   485
quae simul adspexit liquefacta rursus in unda,
non tulit ulterius, sed ut intabescere flavae
igne levi cerae matutinaeque pruinae
sole tepente solent, sic attenuatus amore
liquitur et tecto paulatim carpitur igni;   490
et neque iam color est mixto candore rubori,
nec vigor et vires et quae modo visa placebant,
nec corpus remanet, quondam quod amaverat Echo.
quae tamen ut vidit, quamvis irata memorque,
indoluit, quotiensque puer miserabilis " eheu "   495
dixerat, haec resonis iterabat vocibus " eheu ";
cumque suos manibus percusserat ille lacertos,
haec quoque reddebat sonitum plangoris eundem.
ultima vox solitam fuit haec spectantis in undam :
" heu frustra dilecte puer! " totidemque remisit 500
verba locus, dictoque vale " vale " inquit et Echo.
ille caput viridi fessum submisit in herba,
lumina mors clausit domini mirantia formam :
tum quoque se, postquam est inferna sede receptus,
in Stygia spectabat aqua.   planxere sorores   505
naides et sectos fratri posuere capillos,

the image came back from the troubled pool. As he saw it thus depart, he cried: " Oh, whither do you flee ? Stay here, and desert not him who loves thee, cruel one ! Still may it be mine to gaze on what I may not touch, and by that gaze feed my unhappy passion." While he thus grieves, he plucks away his tunic at its upper fold and beats his bare breast with pallid hands. His breast when it is struck takes on a delicate glow; just as apples sometimes, though white in part, flush red in other part, or as grapes hanging in clusters take on a purple hue when not yet ripe. As soon as he sees this, when the water has become clear again, he can bear no more; but, as the yellow wax melts before a gentle heat, as hoar frost melts before the warm morning sun, so does he, wasted with love, pine away, and is slowly consumed by its hidden fire. No longer has he that ruddy colour mingling with the white, no longer that strength and vigour, and all that lately was so pleasing to behold; scarce does his form remain which once Echo had loved so well. But when she saw it, though still angry and unforgetful, she felt pity; and as often as the poor boy says " Alas ! " again with answering utterance she cries " Alas ! " and as his hands beat his shoulders she gives back the same sounds of woe. His last words as he gazed into the familiar spring were these: " Alas, dear boy, vainly beloved ! " and the place gave back his words. And when he said "Farewell !" "Farewell !" said Echo too. He drooped his weary head on the green grass and death sealed the eyes that marvelled at their master's beauty. And even when he had been received into the infernal abodes, he kept on gazing on his image in the Stygian pool. His naiad-sisters beat their breasts and shore their locks in sign of grief for their dear

planxerunt dryades; plangentibus adsonat Echo.
iamque rogum quassasque faces feretrumque
    parabant:
nusquam corpus erat; croceum pro corpore florem
inveniunt foliis medium cingentibus albis.   510

  Cognita res meritam vati per Achaidas urbes
attulerat famam, nomenque erat auguris ingens;
spernit Echionides tamen hunc ex omnibus unus
contemptor superum Pentheus praesagaque ridet
verba senis tenebrasque et cladem lucis ademptae 515
obicit. ille movens albentia tempora canis
" quam felix esses, si tu quoque luminis huius
orbus " ait " fieres, ne Bacchica sacra videres!
namque dies aderit, quam non procul auguror
    esse,
qua novus huc veniat, proles Semeleia, Liber,   520
quem nisi templorum fueris dignatus honore,
mille lacer spargere locis et sanguine silvas
foedabis matremque tuam matrisque sorores.
eveniet! neque enim dignabere numen honore,
meque sub his tenebris nimium vidisse quereris." 525
talia dicentem proturbat Echione natus;
dicta fides sequitur, responsaque vatis aguntur.

  Liber adest, festisque fremunt ululatibus agri:
turba ruit, mixtaeque viris matresque nurusque
vulgusque proceresque ignota ad sacra feruntur. 530
" Quis furor, anguigenae, proles Mavortia, vestras
attonuit mentes? " Pentheus ait; " aerane tantum
aere repulsa valent et adunco tibia cornu

brother; the dryads, too, lamented, and Echo gave
back their sounds of woe. And now they were pre-
paring the funeral pile, the brandished torches and
the bier; but his body was nowhere to be found.
In place of his body they find a flower, its yellow
centre girt with white petals.

When this story was noised abroad it spread the
well-deserved fame of the seer throughout the cities
of Greece, and great was the name of Tiresias. Yet
Echion's son, Pentheus, the scoffer at gods, alone of all
men flouted the seer, laughed at the old man's words
of prophecy, and taunted him with his darkness and
loss of sight. But he, shaking his hoary head in
warning, said: " How fortunate wouldst thou be if
this light were dark to thee also, so that thou mightst
not behold the rites of Bacchus! For the day will
come—nay, I foresee 'tis near—when the new god
shall come hither, Liber, son of Semele. Unless thou
worship him as is his due, thou shalt be torn into a
thousand pieces and scattered everywhere, and shalt
with thy blood defile the woods and thy mother and
thy mother's sisters. So shall it come to pass; for
thou shalt refuse to honour the god, and shalt com-
plain that in my blindness I have seen all too well."
Even while he speaks the son of Echion flings him
forth; but his words did indeed come true and his
prophecies were accomplished.

The god is now come and the fields resound with
the wild cries of revellers. The people rush out of
the city in throngs, men and women, old and young,
nobles and commons, all mixed together, and hasten
to celebrate the new rites. " What madness, ye
sons of the serpent's teeth, ye seed of Mars, has
dulled your reason? " Pentheus cries. " Can clash-
ing cymbals, can the pipe of crooked horn, can

et magicae fraudes, ut, quos non bellicus ensis,
non tuba terruerit, non strictis agmina telis,   535
femineae voces et mota insania vino
obscenique greges et inania tympana vincant?
vosne, senes, mirer, qui longa per aequora vecti
hac Tyron, hac profugos posuistis sede penates,
nunc sinitis sine Marte capi? vosne, acrior aetas,   540
o iuvenes, propiorque meae, quos arma tenere,
non thyrsos, galeaque tegi, non fronde decebat?
este, precor, memores, qua sitis stirpe creati,
illiusque animos, qui multos perdidit unus,
sumite serpentis! pro fontibus ille lacuque   545
interiit: at vos pro fama vincite vestra!
ille dedit leto fortes: vos pellite molles
et patrium retinete decus! si fata vetabant
stare diu Thebas, utinam tormenta virique
moenia diruerent, ferrumque ignisque sonarent!   550
essemus miseri sine crimine, sorsque querenda,
non celanda foret, lacrimaeque pudore carerent;
at nunc a puero Thebae capientur inermi,
quem neque bella iuvant nec tela nec usus equorum,
sed madidus murra crinis mollesque coronae   555
purpuraque et pictis intextum vestibus aurum,
quem quidem ego actutum (modo vos absistite) cogam
adsumptumque patrem commentaque sacra fateri.
an satis Acrisio est animi, contemnere vanum
numen et Argolicas venienti claudere portas: 560
Penthea terrebit cum totis advena Thebis?
ite citi " (famulis hoc imperat), " ite ducemque

shallow tricks of magic, women's shrill cries, wine-
heated madness, vulgar throngs and empty drums
—can all these vanquish men, for whom real war,
with its drawn swords, the blare of trumpets, and
lines of glittering spears, had no terrors? You, ye
elders, should I give you praise, who sailed the long
reaches of the sea and planted here your Tyre, here
your wandering Penates, and who now permit them
to be taken without a struggle? Or you, ye young
men of fresher age and nearer arms to my own, for whom
once 'twas seemly to bear arms and not the thyrsus,
to be sheltered by helmets and not garlands? Be
mindful, I pray, from what seed you are sprung, and
show the spirit of the serpent, who in his single
strength killed many foes. For his fountain and his
pool he perished; but do you conquer for your glory's
sake! He did to death brave men: do you but put
to flight unmanly men and save your ancestral honour.
If it be the fate of Thebes not to endure for long, I
would the enginery of war and heroes might batter
down her walls and that sword and fire might roar
around her: then should we be unfortunate, but our
honour without stain; we should bewail, not seek to
conceal, our wretched state; then our tears would be
without shame. But now our Thebes shall fall before
an untried boy, whom neither arts of war assist nor
spears nor horsemen, but whose weapons are scented
locks, soft garlands, purple and gold inwoven in em-
broidered robes. But forthwith—only do you stand
aside—I will force him to confess that his father's
name is borrowed and his sacred rites a lie. Did
Acrisius have spirit enough to despise his empty god-
head, and to shut the gates of Argos in his face, and
shall Pentheus and all Thebes tremble at this
wanderer's approach? Go quickly "—this to his

attrahite huc vinctum! iussis mora segnis abesto!"
hunc avus, hunc Athamas, hunc cetera turba suorum
corripiunt dictis frustraque inhibere laborant.   565
acrior admonitu est inritaturque retenta
et crescit rabies remoraminaque ipsa nocebant:
sic ego torrentem, qua nil obstabat eunti,
lenius et modico strepitu decurrere vidi;
at quacumque trabes obstructaque saxa tenebant, 570
spumeus et fervens et ab obice saevior ibat.

Ecce cruentati redeunt et, Bacchus ubi esset,
quaerenti domino Bacchum vidisse negarunt;
" hunc " dixere " tamen comitem famulumque
    sacrorum
cepimus " et tradunt manibus post terga ligatis 575
sacra dei quendam Tyrrhena gente secutum.
adspicit hunc Pentheus oculis, quos ira tremendos
fecerat, et quamquam poenae vix tempora differt,
" o periture tuaque aliis documenta dature
morte," ait, " ede tuum nomen nomenque parentum
et patriam, morisque novi cur sacra frequentes!" 581
ille metu vacuus " nomen mihi " dixit " Acoetes,
patria Maeonia est, humili de plebe parentes.
non mihi quae duri colerent pater arva iuvenci,
lanigerosve greges, non ulla armenta reliquit; 585
pauper et ipse fuit linoque solebat et hamis
decipere et calamo salientis ducere pisces.
ars illi sua census erat; cum traderet artem,
' accipe, quas habeo, studii successor et heres,'
dixit ' opes,' moriensque mihi nihil ille reliquit 590

slaves—" go, bring this plotter hither, and in chains!
Let there be no dull delay to my bidding." His
grandsire addresses him in words of reprimand, and
Athamas, and all his counsellors, and they vainly strive
to curb his will. He is all the more eager for their
warning; his mad rage is fretted by restraint and
grows apace, and their attempts to delay him but
make him worse. So have I seen a river, where
nothing obstructed its course, flow smoothly on with
but a gentle murmur; but, where it was held in check
by dams of timber and stone set in its way, foaming
and boiling it went, fiercer for the obstruction.

But now the slaves come back, all covered with
blood, and, when their master asks where Bacchus
is, they say that they have not seen him; " but
this companion of his," they say, " this priest of his
sacred rites, we have taken," and they deliver up,
his hands bound behind his back, one of Etruscan
stock, a votary of Bacchus. Him Pentheus eyes
awhile with gaze made terrible by his wrath; and,
with difficulty withholding his hand from punish-
ment, he says: " Thou fellow, doomed to perish and
by thy death to serve as a warning to others, tell me
thy name, thy parents, and thy country; and why
thou dost devote thyself to this new cult." He
fearlessly replies: " My name is Acoetes, and my
country is Maeonia; my parents were but humble
folk. My father left me no fields or sturdy bullocks
to till them; no woolly sheep, no cattle. He himself
was poor and used to catch fish with hook and line
and rod and draw them leaping from the stream.
His craft was all his wealth; and when he passed it
on to me he said: 'Take this craft; 'tis all my fortune.
Be you my heir and successor in it.' And in dying
he left me nothing but the waters. This alone can

praeter aquas: unum hoc possum adpellare paternum.
mox ego, ne scopulis haererem semper in isdem,
addidici regimen dextra moderante carinae
flectere et Oleniae sidus pluviale capellae
Taygetenque Hyadasque oculis Arctonque notavi 595
ventorumque domos et portus puppibus aptos.
forte petens Delum Chiae telluris ad oras
adplicor et dextris adducor litora remis
doque levis saltus udaeque inmittor harenae:
nox ibi consumpta est; aurora rubescere primo 600
coeperat: exsurgo laticesque inferre recentis
admoneo monstroque viam, quae ducat ad undas;
ipse quid aura mihi tumulo promittat ab alto
prospicio comitesque voco repetoque carinam.
' adsumus en ' inquit sociorum primus Opheltes, 605
utque putat, praedam deserto nactus in agro,
virginea puerum ducit per litora forma.
ille mero somnoque gravis titubare videtur
vixque sequi; specto cultum faciemque gradumque:
nil ibi, quod credi posset mortale, videbam. 610
et sensi et dixi sociis: ' quod numen in isto
corpore sit, dubito; sed corpore numen in isto est!
quisquis es, o faveas nostrisque laboribus adsis;
his quoque des veniam! ' ' pro nobis mitte precari! '
Dictys ait, quo non alius conscendere summas 615
ocior antemnas prensoque rudente relabi.
hoc Libys, hoc flavus, prorae tutela, Melanthus,
hoc probat Alcimedon et, qui requiemque modumque
voce dabat remis, animorum hortator, Epopeus,
hoc omnes alii: praedae tam caeca cupido est. 620

I call my heritage. Soon, that I might not always
stay planted on the selfsame rocks, I learned to steer
ships with guiding hand; I studied the stars; the rainy
constellation of the Olenian Goat, Taygete, the
Hyades, the Bears; I learned the winds and whence
they blow; I learned what harbours are best for ships.
It chanced that while making for Delos I was driven
out of my course to the shore of Chios and made the
land with well-skilled oars. Light leaping, we landed
on the wet shore and spent the night. As soon as
the eastern sky began to redden I rose and bade my
men go for fresh water, showing them the way that
led to the spring. For my own task, from a high
hill I observed the direction of the wind; then called
my comrades and started back on board. ' Lo, here
we are! ' cried Opheltes, first of all the men, bringing
with him a prize (so he considered it) which he had
found in a deserted field, a little boy with form
beautiful as a girl's. He seemed to stagger, as if
o'ercome with wine and sleep, and could scarce
follow him who led. I gazed on his garb, his face, his
walk; and all I saw seemed more to me than mortal.
This I perceived, and said to my companions:
' What divinity is in that mortal body I know not;
but assuredly a divinity is therein. Whoever thou
art, be gracious unto us and prosper our under-
takings. Grant pardon also to these men.' ' Pray
not for us,' said Dictys, than whom none was more
quick to climb the topmost yard and slide down on
firm-grasped rope. Libys seconded this speech; so
did yellow-haired Melanthus, the look-out, and
Alcimedon and Epopeus, who by his voice marked
the time for the rowers and urged on their flagging
spirits. And all the rest approved, so blind and
heedless was their greed for booty. ' And yet I

' non tamen hanc sacro violari pondere pinum
perpetiar ' dixi : ' pars hic mihi maxima iuris '
inque aditu obsisto : furit audacissimus omni
de numero Lycabas, qui Tusca pulsus ab urbe
exilium dira poenam pro caede luebat ;   625
is mihi, dum resto, iuvenali guttura pugno
rupit et excussum misisset in aequora, si non
haesissem, quamvis amens, in fune retentus.
inpia turba probat factum ; tum denique Bacchus
(Bacchus enim fuerat), veluti clamore solutus   630
sit sopor aque mero redeant in pectora sensus,
' quid facitis ? quis clamor ? ' ait ' qua, dicite, nautae,
huc ope perveni ? quo me deferre paratis ? '
' pone metum ' Proreus, ' et quos contingere portus
ede velis ! ' dixit ; ' terra sistere petita.'   635
' Naxon ' ait Liber ' cursus advertite vestros !
illa mihi domus est, vobis erit hospita tellus.'
per mare fallaces perque omnia numina iurant
sic fore meque iubent pictae dare vela carinae.
dextera Naxos erat : dextra mihi lintea danti   640
' quid facis, o demens ? quis te furor,' inquit
    'Acoete,'
pro se quisque, ' tenet ?[1] laevam pete ! ' maxima nutu
pars mihi significat, pars quid velit ore susurro.
obstipui ' capiat ' que ' aliquis moderamina ! ' dixi
meque ministerio scelerisque artisque removi.   645

---

[1] tenet *Heinsius:* timet *MSS.*

shall not permit this ship to be defiled by such sacrilege,' I said; 'here must my authority have greater weight.' And I resisted their attempt to come on board. Then did Lycabas break out into wrath, the most reckless man of the crew, who, driven from Tuscany, was suffering exile as a punishment for the foul crime of murder. He, while I withstood him, tore at my throat with his strong hands and would have hurled me overboard, if, scarce knowing what I did, I had not clung to a rope that held me back. The godless crew applauded Lycabas. Then at last Bacchus—for it was he—as if aroused from slumber by the outcry, and as if his wine-dimmed senses were coming back, said: 'What are you doing? Why this uproar? And tell me, ye sailor-men, how did I get here and whither are you planning to take me?' 'Be not afraid,' said Proreus, 'tell me what port you wish to make, and you shall be set off at any place you choose.' 'Then turn your course to Naxos,' said Liber; 'that is my home, and there shall you find, yourselves, a friendly land.' By the sea and all its gods the treacherous fellows swore that they would do this, and bade me get the painted vessel under sail. Naxos lay off upon the right; and as I was setting my sails towards the right they severally turn on me, saying: 'What are you doing, you fool? what madness has got into you, Acoetes? Take the left tack.' The most of them by nods and winks let me know their intention, and some by explicit whispers. I could not believe my senses and I said to them: 'Then let someone else take the helm'; and declared that I would have nor part nor lot in their wicked scheme. They all cried out upon me and kept up their wrathful

increpor a cunctis, totumque inmurmurat agmen;
e quibus Aethalion ' te scilicet omnis in uno
nostra salus posita est! ' ait et subit ipse meumque
explet opus Naxoque petit diversa relicta.
tum deus inludens, tamquam modo denique fraudem   650
senserit, e puppi pontum prospectat adunca
et flenti similis ' non haec mihi litora, nautae,
promisistis ' ait, ' non haec mihi terra rogata est!
quo merui poenam facto? quae gloria vestra est,
si puerum iuvenes, si multi fallitis unum? '   655
iamdudum flebam: lacrimas manus inpia nostras
ridet et inpellit properantibus aequora remis.
per tibi nunc ipsum (nec enim praesentior illo
est deus) adiuro, tam me tibi vera referre
quam veri maiora fide: stetit aequore puppis   660
haud aliter, quam si siccam navale teneret.
illi admirantes remorum in verbere perstant
velaque deducunt geminaque ope currere temptant:
inpediunt hederae remos nexuque recurvo
serpunt et gravidis distinguunt vela corymbis.   665
ipse racemiferis frontem circumdatus uvis
pampineis agitat velatam frondibus hastam;
quem circa tigres simulacraque inania lyncum
pictarumque iacent fera corpora pantherarum.
exsiluere viri, sive hoc insania fecit   670
sive timor, primusque Medon nigrescere toto
corpore et expresso spinae curvamine flecti
incipit. huic Lycabas ' in quae miracula ' dixit
' verteris? ' et lati rictus et panda loquenti

mutterings. And one of them, Aethalion, broke out:
' I'd have you know, the safety of us all does not de-
pend on you alone!' So saying, he came and took
my place at the helm and, leaving the course for
Naxos, steered off in another direction. Then the
god, in mockery of them, as if he had just discovered
their faithlessness, looked out upon the sea from the
curved stern, and in seeming tears cried out: ' These
are not the shores you promised me, you sailor-men;
and this is not the land I sought. What have I done
to be so treated? And what glory will you gain if
you, grown men, deceive a little boy? if you, so many,
overcome just one?' I was long since in tears;
but the godless crew mocked my tears and swept the
seas with speeding oars. Now by the god himself I
swear (for there is no god more surely near than he)
that what I speak is truth, though far beyond
belief. The ship stands still upon the waves, as if
held dry in dock. The sailors in amaze redouble
their striving at the oars and make all sail, hoping
thus to speed their way by twofold power. But ivy
twines and clings about the oars, creeps upward
with many a back-flung, catching fold, and decks
the sails with heavy, hanging clusters. The god
himself, with his brow garlanded with clustering
berries, waves a wand wreathed with ivy-leaves.
Around him lie tigers, the forms (though empty all)
of lynxes and of fierce spotted panthers. The men
leap overboard, driven on by madness or by fear.
And first Medon's body begins to darken all over and
his back to be bent in a well-marked curve. Lycabas
says to him: ' Into what strange creature are you
turning?' But as he speaks his own jaws spread
wide, his nose becomes hooked, and his skin be-

naris erat, squamamque cutis durata trahebat.   675
at Libys obstantis dum vult obvertere remos,
in spatium resilire manus breve vidit et illas
iam non esse manus, iam pinnas posse vocari.
alter ad intortos cupiens dare bracchia funes
bracchia non habuit truncoque repandus in undas 680
corpore desiluit: falcata novissima cauda est,
qualia dividuae sinuantur cornua lunae.
undique dant saltus multaque adspergine rorant
emerguntque iterum redeuntque sub aequora rursus
inque chori ludunt speciem lascivaque iactant   685
corpora et acceptum patulis mare naribus efflant.
de modo viginti (tot enim ratis illa ferebat)
restabam solus: pavidum gelidumque trementi
corpore vixque meum firmat deus ' excute ' dicens
' corde metum Diamque tene! ' delatus in illam 690
accessi sacris Baccheaque sacra frequento."
   "Praebuimus longis" Pentheus "ambagibus aures,"
inquit " ut ira mora vires absumere posset.
praecipitem, famuli, rapite hunc cruciataque diris
corpora tormentis Stygiae demittite nocti! "   695
protinus abstractus solidis Tyrrhenus Acoetes
clauditur in tectis; et dum crudelia iussae
instrumenta necis ferrumque ignesque parantur,
sponte sua patuisse fores lapsasque lacertis
sponte sua fama est nullo solvente catenas.   700
   Perstat Echionides, nec iam iubet ire, sed ipse
vadit, ubi electus facienda ad sacra Cithaeron
cantibus et clara bacchantum voce sonabat.

comes hard and covered with scales. But Libys, while he seeks to ply the sluggish oars, sees his hands suddenly shrunk in size to things that can no longer be called hands at all, but fins. Another, catching at a twisted rope with his arms, finds he has no arms and goes plunging backwards with limbless body into the sea: the end of his tail is curved like the horns of a crescent moon. They leap about on every side, sending up showers of spray; they emerge from the water, only to return to the depths again; they sport like a troupe of dancers, tossing their bodies in wanton sport and drawing in and blowing out the water from their broad nostrils. Of but now twenty men—for the ship bore so many—I alone remained. And, as I stood quaking and trembling with cold fear, and hardly knowing what I did, the god spoke words of cheer to me and said: 'Be of good courage, and hold on your course to Naxos.' Arrived there, I have joined the rites and am one of the Bacchanalian throng."

Then Pentheus said: "We have lent ear to this long, rambling tale, that by such delay our anger might lose its might. Ye slaves, now hurry him away, rack his body with fearsome tortures, and so send him down to Stygian night." Straightway Acoetes, the Tyrrhenian, was dragged out and shut up in a strong dungeon. And while the slaves were getting the cruel instruments of torture ready, the iron, the fire—of their own accord the doors flew open wide; of their own accord, with no one loosing them, the chains fell from the prisoner's arms.

But Pentheus stood fixed in his purpose. He no longer sent messengers, but went himself to where Cithaeron, the chosen seat for the god's sacred rites, was resounding with songs and the shrill cries of wor-

ut fremit acer equus, cum bellicus aere canoro
signa dedit tubicen pugnaeque adsumit amorem,   705
Penthea sic ictus longis ululatibus aether
movit, et audito clamore recanduit ira.

Monte fere medio est, cingentibus ultima silvis,
purus ab arboribus, spectabilis undique, campus:
hic oculis illum cernentem sacra profanis   710
prima videt, prima est insano concita cursu,
prima suum misso violavit Penthea thyrso
mater et " o geminae " clamavit " adeste sorores!
ille aper, in nostris errat qui maximus agris,
ille mihi feriendus aper."   ruit omnis in unum   715
turba furens; cunctae coeunt trepidumque sequuntur,
iam trepidum, iam verba minus violenta loquentem,
iam se damnantem, iam se peccasse fatentem.
saucius ille tamen " fer opem, matertera " dixit
"Autonoe! moveant animos Actaeonis umbrae!"   720
illa, quis Actaeon, nescit dextramque precanti
abstulit, Inoo lacerata est altera raptu.
non habet infelix quae matri bracchia tendat,
trunca sed ostendens dereptis vulnera membris
" adspice, mater! " ait.   visis ululavit Agaue   725
collaque iactavit movitque per aera crinem
avulsumque caput digitis conplexa cruentis
clamat: " io comites, opus hoc victoria nostra est! "
non citius frondes autumni frigore tactas
iamque male haerentes alta rapit arbore ventus,   730
quam sunt membra viri manibus direpta nefandis.
talibus exemplis monitae nova sacra frequentant
turaque dant sanctasque colunt Ismenides aras.

shippers. As a spirited horse snorts when the brazen trumpet with tuneful voice sounds out the battle and his eagerness for the fray waxes hot, so did the air, pulsing with the long-drawn cries, stir Pentheus, and the wild uproar in his ears heated his wrath white-hot.

About midway of the mountain, bordered with thick woods, was an open plain, free from trees, in full view from every side. Here, as Pentheus was spying with profane eyes upon the sacred rites, his mother was the first to see him, first to rush madly on him, first with hurled thyrsus to smite her son. "Ho, there, my sisters, come!" she cried, "see that huge boar prowling in our fields. Now must I rend him." The whole mad throng rush on him; from all sides they come and pursue the frightened wretch— yes, frightened now, and speaking milder words, cursing his folly and confessing that he has sinned. Sore wounded, he cries out: "Oh help, my aunt, Autonoë! Let the ghost of Actaeon move your heart." She knows not who Actaeon is, and tears off the suppliant's right arm; Ino in frenzy rends away his left. And now the wretched man has no arms to stretch out in prayer to his mother; but, showing his mangled stumps where his arms have been torn away, he cries: "Oh, mother, see!" Agave howls madly at the sight and tosses her head with wildly streaming hair. Off she tears his head, and holding it in bloody hands, she yells: "See, comrades, this feat spells victory for us!" Not more quickly are leaves, when touched by the first cold of autumn and now lightly clinging, whirled from the lofty tree by the wind than is Pentheus torn limb from limb by those impious hands. Taught by such a warning, the Thebans throng the new god's sacred rites, burn incense, and bow down before his shrines.

BOOK IV

1–415	*The Daughters of Minyas*
55–166	*Pyramus and Thisbe*
167–189	*Mars and Venus*
190–273	*Leucothoe and Clytie*
274–388	*Salmacis and Hermaphroditus*
416–562	*Athamas and Ino*
563–603	*The End of Cadmus*
604–803	*Perseus and Andromeda*

LIBER IV

At non Alcithoe Minyeias orgia censet
accipienda dei, sed adhuc temeraria Bacchum
progeniem negat esse Iovis sociasque sorores
inpietatis habet.   festum celebrare sacerdos
inmunesque operum famulas dominasque suorum   5
pectora pelle tegi, crinales solvere vittas,
serta coma, manibus frondentis sumere thyrsos
iusserat et saevam laesi fore numinis iram
vaticinatus erat: parent matresque nurusque
telasque calathosque infectaque pensa reponunt   10
turaque dant Bacchumque vocant Bromiumque
     Lyaeumque
ignigenamque satumque iterum solumque bimatrem;
additur his Nyseus indetonsusque Thyoneus
et cum Lenaeo genialis consitor uvae
Nycteliusque Eleleusque parens et Iacchus et Euhan,
et quae praeterea per Graias plurima gentes   16
nomina, Liber, habes.   tibi enim inconsumpta iuventa
     est,

---

    [1] " The noisy one."
    [2] " The deliverer from care."
    [3] " Of Nysa," a city in India, connected traditionally with
the infancy of Bacchus.
    [4] " Son of Thyone," the name given to his mother, Semele,
after her translation to the skies.
    [5] " God of the wine-press."
    [6] So named from the fact that his orgies were celebrated in
the night.

178

BOOK IV

But not Minyas' daughter Alcithoë; she will not
have the god's holy revels admitted; nay, so bold
is she that she denies Bacchus to be Jove's son!
And her sisters are with her in the impious deed.
The priest had bidden the people to celebrate a
Bacchic festival: all serving-women must be excused
from toil; with their mistresses they must cover
their breasts with the skins of beasts, they must
loosen the ribands of their hair, and with garlands
upon their heads they must hold in their hands the
vine-wreathed thyrsus. And he had prophesied that
the wrath of the god would be merciless if he were
disregarded. The matrons and young wives all obey,
put by weaving and work-baskets, leave their tasks
unfinished; they burn incense, calling on Bacchus,
naming him also Bromius,[1] Lyaeus,[2] son of the
thunderbolt, twice born, child of two mothers; they
hail him as Nyseus[3] also, Thyoneus[4] of the unshorn
locks, Lenaeus,[5] planter of the joy-giving vine,
Nyctelius,[6] father Eleleus,[7], Iacchus,[8] and Euhan,
and all the many names besides by which thou art
known, O Liber,[9] throughout the towns of Greece.

[7] From the wild cries uttered by his worshippers in the
orgies.
[8] A name identified with Bacchus.
[9] Either from *liber*, " the free," or from *libo*, " he to whom
libations of wine are poured."

tu puer aeternus, tu formosissimus alto
conspiceris caelo; tibi, cum sine cornibus adstas,
virgineum caput est; Oriens tibi victus, adusque 20
decolor extremo qua tinguitur India Gange.
Penthea tu, venerande, bipenniferumque Lycurgum
sacrilegos mactas, Tyrrhenaque mittis in aequor
corpora, tu biiugum pictis insignia frenis
colla premis lyncum. bacchae satyrique sequuntur, 25
quique senex ferula titubantis ebrius artus
sustinet et pando non fortiter haeret asello.
quacumque ingrederis, clamor iuvenalis et una
femineae voces inpulsaque tympana palmis
concavaque aera sonant longoque foramine buxus. 30
    " Placatus mitisque " rogant Ismenides " adsis,"
iussaque sacra colunt; solae Minyeides intus
intempestiva turbantes festa Minerva
aut ducunt lanas aut stamina pollice versant
aut haerent telae famulasque laboribus urguent. 35
e quibus una levi deducens pollice filum
" dum cessant aliae commentaque sacra frequentant,
nos quoque, quas Pallas, melior dea, detinet " inquit,
" utile opus manuum vario sermone levemus
perque vices aliquid, quod tempora longa videri 40
non sinat, in medium vacuas referamus ad aures! "
dicta probant primamque iubent narrare sorores.
illa, quid e multis referat (nam plurima norat),
cogitat et dubia est, de te, Babylonia, narret,
Derceti, quam versa squamis velantibus artus 45
stagna Palaestini credunt motasse figura,

For thine is unending youth, eternal boyhood; thou
art the most lovely in the lofty sky; thy face is
virgin-seeming, if without horns thou stand before
us. The Orient owns thy sway, even to the bounds
where remotest Ganges laves swart India. Pentheus
thou didst destroy, thou awful god, and Lycurgus,
armed with the two-edged battle-axe (impious were
they both), and didst hurl the Tuscan sailors into the
sea. Lynxes, with bright reins harnessed, draw thy
car; bacchant women and satyrs follow thee, and
that old man who, drunk with wine, supports his
staggering limbs on his staff, and clings weakly to his
misshapen ass. Where'er thou goest, glad shouts
of youths and cries of women echo round, with drum
of tambourine, the cymbals' clash, and the shrill
piping of the flute.

"Oh, be thou with us, merciful and mild!" the
Theban women cry; and perform the sacred rites as
the priest bids them. The daughters of Minyas
alone stay within, marring the festival, and out of
due time ply their household tasks, spinning wool,
thumbing the turning threads, or keep close to the
loom, and press their maidens with work. Then one
of them, drawing the thread the while with deft
thumb, says: "While other women are deserting
their tasks and thronging this so-called festival, let
us also, who keep to Pallas, a truer goddess, lighten
with various talk the serviceable work of our hands,
and to beguile the tedious hours, let us take turns
in telling stories, while all the others listen." The
sisters agree and bid her be first to speak. She
mused awhile which she should tell of many tales,
for very many she knew. She was in doubt whether
to tell of thee, Dercetis of Babylon, who, as the
Syrians believe, changed to a fish, all covered with

an magis, ut sumptis illius filia pennis
extremos albis in turribus egerit annos,
nais an ut cantu nimiumque potentibus herbis
verterit in tacitos iuvenalia corpora pisces,   50
donec idem passa est, an, quae poma alba ferebat
ut nunc nigra ferat contactu sanguinis arbor:
hoc placet; hanc, quoniam vulgaris fabula non est,
talibus orsa modis lana sua fila sequente:

    " Pyramus et Thisbe, iuvenum pulcherrimus alter,
altera, quas Oriens habuit, praelata puellis,   56
contiguas tenuere domos, ubi dicitur altam
coctilibus muris cinxisse Semiramis urbem.
notitiam primosque gradus vicinia fecit,
tempore crevit amor; taedae quoque iure coissent, 60
sed vetuere patres: quod non potuere vetare,
ex aequo captis ardebant mentibus ambo.
conscius omnis abest; nutu signisque loquuntur,
quoque magis tegitur, tectus magis aestuat ignis.
fissus erat tenui rima, quam duxerat olim,   65
cum fieret, paries domui communis utrique.
id vitium nulli per saecula longa notatum—
quid non sentit amor?—primi vidistis amantes
et vocis fecistis iter, tutaeque per illud
murmure blanditiae minimo transire solebant.   70
saepe, ubi constiterant hinc Thisbe, Pyramus illinc,
inque vices fuerat captatus anhelitus oris,
' invide ' dicebant ' paries, quid amantibus obstas?'
quantum erat, ut sineres toto nos corpore iungi
aut, hoc si nimium est, vel ad oscula danda pateres?

scales, and swims in a pool; or how her daughter, changed to a pure white dove, spent her last years perched on high battlements; or how a certain nymph, by incantation and herbs too potent, changed the bodies of some boys into mute fishes, and at last herself became a fish; or how the mulberry-tree, which once had borne white fruit, now has fruit dark red, from the bloody stain. The last seems best. This tale, not commonly known as yet, she tells, spinning her wool the while.

" Pyramus and Thisbe—he, the most beautiful youth, and she, loveliest maid of all the East—dwelt in houses side by side, in the city which Semiramis is said to have surrounded with walls of brick. Their nearness made the first steps of their acquaintance. In time love grew, and they would have been joined in marriage, too, but their parents forbade. Still, what no parents could forbid, sore smitten in heart they burned with mutual love. They had no go-between, but communicated by nods and signs; and the more they covered up the fire, the more it burned. There was a slender chink in the party-wall of the two houses, which it had at some former time received when it was building. This chink, which no one had ever discovered through all these years—but what does love not see?—you lovers first discovered and made it the channel of speech. Safe through this your loving words used to pass in tiny whispers. Often, when they had taken their positions, on this side Thisbe, and Pyramus on that, and when each in turn had listened eagerly for the other's breath, ' O envious wall,' they would say, ' why do you stand between lovers? How small a thing 'twould be for you to permit us to embrace each other, or, if this be too much, to open for our kisses! But we are

OVID

nec sumus ingrati: tibi nos debere fatemur,   **76**
quod datus est verbis ad amicas transitus auris.'
talia diversa nequiquam sede locuti
sub noctem dixere ' vale ' partique dedere
oscula quisque suae non pervenientia contra.   **80**
postera nocturnos Aurora removerat ignes,
solque pruinosas radiis siccaverat herbas:
ad solitum coiere locum.   tum murmure parvo
multa prius questi statuunt, ut nocte silenti
fallere custodes foribusque excedere temptent,   **85**
cumque domo exierint, urbis quoque tecta relinquant,
neve sit errandum lato spatiantibus arvo,
conveniant ad busta Nini lateantque sub umbra
arboris: arbor ibi niveis uberrima pomis,
ardua morus, erat, gelido contermina fonti.   **90**
pacta placent; et lux, tarde discedere visa,
praecipitatur aquis, et aquis nox exit ab isdem.

  " Callida per tenebras versato cardine Thisbe
egreditur fallitque suos adopertaque vultum
pervenit ad tumulum dictaque sub arbore sedit.   **95**
audacem faciebat amor. venit ecce recenti
caede leaena boum spumantis oblita rictus
depositura sitim vicini fontis in unda;
quam procul ad lunae radios Babylonia Thisbe
vidit et obscurum timido pede fugit in antrum,   **100**
dumque fugit, tergo velamina lapsa reliquit.
ut lea saeva sitim multa conpescuit unda,
dum redit in silvas, inventos forte sine ipsa
ore cruentato tenues laniavit amictus.

184

not ungrateful. We owe it to you, we admit, that a passage is allowed by which our words may go through to loving ears.' So, separated all to no purpose, they would talk, and as night came on they said good-bye and printed, each on his own side of the wall, kisses that did not go through. The next morning had put out the starry beacons of the night, and the sun's rays had dried the frosty grass; they came together at the accustomed place. Then first in low whispers they lamented bitterly, then decided when all had become still that night to try to elude their guardians' watchful eyes and steal out of doors; and, when they had gotten out, they would leave the city as well; and that they might not run the risk of missing one another, as they wandered in the open country, they were to meet at Ninus' tomb and hide in the shade of a tree. Now there was a tree there hanging full of snow-white berries, a tall mulberry, and not far away was a cool spring. They liked the plan, and slow the day seemed to go. But at last the sun went plunging down beneath the waves, and from the same waves the night came up.

" Now Thisbe, carefully opening the door, steals out through the darkness, seen of none, and arrives duly at the tomb with her face well veiled and sits down under the trysting-tree. Love made her bold. But see! here comes a lioness, her jaws all dripping with the blood of fresh-slain cattle, to slake her thirst at the neighbouring spring. Far off under the rays of the moon Babylonian Thisbe sees her, and flees with trembling feet into the deep cavern, and as she flees she leaves her cloak on the ground behind her. When the savage lioness has quenched her thirst by copious draughts of water, returning to the woods she comes by chance upon the light garment (but without the

serius egressus vestigia vidit in alto   105
pulvere certa ferae totoque expalluit ore
Pyramus; ut vero vestem quoque sanguine tinctam
repperit, ' una duos ' inquit ' nox perdet amantes,
e quibus illa fuit longa dignissima vita;
nostra nocens anima est. ego te, miseranda, peremi,
in loca plena metus qui iussi nocte venires   111
nec prior huc veni. nostrum divellite corpus
et scelerata fero consumite viscera morsu,
o quicumque sub hac habitatis rupe leones!
sed timidi est optare necem.' velamina Thisbes 115
tollit et ad pactae secum fert arboris umbram,
utque dedit notae lacrimas, dedit oscula vesti,
' accipe nunc ' inquit ' nostri quoque sanguinis
    haustus!'
quoque erat accinctus, demisit in ilia ferrum,
nec mora, ferventi moriens e vulnere traxit.   120
ut iacuit resupinus humo, cruor emicat alte,
non aliter quam cum vitiato fistula plumbo
scinditur et tenui stridente foramine longas
eiaculatur aquas atque ictibus aera rumpit.
arborei fetus adspergine caedis in atram   125
vertuntur faciem, madefactaque sanguine radix
purpureo tinguit pendentia mora colore.

  " Ecce metu nondum posito, ne fallat amantem,
illa redit iuvenemque oculis animoque requirit,
quantaque vitarit narrare pericula gestit;   130
utque locum et visa cognoscit in arbore formam,
sic facit incertam pomi color: haeret, an haec sit.

girl herself!) and tears it with bloody jaws. Pyramus, coming out a little later, sees the tracks of the beast plain in the deep dust and grows deadly pale at the sight. But when he saw the cloak too, smeared with blood, he cried: ' One night shall bring two lovers to death. But she of the two was more worthy of long life; on my head lies all the guilt. Oh, I have been the cause of your death, poor girl, in that I bade you come forth by night into this dangerous place, and did not myself come hither first. Come, rend my body and devour my guilty flesh with your fierce fangs, O all ye lions who have your lairs beneath this cliff! But 'tis a coward's part merely to pray for death.' He picks up Thisbe's cloak and carries it to the shade of the trysting-tree. And while he kisses the familiar garment and bedews it with his tears he cries: ' Drink now my blood too.' So saying, he drew the sword which he wore girt about him, plunged the blade into his side, and straightway, with his dying effort, drew the sword from his warm wound. As he lay stretched upon the earth the spouting blood leaped high; just as when a pipe has broken at a weak spot in the lead and through the small hissing aperture sends spurting forth long streams of water, cleaving the air with its jets. The fruit of the tree, sprinkled with the blood, was changed to a dark red colour; and the roots, soaked with his gore, also tinged the hanging berries with the same purple hue.

" And now comes Thisbe from her hiding-place, still trembling, but fearful also that her lover will miss her; she seeks for him both with eyes and soul, eager to tell him how great perils she has escaped. And while she recognizes the place and the shape of the well-known tree, still the colour

dum dubitat, tremebunda videt pulsare cruentum
membra solum, retroque pedem tulit, oraque buxo
pallidiora gerens exhorruit aequoris instar,   135
quod tremit, exigua cum summum stringitur aura.
sed postquam remorata suos cognovit amores,
percutit indignos claro plangore lacertos
et laniata comas amplexaque corpus amatum
vulnera supplevit lacrimis fletumque cruori   140
miscuit et gelidis in vultibus oscula figens
' Pyrame,' clamavit, ' quis te mihi casus ademit?
Pyrame, responde! tua te carissima Thisbe
nominat; exaudi vultusque attolle iacentes!'
ad nomen Thisbes oculos iam morte gravatos   145
Pyramus erexit visaque recondidit illa.

   "Quae postquam vestemque suam cognovit et ense
vidit ebur vacuum, ' tua te manus ' inquit ' amorque
perdidit, infelix! est et mihi fortis in unum
hoc manus, est et amor: dabit hic in vulnera vires.
persequar extinctum letique miserrima dicar   151
causa comesque tui: quique a me morte revelli
heu sola poteras, poteris nec morte revelli.
hoc tamen amborum verbis estote rogati,
o multum miseri meus illiusque parentes,   155
ut, quos certus amor, quos hora novissima iunxit,
conponi tumulo non invideatis eodem;
at tu quae ramis arbor miserabile corpus
nunc tegis unius, mox es tectura duorum,
signa tene caedis pullosque et luctibus aptos   160
semper habe fetus, gemini monimenta cruoris.'

of its fruit mystifies her. She doubts if it be this. While she hesitates, she sees somebody's limbs writhing on the bloody ground, and starts back, paler than boxwood, and shivering like the sea when a slight breeze ruffles its surface. But when after a little while she recognizes her lover, she smites her innocent arms with loud blows of grief, and tears her hair; and embracing the well-beloved form, she fills his wounds with tears, mingling these with his blood. And as she kissed his lips, now cold in death, she wailed: ' O my Pyramus, what mischance has reft you from me? Pyramus! answer me. 'Tis your dearest Thisbe calling you. Oh, listen, and lift your drooping head! ' At the name of Thisbe, Pyramus lifted his eyes, now heavy with death, and having looked upon her face, closed them again.

" Now when she saw her own cloak and the ivory scabbard empty of the sword, she said: ' 'Twas your own hand and your love, poor boy, that took your life. I, too, have a hand brave for this one deed; I, too, have love. This shall give me strength for the fatal blow. I will follow you in death, and men shall say that I was the most wretched cause and comrade of your fate. Whom death alone had power to part from me, not even death shall have power to part from me. O wretched parents, mine and his, be ye entreated of this by the prayers of us both, that you begrudge us not that we, whom faithful love, whom the hour of death has joined, should be laid together in the same tomb. And do you, O tree, who now shade with your branches the poor body of one, and soon will shade two, keep the marks of our death and always bear your fruit of a dark colour, meet for mourning, as a memorial of our double death.'

dixit et aptato pectus mucrone sub imum
incubuit ferro, quod adhuc a caede tepebat.
vota tamen tetigere deos, tetigere parentes;
nam color in pomo est, ubi permaturuit, ater,   165
quodque rogis superest, una requiescit in urna."

   Desierat: mediumque fuit breve tempus, et orsa est
dicere Leuconoe: vocem tenuere sorores.
" hunc quoque, siderea qui temperat omnia luce,
cepit amor Solem: Solis referemus amores.   170
primus adulterium Veneris cum Marte putatur
hic vidisse deus; videt hic deus omnia primus.
indoluit facto Iunonigenaeque marito
furta tori furtique locum monstravit, at illi
et mens et quod opus fabrilis dextra tenebat   175
excidit: extemplo graciles ex aere catenas
retiaque et laqueos, quae lumina fallere possent,
elimat.   non illud opus tenuissima vincant
stamina, non summo quae pendet aranea tigno;
utque levis tactus momentaque parva sequantur,   180
efficit et lecto circumdata collocat arte.
ut venere torum coniunx et adulter in unum,
arte viri vinclisque nova ratione paratis
in mediis ambo deprensi amplexibus haerent.
Lemnius extemplo valvas patefecit eburnas   185
inmisitque deos; illi iacuere ligati
turpiter, atque aliquis de dis non tristibus optat
sic fieri turpis; superi risere, diuque
haec fuit in toto notissima fabula caelo.
   " Exigit indicii memorem Cythereia poenam   190

She spoke, and fitting the point beneath her breast, she fell forward on the sword which was still warm with her lover's blood. Her prayers touched the gods and touched the parents; for the colour of the mulberry fruit is dark red when it is ripe, and all that remained from both funeral pyres rests in a common urn."

The tale was done. Then, after a brief interval, Leuconoë began, while her sisters held their peace. "Even the Sun, who with his central light guides all the stars, has felt the power of love. The Sun's loves we will relate. This god was first, 'tis said, to see the shame of Mars and Venus; this god sees all things first. Shocked at the sight, he revealed her sin to the goddess' husband, Vulcan, Juno's son, and where it was committed. Then Vulcan's mind reeled and the work upon which he was engaged fell from his hands. Straightway he fashioned a net of fine links of bronze, so thin that they would escape detection of the eye. Not the finest threads of wool would surpass that work; no, not the web which the spider lets down from the ceiling beam. He made the web in such a way that it would yield to the slightest touch, the least movement, and then he spread it deftly over the couch. Now when the goddess and her paramour had come thither, by the husband's art and by the net so cunningly prepared they were both caught and held fast in each other's arms. Straightway Vulcan, the Lemnian, opened wide the ivory doors and let in the other gods. There lay the two in chains, disgracefully, and some one of the merry gods prayed that he might be so disgraced. The gods laughed, and for a long time this story was the talk of heaven.

"But the goddess of Cythera did not forget the one

inque vices illum, tectos qui laesit amores,
laedit amore pari.   quid nunc, Hyperione nate,
forma colorque tibi radiataque lumina prosunt?
nempe, tuis omnes qui terras ignibus uris,
ureris igne novo; quique omnia cernere debes,   195
Leucothoen spectas et virgine figis in una,
quos mundo debes, oculos.   modo surgis Eoo
temperius caelo, modo serius incidis undis,
spectandique mora brumalis porrigis horas;
deficis interdum, vitiumque in lumina mentis   200
transit et obscurus mortalia pectora terres.
nec tibi quod lunae terris propioris imago
obstiterit, palles: facit hunc amor iste colorem.
diligis hanc unam, nec te Clymeneque Rhodosque
nec tenet Aeaeae genetrix pulcherrima Circes   205
quaeque tuos Clytie quamvis despecta petebat
concubitus ipsoque illo grave vulnus habebat
tempore: Leucothoe multarum oblivia fecit,
gentis odoriferae quam formosissima partu
edidit Eurynome; sed postquam filia crevit,   210
quam mater cunctas, tam matrem filia vicit.
rexit Achaemenias urbes pater Orchamus isque
septimus a prisco numeratur origine Belo.

" Axe sub Hesperio sunt pascua Solis equorum:
ambrosiam pro gramine habent; ea fessa diurnis   215
membra ministeriis nutrit reparatque labori.
dumque ibi quadrupedes caelestia pabula carpunt
noxque vicem peragit, thalamos deus intrat
    amatos,

who had spied on her, and took fitting vengeance on him; and he that betrayed her stolen love was equally betrayed in love. What now avail, O son of Hyperion, thy beauty and brightness and radiant beams? For thou, who dost inflame all lands with thy fires, art thyself inflamed by a strange fire. Thou who shouldst behold all things, dost gaze on Leucothoë alone, and on one maiden dost thou fix those eyes which belong to the whole world. Anon too early dost thou rise in the eastern sky, and anon too late dost thou sink beneath the waves, and through thy long lingering over her dost prolong the short wintry hours. Sometimes thy beams fail utterly, thy heart's darkness passing to thy rays, and darkened thou dost terrify the hearts of men. Nor is it that the moon has come 'twixt thee and earth that thou art dark; 'tis that love of thine alone that makes thy face so wan. Thou delightest in her alone. Now neither Clymene seems fair to thee, nor the maid of Rhodes, nor Aeaean Circes' mother, though most beautiful, nor Clytie, who, although scorned by thee, still seeks thy love and even now bears its deep wounds in her heart. Leucothoë makes thee forgetful of them all, she whom most fair Eurynome bore in the land of spices. But, after the daughter came to womanhood, as the mother surpassed all in loveliness, so did the daughter surpass her. Her father, Orchamus, ruled over the cities of Persia, himself the seventh in line from ancient Belus.

"Beneath the western skies lie the pastures of the Sun's horses. Here not common grass, but ambrosia is their food. On this their bodies, weary with their service of the day, are refreshed and gain new strength for toil. While here his horses crop their celestial pasturage and Night takes her turn of toil, the

versus in Eurynomes faciem genetricis, et inter
bis sex Leucothoen famulas ad lumina cernit   220
levia versato ducentem stamina fuso.
ergo ubi ceu mater carae dedit oscula natae,
' res ' ait ' arcana est: famulae, discedite neve
eripite arbitrium matri secreta loquendi.'
paruerant, thalamoque deus sine teste relicto   225
' ille ego sum ' dixit, ' qui longum metior annum,
omnia qui video, per quem videt omnia tellus,
mundi oculus: mihi, crede, places.'   pavet illa,
          metuque
et colus et fusus digitis cecidere remissis.
ipse timor decuit.   nec longius ille moratus   230
in veram rediit speciem solitumque nitorem;
at virgo quamvis inopino territa visu
victa nitore dei posita vim passa querella est.

    " Invidit Clytie (neque enim moderatus in illa
Solis amor fuerat) stimulataque paelicis ira   235
vulgat adulterium diffamatamque parenti
indicat.   ille ferox inmansuetusque precantem
tendentemque manus ad lumina Solis et ' ille
vim tulit invitae ' dicentem defodit alta
crudus humo tumulumque super gravis addit
          harenae.   240
dissipat hunc radiis Hyperione natus iterque
dat tibi, qua possis defossos promere vultus;
nec tu iam poteras enectum pondere terrae
tollere, nympha, caput corpusque exsangue iacebas:
nil illo fertur volucrum moderator equorum   245

god enters the apartments of his love, assuming the form of Eurynome, her mother. There he discovers Leucothoë, surrounded by her twelve maidens, spinning fine wool with whirling spindle. Then having kissed her, just as her mother would have kissed her dear daughter, he says: ' Mine is a private matter. Retire, ye slaves, and let not a mother want the right to a private speech.' The slaves obey; and now the god, when the last witness has left the room, declares: ' Lo, I am he who measure out the year, who behold all things, by whom the earth beholds all things— the world's eye. I tell thee thou hast found favour in my sight.' The nymph is filled with fear; distaff and spindle fall unheeded from her limp fingers. Her very fear becomes her. Then he, no longer tarrying, resumes his own form and his wonted splendour. But the maiden, though in terror at this sudden apparition, yet, overwhelmed by his radiance, at last without protest suffers the ardent wooing of the god.

" Clytie was jealous, for love of the Sun still burned uncontrolled in her. Burning now with wrath at the sight of her rival, she spread abroad the story, and especially to the father did she tell his daughter's shame. He, fierce and merciless, unheeding her prayers, unheeding her arms stretched out to the Sun, and unheeding her cry, ' He overbore my will,' with brutal cruelty buried her deep in the earth, and heaped on the spot a heavy mound of sand. The son of Hyperion rent this with his rays, and made a way by which you might put forth your buried head; but too late, for now, poor nymph, you could not lift your head, crushed beneath the heavy earth, and you lay there, a lifeless corpse. Naught more pitiful than that sight, they say, did the driver of the swift steeds

post Phaethonteos vidisse dolentius ignes.
ille quidem gelidos radiorum viribus artus
si queat in vivum temptat revocare calorem;
sed quoniam tantis fatum conatibus obstat,
nectare odorato sparsit corpusque locumque   250
multaque praequestus ' tanges tamen aethera ' dixit.
protinus inbutum caelesti nectare corpus
deliquit terramque suo madefecit odore,
virgaque per glaebas sensim radicibus actis
turea surrexit tumulumque cacumine rupit.   255
    " At Clytien, quamvis amor excusare dolorem
indiciumque dolor poterat, non amplius auctor
lucis adit Venerisque modum sibi fecit in illa.
tabuit ex illo dementer amoribus usa;
nympharum inpatiens et sub Iove nocte dieque   260
sedit humo nuda nudis incompta capillis,
perque novem luces expers undaeque cibique
rore mero lacrimisque suis ieiunia pavit
nec se movit humo; tantum spectabat euntis
ora dei vultusque suos flectebat ad illum.   265
membra ferunt haesisse solo, partemque coloris
luridus exsangues pallor convertit in herbas;
est in parte rubor violaeque simillimus ora
flos tegit.   illa suum, quamvis radice tenetur,
vertitur ad Solem mutataque servat amorem."   270
dixerat, et factum mirabile ceperat auris;
pars fieri potuisse negant, pars omnia veros
posse deos memorant: sed non est Bacchus in illis.
    Poscitur Alcithoe, postquam siluere sorores.

see since Phaëthon's burning death. He tried, indeed, by his warm rays to recall those death-cold limbs to the warmth of life. But since grim fate opposed all his efforts, he sprinkled the body and the ground with fragrant nectar, and preluding with many words of grief, he said: ' In spite of fate shalt thou reach the upper air.' Straightway the body, soaked with the celestial nectar, melted away and filled the earth around with its sweet fragrance. Then did a shrub of frankincense, with deep-driven roots, rise slowly through the soil and its top cleaved the mound.

"But Clytie, though love could excuse her grief, and grief her tattling, was sought no more by the great light-giver, nor did he find aught to love in her. Thereafter she pined away, her love turned to madness. Unable to endure her sister nymphs, beneath the open sky, by night and day, she sat upon the bare ground, naked, bareheaded, unkempt. For nine whole days she sat, tasting neither drink nor food, her hunger fed by naught save pure dew and tears, and moved not from the ground. Only she gazed on the face of her god as he went his way, and turned her face towards him. They say that her limbs grew fast to the soil and her deathly pallor changed in part to a bloodless plant; but in part 'twas red, and a flower, much like a violet, came where her face had been. Still, though roots hold her fast, she turns ever towards the sun and, though changed herself, preserves her love unchanged." The story-teller ceased; the wonderful tale had held their ears. Some of the sisters say that such things could not happen; others declare that true gods can do anything. But Bacchus is not one of these.

Alcithoë is next called for when the sisters have

quae radio stantis percurrens stamina telae   275
" vulgatos taceo " dixit " pastoris amores
Daphnidis Idaei, quem nymphe paelicis ira
contulit in saxum : tantus dolor urit amantes ;
nec loquor, ut quondam naturae iure novato
ambiguus fuerit modo vir, modo femina Sithon.   280
te quoque, nunc adamas, quondam fidissime parvo,
Celmi, Iovi largoque satos Curetas ab imbri
et Crocon in parvos versum cum Smilace flores
praetereo dulcique animos novitate tenebo.

"Unde sit infamis, quare male fortibus undis   285
Salmacis enervet tactosque remolliat artus,
discite.   causa latet, vis est notissima fontis.
Mercurio puerum diva Cythereide natum
naides Idaeis enutrivere sub antris,
cuius erat facies, in qua materque paterque   290
cognosci possent ; nomen quoque traxit ab illis.
is tria cum primum fecit quinquennia, montes
deseruit patrios Idaque altrice relicta
ignotis errare locis, ignota videre
flumina gaudebat, studio minuente laborem.   295
ille etiam Lycias urbes Lyciaeque propinquos
Caras adit : videt hic stagnum lucentis ad imum
usque solum lymphae ; non illic canna palustris
nec steriles ulvae nec acuta cuspide iunci ;
perspicuus liquor est ; stagni tamen ultima vivo 300
caespite cinguntur semperque virentibus herbis.
nympha colit, sed nec venatibus apta nec arcus
flectere quae soleat nec quae contendere cursu,

198

become silent again. Running her shuttle swiftly through the threads of her loom, she said: "I will pass by the well-known love of Daphnis, the shepherd-boy of Ida, whom a nymph, in anger at her rival, changed to stone: so great is the burning smart which jealous lovers feel. Nor will I tell how once Sithon, the natural laws reversed, lived of changing sex, now woman and now man. How you also, Celmis, now adamant, were once most faithful friend of little Jove; how the Curetes sprang from copious showers; how Crocus and his beloved Smilax were changed into tiny flowers. All these stories I will pass by and will charm your minds with a tale that is pleasing because new.

"How the fountain of Salmacis is of ill-repute, how it enervates with its enfeebling waters and renders soft and weak all men who bathe therein, you shall now hear. The cause is hidden; but the enfeebling power of the fountain is well known. A little son of Hermes and of the goddess of Cythera the naiads nursed within Ida's caves. In his fair face mother and father could be clearly seen; his name also he took from them. When fifteen years had passed, he left his native mountains and abandoned his foster-mother, Ida, delighting to wander in unknown lands and to see strange rivers, his eagerness making light of toil. He came even to the Lycian cities and to the Carians, who dwell hard by the land of Lycia. Here he saw a pool of water crystal clear to the very bottom. No marshy reeds grew there, no unfruitful swamp-grass, nor spiky rushes; it is clear water. But the edges of the pool are bordered with fresh grass, and herbage ever green. A nymph dwells in the pool, one that loves not hunting, nor is wont to bend the bow or strive with speed of foot. She

solaque naiadum celeri non nota Dianae.
saepe suas illi fama est dixisse sorores   305
' Salmaci, vel iaculum vel pictas sume pharetras
et tua cum duris venatibus otia misce!'
nec iaculum sumit nec pictas illa pharetras,
nec sua cum duris venatibus otia miscet,
sed modo fonte suo formosos perluit artus,   310
saepe Cytoriaco deducit pectine crines
et, quid se deceat, spectatas consulit undas;
nunc perlucenti circumdata corpus amictu
mollibus aut foliis aut mollibus incubat herbis,
saepe legit flores. et tum quoque forte legebat, 315
cum puerum vidit visumque optavit habere.

   " Nec tamen ante adiit, etsi properabat adire,
quam se conposuit, quam circumspexit amictus
et finxit vultum et meruit formosa videri.
tunc sic orsa loqui: ' puer o dignissime credi   320
esse deus, seu tu deus es, potes esse Cupido,
sive es mortalis, qui te genuere, beati,
et frater felix, et fortunata profecto,
si qua tibi soror est, et quae dedit ubera nutrix;
sed longe cunctis longeque beatior illa,   325
si qua tibi sponsa est, si quam dignabere taeda.
haec tibi sive aliqua est, mea sit furtiva voluptas,
seu nulla est, ego sim, thalamumque ineamus
        eundem.'
nais ab his tacuit. pueri rubor ora notavit;
nescit, enim, quid amor; sed et erubuisse decebat:
hic color aprica pendentibus arbore pomis   331
aut ebori tincto est aut sub candore rubenti,
cum frustra resonant aera auxiliaria, lunae.
poscenti nymphae sine fine sororia saltem

only of the naiads follows not in swift Diana's train.
Often, 'tis said, her sisters would chide her: ' Sal-
macis, take now either hunting-spear or painted
quiver, and vary your ease with the hardships of the
hunt.' But she takes no hunting-spear, no painted
quiver, nor does she vary her ease with the hardships
of the hunt; but at times she bathes her shapely
limbs in her own pool; often combs her hair with a
boxwood comb, often looks in the mirror-like waters to
see what best becomes her. Now, wrapped in a trans-
parent robe, she lies down to rest on the soft grass
or the soft herbage. Often she gathers flowers; and
on this occasion, too, she chanced to be gathering
flowers when she saw the boy and longed to possess
what she saw.

" Not yet, however, did she approach him, though
she was eager to do so, until she had calmed herself,
until she had arranged her robes and composed her
countenance, and taken all pains to appear beautiful.
Then did she speak: ' O youth, most worthy to be
believed a god, if thou art indeed a god, thou must be
Cupid; or if thou art mortal, happy are they who
gave thee birth, blest is thy brother, fortunate indeed
any sister of thine and thy nurse who gave thee suck.
But far, oh, far happier than they all is she, if any be
thy promised bride, if thou shalt deem any worthy to
be thy wife. If there be any such, let mine be stolen
joy; if not, may I be thine, thy bride, and may we be
joined in wedlock.' The maiden said no more. But the
boy blushed rosy red; for he knew not what love is.
But still the blush became him well. Such colour have
apples hanging in sunny orchards, or painted ivory;
such has the moon, eclipsed, red under white, when
brazen vessels clash vainly for her relief. When the
nymph begged and prayed for at least a sister's kiss,

oscula iamque manus ad eburnea colla ferenti   335
' desinis, an fugio tecumque ' ait ' ista relinquo?'
Salmacis extimuit ' loca ' que ' haec tibi libera
    trado,
hospes ' ait simulatque gradu discedere verso,
tum quoque respiciens, fruticumque recondita
    silva
delituit flexuque genu submisit; at ille,   340
scilicet ut vacuis et inobservatus in herbis,
huc it et hinc illuc et in adludentibus undis
summa pedum taloque tenus vestigia tinguit;
nec mora, temperie blandarum captus aquarum
mollia de tenero velamina corpore ponit.   345
tum vero placuit, nudaeque cupidine formae
Salmacis exarsit; flagrant quoque lumina nymphae,
non aliter quam cum puro nitidissimus orbe
opposita speculi referitur imagine Phoebus;
vixque moram patitur, vix iam sua gaudia differt,   350
iam cupit amplecti, iam se male continet amens.
ille cavis velox adplauso corpore palmis
desilit in latices alternaque bracchia ducens
in liquidis translucet aquis, ut eburnea si quis
signa tegat claro vel candida lilia vitro.   355
' vicimus et meus est ' exclamat nais, et omni
veste procul iacta mediis inmittitur undis,
pugnantemque tenet, luctantiaque oscula carpit,
subiectatque manus, invitaque pectora tangit,
et nunc hac iuveni, nunc circumfunditur illac;   360
denique nitentem contra elabique volentem
inplicat ut serpens, quam regia sustinet ales
sublimemque rapit: pendens caput illa pedesque
adligat et cauda spatiantes inplicat alas;
utve solent hederae longos intexere truncos,   365
utque sub aequoribus deprensum polypus hostem

and was in act to throw her arms round his snowy
neck, he cried: ' Have done, or I must flee and leave
this spot—and you.' Salmacis trembled at this threat
and said: ' I yield the place to you, fair stranger,'
and turning away, pretended to depart. But even so
she often looked back, and deep in a neighbouring
thicket she hid herself, crouching on bended knees.
But the boy, freely as if unwatched and alone, walks
up and down on the grass, dips his toes in the lapping
waters, and his feet. Then quickly, charmed with the
coolness of the soothing stream, he threw aside the
thin garments from his slender form. Then did he
truly attract her, and the nymph's love kindled as she
gazed at the naked form. Her eyes shone bright as
when the sun's dazzling face is reflected from the
surface of a glass held opposite his rays. Scarce can
she endure delay, scarce bear her joy postponed, so
eager to hold him in her arms, so madly incontinent.
He, clapping his body with hollow palms, dives into
the pool, and swimming with alternate strokes flashes
with gleaming body through the transparent flood, as
if one should encase ivory figures or white lilies in
translucent glass. ' I win, and he is mine! ' cries the
naiad, and casting off all her garments dives also into
the waters: she holds him fast though he strives
against her, steals reluctant kisses, fondles him,
touches his unwilling breast, clings to him on this
side and on that. At length, as he tries his best to
break away from her, she wraps him round with her
embrace, as a serpent, when the king of birds has
caught her and is bearing her on high: which, hang-
ing from his claws, wraps her folds around his head
and feet and entangles his flapping wings with her
tail; or as the ivy oft-times embraces great trunks of
trees, or as the sea-polyp holds its enemy caught

continet ex omni dimissis parte flagellis.
perstat Atlantiades sperataque gaudia nymphae
denegat; illa premit commissaque corpore toto
sicut inhaerebat, ' pugnes licet, inprobe,' dixit,   370
' non tamen effugies.   ita, di, iubeatis, et istum
nulla dies a me nec me deducat ab isto.'
vota suos habuere deos; nam mixta duorum
corpora iunguntur, faciesque inducitur illis
una.   velut, si quis conducat cortice ramos,   375
crescendo iungi pariterque adolescere cernit,
sic ubi conplexu coierunt membra tenaci,
nec duo sunt et forma duplex, nec femina dici
nec puer ut possit, neutrumque et utrumque videntur.
   " Ergo ubi se liquidas, quo vir descenderat, undas
semimarem fecisse videt mollitaque in illis   381
membra, manus tendens, sed iam non voce virili
Hermaphroditus ait: ' nato date munera vestro,
et pater et genetrix, amborum nomen habenti:
quisquis in hos fontes vir venerit, exeat inde   385
semivir et tactis subito mollescat in undis! '
motus uterque parens nati rata verba biformis
fecit et incesto fontem medicamine tinxit."
   Finis erat dictis, et adhuc Minyeia proles
urguet opus spernitque deum festumque profanat,
tympana cum subito non adparentia raucis   391
obstrepuere sonis, et adunco tibia cornu
tinnulaque aera sonant; redolent murraeque crocique,
resque fide maior, coepere virescere telae
inque hederae faciem pendens frondescere vestis; 395
pars abit in vites, et quae modo fila fuerunt,

beneath the sea, its tentacles embracing him on every side. The son of Atlas resists as best he may and denies the nymph the joy she craves; but she holds on, and clings as if grown fast to him. 'Strive as you may, wicked boy,' she cries, 'still shall you not escape me. Grant me this, ye gods, and may no day ever come that shall separate him from me or me from him.' The gods heard her prayer. For their two bodies, joined together as they were, were merged in one, with one face and form for both. As when one grafts a twig on some tree, he sees the branches grow one, and with common life come to maturity, so were these two bodies knit in close embrace: they were no longer two, nor such as to be called, one, woman, and one, man. They seemed neither, and yet both.

"When now he saw that the waters into which he had plunged had made him but half-man, and that his limbs had become enfeebled there, stretching out his hands and speaking, though not with manly tones, Hermaphroditus cried: 'Oh, grant this boon, my father and my mother, to your son who bears the names of both: whoever comes into this pool as man may he go forth half-man, and may he weaken at touch of the water.' His parents heard the prayer of their two-formed son and charged the waters with that uncanny power."

Alcithoë was done; but still did the daughters of Minyas ply their tasks, despising the god and profaning his holy day: when suddenly unseen timbrels sounded harshly in their ears, and flutes, with curving horns, and tinkling cymbals; the air was full of the sweet scent of saffron and of myrrh; and, past all belief, their weft turned green, the hanging cloth changed into vines of ivy; part became grape-vines, and what were but now threads became clinging

palmite mutantur; de stamine pampinus exit;
purpura fulgorem pictis adcommodat uvis.
iamque dies exactus erat, tempusque subibat,
quod tu nec tenebras nec possis dicere lucem,⠀⠀⠀400
sed cum luce tamen dubiae confinia noctis:
tecta repente quati pinguesque ardere videntur
lampades et rutilis conlucere ignibus aedes
falsaque saevarum simulacra ululare ferarum,
fumida iamdudum latitant per tecta sorores⠀⠀⠀405
diversaeque locis ignes ac lumina vitant,
dumque petunt tenebras, parvos membrana per artus
porrigitur tenuique includit bracchia pinna;
nec qua perdiderint veterem ratione figuram,
scire sinunt tenebrae: non illas pluma levavit,⠀⠀⠀410
sustinuere tamen se perlucentibus alis
conataeque loqui minimam et pro corpore vocem
emittunt peraguntque levi stridore querellas.
tectaque, non silvas celebrant lucemque perosae
nocte volant seroque tenent a vespere nomen.⠀⠀⠀415

⠀⠀Tum vero totis Bacchi memorabile Thebis
numen erat, magnasque novi matertera vires
narrat ubique dei de totque sororibus expers
una doloris erat, nisi quem fecere sorores:
adspicit hanc natis thalamoque Athamantis habentem
sublimes animos et alumno numine Iuno⠀⠀⠀421
nec tulit et secum: " potuit de paelice natus

tendrils; vine-leaves sprang out along the warp, and bright-hued clusters matched the purple tapestry. And now the day was ended, and the time was come when you could not say 'twas dark or light; it was the borderland of night, yet with a gleam of day. Suddenly the whole house seemed to tremble, the oil-fed lamps to flare up, and all the rooms to be ablaze with ruddy fires, while ghostly beasts howled round. Meanwhile the sisters are seeking hiding-places through the smoke-filled rooms, in various corners trying to avoid the flames and glare of light. And while they seek to hide, a skinny covering overspreads their slender limbs, and thin wings enclose their arms. And in what fashion they have lost their former shape they know not for the darkness. No feathered pinions uplift them, yet they sustain themselves on transparent wings. They try to speak, but utter only the tiniest sound as befits their shrivelled forms, and give voice to their grief in thin squeaks. Houses, not forests, are their favourite haunts; and, hating the light of day, they flit by night and from late eventide derive their name.[1]

Then, truly, was the divinity of Bacchus acknowledged throughout all Thebes, and his mother's sister, Ino, would be telling of the wonderful powers of the new god everywhere. She alone of all her sisters knew naught of grief, except what she felt for them. She, proud of her children, of her husband, Athamas, and proud above all of her divine foster-son, is seen by Juno, who could not bear the sight. "That child of my rival," she said, communing with herself, "had power to change the

[1] i.e. vespertiliones, "creatures that flit about in the twilight," i.e. bats.

vertere Maeonios pelagoque inmergere nautas
et laceranda suae nati dare viscera matri
et triplices operire novis Minyeidas alis: 425
nil poterit Iuno nisi inultos flere dolores?
idque mihi satis est? haec una potentia nostra est?
ipse docet, quid agam (fas est et ab hoste doceri),
quidque furor valeat, Penthea caede satisque
ac super ostendit: cur non stimuletur eatque   430
per cognata suis exempla furoribus Ino? "

Est via declivis funesta nubila taxo:
ducit ad infernas per muta silentia sedes;
Styx nebulas exhalat iners, umbraeque recentes
descendunt illac simulacraque functa sepulcris: 435
pallor hiemsque tenent late loca senta, novique,
qua sit iter, manes, Stygiam quod ducat ad urbem,
ignorant, ubi sit nigri fera regia Ditis.
mille capax aditus et apertas undique portas
urbs habet, utque fretum de tota flumina terra,   440
sic omnes animas locus accipit ille nec ulli
exiguus populo est turbamve accedere sentit.
errant exsangues sine corpore et ossibus umbrae,
parsque forum celebrant, pars imi tecta tyranni,
pars aliquas artes, antiquae imitamina vitae.[1]   445

Sustinet ire illuc caelesti sede relicta   447
(tantum odiis iraeque dabat) Saturnia Iuno;
quo simul intravit sacroque a corpore pressum
ingemuit limen, tria Cerberus extulit ora   450

---

[1] 446 exercent, aliam partem sua poena coercet. *This line,
included in some manuscripts, is rejected by most editors.*

208

Maeonian sailors and plunge them in the sea, to
cause the flesh of a son to be torn in pieces by his
own mother, and to enwrap the three daughters of
Minyas with strange wings; and shall naught be
given to Juno, save to bemoan her wrongs still
unavenged? Does that suffice me? Is this my
only power? But he himself teaches me what to
do. 'Tis proper to learn even from an enemy. To
what length madness can go he has proved enough and
to spare by the slaughter of Pentheus. Why should
not Ino be stung to madness too, and, urged by her
fury, go where her kinswomen have led the way?"

There is a down-sloping path, by deadly yew-trees
shaded, which leads through dumb silence to the
infernal realms. The sluggish Styx there exhales its
vaporous breath; and by that way come down the
spirits of the new-dead, shades of those who have
received due funeral rites. This is a wide-extending
waste, wan and cold; and the shades newly arrived
know not where the road is which leads to the Stygian
city where lies the dread palace of black Dis. This
city has a thousand wide approaches and gates open
on all sides; and as the ocean receives the rivers that
flow down from all the earth, so does this place
receive all souls; it is not too small for any people,
nor does it feel the accession of a throng. There
wander the shades bloodless, without body and bone.
Some throng the forum, some the palace of the under-
world king; others ply some craft in imitation of their
former life.

Thither, leaving her abode in heaven, Saturnian
Juno endured to go; so much did she grant to her
hate and wrath. When she made entrance there,
and the threshold groaned beneath the weight of her
sacred form, Cerberus reared up his threefold head

et tres latratus semel edidit; illa sorores
Nocte vocat genitas, grave et inplacabile numen:
carceris ante fores clausas adamante sedebant
deque suis atros pectebant crinibus angues.
quam simul agnorunt inter caliginis umbras,   455
surrexere deae; sedes scelerata vocatur:
viscera praebebat Tityos lanianda novemque
iugeribus distentus erat; tibi, Tantale, nullae
deprenduntur aquae, quaeque inminet, effugit
    arbor;
aut petis aut urgues rediturum, Sisyphe, saxum; 460
volvitur Ixion et se sequiturque fugitque,
molirique suis letum patruelibus ausae
adsiduae repetunt, quas perdant, Belides undas.

    Quos omnes acie postquam Saturnia torva
vidit et ante omnes Ixiona, rursus ab illo   465
Sisyphon adspiciens " cur hic e fratribus " inquit
" perpetuas patitur poenas, Athamanta superbum
regia dives habet, qui me cum coniuge semper
sprevit? " et exponit causas odiique viaeque,
quidque velit: quod vellet, erat, ne regia Cadmi 470
staret, et in facinus traherent Athamanta sorores.
imperium, promissa, preces confundit in unum
sollicitatque deas: sic haec Iunone locuta,
Tisiphone canos, ut erat, turbata capillos
movit et obstantes reiecit ab ore colubras   475
atque ita " non longis opus est ambagibus," inquit;
" facta puta, quaecumque iubes; inamabile regnum
desere teque refer caeli melioris ad auras."

and uttered his threefold baying. The goddess summoned the Furies, sisters born of Night, divinities deadly and implacable. Before hell's closed gates of adamant they sat, combing the while black snakes from their hair. When they recognized Juno approaching through the thick gloom, the goddesses arose. This place is called the Accursed Place. Here Tityos offered his vitals to be torn, lying stretched out over nine broad acres. Thy lips can catch no water, Tantalus, and the tree that overhangs ever eludes thee. Thou, Sisyphus, dost either push or chase the rock that must always return upon its tracks. There whirls Ixion on his wheel, both following himself and fleeing, all in one; and the Belides, for daring to work destruction on their cousin-husbands, with unremitting toil seek again and again the waters, only to lose them.

On all these Saturnia looks with frowning eyes, but especially on Ixion; then, turning her gaze from him to Sisyphus, she says: "Why does this of all the brothers suffer unending pains, while Athamas dwells proudly in a rich palace—Athamas, who with his wife has always scorned my godhead?" And she explains the causes of her hatred and of her journey hither, and what she wants. What she wanted was that the house of Cadmus should fall, and that the Fury-sisters should drive Athamas to madness. Commands, promises, prayers she poured out all in one, and begged the goddesses to aid her. When Juno had done, Tisiphone, just as she was, shook her tangled grey locks, tossed back the straggling snakes from her face, and said: "There is no need of long explanations; consider done all that you ask. Leave this unlovely realm and go back to the sweeter airs of your native skies." Juno went back rejoicing;

OVID

laeta redit Iuno, quam caelum intrare parantem
roratis lustravit aquis Thaumantias Iris.　　480
　　Nec mora, Tisiphone madefactam sanguine sumit
inportuna facem, fluidoque cruore rubentem
induitur pallam, tortoque incingitur angue
egrediturque domo.　Luctus comitatur euntem
et Pavor et Terror trepidoque Insania vultu.　485
limine constiterat: postes tremuisse feruntur
Aeolii pallorque fores infecit acernas [1]
solque locum fugit. monstris est territa coniunx,
territus est Athamas, tectoque exire parabant:
obstitit infelix aditumque obsedit Erinys,　490
nexaque vipereis distendens bracchia nodis
caesariem excussit: motae sonuere colubrae,
parsque iacent umeris, pars circum pectora lapsae
sibila dant saniemque vomunt linguisque coruscant.
inde duos mediis abrumpit crinibus angues　495
pestiferaque manu raptos inmisit, at illi
Inoosque sinus Athamanteosque pererrant
inspirantque graves animas; nec vulnera membris
ulla ferunt: mens est, quae diros sentiat ictus.
attulerat secum liquidi quoque monstra veneni,　500
oris Cerberei spumas et virus Echidnae
erroresque vagos caecaeque oblivia mentis
et scelus et lacrimas rabiemque et caedis amorem,
omnia trita simul, quae sanguine mixta recenti
coxerat aere cavo viridi versata cicuta;　505
dumque pavent illi, vergit furiale venenum
pectus in amborum praecordiaque intima movit.

[1] acernas *MSS.*: Avernus *Merkel.*

212

and as she was entering heaven, Iris, the daughter of Thaumus, sprinkled her o'er with purifying water.

Straightway the fell Tisiphone seized a torch which had been steeped in gore, put on a robe red with dripping blood, girt round her waist a writhing snake, and started forth. Grief went along with her, Terror and Dread and Madness, too, with quivering face. She stood upon the doomed threshold. They say the very door-posts of the house of Aeolus [1] shrank away from her; the polished oaken doors grew dim and the sun hid his face. Ino was filled with terror at the monstrous sight, and her husband, Athamas, was filled with terror, too. They made to leave their palace, but the baleful Fury stood in their way and blocked their exit. And stretching her arms, wreathed with vipers, she shook out her locks: disturbed, the serpents hissed horribly. A part lay on her shoulders, part twined round her breast, hissing, vomiting venomous gore, and darting out their tongues. Then she tears away two serpents from the midst of her tresses, and with deadly aim hurls them at her victims. The snakes go gliding over the breasts of Ino and of Athamas and breathe upon them their pestilential breath. No wounds their bodies suffer; 'tis their minds that feel the deadly stroke. The Fury, not content with this, had brought horrid poisons too—froth of Cerberus' jaws, the venom of the Hydra, strange hallucinations and utter forgetfulness, crime and tears, mad love of slaughter, all mixed together with fresh blood, brewed in a brazen cauldron and stirred with a green hemlock-stalk. And while they stood quaking there, over the breasts of both she poured this maddening poison brew, and made it sink to their being's core.

[1] The father of Athamas.

tum face iactata per eundem saepius orbem
consequitur motis velociter ignibus ignes.
sic victrix iussique potens ad inania magni   510
regna redit Ditis sumptumque recingitur anguem.
　Protinus Aeolides media furibundus in aula
clamat " io, comites, his retia tendite silvis!
hic modo cum gemina visa est mihi prole leaena "
utque ferae sequitur vestigia coniugis amens   515
deque sinu matris ridentem et parva Learchum
bracchia tendentem rapit et bis terque per auras
more rotat fundae rigidoque infantia saxo
discutit ora ferox; tum denique concita mater,
seu dolor hoc fecit seu sparsi causa veneni,   520
exululat passisque fugit male sana capillis
teque ferens parvum nudis, Melicerta, lacertis
" euhoe Bacche " sonat: Bacchi sub nomine Iuno
risit et " hos usus praestet tibi " dixit " alumnus! "
inminet aequoribus scopulus: pars ima cavatur   525
fluctibus et tectas defendit ab imbribus undas,
summa riget frontemque in apertum porrigit
　　aequor;
occupat hunc (vires insania fecerat) Ino
seque super pontum nullo tardata timore
mittit onusque suum; percussa recanduit unda.   530
　At Venus, inmeritae neptis miserata labores,
sic patruo blandita suo est " o numen aquarum,
proxima cui caelo cessit, Neptune, potestas,

Then, catching up her torch, she whirled it rapidly round and round and kindled fire by the swiftly moving fire. So, her task accomplished and her victory won, she retraced her way to the unsubstantial realm of mighty Dis, and there laid off the serpents she had worn.

Straightway cried Athamas, the son of Aeolus, madly raving in his palace halls: "Ho! my comrades, spread the nets here in these woods! I saw here but now a lioness with her two cubs"; and madly pursued his wife's tracks as if she were a beast of prey. His son, Learchus, laughing and stretching out his little hands in glee, he snatched from the mother's arms, and whirling him round and round through the air like a sling, he madly dashed the baby's head against a rough rock. Then the mother, stung to madness too, either by grief or by the sprinkled poison's force, howled wildly, and, quite bereft of sense, with hair streaming, she fled away, bearing thee, little Melicerta, in her naked arms, and shouting "Ho! Bacchus!" as she fled. At the name of Bacchus, Juno laughed in scorn and said: "So may your foster-son ever bless you!" A cliff o'erhung the sea, the lower part of which had been hollowed out by the beating waves, and sheltered the waters underneath from the rain. Its top stood high and sharp and stretched far out in front over the deep. To this spot—for madness had made her strong—Ino climbed, and held by no natural fears, she leaped with her child far out above the sea. The water where she fell was churned white with foam.

But Venus, pitying the undeserved sufferings of her granddaughter, thus addressed her uncle with coaxing words: "O Neptune, god of waters, whose

magna quidem posco, sed tu miserere meorum,
iactari quos cernis in Ionio inmenso, 535
et dis adde tuis.   aliqua et mihi gratia ponto est,
si tamen in medio quondam concreta profundo
spuma fui Graiumque manet mihi nomen ab
    illa."
adnuit oranti Neptunus et abstulit illis,
quod mortale fuit, maiestatemque verendam 540
inposuit nomenque simul faciemque novavit
Leucothoeque deum cum matre Palaemona dixit.

  Sidoniae comites, quantum valuere secutae
signa pedum, primo videre novissima saxo;
nec dubium de morte ratae Cadmeida palmis 545
deplanxere domum scissae cum veste capillos,
utque parum iustae nimiumque in paelice saevae
invidiam fecere deae.   convicia Iuno
non tulit et " faciam vos ipsas maxima " dixit
" saevitiae monimenta meae "; res dicta secuta
    est. 550
nam quae praecipue fuerat pia, " persequar " inquit
" in freta reginam " saltumque datura moveri
haud usquam potuit scopuloque adfixa cohaesit;
altera, dum solito temptat plangore ferire
pectora, temptatos sensit riguisse lacertos; 555
illa, manus ut forte tetenderat in maris undas;
saxea facta manus in easdem porrigit undas;
huius, ut arreptum laniabat vertice crinem,
duratos subito digitos in crine videres:
216

power is second to heaven alone, I ask great things,
I know; but do thou pity these my friends, whom
thou seest plunged in the broad Ionian sea, and
receive them among thy sea-deities. Some favour is
due to me from the sea, if in the middle of its depths
my being sprang once from foam, and in the Greek
tongue I have a name from this." Neptune con-
sented to her prayer and, taking from Ino and her
son all that was mortal, gave them a being to be
revered, changing both name and form; for he
called the new god Palaemon, and his goddess-
mother, Leucothoë.

The Theban women who had been Ino's com-
panions followed on her track as best they could,
and saw her last act from the edge of the rock.
Nothing doubting that she had been killed, in
mourning for the house of Cadmus they beat their
breasts with their hands, tore their hair, and rent
their garments; and they upbraided Juno, saying
that she was unjust and too cruel to the woman
who had wronged her. Juno could not brook their
reproaches and said: " I will make yourselves the
greatest monument of my cruelty." No sooner said
than done. For she who had been most devoted to
the queen cried: " I shall follow my queen into the
sea "; and was just about to take the leap when she
was unable to move at all, and stood fixed fast to the
rock. A second, while she was preparing again to
smite her breasts as she had been doing, felt her
lifted arms grow stiff. Another had by chance
stretched out her hands towards the waters of the
sea, but now 'twas a figure of stone that stretched
out hands to those same waters. Still another,
plucking at her hair to tear it out, you might
see with sudden stiffened fingers still in act to

quo quaeque in gestu deprensa est, haesit in illo. 560
pars volucres factae, quae nunc quoque gurgite in
    illo
aequora destringunt summis Ismenides alis.
    Nescit Agenorides natam parvumque nepotem
aequoris esse deos; luctu serieque malorum
victus et ostentis, quae plurima viderat, exit   565
conditor urbe sua, tamquam fortuna locorum,
non sua se premeret, longisque erroribus actus
contigit Illyricos profuga cum coniuge fines.
iamque malis annisque graves dum prima retractant
fata domus releguntque suos sermone labores,   570
" num sacer ille mea traiectus cuspide serpens "
Cadmus ait " fuerat, tum cum Sidone profectus
vipereos sparsi per humum, nova semina, dentes?
quem si cura deum tam certa vindicat ira,
ipse precor serpens in longam porrigar alvum."   575
dixit, et ut serpens in longam tenditur alvum
durataeque cuti squamas increscere sentit
nigraque caeruleis variari corpora guttis
in pectusque cadit pronus, commissaque in unum
paulatim tereti tenuantur acumine crura.   580
bracchia iam restant: quae restant bracchia tendit
et lacrimis per adhuc humana fluentibus ora
" accede, o coniunx, accede, miserrima " dixit,
" dumque aliquid superest de me, me tange
    manumque
accipe, dum manus est, dum non totum occupat
    anguis."   585

tear. Each turned to stone and kept the pose in which she was overtaken. Still others were changed to birds, and they also, once Theban women, now on light wings skim the water over that pool.

Cadmus was all unaware that his daughter and little grandson had been changed to deities of the sea. Overcome with grief at the misfortunes which had been heaped upon him, and awed by the many portents he had seen, he fled from the city which he had founded, as if the fortune of the place and not his own evil fate were overwhelming him. Driven on through long wanderings, at last his flight brought him with his wife to the borders of Illyria. Here, overborne by the weight of woe and age, they reviewed the early misfortunes of their house and their own troubles. Cadmus said: " Was that a sacred serpent which my spear transfixed long ago when, fresh come from Sidon, I scattered his teeth on the earth, seed of a strange crop of men? If it be this the gods have been avenging with such unerring wrath, I pray that I, too, may be a serpent, and stretch myself in long snaky form——" Even as he spoke he was stretched out in long snaky form; he felt his skin hardening and scales growing on it, while iridescent spots besprinkled his darkening body. He fell prone upon his belly, and his legs were gradually moulded together into one and drawn out into a slender, pointed tail. His arms yet remained; while they remained, he stretched them out, and with tears flowing down his still human cheeks he cried: " Come near, oh, come, my most wretched wife, and while still there is something left of me, touch me, take my hand, while I have a hand, while still the serpent does not usurp me quite." He wanted to

ille quidem vult plura loqui, sed lingua repente
in partes est fissa duas, nec verba volenti
sufficiunt, quotiensque aliquos parat edere questus,
sibilat: hanc illi vocem natura reliquit.
nuda manu feriens exclamat pectora coniunx: 590
" Cadme, mane teque, infelix, his exue monstris!
Cadme, quid hoc? ubi pes, ubi sunt umerique
    manusque
et color et facies et, dum loquor, omnia? cur non
me quoque, caelestes, in eandem vertitis anguem? "
dixerat, ille suae lambebat coniugis ora   595
inque sinus caros, veluti cognosceret, ibat
et dabat amplexus adsuetaque colla petebat.
quisquis adest (aderant comites), terretur; at illa
lubrica permulcet cristati colla draconis,
et subito duo sunt iunctoque volumine serpunt,   600
donec in adpositi nemoris subiere latebras,
nunc quoque nec fugiunt hominem nec vulnere
    laedunt
quidque prius fuerint, placidi meminere dracones.
    Sed tamen ambobus versae solacia formae
magna nepos dederat, quem debellata colebat   605
India, quem positis celebrabat Achaïa templis;
solus Abantiades ab origine cretus eadem
Acrisius superest, qui moenibus arceat urbis
Argolicae contraque deum ferat arma genusque
non putet esse Iovis: neque enim Iovis esse putabat
Persea, quem pluvio Danae conceperat auro.   611
mox tamen Acrisium (tanta est praesentia veri)
tam violasse deum quam non agnosse nepotem

say much more, but his tongue was of a sudden cleft in two; words failed him, and whenever he tried to utter some sad complaint, it was a hiss; this was the only voice which Nature left him. Then his wife, smiting her naked breasts with her hands, cried out: " O Cadmus, stay, unhappy man, and put off this monstrous form! Cadmus, what does this mean? Where are your feet? Where are your shoulders and your hands, your colour, face, and, while I speak, your—everything? Why, O ye gods of heaven, do you not change me also into the same serpent form? " She spoke; he licked his wife's face and glided into her dear breasts as if familiar there, embraced her, and sought his wonted place about her neck. All who were there—for they had comrades with them—were filled with horror. But she only stroked the sleek neck of the crested dragon, and suddenly there were two serpents there with intertwining folds, which after a little while crawled off and hid in the neighbouring woods. Now also, as of yore, they neither fear mankind nor wound them, mild creatures, remembering what once they were.

But both in their altered form found great comfort in their grandson, whom conquered India now worshipped, whose temples Greece had filled with adoring throngs. There was one only, Acrisius, the son of Abas, sprung from the same stock, who forbade the entrance of Bacchus within the walls of his city, Argos, who violently opposed the god, and did not admit that he was the son of Jove. Nor did he admit that Perseus was son of Jove, whom Danaë had conceived of a golden shower. And yet, such is the power of truth, Acrisius in the end was sorry that he had repulsed the god and had not acknowledged his grandson. The one had now been received to a

paenitet: inpositus iam caelo est alter, at alter
viperei referens spolium memorabile monstri   615
aera carpebat tenerum stridentibus alis,
cumque super Libycas victor penderet harenas,
Gorgonei capitis guttae cecidere cruentae;
quas humus exceptas varios animavit in angues,
unde frequens illa est infestaque terra colubris.   620
    Inde per inmensum ventis discordibus actus
nunc huc, nunc illuc exemplo nubis aquosae
fertur et ex alto seductas aethere longe
despectat terras totumque supervolat orbem.
ter gelidas Arctos, ter Cancri bracchia vidit,   625
saepe sub occasus, saepe est ablatus in ortus,
iamque cadente die, veritus se credere nocti,
constitit Hesperio, regnis Atlantis, in orbe
exiguamque petit requiem, dum Lucifer ignes
evocet Aurorae, currus Aurora diurnos.   630
hic hominum cunctos ingenti corpore praestans
Iapetionides Atlas fuit: ultima tellus
rege sub hoc et pontus erat, qui Solis anhelis
aequora subdit equis et fessos excipit axes.
mille greges illi totidemque armenta per herbas   635
errabant, et humum vicinia nulla premebat;
arboreae frondes auro radiante nitentes
ex auro ramos, ex auro poma tegebant.
" hospes " ait Perseus illi, " seu gloria tangit
te generis magni, generis mihi Iuppiter auctor;   640
sive es mirator rerum, mirabere nostras;
hospitium requiemque peto."   memor ille vetustae
sortis erat; Themis hanc dederat Parnasia sortem:

place in heaven; but the other, bearing the wonderful spoil of the snake-haired monster, was taking his way through the thin air on whirring wings. As he was flying over the sandy wastes of Libya, bloody drops from the Gorgon's head fell down; and the earth received them as they fell and changed them into snakes of various kinds. And for this cause the land of Libya is full of deadly serpents.

From there he was driven through the vast stretches of air by warring winds and borne, now hither, now thither, like a cloud of mist. He looked down from his great height upon the lands lying below and flew over the whole world. Thrice did he see the cold Bears, and thrice the Crab's spreading claws; time and again to the west, and as often back to the east was he carried. And now, as daylight was fading, fearing to trust himself to flight by night, he alighted on the borders of the West, in the realm of Atlas. Here he sought a little rest until the morning star should wake the fires of dawn and the dawn lead out the fiery car of day. Here, far surpassing all men in huge bulk of body, was Atlas, of the stock of Iapetus. He ruled this edge of the world and the sea which spread its waters to receive the Sun's panting horses and his weary car. A thousand flocks he had, and as many herds, wandering at will over the grassy plains; and no other realm was near to hem in his land. A tree he had whose leaves were of gleaming gold, concealing golden branches and golden fruits. " Good sir," said Perseus, addressing him, " if glory of high birth means anything to you, Jove is my father; or if you admire great deeds, you surely will admire mine. I crave your hospitality and a chance to rest." But Atlas bethought him of an old oracle, which Themis of Parnasus had given:

" tempus, Atlas, veniet, tua quo spoliabitur auro
arbor, et hunc praedae titulum Iove natus habebit."
id metuens solidis pomaria clauserat Atlas   646
moenibus et vasto dederat servanda draconi
arcebatque suis externos finibus omnes.
huic quoque " vade procul, ne longe gloria rerum,
quam mentiris" ait, "longe tibi Iuppiter absit!"   650
vimque minis addit manibusque expellere temptat
cunctantem et placidis miscentem fortia dictis.
viribus inferior (quis enim par esset Atlantis
viribus?) " at, quoniam parvi tibi gratia nostra est,
accipe munus! " ait laevaque a parte Medusae   655
ipse retro versus squalentia protulit ora.
quantus erat, mons factus Atlas: nam barba comaeque
in silvas abeunt, iuga sunt umerique manusque,
quod caput ante fuit, summo est in monte cacumen,
ossa lapis fiunt; tum partes altus in omnes   660
crevit in inmensum (sic, di, statuistis) et omne
cum tot sideribus caelum requievit in illo.

    Clauserat Hippotades Aetnaeo carcere ventos,
admonitorque operum caelo clarissimus alto
Lucifer ortus erat: pennis ligat ille resumptis   665
parte ab utraque pedes teloque accingitur unco
et liquidum motis talaribus aera findit.
gentibus innumeris circumque infraque relictis
Aethiopum populos Cepheaque conspicit arva.
illic inmeritam maternae pendere linguae   670
Andromedan poenas iniustus iusserat Ammon;
224

" Atlas, the time will come when your tree will be spoiled of its gold, and he who gets the glory of this spoil will be Jove's son." Fearing this, Atlas had enclosed his orchard with massive walls and had put a huge dragon there to watch it; and he kept off all strangers from his boundaries. And now to Perseus, too, he said: " Hence afar, lest the glory of your deeds, which you falsely brag of, and lest this Jupiter of yours be far from aiding you." He added force to threats, and was trying to thrust out the other, who held back and manfully resisted while he urged his case with soothing speech. At length, finding himself unequal in strength—for who would be a match in strength for Atlas?—he said: " Well, since so small a favour you will not grant to me, let me give you a boon "; and, himself turning his back, he held out from his left hand the ghastly Medusa-head. Straightway Atlas became a mountain huge as the giant had been; his beard and hair were changed to trees, his shoulders and arms to spreading ridges; what had been his head was now the mountain's top, and his bones were changed to stones. Then he grew to monstrous size in all his parts—for so, O gods, ye had willed it—and the whole heaven with all its stars rested upon his head.

Now Aeolus, the son of Hippotas, had shut the winds in their prison beneath Etna, and the bright morning star that wakes men to their toil had risen in the heavens. Then Perseus bound on both his feet the wings he had laid by, girt on his hooked sword, and soon in swift flight was cleaving the thin air. Having left behind countless peoples all around him and below, he spied at last the Ethiopians and Cepheus' realm. There unrighteous Ammon had bidden Andromeda, though innocent, to

quam simul ad duras religatam bracchia cautes
vidit Abantiades, nisi quod levis aura capillos
moverat et tepido manabant lumina fletu,
marmoreum ratus esset opus; trahit inscius ignes 675
et stupet et visae correptus imagine formae
paene suas quatere est oblitus in aere pennas.
ut stetit, " o " dixit " non istis digna catenis,
sed quibus inter se cupidi iunguntur amantes,
pande requirenti nomen terraeque tuumque, 680
et cur vincla geras." primo silet illa nec audet
adpellare virum virgo, manibusque modestos
celasset vultus, si non religata fuisset;
lumina, quod potuit, lacrimis inplevit obortis.
saepius instanti, sua ne delicta fateri 685
nolle videretur, nomen terraeque suumque,
quantaque maternae fuerit fiducia formae,
indicat, et nondum memoratis omnibus unda
insonuit, veniensque inmenso belua ponto
inminet et latum sub pectore possidet aequor. 690
conclamat virgo : genitor lugubris et una
mater adest, ambo miseri, sed iustius illa,
nec secum auxilium, sed dignos tempore fletus
plangoremque ferunt vinctoque in corpore adhaerent.
cum sic hospes ait " lacrimarum longa manere 695
tempora vos poterunt, ad opem brevis hora ferendam
    est.
hanc ego si peterem Perseus Iove natus et illa,
quam clausam inplevit fecundo Iuppiter auro,
Gorgonis anguicomae Perseus superator et alis
aerias ausus iactatis ire per auras, 700

pay the penalty of her mother's words. As soon as
Perseus saw her there bound by the arms to a rough
cliff—save that her hair gently stirred in the breeze,
and the warm tears were trickling down her cheeks,
he would have thought her a marble statue—he
took fire unwitting, and stood dumb. Smitten by the
sight of the beauty he sees, he almost forgot to
move his wings in the air. Then, when he alighted
near the maiden, he said: " Oh! those are not the
chains you deserve to wear, but rather those that link
fond lovers together! Tell me, for I would know,
your country's name and yours, and why you are
chained here." She was silent at first, for, being a
maid, she did not dare address a man; she would have
hidden her face modestly with her hands but that
her hands were bound. Her eyes were free, and
these filled with rising tears. As he continued to
urge her, she, lest she should seem to be trying to
conceal some fault of her own, told him her name
and her country, and what sinful boasting her mother
had made of her own beauty. While she was yet
speaking, there came a loud sound from the sea, and
there, advancing over the broad expanse, a monstrous
creature loomed up, breasting the wide waves. The
maiden shrieked. The grieving father and the mother
are at hand, both wretched, but she more justly so.
They have no help to give, but only wailings and loud
beatings of the breast, befitting the occasion, and
they hang to the girl's chained form. Then speaks
the stranger: " There will be long time for weeping
by and by; but time for helping is very short. If I
sought this maid as Perseus, son of Jove and that
imprisoned one whom Jove filled with his life-giving
shower; if as Perseus, victor over Gorgon of the
snaky locks, and as he who has dared to ride the

praeferrer cunctis certe gener; addere tantis
dotibus et meritum, faveant modo numina, tempto:
ut mea sit servata mea virtute, paciscor."
accipiunt legem (quis enim dubitaret?) et orant
promittuntque super regnum dotale parentes.   705

    Ecce, velut navis praefixo concita rostro
sulcat aquas iuvenum sudantibus acta lacertis,
sic fera dimotis inpulsu pectoris undis;
tantum aberat scopulis, quantum Balearica torto
funda potest plumbo medii transmittere caeli,   710
cum subito iuvenis pedibus tellure repulsa
arduus in nubes abiit: ut in aequore summo
umbra viri visa est, visam fera saevit in umbram,
utque Iovis praepes, vacuo cum vidit in arvo
praebentem Phoebo liventia terga draconem,   715
occupat aversum, neu saeva retorqueat ora,
squamigeris avidos figit cervicibus ungues,
sic celeri missus praeceps per inane volatu
terga ferae pressit dextroque frementis in armo
Inachides ferrum curvo tenus abdidit hamo.   720
vulnere laesa gravi modo se sublimis in auras
attollit, modo subdit aquis, modo more ferocis
versat apri, quem turba canum circumsona terret.
ille avidos morsus velocibus effugit alis
quaque patet, nunc terga cavis super obsita conchis,
nunc laterum costas, nunc qua tenuissima cauda   726
desinit in piscem, falcato verberat ense;
228

winds of the air on fluttering wings, surely I should be preferred to all suitors as your son-in-law. But now I shall try to add to these great gifts the gift of service, too, if only the gods will favour me. That she be mine if saved by my valour is my bargain." The parents accept the condition—for who would refuse? —and beg him to save her, promising him a kingdom as dowry in addition.

But see! as a swift ship with its sharp beak plows the waves, driven by stout rowers' sweating arms, so does the monster come, rolling back the water from either side as his breast surges through. And now he was as far from the cliff as is the space through which a Balearic sling can send its whizzing bullet; when suddenly the youth, springing up from the earth, mounted high into the clouds. When the monster saw the hero's shadow on the surface of the sea, he savagely attacked the shadow. And as the bird of Jove, when it has seen in an open field a serpent sunning its mottled body, swoops down upon him from behind; and, lest the serpent twist back his deadly fangs, the bird buries deep his sharp claws in the creature's scaly neck; so did Perseus, plunging headlong in a swift swoop through the empty air, attack the roaring monster from above, and in his right shoulder buried his sword clear down to the curved hook. Smarting under the deep wound, the creature now reared himself high in air, now plunged beneath the waves, now turned like a fierce wild-boar when around him a noisy pack of hounds give tongue. Perseus eludes the greedy fangs by help of his swift wings; and where the vulnerable points lie open to attack, he smites with his hooked sword, now at the back, thick-set with barnacles, now on the sides, now where the tail is most slender and changes into

belua puniceo mixtos cum sanguine fluctus
ore vomit: maduere graves adspergine pennae.
nec bibulis ultra Perseus talaribus ausus   730
credere conspexit scopulum, qui vertice summo
stantibus exstat aquis, operitur ab aequore moto.
nixus eo rupisque tenens iuga prima sinistra
ter quater exegit repetita per ilia ferrum.
litora cum plausu clamor superasque deorum   735
inplevere domos: gaudent generumque salutant
auxiliumque domus servatoremque fatentur
Cassiope Cepheusque pater; resoluta catenis
incedit virgo, pretiumque et causa laboris.
ipse manus hausta victrices abluit unda,   740
anguiferumque caput dura ne laedat harena,
mollit humum foliis natasque sub aequore virgas
sternit et inponit Phorcynidos ora Medusae.
virga recens bibulaque etiamnum viva medulla
vim rapuit monstri tactuque induruit huius   745
percepitque novum ramis et fronde rigorem.
at pelagi nymphae factum mirabile temptant
pluribus in virgis et idem contingere gaudent
seminaque ex illis iterant iactata per undas:
nunc quoque curaliis eadem natura remansit,   750
duritiam tacto capiant ut ab aere quodque
vimen in aequore erat, fiat super aequora saxum.
   Dis tribus ille focos totidem de caespite ponit,
laevum Mercurio, dextrum tibi, bellica virgo,
ara Iovis media est; mactatur vacca Minervae,   755
alipedi vitulus, taurus tibi, summe deorum.

the form of fish. The beast belches forth waters mixed with purple blood. Meanwhile Perseus' wings are growing heavy, soaked with spray, and he dares not depend further on his drenched pinions. He spies a rock whose top projects above the surface when the waves are still, but which is hidden by the roughened sea. Resting on this and holding an edge of the rock with his left hand, thrice and again he plunges his sword into the vitals of the monster. At this the shores and the high seats of the gods re-echo with wild shouts of applause. Cassiope and Cepheus rejoice and salute the hero as son-in-law, calling him prop and saviour of their house. The maiden also now comes forward, freed from chains, she, the prize as well as cause of his feat. He washes his victorious hands in water drawn for him; and, that the Gorgon's snaky head may not be bruised on the hard sand, he softens the ground with leaves, strews seaweed over these, and lays on this the head of Medusa, daughter of Phorcys. The fresh weed twigs, but now alive and porous to the core, absorb the power of the monster and hardens at its touch and take a strange stiffness in their stems and leaves. And the sea-nymphs test the wonder on more twigs and are delighted to find the same thing happening to them all; and, by scattering these twigs as seeds, propagate the wondrous thing throughout their waters. And even till this day the same nature has remained in coral so that they harden when exposed to air, and what was a pliant twig beneath the sea is turned to stone above.

Now Perseus builds to three gods three altars of turf, the left to Mercury, the right to thee, O warlike maid, and the central one to Jove. To Minerva he slays a cow, a young bullock to the winged god, and

protinus Andromedan et tanti praemia facti
indotata rapit; taedas Hymenaeus Amorque
praecutiunt; largis satiantur odoribus ignes,
sertaque dependent tectis et ubique lyraeque   760
tibiaque et cantus, animi felicia laeti
argumenta, sonant; reseratis aurea valvis
atria tota patent, pulchroque instructa paratu
Cepheni proceres ineunt convivia regis.

    Postquam epulis functi generosi munere Bacchi 765
diffudere animos, cultusque genusque locorum
quaerit Lyncides moresque animumque virorum; 767
qui simul edocuit, " nunc, o fortissime," dixit   769
" fare, precor, Perseu, quanta virtute quibusque 770
artibus abstuleris crinita draconibus ora! "
narrat Agenorides gelido sub Atlante iacentem
esse locum solidae tutum munimine molis;
cuius in introitu geminas habitasse sorores
Phorcidas unius partitas luminis usum;   775
id se sollerti furtim, dum traditur, astu
supposita cepisse manu perque abdita longe
deviaque et silvis horrentia saxa fragosis
Gorgoneas tetigisse domos passimque per agros
perque vias vidisse hominum simulacra ferarumque
in silicem ex ipsis visa conversa Medusa.   781
se tamen horrendae clipei, quem laeva gerebat,
aere repercusso formam adspexisse Medusae,
dumque gravis somnus colubrasque ipsamque tenebat,
eripuisse caput collo; pennisque fugacem   785
Pegason et fratrem matris de sanguine natos.

a bull to thee, thou greatest of the gods. Forthwith
the hero claims Andromeda as the prize of his great
deed, seeking no further dowry. Hymen and Love
shake the marriage torch; the fires are fed full with
incense rich and fragrant, garlands deck the dwell-
ings, and everywhere lyre and flute and songs
resound, blessed proofs of inward joy. The huge
folding-doors swing back and reveal the great
golden palace-hall with a rich banquet spread,
where Cepheus' princely courtiers grace the feast.

When they have had their fill of food, and their
hearts have expanded with Bacchus' generous gift,
then Perseus seeks to know the manner of the region
thereabouts, its peoples, customs, and the spirit of its
men. The prince who answered him then said:
" Now tell us, pray, O Perseus, by what wondrous
valour, by what arts you won the Gorgon's snaky
head." The hero, answering, told how beneath cold
Atlas there was a place safe under the protection of
the rocky mass. At the entrance to this place two
sisters dwelt, both daughters of old Phorcys, who
shared one eye between them. This eye by craft
and stealth, while it was being passed from one
sister to the other, Perseus stole away, and travelling
far through trackless and secret ways, rough woods,
and bristling rocks, he came at last to where the
Gorgons lived. On all sides through the fields and
along the ways he saw the forms of men and beasts
changed into stone by one look at Medusa's face.
But he himself had looked upon the image of that
dread face reflected from the bright bronze shield his
left hand bore; and while deep sleep held fast both
the snakes and her who wore them, he smote her head
clean from her neck, and from the blood of his mother
swift-winged Pegasus and his brother sprang.

Addidit et longi non falsa pericula cursus,
quae freta, quas terras sub se vidisset ab alto
et quae iactatis tetigisset sidera pennis;
ante exspectatum tacuit tamen.   excipit unus   790
ex numero procerum quaerens, cur sola sororum
gesserit alternis inmixtos crinibus angues.
hospes ait: " quoniam scitaris digna relatu,
accipe quaesiti causam.   clarissima forma
multorumque fuit spes invidiosa procorum   795
illa, nec in tota conspectior ulla capillis
pars fuit: inveni, qui se vidisse referret.
hanc pelagi rector templo vitiasse Minervae
dicitur: aversa est et castos aegide vultus
nata Iovis texit, neve hoc inpune fuisset,   800
Gorgoneum crinem turpes mutavit in hydros.
nunc quoque, ut attonitos formidine terreat hostes,
pectore in adverso, quos fecit, sustinet angues."

The hero further told of his long journeys and
perils passed, all true, what seas, what lands he had
beheld from his high flight, what stars he had
touched on beating wings. He ceased, while they
waited still to hear more. But one of the princes
asked him why Medusa only of the sisters wore
serpents mingled with her hair. The guest replied:
" Since what you ask is a tale well worth the telling,
hear then the cause. She was once most beautiful
in form, and the jealous hope of many suitors. Of
all her beauties, her hair was the most beautiful—
for so I learned from one who said he had seen
her. 'Tis said that in Minerva's temple Neptune,
lord of the Ocean, ravished her. Jove's daughter
turned away and hid her chaste eyes behind her
aegis. And, that the deed might be punished as was
due, she changed the Gorgon's locks to ugly snakes.
And now to frighten her fear-numbed foes, she still
wears upon her breast the snakes which she has
made."

BOOK V

1–249	*Perseus and Phineus*
250–678	*Minerva on Helicon*
269–293	*Pyreneus*
318–331	*Typhoeus*
346–571	*The Rape of Proserpine*
572–641	*Arethusa*
642–661	*Lyncus*
662–678	*The Pierides*

LIBER V

Dvmqve ea Cephenum medio Danaeius heros
agmine commemorat, fremida regalia turba
atria conplentur, nec coniugialia festa
qui canat est clamor, sed qui fera nuntiet arma;
inque repentinos convivia versa tumultus   5
adsimilare freto possis, quod saeva quietum
ventorum rabies motis exasperat undis.
primus in his Phineus, belli temerarius auctor,
fraxineam quatiens aeratae cuspidis hastam
"en" ait, "en adsum praereptae coniugis ultor;   10
nec mihi te pennae nec falsum versus in aurum
Iuppiter eripiet!" conanti mittere Cepheus
"quid facis?" exclamat, "quae te, germane,
      furentem
mens agit in facinus? meritisne haec gratia tantis
redditur? hac vitam servatae dote rependis?   15
quam tibi non Perseus, verum si quaeris, ademit,
sed grave Nereidum numen, sed corniger Ammon,
sed quae visceribus veniebat belua ponti
exsaturanda meis; illo tibi tempore rapta est,
quo peritura fuit, nisi si, crudelis, id ipsum   20
exigis, ut pereat, luctuque levabere nostro.

238

BOOK V

WHILE the heroic son of Danaë is relating these adventures amongst the Ethiopian chiefs, the royal halls are filled with confused uproar: not the loud sound that sings a song of marriage, but one that presages the fierce strife of arms. And the feast, turned suddenly to tumult, you could liken to the sea, whose peaceful waters the raging winds lash to boisterous waves. First among them is Phineus, brother of the king, rash instigator of strife, who brandishes an ashen spear with bronze point. "Behold," says he, "here am I, come to avenge the theft of my bride. Your wings shall not save you this time, nor Jove, changed to seeming gold." As he was in the act of hurling his spear, Cepheus cried out: "What are you doing, brother? What mad folly is driving you to crime? Is this the way you thank our guest for his brave deeds? Is this the dower you give for the maiden saved? If 'tis the truth you want, it was not Perseus who took her from you, but the dread deity of the Nereids, but horned Ammon, but that sea-monster who came to glut his maw upon my own flesh and blood. 'Twas then you lost her when she was exposed to die; unless, perchance, your cruel heart demands this very thing—her death, and seeks by my grief to ease its own. It seems it is not enough that you saw her chained, and that you brought no aid, uncle though

239

scilicet haud satis est, quod te spectante revincta est
et nullam quod opem patruus sponsusve tulisti;
insuper, a quoquam quod sit servata, dolebis
praemiaque eripies? quae si tibi magna videntur, 25
ex illis scopulis, ubi erant adfixa, petisses.
nunc sine, qui petiit, per quem haec non orba
    senectus,
ferre, quod et meritis et voce est pactus, eumque
non tibi, sed certae praelatum intellege morti."

    Ille nihil contra, sed et hunc et Persea vultu 30
alterno spectans petat hunc ignorat an illum:
cunctatusque brevi contortam viribus hastam,
quantas ira dabat, nequiquam in Persea misit.
ut stetit illa toro, stratis tum denique Perseus
exsiluit teloque ferox inimica remisso 35
pectora rupisset, nisi post altaria Phineus
isset: et (indignum) scelerato profuit ara.
fronte tamen Rhoeti non inrita cuspis adhaesit,
qui postquam cecidit ferrumque ex osse revulsum est
calcitrat et positas adspergit sanguine mensas. 40
tum vero indomitas ardescit vulgus in iras,
telaque coniciunt, et sunt, qui Cephea dicunt
cum genero debere mori; sed limine tecti
exierat Cepheus testatus iusque fidemque
hospitiique deos, ea se prohibente moveri. 45
bellica Pallas adest et protegit aegide fratrem
datque animos.

       Erat Indus Athis, quem flumine Gange
edita Limnaee vitreis peperisse sub undis

you were, and promised husband: will you grieve, besides, that someone did save her, and will you rob him of his prize? If this prize seems so precious in your sight, you should have taken it from those rocks where it was chained. Now let the man who did take it, by whom I have been saved from childlessness in my old age, keep what he has gained by his deserving deeds and by my promise. And be assured of this: that he has not been preferred to you, but to certain death."

Phineus made no reply; but, looking now on him and now on Perseus, he was in doubt at which to aim his spear. Delaying a little space, he hurled it with all the strength that wrath gave at Perseus; but in vain. When the weapon struck and stood fast in the bench, then at last Perseus leapt gallantly up and hurled back the spear, which would have pierced his foeman's heart; but Phineus had already taken refuge behind the altar, and, shame! the wretch found safety there. Still was the weapon not without effect, for it struck full in Rhoetus' face. Down he fell, and when the spear had been wrenched forth from the bone he writhed about and sprinkled the well-spread table with his blood. And now the mob was fired to wrath unquenchable. They hurled their spears, and there were some who said that Cepheus ought to perish with his son-in-law. But Cepheus had already withdrawn from the palace, calling to witness Justice, Faith, and the gods of hospitality that this was done against his protest. Then came warlike Pallas, protecting her brother with her shield, and making him stout of heart.

There was an Indian youth, Athis by name, whom Limnaee, a nymph of Ganges' stream, is said to have

OVID

creditur, egregius forma, quam divite cultu
augebat, bis adhuc octonis integer annis, 50
indutus chlamydem Tyriam, quam limbus obibat
aureus; ornabant aurata monilia collum
et madidos murra curvum crinale capillos;
ille quidem iaculo quamvis distantia misso
figere doctus erat, sed tendere doctior arcus. 55
tum quoque lenta manu flectentem cornua Perseus
stipite, qui media positus fumabat in ara,
perculit et fractis confudit in ossibus ora.

Hunc ubi laudatos iactantem in sanguine vultus
Assyrius vidit Lycabas, iunctissimus illi 60
et comes et veri non dissimulator amoris,
postquam exhalantem sub acerbo vulnere vitam
deploravit Athin, quos ille tetenderat arcus
arripit et " mecum tibi sint certamina! " dixit;
" nec longum pueri fato laetabere, quo plus 65
invidiae quam laudis habes." haec omnia nondum
dixerat: emicuit nervo penetrabile telum
vitatumque tamen sinuosa veste pependit.
vertit in hunc harpen spectatam caede Medusae
Acrisioniades adigitque in pectus; at ille 70
iam moriens oculis sub nocte natantibus atra
circumspexit Athin seque adclinavit ad illum
et tulit ad manes iunctae solacia mortis.

Ecce Syenites, genitus Metione, Phorbas
et Libys Amphimedon, avidi committere pugnam, 75
sanguine, quo late tellus madefacta tepebat,
conciderant lapsi; surgentibus obstitit ensis,
alterius costis, iugulo Phorbantis adactus.

242

brought forth beneath her crystal waters. He was
of surpassing beauty, which his rich robes enhanced,
a sturdy boy of sixteen years, clad in a purple mantle
fringed with gold; a golden chain adorned his neck,
and a golden circlet held his locks in place, perfumed
with myrrh. He was well skilled to hurl the javelin
at the most distant mark, but with more skill could
bend the bow. When now he was in the very act of
bending his stout bow, Perseus snatched up a brand
which lay smouldering on the altar and smote the
youth, crushing his face to splintered bones.

When Assyrian Lycabas beheld him, his lovely
features defiled with blood—Lycabas, his closest
comrade and his declared true lover—he wept aloud
for Athis, who lay gasping out his life beneath that
bitter wound; then he caught up the bow which
Athis had bent, and cried: " Now you have me to
fight, and not long shall you plume yourself on a
boy's death, which brings you more contempt than
glory." Before he had finished speaking the keen
arrow fleshed from the bowstring; but it missed its
mark and stuck harmless in a fold of Perseus' robe.
Acrisius' grandson quickly turned on him that hook
which had been fleshed in Medusa's death, and drove
it into his breast. But he, even in death, with his
eyes swimming in the black darkness, looked round
for Athis, fell down by his side, and bore to the
shadows this comfort, that in death they were not
divided.

Then Phorbas of Syene, Metion's son, and Libyan
Amphimedon, eager to join in the fray, slipped and
fell in the blood with which all the floor was wet. As
they strove to rise the sword met them, driven
through the ribs of one and through the other's
throat.

At non Actoriden Erytum, cui lata bipennis
telum erat, hamato Perseus petit ense, sed altis   80
exstantem signis multaeque in pondere massae
ingentem manibus tollit cratera duabus
infligitque viro; rutilum vomit ille cruorem
et resupinus humum moribundo vertice pulsat.
inde Semiramio Polydegmona sanguine cretum   85
Caucasiumque Abarin Sperchionidenque Lycetum
intonsumque comas Helicen Phlegyanque Clytumque
sternit et exstructos morientum calcat acervos.

Nec Phineus ausus concurrere comminus hosti
intorquet iaculum, quod detulit error in Idan,   90
expertem frustra belli et neutra arma secutum.
ille tuens oculis inmitem Phinea torvis
" quandoquidem in partes " ait " abstrahor, accipe,
        Phineu,
quem fecisti, hostem pensaque hoc vulnere vulnus! "
iamque remissurus tractum de corpore telum   95
sanguine defectos cecidit conlapsus in artus.

Tum quoque Cephenum post regem primus Hodites
ense iacet Clymeni, Prothoenora percutit Hypseus,
Hypsea Lyncides.   fuit et grandaevus in illis
Emathion, aequi cultor timidusque deorum,   100
qui, quoniam prohibent anni bellare, loquendo
pugnat et incessit scelerataque devovet arma;
huic Chromis amplexo tremulis altaria palmis
decutit ense caput, quod protinus incidit arae
atque ibi semianimi verba exsecrantia lingua   105
edidit et medios animam exspiravit in ignes.

But Eurytus, the son of Actor, who wielded a broad, two-edged battle-axe, Perseus did not attack with his hooked sword, but lifting high in both hands a huge mixing-bowl heavily embossed and ponderous, he hurled it crashing at the man. The red blood spouted forth as he lay dying on his back, beating the floor with his head. Then in rapid succession Perseus laid low Polydegmon, descended from Queen Semiramis, Caucasian Abaris, Lycetus who dwelt by Sperchros, Helices of unshorn locks, Phlegyas and Clytus, treading the while on heaps of dying men.

Phineus did not dare to come to close combat with his enemy, but hurled his javelin. This was ill-aimed and struck Idas, who all to no purpose had kept out of the fight, taking sides with neither party. He, gazing with angry eyes upon cruel Phineus, said: "Since I am forced into the strife, O Phineus, accept the foeman you have made, and score me wound for wound." And he was just about to hurl back the javelin which he had drawn out of his own body, when he fell fainting, his limbs all drained of blood.

Then also Hodites, first of the Ethiopians after the king, fell by the sword of Clymenus; Hypseus smote Prothoënor; Lyncides, Hypseus. Amid the throng was one old man, Emathion, who loved justice and revered the gods. He, since his years forbade warfare, fought with the tongue, and strode forward and cursed their impious arms. As he clung to the altar-horns with age-enfeebled hands Chromis struck off his head with his sword: the head fell straight on the altar, and there the still half-conscious tongue kept up its execrations and the life was breathed out in the midst of the altar-fires.

OVID

Hinc gemini fratres Broteasque et caestibus
    Ammon
invicti, vinci si possent caestibus enses,
Phinea cecidere manu Cererisque sacerdos
Ampycus albenti velatus tempora vitta,   110
tu quoque, Lampetide, non hos adhibendus ad
    usus,
sed qui, pacis opus, citharam cum voce moveres;
iussus eras celebrare dapes festumque canendo.
quem procul adstantem plectrumque inbelle
    tenentem
Pedasus inridens " Stygiis cane cetera " dixit   115
" manibus! " et laevo mucronem tempore fixit;
concidit et digitis morientibus ille retemptat
fila lyrae, casuque ferit miserabile carmen.
nec sinit hunc inpune ferox cecidisse Lycormas
raptaque de dextro robusta repagula posti   120
ossibus inlisit mediae cervicis, at ille
procubuit terrae mactati more iuvenci.
demere temptabat laevi quoque robora postis
Cinyphius Pelates; temptanti dextera fixa est
cuspide Marmaridae Corythi lignoque cohaesit;   125
haerenti latus hausit Abas, nec corruit ille,
sed retinente manum moriens e poste pependit.
sternitur et Melaneus, Perseia castra secutus,
et Nasamoniaci Dorylas ditissimus agri,
dives agri Dorylas, quo non possederat alter   130
latius aut totidem tollebat turis acervos.
huius in obliquo missum stetit inguine ferrum:
letifer ille locus.   quem postquam vulneris auctor
singultantem animam et versantem lumina vidit
Bactrius Halcyoneus, " hoc, quod premis," inquit
    " habeto   135
de tot agris terrae! " corpusque exsangue reliquit.
torquet in hunc hastam calido de vulnere raptam

Next fell two brothers by Phineus' hand, Broteas
and Ammon, invincible with gauntlets, if gauntlets
could but contend with swords; and Ampycus, Ceres'
priest, his temples wreathed with white fillets. You,
too, Lampetides, not intended for such a scene as this,
but for a peaceful task, to ply lute and voice: you had
been bidden to grace the feast and sing the festal
song. To him standing apart and holding his
peaceful quill, Pedasus mocking cried: "Go sing
the rest of your song to the Stygian shades," and
pierced the left temple with his steel. He fell, and
with dying fingers again essays the strings, and as
he fell he struck a discordant sound. Nor did
Lycormas, maddened at the sight, suffer him to
perish unavenged; but, tearing out a stout bar from
the door-post on the right, he broke the murderer's
neck with a crashing blow. And Pedasus fell to the
earth like a slaughtered bull. Cinyphian Pelates
essayed to tear away another bar from the left post,
but in the act his right hand was pierced by the spear
of Corythus of Marmarida, and pinned to the wood.
There fastened, Abas thrust him through the side;
nor did he fall, but, dying, hung down from the post
to which his hand was nailed. Melaneus, too, was
slain, one of Perseus' side; and Dorylas, the richest
man in the land of Nasamonia—Dorylas, rich in
land, than whom none held a wider domain, none
heaped so many piles of spices. Into his groin a
spear hurled from the side struck; that place is fatal.
When Bactrian Halcyoneus, who hurled the spear,
beheld him gasping out his life and rolling his eyes
in death, he said: "This land alone on which you lie
of all your lands shall you possess," and left the lifeless
body. Against him Perseus, swift to avenge, hurled
the spear snatched from the warm wound, which,

ultor Abantiades; media quae nare recepta
cervice exacta est in partesque eminet ambas;
dumque manum Fortuna iuvat, Clytiumque
    Claninque,   140
matre satos una, diverso vulnere fudit:
nam Clytii per utrumque gravi librata lacerto
fraxinus acta femur, iaculum Clanis ore momor-
    dit.
occidit et Celadon Mendesius, occidit Astreus
matre Palaestina dubio genitore creatus,   145
Aethionque sagax quondam ventura videre,
tunc ave deceptus falsa, regisque Thoactes
armiger et caeso genitore infamis Agyrtes.
    Plus tamen exhausto superest; namque omnibus
        unum
opprimere est animus, coniurata undique pugnant 150
agmina pro causa meritum inpugnante fidemque;
hac pro parte socer frustra pius et nova coniunx
cum genetrice favent ululatuque atria conplent,
sed sonus armorum superat gemitusque cadentum,
pollutosque simul multo Bellona penates   155
sanguine perfundit renovataque proelia miscet.
    Circueunt unum Phineus et mille secuti
Phinea: tela volant hiberna grandine plura
praeter utrumque latus praeterque et lumen et
        aures.
adplicat hic umeros ad magnae saxa columnae   160
tutaque terga gerens adversaque in agmina versus
sustinet instantes: instabat parte sinistra
Chaonius Molpeus, dextra Nabataeus Ethemon.
tigris ut auditis diversa valle duorum
exstimulata fame mugitibus armentorum   165
nescit, utro potius ruat, et ruere ardet utroque,
sic dubius Perseus, dextra laevane feratur,
Molpea traiecti submovit vulnere cruris
248

striking the nose, was driven through the neck, and
stuck out on both sides. And, while fortune favoured
him, he slew also Clytius and Clanis, both born of
one mother, but each with a different wound. For
through both thighs of Clytius went the ashen spear,
hurled by his mighty arm; the other dart Clanis
crunched with his jaw. There fell also Mendesian
Celadon; Astreus, too, whose mother was a Syrian,
and his father unknown; Aethion, once wise to see
what is to come, but now tricked by a false omen;
Thoactes, armour-bearer of the king; Agyrtes,
infamous for that he had slain his sire.

Yet more remains, faint with toil though he is;
for all are bent on crushing him alone. On all sides
the banded lines assail him, in a cause that repudiated
merit and plighted word. On his side his father-in-
law with useless loyalty and his bride and her mother
range themselves, and fill all the hall with their
shrieks. But their cries are drowned in the clash
of arms and the groans of dying men; while Bellona
drenches and pollutes with blood the sacred home,
and ever renews the strife.

Now he stands alone where Phineus and a thousand
followers close round him. Thicker than winter hail
fly the spears, past right side and left, past eyes and
ears. He stands with his back against a great stone
column and, so protected in the rear, faces the
opposing crowds and their impetuous attack. The
attack is made on the left by Chaonian Molpeus, and
by Arabian Ethemon on the right. Just as a tigress,
pricked by hunger, that hears the bellowing of two
herds in two several valleys, knows not which to rush
upon, but burns to rush on both; so Perseus hesi-
tates whether to smite on right or left; he stops
Molpeus with a wound through the leg and was

contentusque fuga est; neque enim dat tempus
    Ethemon,
sed furit et cupiens alto dare vulnera collo   170
non circumspectis exactum viribus ensem
fregit, in extrema percussae parte columnae:
lamina dissiluit dominique in gutture fixa est.
non tamen ad letum causas satis illa valentes
plaga dedit; trepidum Perseus et inermia frustra 175
bracchia tendentem Cyllenide confodit harpe.
    Verum ubi virtutem turbae succumbere vidit,
" auxilium " Perseus, " quoniam sic cogitis ipsi,"
dixit " ab hoste petam: vultus avertite vestros,
si quis amicus adest!" et Gorgonis extulit ora.   180
" quaere alium, tua quem moveant miracula " dixit
Thescelus; utque manu iaculum fatale parabat
mittere, in hoc haesit signum de marmore gestu.
proximus huic Ampyx animi plenissima magni
pectora Lyncidae gladio petit: inque petendo   185
dextera diriguit nec citra mota nec ultra est.
at Nileus, qui se genitum septemplice Nilo
ementitus erat, clipeo quoque flumina septem
argento partim, partim caelaverat auro,
" adspice " ait " Perseu, nostrae primordia gentis: 190
magna feres tacitas solacia mortis ad umbras,
a tanto cecidisse viro "; pars ultima vocis
in medio suppressa sono est, adapertaque velle
ora loqui credas, nec sunt ea pervia verbis.
increpat hos " vitio " que " animi, non viribus "
    inquit   195
" Gorgoneis torpetis " Eryx. " incurrite mecum

content to let him go; but Ethemon gives him no time, and comes rushing on, eager to wound him in the neck, and drives his sword with mighty power but careless aim, and breaks it on the edge of the great stone column: the blade flies off and sticks in its owner's throat. The stroke indeed is not deep enough for death; but as he stands there trembling and stretching out his empty hands (but all in vain), Perseus thrusts him through with Mercury's hooked sword.

But when Perseus saw his own strength was no match for the superior numbers of his foes, he exclaimed: "Since you yourselves force me to it, I shall seek aid from my own enemy. Turn away your faces, if any friend be here." So saying, he raised on high the Gorgon's head. "Seek someone else to frighten with your magic arts," cried Thescelus, and raised his deadly javelin in act to throw; but in that very act he stood immovable, a marble statue. Next after him Ampyx thrust his sword full at the heart of the great-souled Perseus; but in that thrust his right hand stiffened and moved neither this way nor that. But Nileus, who falsely claimed that he was sprung from the sevenfold Nile, and who had on his shield engraved the image of the stream's seven mouths, part silver and part gold, cried: "See, O Perseus, the source whence I have sprung. Surely a great consolation for your death will you carry to the silent shades, that you have fallen by so great a man "—his last words were cut off in mid-speech; you would suppose that his open lips still strove to speak, but they no longer gave passage to his words. These two Eryx rebuked, saying: "'Tis from defect of courage, not from any power of the Gorgon's head, that you stand rigid. Rush in with me and hurl to

et prosternite humi iuvenem magica arma moven-
    tem!"
incursurus erat: tenuit vestigia tellus,
inmotusque silex armataque mansit imago.

Hi tamen ex merito poenas subiere, sed unus   200
miles erat Persei: pro quo dum pugnat, Aconteus
Gorgone conspecta saxo concrevit oborto;
quem ratus Astyages etiamnum vivere, longo
ense ferit: sonuit tinnitibus ensis acutis.
dum stupet Astyages, naturam traxit eandem,   205
marmoreoque manet vultus mirantis in ore.
nomina longa mora est media de plebe virorum
dicere: bis centum restabant corpora pugnae,
Gorgone bis centum riguerunt corpora visa.

Paenitet iniusti tum denique Phinea belli;   210
sed quid agat? simulacra videt diversa figuris
adgnoscitque suos et nomine quemque vocatum
poscit opem credensque parum sibi proxima tangit
corpora: marmor erant; avertitur atque ita supplex
confessasque manus obliquaque bracchia tendens   215
"vincis" ait, "Perseu! remove tua monstra tuaeque
saxificos vultus, quaecumque est, tolle Medusae,
tolle, precor! non nos odium regnique cupido
conpulit ad bellum, pro coniuge movimus arma!
causa fuit meritis melior tua, tempore nostra: 220
non cessisse piget; nihil, o fortissime, praeter
hanc animam concede mihi, tua cetera sunto!"
talia dicenti neque eum, quem voce rogabat,
respicere audenti "quod" ait, "timidissime Phineu,

the earth this fellow and his magic arms!" He had begun the rush, but the floor held his feet fast and there he stayed, a motionless rock, an image in full armour.

These, indeed, deserved the punishment they received. But there was one, Aconteus, a soldier on Perseus' side, who, while fighting for his friend, chanced to look upon the Gorgon's face and hardened into stone. Astyages, thinking him still a living man, smote upon him with his long sword. The sword gave out a sharp clanging sound; and while Astyages stood amazed, the same strange power got hold on him, and he stood there still with a look of wonder on his marble face. It would take too long to tell the names of the rank and file who perished. Two hundred men survived the fight; two hundred saw the Gorgon and turned to stone.

But now at last Phineus repents him of this unrighteous strife. But what is he to do? He sees images in various attitudes and knows the men for his own; he calls each one by name, prays for his aid, and hardly believing his eyes, he touches those who are nearest him: marble, all! He turns his face away, and so stretching out sideways suppliant hands that confess defeat, he says: "Perseus, you are my conqueror. Remove that dreadful thing; that petrifying Medusa-head of yours—whosoever she may be, oh, take it away, I beg. It was not hate of you and lust for the kingly power that drove me to this war. It was my wife I fought for. Your claim was better in merit, mine in time. I am content to yield. Grant me now nothing, O bravest of men, save this my life. All the rest be yours." As he thus spoke, not daring to look at him to whom he prayed, Perseus replied: "Most craven Phineus, dismiss your

et possum tribuisse et magnum est munus inerti,—
pone metum!—tribuam: nullo violabere ferro. 226
quin etiam mansura dabo monimenta per aevum,
inque domo soceri semper spectabere nostri,
ut mea se sponsi soletur imagine coniunx."
dixit et in partem Phorcynida transtulit illam, 230
ad quam se trepido Phineus obverterat ore.
tum quoque conanti sua vertere lumina cervix
deriguit, saxoque oculorum induruit umor,
sed tamen os timidum vultusque in marmore supplex
submissaeque manus faciesque obnoxia mansit. 235

Victor Abantiades patrios cum coniuge muros
intrat et inmeriti vindex ultorque parentis
adgreditur Proetum; nam fratre per arma fugato
Acrisioneas Proetus possederat arces.
sed nec ope armorum nec, quam male ceperat, arce
torva colubriferi superavit lumina monstri. 241

Te tamen, o parvae rector, Polydecta, Seriphi,
nec iuvenis virtus per tot spectata labores
nec mala mollierant, sed inexorabile durus
exerces odium, nec iniqua finis in ira est; 245
detrectas etiam laudem fictamque Medusae
arguis esse necem. " dabimus tibi pignora veri.
parcite luminibus!" Perseus ait oraque regis
ore Medusaeo silicem sine sanguine fecit.

Hactenus aurigenae comitem Tritonia fratri 250

fears; what I can give (and 'tis a great boon for your
coward soul), I will grant: you shall not suffer by the
sword. Nay, but I will make of you a monument
that shall endure for ages; and in the house of my
father-in-law you shall always stand on view, that so
my wife may find solace in the statue of her promised
lord." So saying, he bore the Gorgon-head where
Phineus had turned his fear-struck face. Then, even
as he strove to avert his eyes, his neck grew hard
and the very tears upon his cheeks were changed to
stone. And now in marble was fixed the cowardly
face, the suppliant look, the pleading hands, the
whole cringing attitude.

Victorious Perseus, together with his bride, now
returns to his ancestral city; and there, to avenge
his grandsire, who little deserved this championship,
he wars on Proetus. For Proetus had driven his
brother out by force of arms, and seized the strong-
hold of Acrisius. But neither by the force of arms,
nor by the stronghold he had basely seized, could he
resist the baleful gaze of that dread snake-wreathed
monster.

But you, O Polydectes, ruler of Little Seriphus,
were not softened by the young man's valour, tried
in so many feats, nor by his troubles; but you were
hard and unrelenting in hate, and your unjust anger
knew no end. You even refused him his honour,
and declared that the death of Medusa was all a lie.
"We will give you proof of that," then Perseus said;
"protect your eyes!" (this to his friends). And
with the Medusa-face he changed the features of
the king to bloodless stone.

During all this time Tritonia [1] had been the
comrade of her brother born of the golden shower.

[1] Athena.

OVID

se dedit; inde cava circumdata nube Seriphon
deserit, a dextra Cythno Gyaroque relictis,
quaque super pontum via visa brevissima, Thebas
virgineumque Helicona petit.   quo monte potita
constitit et doctas sic est adfata sorores: 255
" fama novi fontis nostras pervenit ad aures,
dura Medusaei quem praepetis ungula rupit.
is mihi causa viae; volui mirabile factum
cernere; vidi ipsum materno sanguine nasci."
excipit Uranie: "quaecumque est causa videndi   260
has tibi, diva, domos, animo gratissima nostro es.
vera tamen fama est: est Pegasus huius origo
fontis " et ad latices deduxit Pallada sacros.
quae mirata diu factas pedis ictibus undas
silvarum lucos circumspicit antiquarum   265
antraque et innumeris distinctas floribus herbas
felicesque vocat pariter studioque locoque
Mnemonidas; quam sic adfata est una sororum:
" o, nisi te virtus opera ad maiora tulisset,
in partem ventura chori Tritonia nostri,   270
vera refers meritoque probas artesque locumque,
et gratam sortem, tutae modo simus, habemus.
sed (vetitum est adeo sceleri nihil) omnia terrent
virgineas mentes, dirusque ante ora Pyreneus
vertitur, et nondum tota me mente recepi.   275
Daulida Threicio Phoceaque milite rura
ceperat ille ferox iniustaque regna tenebat;
templa petebamus Parnasia: vidit euntes
nostraque fallaci veneratus numina vultu   279
' Mnemonides ' (cognorat enim), ' consistite ' dixit

256

But now, wrapped in a hollow cloud, she left Seriphus, and, passing Cythnus and Gyarus on the right, by the shortest course over the sea she made for Thebes and Helicon, home of the Muses. On this mountain she alighted, and thus addressed the sisters versed in song: "The fame of a new spring has reached my ears, which broke out under the hard hoof of the winged horse of Medusa. This is the cause of my journey: I wished to see the marvellous thing. The horse himself I saw born from his mother's blood." Urania replied: "Whatever cause has brought thee to see our home, O goddess, thou art most welcome to our hearts. But the tale is true, and Pegasus did indeed produce our spring." And she led Pallas aside to the sacred waters. She long admired the spring made by the stroke of the horse's hoof; then looked round on the ancient woods, the grottoes, and the grass, spangled with countless flowers. She declared the daughters of Mnemosyne to be happy alike in their favourite pursuits and in their home. And thus one of the sisters answered her: "O thou, Tritonia, who wouldst so fitly join our band, had not thy merits raised thee to far greater tasks, thou sayest truth and dost justly praise our arts and our home. We have indeed a happy lot—were we but safe in it. But (such is the licence of the time) all things affright our virgin souls, and the vision of fierce Pyreneus is ever before our eyes, and I have not yet recovered from my fear. This bold king with his Thracian soldiery had captured Daulis and the Phocian fields, and ruled that realm which he had unjustly gained. It chanced that we were journeying to the temple on Parnasus. He saw us going, and feigning a reverence for our divinity, he said: 'O daughters of Mnemosyne'—for he knew us—'stay your steps and do not hesitate

' nec dubitate, precor, tecto grave sidus et imbrem '
(imber erat) ' vitare meo; subiere minores
saepe casas superi.' dictis et tempore motae
adnuimusque viro primasque intravimus aedes.
desierant imbres, victoque aquilonibus austro   285
fusca repurgato fugiebant nubila caelo:
inpetus ire fuit; claudit sua tecta Pyreneus
vimque parat, quam nos sumptis effugimus alis.
ipse secuturo similis stetit arduus arce
' qua ' que ' via est vobis, erit et mihi ' dixit ' eadem '
seque iacit vecors e summae culmine turris   291
et cadit in vultus discussisque ossibus oris
tundit humum moriens scelerato sanguine tinctam."

Musa loquebatur: pennae sonuere per auras,
voxque salutantum ramis veniebat ab altis.   295
suspicit et linguae quaerit tam certa loquentes
unde sonent hominemque putat Iove nata locutum;
ales erat. numeroque novem sua fata querentes
institerant ramis imitantes omnia picae.
miranti sic orsa deae dea " nuper et istae   300
auxerunt volucrum victae certamine turbam.
Pieros has genuit Pellaeis dives in arvis,
Paeonis Euippe mater fuit; illa potentem
Lucinam noviens, noviens paritura, vocavit.
intumuit numero stolidarum turba sororum   305
perque tot Haemonias et per tot Achaidas urbes
huc venit et tali committit proelia voce:
' desinite indoctum vana dulcedine vulgus
fallere; nobiscum, si qua est fiducia vobis,

to take shelter beneath my roof against the lowering sky and the rain '—for rain was falling—' gods have often entered a humbler home.' Moved by his words and by the storm, we yielded to the man and entered his portal. And now the rain had ceased, the south wind had been routed by the north, and the dusky clouds were in full flight from the brightening sky. We were fain to go on our way; but Pyreneus shut his doors, and offered us violence. This we escaped by donning our wings. He, as if he would follow us, took his stand on a lofty battlement and cried to us: ' What way you take, the same will I take also '; and, quite bereft of sense, he leaped from the pinnacle of the tower. Headlong he fell, crushing his bones and dyeing the ground in death with his accursed blood."

While the muse was still speaking, the sound of whirring wings was heard and words of greeting came from the high branches of the trees. Jove's daughter looked up and tried to see whence came the sound which was so clearly speech. She thought some human being spoke; but it was a bird. Nine birds, lamenting their fate, had alighted in the branches, magpies, which can imitate any sound they please. When Minerva wondered at the sight, the other addressed her, goddess to goddess: " 'Tis but lately those creatures also, conquered in a strife, have been added to the throng of birds. Pierus, lord of the rich domain of Pella, was their father, and Euippe of Paeonia was their mother. Nine times brought to the birth, nine times she called for help on mighty Lucina. Swollen with pride of numbers, this throng of senseless sisters journeyed through all the towns of Haemonia and all the towns of Achaia to us, and thus defied us to a contest in song: ' Cease to deceive the unsophisticated rabble with your pretence

Thespiades, certate, deae. nec voce, nec arte   310
vincemur totidemque sumus: vel cedite victae
fonte Medusaeo et Hyantea Aganippe,
vel nos Emathiis ad Paeonas usque nivosos
cedemus campis! dirimant certamina nymphae.'
  " Turpe quidem contendere erat, sed cedere visum
turpius; electae iurant per flumina nymphae   316
factaque de vivo pressere sedilia saxo.
tunc sine sorte prior quae se certare professa est,
bella canit superum falsoque in honore gigantas
ponit et extenuat magnorum facta deorum;   320
emissumque ima de sede Typhoea terrae
caelitibus fecisse metum cunctosque dedisse
terga fugae, donec fessos Aegyptia tellus
ceperit et septem discretus in ostia Nilus.
huc quoque terrigenam venisse Typhoea narrat   325
et se mentitis superos celasse figuris;
' duxque gregis ' dixit ' fit Iuppiter: unde recurvis
nunc quoque formatus Libys est cum cornibus Ammon;
Delius in corvo, proles Semeleia capro,
fele soror Phoebi, nivea Saturnia vacca,   330
pisce Venus latuit, Cyllenius ibidis alis.'
  " Hactenus ad citharam vocalia moverat ora:
poscimur Aonides,—sed forsitan otia non sint,
nec nostris praebere vacet tibi cantibus aures."
" ne dubita vestrumque mihi refer ordine carmen! "
Pallas ait nemorisque levi consedit in umbra;   336
Musa refert: " dedimus summam certaminis uni;
surgit et inmissos hedera collecta capillos
Calliope querulas praetemptat pollice chordas

of song. Come, strive with us, ye Thespian goddesses, if you dare. Neither in voice nor in skill can we be conquered, and our numbers are the same. If you are conquered, yield us Medusa's spring and Boeotian Aganippe; or we will yield to you the Emathian plains even to snow-clad Paeonia; and let the nymphs be judges of our strife.'

" It was a shame to strive with them, but it seemed greater shame to yield. So the nymphs were chosen judges and took oath by their streams, and they set them down upon benches of living rock. Then without drawing lots she who had proposed the contest first began. She sang of the battle of the gods and giants, ascribing undeserved honour to the giants, and belittling the deeds of the mighty gods: how Typhoeus, sprung from the lowest depths of earth, inspired the heavenly gods with fear, and how they all turned their backs and fled, until, weary, they found refuge in the land of Egypt and the seven-mouthed Nile. How even there Typhoeus, son of earth, pursued them, and the gods hid themselves in lying shapes: ' Jove thus became a ram,' said she, ' the lord of flocks, whence Libyan Ammon even to this day is represented with curving horns; Apollo hid in a crow's shape, Bacchus in a goat; the sister of Phoebus, in a cat, Juno in a snow-white cow, Venus in a fish, Mercury in an ibis bird.'

" So far had she sung, tuning voice to harp; we, the Aonian sisters, were challenged to reply—but perhaps you have not leisure, and care not to listen to our song?" "Nay, have no doubt," Pallas exclaimed, " but sing now your song in due order." And she took her seat in the pleasant shade of the forest. The muse replied: " We gave the conduct of our strife to one, Calliope; who rose and, with her flowing tresses

atque haec percussis subiungit carmina nervis : 340
' Prima Ceres unco glaebam dimovit aratro,
prima dedit fruges alimentaque mitia terris,
prima dedit leges; Cereris sunt omnia munus;
illa canenda mihi est.   utinam modo dicere possim
carmina digna dea! certe dea carmine digna est. 345
    " ' Vasta giganteis ingesta est insula membris
Trinacris et magnis subiectum molibus urguet
aetherias ausum sperare Typhoea sedes.
nititur ille quidem pugnatque resurgere saepe,
dextra sed Ausonio manus est subiecta Peloro, 350
laeva, Pachyne, tibi, Lilybaeo crura premuntur,
degravat Aetna caput, sub qua resupinus harenas
eiectat flammamque ferox vomit ore Typhoeus.
saepe remoliri luctatur pondera terrae
oppidaque et magnos devolvere corpore montes : 355
inde tremit tellus, et rex pavet ipse silentum,
ne pateat latoque solum retegatur hiatu
inmissusque dies trepidantes terreat umbras.
hanc metuens cladem tenebrosa sede tyrannus
exierat curruque atrorum vectus equorum 360
ambibat Siculae cautus fundamina terrae.
postquam exploratum satis est loca nulla labare
depositoque metu, videt hunc Erycina vagantem
monte suo residens natumque amplexa volucrem
" arma manusque meae, mea, nate, potentia " dixit,
" illa, quibus superas omnes, cape tela, Cupido, 366
262

bound in an ivy wreath, tried the plaintive chords
with her thumb, and then, with sweeping chords, she
sang this song: 'Ceres was the first to turn the glebe
with the hooked plowshare; she first gave corn and
kindly sustenance to the world; she first gave laws.
All things are the gift of Ceres; she must be the
subject of my song. Would that I could worthily sing
of her; surely the goddess is worthy of my song.

" ' The huge island of Sicily had been heaped upon
the body of the giant, and with its vast weight was
resting on Typhoeus, who had dared to aspire to the
heights of heaven. He struggles indeed, and strives
often to rise again; but his right hand is held down
by Ausonian Pelorus and his left by you, Pachynus.
Lilybaeum rests on his legs, and Aetna's weight is on
his head. Flung on his back beneath this mountain,
the fierce Typhoeus spouts forth ashes and vomits
flames from his mouth. Often he puts forth all his
strength to push off the weight of earth and to roll the
cities and great mountains from his body: then the
earth quakes, and even the king of the silent land is
afraid lest the crust of the earth split open in wide
seams and lest the light of day be let in and affright
the trembling shades. Fearing this disaster, the king
of the lower world had left his gloomy realm and,
drawn in his chariot with its sable steeds, was tra-
versing the land of Sicily, carefully examining its
foundations. After he had examined all to his
satisfaction, and found that no points were giving
way, he put aside his fears. Then Venus Erycina saw
him wandering to and fro, as she was seated on her
sacred mountain, and embracing her winged son,
she exclaimed: " O son, both arms and hands to
me, and source of all my power, take now those
shafts, Cupid, with which you conquer all, and shoot

OVID

inque dei pectus celeres molire sagittas,
cui triplicis cessit fortuna novissima regni.
tu superos ipsumque Iovem, tu numina ponti
victa domas ipsumque, regit qui numina ponti: 370
Tartara quid cessant? cur non matrisque tuumque
imperium profers? agitur pars tertia mundi,
et tamen in caelo, quae iam patientia nostra est,
spernimur, ac mecum vires minuuntur Amoris.
Pallada nonne vides iaculatricemque Dianam   375
abscessisse mihi? Cereris quoque filia virgo,
si patiemur, erit; nam spes adfectat easdem.
at tu pro socio, si qua est ea gratia, regno
iunge deam patruo." dixit Venus; ille pharetram
solvit et arbitrio matris de mille sagittis   380
unam seposuit, sed qua nec acutior ulla
nec minus incerta est nec quae magis audiat arcus,
oppositoque genu curvavit flexile cornum
inque cor hamata percussit harundine Ditem.

   "'Haud procul Hennaeis lacus est a moenibus altae,
nomine Pergus, aquae: non illo plura Caystros   386
carmina cycnorum labentibus audit in undis.
silva coronat aquas cingens latus omne suisque
frondibus ut velo Phoebeos submovet ictus;
frigora dant rami, Tyrios humus umida flores: 390
perpetuum ver est. quo dum Proserpina luco
ludit et aut violas aut candida lilia carpit,
dumque puellari studio calathosque sinumque
inplet et aequales certat superare legendo,
paene simul visa est dilectaque raptaque Diti: 395
usque adeo est properatus amor. dea territa maesto

your swift arrows into the heart of that god to whom
the final lot of the triple kingdom fell. You rule the
gods, and Jove himself; you conquer and control the
deities of the sea, and the very king that rules
the deities of the sea. Why does Tartarus hold back?
Why do you not extend your mother's empire and
your own? The third part of the world is at stake.
And yet in heaven, such is our long-suffering, we are
despised, and with my own, the power of love is
weakening. Do you not see that Pallas and huntress
Diana have revolted against me? And Ceres'
daughter, too, will remain a virgin if we suffer it;
for she aspires to be like them. But do you, in
behalf of our joint sovereignty, if you take any pride
in that, join the goddess to her uncle in the bonds of
love." So Venus spoke. The god of love loosed his
quiver at his mother's bidding and selected from his
thousand arrows one, the sharpest and the surest and
the most obedient to the bow. Then he bent the
pliant bow across his knee and with his barbed arrow
smote Dis through the heart.

" ' Not far from Henna's walls there is a deep pool
of water, Pergus by name. Not Cayster on its gliding
waters hears more songs of swans than does this pool.
A wood crowns the heights around its waters on every
side, and with its foliage as with an awning keeps off
the sun's hot rays. The branches afford a pleasing
coolness, and the well-watered ground bears bright-
coloured flowers. There spring is everlasting. Within
this grove Proserpina was playing, and gathering
violets or white lilies. And while with girlish eager-
ness she was filling her basket and her bosom, and
striving to surpass her mates in gathering, almost in
one act did Pluto see and love and carry her away:
so precipitate was his love. The terrified girl called

et matrem et comites, sed matrem saepius, ore
clamat, et ut summa vestem laniarat ab ora,
collecti flores tunicis cecidere remissis,
tantaque simplicitas puerilibus adfuit annis,   400
haec quoque virgineum movit iactura dolorem.
raptor agit currus et nomine quemque vocando
exhortatur equos, quorum per colla iubasque
excutit obscura tinctas ferrugine habenas,
perque lacus altos et olentia sulphure fertur   405
stagna Palicorum rupta ferventia terra
et qua Bacchiadae, bimari gens orta Corintho,
inter inaequales posuerunt moenia portus.

   " ' Est medium Cyanes et Pisaeae Arethusae,
quod coit angustis inclusum cornibus aequor: 410
hic fuit, a cuius stagnum quoque nomine dictum
     est,
inter Sicelidas Cyane celeberrima nymphas.
gurgite quae medio summa tenus exstitit alvo
adgnovitque deam "ne" c "longius ibitis!" inquit;
" non potes invitae Cereris gener esse: roganda, 415
non rapienda fuit.   quodsi conponere magnis
parva mihi fas est, et me dilexit Anapis;
exorata tamen, nec, ut haec, exterrita nupsi."
dixit et in partes diversas bracchia tendens
obstitit.   haud ultra tenuit Saturnius iram   420
terribilesque hortatus equos in gurgitis ima
contortum valido sceptrum regale lacerto
condidit; icta viam tellus in Tartara fecit
et pronos currus medio cratere recepit.

plaintively on her mother and her companions, but more often upon her mother. And since she had torn her garment at its upper edge, the flowers which she had gathered fell out of her loosened tunic; and such was the innocence of her girlish years, the loss of her flowers even at such a time aroused new grief. Her captor sped his chariot and urged on his horses, calling each by name, and shaking the dark-dyed reins on their necks and manes. Through deep lakes he galloped, through the pools of the Palici, reeking with sulphur and boiling up from a crevice of the earth, and where the Bacchiadae, a race sprung from Corinth between two seas, had built a city between two harbours of unequal size.

" ' There is between Cyane and Pisaean Arethusa a bay of the sea, its waters confined by narrowing points of land. Here was Cyane, the most famous of the Sicilian nymphs, from whose name the pool itself was called. She stood forth from the midst of her pool as far as her waist, and recognizing the goddess cried to Dis: " No further shall you go! Thou canst not be the son-in-law of Ceres against her will. The maiden should have been wooed, not ravished. But, if it is proper for me to compare small things with great, I also have been wooed, by Anapis, and I wedded him, too, yielding to prayer, however, not to fear, like this maiden." She spoke and, stretching her arms on either side, blocked his way. No longer could the son of Saturn hold his wrath, and urging on his terrible steeds, he whirled his royal sceptre with strong right arm and smote the pool to its bottom. The smitten earth opened up a road to Tartarus and received the down-plunging chariot in her cavernous depths.

OVID

" ' At Cyane, raptamque deam contemptaque fontis
iura sui maerens, inconsolabile vulnus   426
mente gerit tacita lacrimisque absumitur omnis
et, quarum fuerat magnum modo numen, in illas
extenuatur aquas : molliri membra videres,
ossa pati flexus, ungues posuisse rigorem ;   430
primaque de tota tenuissima quaeque liquescunt,
caerulei crines digitique et crura pedesque
(nam brevis in gelidas membris exilibus undas
transitus est); post haec umeri tergusque latusque
pectoraque in tenues abeunt evanida rivos ;   435
denique pro vivo vitiatas sanguine venas
lympha subit, restatque nihil, quod prendere possis.
" ' Interea pavidae nequiquam filia matri
omnibus est terris, omni quaesita profundo.
illam non udis veniens Aurora capillis   440
cessantem vidit, non Hesperus ; illa duabus
flammiferas pinus manibus succendit ab Aetna
perque pruinosas tulit inrequieta tenebras ;
rursus ubi alma dies hebetarat sidera, natam
solis ab occasu solis quaerebat ad ortus.   445
fessa labore sitim conceperat, oraque nulli
conluerant fontes, cum tectam stramine vidit
forte casam parvasque fores pulsavit ; at inde
prodit anus divamque videt lymphamque roganti
dulce dedit, tosta quod texerat ante polenta. 450
dum bibit illa datum, duri puer oris et audax
constitit ante deam risitque avidamque vocavit.
offensa est neque adhuc epota parte loquentem
cum liquido mixta perfudit diva polenta :
conbibit os maculas et, quae modo bracchia gessit,
crura gerit ; cauda est mutatis addita membris, 456
inque brevem formam, ne sit vis magna nocendi,

268

" ' But Cyane, grieving for the rape of the goddess and for her fountain's rights thus set at naught, nursed an incurable wound in her silent heart, and dissolved all away in tears; and into those very waters was she melted whose great divinity she had been but now. You might see her limbs softening, her bones becoming flexible, her nails losing their hardness. And first of all melt the slenderest parts: her dark hair, her fingers, legs and feet; for it is no great change from slender limbs to cool water. Next after these, her shoulders, back and sides and breasts vanish into thin watery streams. And finally, in place of living blood, clear water flows through her weakened veins and nothing is left that you can touch.

" ' Meanwhile all in vain the affrighted mother seeks her daughter in every land, on every deep. Not Aurora, rising with dewy tresses, not Hesperus sees her pausing in the search. She kindles two pine torches in the fires of Aetna, and wanders without rest through the frosty shades of night; again, when the genial day had dimmed the stars, she was still seeking her daughter from the setting to the rising of the sun. Faint with toil and athirst, she had moistened her lips in no fountain, when she chanced to see a hut thatched with straw, and knocked at its lowly door. Then out came an old woman and beheld the goddess, and when she asked for water gave her a sweet drink with parched barley floating upon it. While she drank, a coarse, saucy boy stood watching her, and mocked her and called her greedy. She was offended, and threw what she had not yet drunk, with the barley grains, full in his face Straightway his face was spotted, his arms were changed to legs, and a tail was added to his transformed limbs; he shrank to tiny size, that he might have no great

contrahitur, parvaque minor mensura lacerta est.
mirantem flentemque et tangere monstra parantem
fugit anum latebramque petit aptumque pudori   460
nomen habet variis stellatus corpora guttis.

  " ' Quas dea per terras et quas erraverit undas,
dicere longa mora est; quaerenti defuit orbis;
Sicaniam repetit, dumque omnia lustrat eundo,
venit et ad Cyanen.   ea ni mutata fuisset,   465
omnia narrasset; sed et os et lingua volenti
dicere non aderant, nec, quo loqueretur, habebat;
signa tamen manifesta dedit notamque parenti,
illo forte loco delapsam in gurgite sacro
Persephones zonam summis ostendit in undis.   470
quam simul agnovit, tamquam tum denique raptam
scisset, inornatos laniavit diva capillos
et repetita suis percussit pectora palmis.
nescit adhuc, ubi sit; terras tamen increpat omnes
ingratasque vocat nec frugum munere dignas,   475
Trinacriam ante alias, in qua vestigia damni
repperit.   ergo illic saeva vertentia glaebas
fregit aratra manu, parilique irata colonos
ruricolasque boves leto dedit arvaque iussit
fallere depositum vitiataque semina fecit.   480
fertilitas terrae latum vulgata per orbem
falsa iacet: primis segetes moriuntur in herbis,
et modo sol nimius, nimius modo corripit imber;
sideraque ventique nocent, avidaeque volucres

power to harm, and became in form a lizard, though yet smaller in size. The old woman wondered and wept, and reached out to touch the marvellous thing, but he fled from her and sought a hiding-place. He has a name [1] suited to his offence, since his body is starred with bright-coloured spots.

" ' Over what lands and what seas the goddess wandered it would take long to tell. When there was no more a place to search in, she came back to Sicily, and in the course of her wanderings here she came to Cyane. If the nymph had not been changed to water, she would have told her all. But, though she wished to tell, she had neither lips nor tongue, nor aught wherewith to speak. But still she gave clear evidence, and showed on the surface of her pool what the mother knew well, Persephone's girdle, which had chanced to fall upon the sacred waters. As soon as she knew this, just as if she had then for the first time learned that her daughter had been stolen, the goddess tore her unkempt locks and smote her breast again and again with her hands. She did not know as yet where her child was; still she reproached all lands, calling them ungrateful and unworthy of the gift of corn; but Sicily above all other lands, where she had found traces of her loss. So there with angry hand she broke in pieces the plows that turn the glebe, and in her rage she gave to destruction farmers and cattle alike, and bade the plowed fields to betray their trust, and blighted the seed. The fertility of this land, famous throughout the world, lay false to its good name: the crops died in early blade, now too much heat, now too much rain destroying them. Stars and winds were baleful, and greedy birds ate up the seed as soon as it was

---

[1] *i.e. stellio,* a lizard or newt.

semina iacta legunt; lolium tribulique fatigant   485
triticeas messes et inexpugnabile gramen.
  " ' Tum caput Eleis Alpheias extulit undis
rorantesque comas a fronte removit ad aures
atque ait " o toto quaesitae virginis orbe
et frugum genetrix, inmensos siste labores   490
neve tibi fidae violenta irascere terrae.
terra nihil meruit patuitque invita rapinae,
nec sum pro patria supplex: huc hospita veni.
Pisa mihi patria est et ab Elide ducimus ortus,
Sicaniam peregrina colo, sed gratior omni   495
haec mihi terra solo est: hos nunc Arethusa penates,
hanc habeo sedem.   quam tu, mitissima, serva.
mota loco cur sim tantique per aequoris undas
advehar Ortygiam, veniet narratibus hora
tempestiva meis, cum tu curaque levata   500
et vultus melioris eris. mihi pervia tellus
praebet iter, subterque imas ablata cavernas
hic caput attollo desuetaque sidera cerno.
ergo dum Stygio sub terris gurgite labor,
visa tua est oculis illic Proserpina nostris: 505
illa quidem tristis neque adhuc interrita vultu,
sed regina tamen, sed opaci maxima mundi,
sed tamen inferni pollens matrona tyranni! "
Mater ad auditas stupuit ceu saxea voces
attonitaeque diu similis fuit, utque dolore   510
pulsa gravi gravis est amentia, curribus oras
exit in aetherias: ibi toto nubila vultu
ante Iovem passis stetit invidiosa capillis

272

sown; tares and thorns and stubborn grasses choked the wheat.

" ' Then did Arethusa, Alpheus' daughter, lift her head from her Elean pool and, brushing her dripping locks back from her brows, thus addressed the goddess: " O thou mother of the maiden sought through all the earth, thou mother of fruits, cease now thy boundless toils and do not be so grievously wroth with the land which has been true to thee. The land is innocent; against its will it opened to the robbery. It is not for my own country that I pray, for I came a stranger hither. Pisa is my native land, and from Elis have I sprung; I dwell in Sicily a foreigner. But I love this country more than all; this is now my home, here is my dwelling-place. And now, I pray thee, save it, O most merciful. Why I moved from my place and why I came to Sicily, through such wastes of sea, a fitting time will come to tell thee, when thou shalt be free from care and of a more cheerful countenance. The solid earth opened a way before me, and passing through the lowest depths, I here lifted my head again and beheld the stars that had grown unfamiliar. Therefore, while I was gliding beneath the earth in my Stygian stream, I saw Proserpina there with these very eyes. She seemed sad indeed, and her face was still perturbed with fear; but yet she was a queen, the great queen of that world of darkness, the mighty consort of the tyrant of the underworld." The mother upon hearing these words stood as if turned to stone, and was for a long time like one bereft of reason. But when her overwhelming frenzy had given way to overwhelming pain, she set forth in her chariot to the realms of heaven. There, with clouded countenance, with dishevelled hair, and full of indignation, she appeared before Jove and said: " I have come, O Jupiter, as

273

" pro " que " meo veni supplex tibi, Iuppiter," inquit
" sanguine proque tuo: si nulla est gratia matris,   515
nata patrem moveat, neu sit tibi cura, precamur,
vilior illius, quod nostro est edita partu.
en quaesita diu tandem mihi nata reperta est,
si reperire vocas amittere certius, aut si
scire, ubi sit, reperire vocas.   quod rapta, feremus,   520
dummodo reddat eam!   neque enim praedone marito
filia digna tua est, si iam mea filia non est."
Iuppiter excepit " commune est pignus onusque
nata mihi tecum;   sed si modo nomina rebus
addere vera placet, non hoc iniuria factum,   525
verum amor est;   neque erit nobis gener ille pudori,
tu modo, diva, velis.   ut desint cetera, quantum est
esse Iovis fratrem!   quid, quod nec cetera desunt
nec cedit nisi sorte mihi?—sed tanta cupido
si tibi discidii est, repetet Proserpina caelum,   530
lege tamen certa, si nullos contigit illic
ore cibos;   nam sic Parcarum foedere cautum est."

" ' Dixerat, at Cereri certum est educere natam;
non ita fata sinunt, quoniam ieiunia virgo
solverat et, cultis dum simplex errat in hortis,   535
puniceum curva decerpserat arbore pomum
sumptaque pallenti septem de cortice grana
presserat ore suo, solusque ex omnibus illud
Ascalaphus vidit, quem quondam dicitur Orphne,
inter Avernales haud ignotissima nymphas,   540
ex Acheronte suo silvis peperisse sub atris;
vidit et indicio reditum crudelis ademit.

suppliant in behalf of my child and your own. If you have no regard for the mother, at least let the daughter touch her father's heart. And let not your care for her be less because I am her mother. See, my daughter, sought so long, has at last been found, if you call it finding more certainly to lose her, or if you call it finding merely to know where she is. That she has been stolen, I will bear, if only he will bring her back; for your daughter does not deserve to have a robber for a husband—if now she is not mine." And Jove replied: "She is, indeed, our daughter, yours and mine, our common pledge and care. But if only we are willing to give right names to things, this is no harm that has been done, but only love. Nor will he shame us for a son-in-law—do you but consent, goddess. Though all else be lacking, how great a thing it is to be Jove's brother! But what that other things are not lacking, and that he does not yield place to me—save only by the lot? But if you so greatly desire to separate them, Proserpina shall return to heaven, but on one condition only: if in the lower-world no food has as yet touched her lips. For so have the fates decreed."

"'He spoke; but Ceres was resolved to have her daughter back. Not so the fates; for the girl had already broken her fast, and while, simple child that she was, she wandered in the trim gardens, she had plucked a purple pomegranate hanging from a bending bough, and peeling off the yellowish rind, she had eaten seven of the seeds. The only one who saw the act was Ascalaphus, whom Orphne, not the least famous of the Avernal nymphs, is said to have borne to her own Acheron within the dark groves of the lower-world. The boy saw, and by his cruel tattling thwarted the girl's return to earth. Then

ingemuit regina Erebi testemque profanam
fecit avem sparsumque caput Phlegethontide lympha
in rostrum et plumas et grandia lumina vertit.   545
ille sibi ablatus fulvis amicitur in alis
inque caput crescit longosque reflectitur ungues
vixque movet natas per inertia bracchia pennas
foedaque fit volucris, venturi nuntia luctus,
ignavus bubo, dirum mortalibus omen.   550
   " ' Hic tamen indicio poenam linguaque videri
commeruisse potest; vobis, Acheloides, unde
pluma pedesque avium, cum virginis ora geratis?
an quia, cum legeret vernos Proserpina flores,
in comitum numero, doctae Sirenes, eratis?   555
quam postquam toto frustra quaesistis in orbe,
protinus, et vestram sentirent aequora curam,
posse super fluctus alarum insistere remis
optastis facilesque deos habuistis et artus
vidistis vestros subitis flavescere pennis.   560
ne tamen ille canor mulcendas natus ad aures
tantaque dos oris linguae deperderet usum,
virginei vultus et vox humana remansit.
   " ' At medius fratrisque sui maestaeque sororis
Iuppiter ex aequo volventem dividit annum: 565
nunc dea, regnorum numen commune duorum,
cum matre est totidem, totidem cum coniuge
      menses.
vertitur extemplo facies et mentis et oris;
nam modo quae poterat Diti quoque maesta videri,
laeta deae frons est, ut sol, qui tectus aquosis   570
nubibus ante fuit, victis e nubibus exit.

276

was the queen of Erebus enraged, and changed the informer into an ill-omened bird; throwing in his face a handful of water from the Phlegethon, she gave him a beak and feathers and big eyes. Robbed of. himself, he is now clothed in yellow wings; he grows into a head and long, hooked claws; but he scarce moves the feathers that sprout all over his sluggish arms. He has become a loathsome bird, prophet of woe, the slothful screech-owl, a bird of evil omen to men.

" ' He indeed can seem to have merited his punishment because of his tattling tongue. But, daughters of Acheloüs, why have you the feathers and feet of birds, though you still have maidens' features? Is it because, when Proserpina was gathering the spring flowers, you were among the number of her companions, ye Sirens, skilled in song? After you had sought in vain for her through all the lands, that the sea also might know your search, you prayed that you might float on beating wings above the waves: you found the gods ready, and suddenly you saw your limbs covered with golden plumage. But, that you might not lose your tuneful voices, so soothing to the ear, and that rich dower of song, maiden features and human voice remained.

" ' But now Jove, holding the balance between his brother and his grieving sister, divides the revolving year into two equal parts. Now the goddess, the common divinity of two realms, spends half the months with her mother and with her husband, half. Straightway the bearing of her heart and face is changed. For she who but lately even to Dis seemed sad, now wears a joyful countenance; like the sun which, long concealed behind dark and misty clouds, disperses the clouds and reveals his face.

OVID

" ' Exigit alma Ceres nata secura recepta,
quae tibi causa fugae, cur sis, Arethusa, sacer fons.
conticuere undae, quarum dea sustulit alto
fonte caput viridesque manu siccata capillos   575
fluminis Elei veteres narravit amores.
" pars ego nympharum, quae sunt in Achaide," dixit
" una fui, nec me studiosius altera saltus
legit nec posuit studiosius altera casses.
sed quamvis formae numquam mihi fama petita est,
quamvis fortis eram, formosae nomen habebam, 581
nec mea me facies nimium laudata iuvabat,
quaque aliae gaudere solent, ego rustica dote
corporis erubui crimenque placere putavi.
lassa revertebar (memini) Stymphalide silva;   585
aestus erat, magnumque labor geminaverat aestum:
invenio sine vertice aquas, sine murmure euntes,
perspicuas ad humum, per quas numerabilis alte
calculus omnis erat, quas tu vix ire putares.
cana salicta dabant nutritaque populus unda   590
sponte sua natas ripis declivibus umbras.
accessi primumque pedis vestigia tinxi,
poplite deinde tenus; neque eo contenta, recingor
molliaque inpono salici velamina curvae
nudaque mergor aquis.   quas dum ferioque trahoque
mille modis labens excussaque bracchia iacto,   596
nescio quod medio sensi sub gurgite murmur
territaque insisto propioris margine ripae.
' quo properas, Arethusa?' suis Alpheos ab undis,
' quo properas?' iterum rauco mihi dixerat ore. 600

" ' Now kindly Ceres, happy in the recovery of her daughter, asks of you, Arethusa, why you fled, why you are now a sacred spring. The waters fall silent while their goddess lifts her head from her deep spring, and dries her green locks with her hands, and tells the old story of the Elean river's love. " I used to be one of the nymphs," she says, " who have their dwelling in Achaia, and no other was more eager in scouring the glades, or in setting the hunting-nets. But although I never sought the fame of beauty, although I was brave, I had the name of beautiful. Nor did my beauty, all too often praised, give me any joy; and my dower of charming form, in which other maids rejoice, made me blush like a country girl, and I deemed it wrong to please. Wearied with the chase, I was returning, I remember, from the Stymphalian wood; the heat was great and my toil had made it double. I came upon a stream flowing without eddy, and without sound, crystal-clear to the bottom, in whose depths you might count every pebble, waters which you would scarcely think to be moving. Silvery willows and poplars fed by the water gave natural shade to the soft-sloping banks. I came to the water's edge and first dipped my feet, then in I went up to the knees: not satisfied with this, I removed my robes, and hanging the soft garments on a drooping willow, naked I plunged into the waters. And while I beat them, drawing them and gliding in a thousand turns and tossing my arms, I though I heard a kind of murmur deep in the pool. In terror I leaped on the nearer bank. Then Alpheus called from his waters: ' Whither in haste, Arethusa? Whither in such haste? ' Twice in his hoarse voice he called to me. As I was, without my robes, I fled; for my robes were

OVID

sicut eram, fugio sine vestibus (altera vestes
ripa meas habuit): tanto magis instat et ardet,
et quia nuda fui, sum visa paratior illi.
sic ego currebam, sic me ferus ille premebat,
ut fugere accipitrem penna trepidante columbae, 605
ut solet accipiter trepidas urguere columbas.
usque sub Orchomenon Psophidaque Cyllenenque
Maenaliosque sinus gelidumque Erymanthon et Elin
currere sustinui, nec me velocior ille;
sed tolerare diu cursus ego viribus inpar 610
non poteram, longi patiens erat ille laboris.
per tamen et campos, per opertos arbore montes,
saxa quoque et rupes et, qua via nulla, cucurri.
sol erat a tergo: vidi praecedere longam
ante pedes umbram, nisi si timor illa videbat; 615
sed certe sonitusque pedum terrebat et ingens
crinales vittas adflabat anhelitus oris.
fessa labore fugae ' fer opem, deprendimur,' inquam
' armigerae, Diana, tuae, cui saepe dedisti
ferre tuos arcus inclusaque tela pharetra! ' 620
mota dea est spissisque ferens e nubibus unam
me super iniecit: lustrat caligine tectam
amnis et ignarus circum cava nubila quaerit
bisque locum, quo me dea texerat, inscius ambit
et bis ' io Arethusa ' vocavit, ' io Arethusa! ' 625
quid mihi tunc animi miserae fuit? anne quod agnae
      est,
si qua lupos audit circum stabula alta frementes,
aut lepori, qui vepre latens hostilia cernit
ora canum nullosque audet dare corpore motus?
non tamen abscedit; neque enim vestigia cernit 630
longius ulla pedum: servat nubemque locumque.
occupat obsessos sudor mihi frigidus artus,
caeruleaeque cadunt toto de corpore guttae,

on the other bank. So much the more he pressed on and burned with love; naked I seemed readier for his taking. So did I flee and so did he hotly press after me, as doves on fluttering pinions flee the hawk, as the hawk pursues the frightened doves. Even past Orchomenus, past Psophis and Cyllene, past the combs of Maenalus, chill Erymanthus and Elis, I kept my flight; nor was he swifter of foot than I. But I, being ill-matched in strength, could not long keep up my speed, while he could sustain a long pursuit. Yet through level plains, over mountains covered with trees, over rocks also and cliffs, and where there was no way at all, I ran. The sun was at my back. I saw my pursuer's long shadow stretching out ahead of me—unless it was fear that saw it—but surely I heard the terrifying sound of feet, and his deep-panting breath fanned my hair. Then, forspent with the toil of flight, I cried aloud: 'O help me or I am caught, help thy armour-bearer, goddess of the hunt, to whom so often thou hast given thy bow to bear and thy quiver, with all its arrows!' The goddess heard, and threw an impenetrable cloud of mist about me. The river-god circled around me, wrapped in the darkness, and at fault quested about the hollow mist. And twice he went round the place where the goddess had hidden me, unknowing, and twice he called, 'Arethusa! O Arethusa!' How did I feel then, poor wretch! Was I not as the lamb, when it hears the wolves howling around the fold? or the hare which, hiding in the brambles, sees the dogs' deadly muzzles and dares not make the slightest motion? But he went not far away, for he saw no traces of my feet further on; he watched the cloud and the place. Cold sweat poured down my beleaguered limbs and the dark drops rained down from my whole body.

quaque pedem movi, manat lacus, eque capillis
ros cadit, et citius, quam nunc tibi facta renarro,   635
in latices mutor.   sed enim cognoscit amatas
amnis aquas positoque viri, quod sumpserat, ore
vertitur in proprias, et se mihi misceat, undas.
Delia rupit humum, caecisque ego mersa cavernis
advehor Ortygiam, quae me cognomine divae   640
grata meae superas eduxit prima sub auras."

    " 'Hac Arethusa tenus; geminos dea fertilis angues
curribus admovit frenisque coercuit ora
et medium caeli terraeque per aera vecta est
atque levem currum Tritonida misit in urbem   645
Triptolemo partimque rudi data semina iussit
spargere humo, partim post tempora longa recultae.
iam super Europen sublimis et Asida terram
vectus erat iuvenis: Scythicas advertitur oras.
rex ibi Lyncus erat; regis subit ille penates.   650
qua veniat, causamque viae nomenque rogatus
et patriam, "patria est clarae mihi" dixit "Athenae;
Triptolemus nomen; veni nec puppe per undas,
nec pede per terras: patuit mihi pervius aether.
dona fero Cereris, latos quae sparsa per agros   655
frugiferas messes alimentaque mitia reddant."
barbarus invidit tantique ut muneris auctor
ipse sit, hospitio recipit somnoque gravatum
adgreditur ferro: conantem figere pectus

Wherever I put my foot a pool trickled out, and from my hair fell the drops; and sooner than I can now tell the tale I was changed to a stream of water. But sure enough he recognized in the waters the maid he loved; and laying aside the form of a man which he had assumed, he changed back to his own watery shape to mingle with me. My Delian goddess cleft the earth, and I, plunging down into the dark depths, was borne hither to Ortygia, which I love because it bears my goddess' name, and this first received me to the upper air."

" ' With this, Arethusa's tale was done. Then the goddess of fertility yoked her two dragons to her car, curbing their mouths with the bit, and rode away through the air midway between heaven and earth, until she came at last to Pallas' city. Here she gave her fleet car to Triptolemus, and bade him scatter the seeds of grain she gave, part in the untilled earth and part in fields that had long lain fallow. And now high over Europe and the land of Asia the youth held his course and came to Scythia, where Lyncus ruled as king. He entered the royal palace. The king asked him how he came and why, what was his name and country: he said: " My country is far-famed Athens; Triptolemus, my name. I came neither by ship over the sea, nor on foot by land; the air opened a path for me. I bring the gifts of Ceres, which, if you sprinkle them over your wide fields, will give a fruitful harvest and food not wild." The barbaric king heard with envy. And, that he himself might be the giver of so great a boon, he received his guest with hospitality, and when he was heavy with sleep, he attacked him with the sword. Him, in the very act of piercing the stranger's breast, Ceres transformed into a lynx; and back

lynca Ceres fecit rursusque per aera iussit   660
Mopsopium iuvenem sacros agitare iugales.'
  " Finierat doctos e nobis maxima cantus;
at nymphae vicisse deas Helicona colentes
concordi dixere sono: convicia victae
cum iacerent, ' quoniam ' dixi ' certamine vobis   665
supplicium meruisse parum est maledictaque culpae
additis et non est patientia libera nobis,
ibimus in poenas et, qua vocat ira, sequemur.'
rident Emathides spernuntque minacia verba,
conantesque loqui et magno clamore protervas   670
intentare manus pennas exire per ungues
adspexere suos, operiri bracchia plumis,
alteraque alterius rigido concrescere rostro
ora videt volucresque novas accedere silvis;
dumque volunt plangi, per bracchia mota levatae 675
aere pendebant, nemorum convicia, picae.
Nunc quoque in alitibus facundia prisca remansit
raucaque garrulitas studiumque inmane loquendi."

through the air she bade the Athenian drive her sacred team.'

"Our eldest sister here brought to an end her able recital; then the nymphs with one voice agreed that the goddesses of Helicon had won. When the conquered sisters retorted with reviling, I made answer: 'Since it was not enough that you have earned punishment by your challenge and you add insults to your offence, and since our patience is not without end, we shall proceed to punishment and indulge our resentment.' The Pierides mocked, and scorned her threatening words. But as they tried to speak, and with loud outcries brandished their hands in saucy gestures, they saw feathers sprouting on their fingers, and plumage covering their arms; each saw another's face stiffening into a hard beak, and new forms of birds added to the woods. And while they strove to beat their breasts, uplifted by their flapping arms, they hung in the air, magpies, the noisy scandal of the woods. Even now in their feathered form their old-time gift of speech remains, their hoarse garrulity, their boundless passion for talk."

BOOK VI

1–145	*Minerva and Arachne*
146–312	*Niobe*
313–381	*The Lycian Peasants*
382–400	*Marsyas*
401–674	*Tereus, Procne, Philomela*
675–721	*Boreas and Orithyia*

LIBER VI

Praebverat dictis Tritonia talibus aures
carminaque Aonidum iustamque probaverat iram;
tum secum: " laudare parum est, laudemur et ipsae
numina nec sperni sine poena nostra sinamus."
Maeoniaeque animum fatis intendit Arachnes,   5
quam sibi lanificae non cedere laudibus artis
audierat.   non illa loco nec origine gentis
clara, sed arte fuit: pater huic Colophonius Idmon
Phocaico bibulas tinguebat murice lanas;
occiderat mater, sed et haec de plebe suoque   10
aequa viro fuerat; Lydas tamen illa per urbes
quaesierat studio nomen memorabile, quamvis
orta domo parva parvis habitabat Hypaepis.
huius ut adspicerent opus admirabile, saepe
deseruere sui nymphae vineta Timoli,   15
deseruere suas nymphae Pactolides undas.
nec factas solum vestes, spectare iuvabat
tum quoque, cum fierent: tantus decor adfuit arti,
sive rudem primos lanam glomerabat in orbes,
seu digitis subigebat opus repetitaque longo   20
vellera mollibat nebulas aequantia tractu,
sive levi teretem versabat pollice fusum,

288

BOOK VI

Tritonia had listened to this tale, and had approved of the muses' song and their just resentment. And then to herself she said: " To praise is not enough; let me be praised myself and not allow my divinity to be scouted without punishment." So saying, she turned her mind to the fate of Maeonian Arachne, who she had heard would not yield to her the palm in the art of spinning and weaving wool. Neither for place of birth nor birth itself had the girl fame, but only for her skill. Her father, Idmon of Colophon, used to dye the absorbent wool for her with Phocaean purple. Her mother was now dead; but she was low-born herself, and had a husband of the same degree. Nevertheless, the girl, Arachne, had gained fame for her skill throughout the Lydian towns, although she herself had sprung from a humble home and dwelt in the hamlet of Hypaepa. Often, to watch her wondrous skill, the nymphs would leave their own vineyards on Timolus' slopes, and the water-nymphs of Pactolus would leave their waters. And 'twas a pleasure not alone to see her finished work, but to watch her as she worked; so graceful and deft was she. Whether she was winding the rough yarn into a new ball, or shaping the stuff with her fingers, reaching back to the distaff for more wool, fleecy as a cloud, to draw into long soft threads, or giving a twist with practised thumb to the graceful spindle, or

seu pingebat acu; scires a Pallade doctam.
quod tamen ipsa negat tantaque offensa magistra
"certet" ait "mecum: nihil est, quod victa re-
    cusem!"   25
   Pallas anum simulat: falsosque in tempora canos
addit et infirmos, baculo quos sustinet, artus.
tum sic orsa loqui "non omnia grandior aetas,
quae fugiamus, habet: seris venit usus ab annis.
consilium ne sperne meum: tibi fama petatur   30
inter mortales faciendae maxima lanae;
cede deae veniamque tuis, temeraria, dictis
supplice voce roga: veniam dabit illa roganti."
adspicit hanc torvis inceptaque fila relinquit
vixque manum retinens confessaque vultibus iram   35
talibus obscuram resecuta est Pallada dictis:
"mentis inops longaque venis confecta senecta,
et nimium vixisse diu nocet.   audiat istas,
si qua tibi nurus est, si qua est tibi filia, voces;
consilii satis est in me mihi, neve monendo   40
profecisse putes, eadem est sententia nobis.
cur non ipsa venit? cur haec certamina vitat?"
tum dea "venit!" ait formamque removit anilem
Palladaque exhibuit: venerantur numina nymphae
Mygdonidesque nurus; sola est non territa virgo, 45
sed tamen erubuit, subitusque invita notavit
ora rubor rursusque evanuit, ut solet aer
purpureus fieri, cum primum Aurora movetur,
et breve post tempus candescere solis ab ortu.

embroidering with her needle: you could know that Pallas had taught her. Yet she denied it, and, offended at the suggestion of a teacher ever so great, she said: "Let her but strive with me; and if I lose there is nothing which I would not forfeit."

Then Pallas assumed the form of an old woman, put false locks of grey upon her head, took a staff in her hand to sustain her tottering limbs, and thus she began: "Old age has some things at least that are not to be despised; experience comes with riper years. Do not scorn my advice: seek all the fame you will among mortal men for handling wool; but yield place to the goddess, and with humble prayer beg her pardon for your words, reckless girl. She will grant you pardon if you ask it." But she regarded the old woman with sullen eyes, dropped the threads she was working, and, scarce holding her hand from violence, with open anger in her face she answered the disguised Pallas: "Doting in mind, you come to me, and spent with old age; and it is too long life that is your bane. Go, talk to your daughter-in-law, or to your daughter, if such you have. I am quite able to advise myself. To show you that you have done no good by your advice, we are both of the same opinion. Why does not your goddess come herself? Why does she avoid a contest with me?" Then the goddess exclaimed: "She has come!" and throwing aside her old woman's disguise, she revealed Pallas. The nymphs worshipped her godhead, and the Mygdonian women; Arachne alone remained unafraid, though she did turn red, for a sudden flush marked her unwilling cheeks and again faded: as when the sky grows crimson when the dawn first appears, and after a little while when the sun is up it pales again. Still she persists in her

OVID

perstat in incepto stolidaeque cupidine palmae   50
in sua fata ruit; neque enim Iove nata recusat
nec monet ulterius nec iam certamina differt.
haud mora, constituunt diversis partibus ambae
et gracili geminas intendunt stamine telas:
tela iugo vincta est, stamen secernit harundo,   55
inseritur medium radiis subtemen acutis,
quod digiti expediunt, atque inter stamina ductum
percusso paviunt insecti pectine dentes.
utraque festinant cinctaeque ad pectora vestes
bracchia docta movent, studio fallente laborem.   60
illic et Tyrium quae purpura sensit aenum
texitur et tenues parvi discriminis umbrae;
qualis ab imbre solent percussis solibus arcus
inficere ingenti longum curvamine caelum;
in quo diversi niteant cum mille colores,   65
transitus ipse tamen spectantia lumina fallit:
usque adeo, quod tangit, idem est; tamen ultima
    distant.
illic et lentum filis inmittitur aurum
et vetus in tela deducitur argumentum.

Cecropia Pallas scopulum Mavortis in arce   70
pingit et antiquam de terrae nomine litem.
bis sex caelestes medio Iove sedibus altis
augusta gravitate sedent; sua quemque deorum
inscribit facies: Iovis est regalis imago;
stare deum pelagi longoque ferire tridente   75
aspera saxa facit, medioque e vulnere saxi
exsiluisse fretum, quo pignore vindicet urbem;
at sibi dat clipeum, dat acutae cuspidis hastam,

292

challenge, and stupidly confident and eager for victory, she rushes on her fate. For Jove's daughter refuses not, nor again warns her or puts off the contest any longer. They both set up the looms in different places without delay and they stretch the fine warp upon them. The web is bound upon the beam, the reed separates the threads of the warp, the woof is threaded through them by the sharp shuttles which their busy fingers ply, and when shot through the threads of the warp, the notched teeth of the hammering slay tap it into place. They speed on the work with their mantles close girt about their breasts and move back and forth their well-trained hands, their eager zeal beguiling their toil. There are inwoven the purple threads dyed in Tyrian kettles, and lighter colours insensibly shading off from these. As when after a storm of rain the sun's rays strike through, and a rainbow, with its huge curve, stains the wide sky, though a thousand different colours shine in it, the eye cannot detect the change from each one to the next; so like appear the adjacent colours, but the extremes are plainly different. There, too, they weave in pliant threads of gold, and trace in the weft some ancient tale.

Pallas pictures the hills of Mars on the citadel of Cecrops [1] and that old dispute over the naming of the land. There sit twelve heavenly gods on lofty thrones in awful majesty, Jove in their midst; each god she pictures with his own familiar features; Jove's is a royal figure. There stands the god of ocean, and with his long trident smites the rugged cliff, and from the cleft rock sea-water leaps forth; a token to claim the city for his own. To herself

---

[1] Ovid here confuses the Acropolis with the Areopagus. See Herod., viii. 55; Apollodorus, iii. 14, 1.

OVID

dat galeam capiti, defenditur aegide pectus,
percussamque sua simulat de cuspide terram   80
edere cum bacis fetum canentis olivae;
mirarique deos: operis Victoria finis.
ut tamen exemplis intellegat aemula laudis,
quod pretium speret pro tam furialibus ausis
quattuor in partes certamina quattuor addit,   85
clara colore suo, brevibus distincta sigillis:
Threiciam Rhodopen habet angulus unus et Haemum,
nunc gelidos montes, mortalia corpora quondam,
nomina summorum sibi qui tribuere deorum;
altera Pygmaeae fatum miserabile matris   90
pars habet: hanc Iuno victam certamine iussit
esse gruem populisque suis indicere bellum;
pinxit et Antigonen, ausam contendere quondam
cum magni consorte Iovis, quam regia Iuno
in volucrem vertit, nec profuit Ilion illi   95
Laomedonve pater, sumptis quin candida pennis
ipsa sibi plaudat crepitante ciconia rostro;
qui superest solus, Cinyran habet angulus orbum;
isque gradus templi, natarum membra suarum,
amplectens saxoque iacens lacrimare videtur.   100
circuit extremas oleis pacalibus oras
(is modus est) operisque sua facit arbore finem.
  Maeonis elusam designat imagine tauri
Europam: verum taurum, freta vera putares;
ipsa videbatur terras spectare relictas   105
et comites clamare suas tactumque vereri
adsilientis aquae timidasque reducere plantas.
fecit et Asterien aquila luctante teneri,

the goddess gives a shield and a sharp-pointed spear,
and a helmet for her head; the aegis guards her
breast; and from the earth smitten by her spear's
point upsprings a pale-green olive-tree hanging
thick with fruit; and the gods look on in wonder.
Victory crowns her work. Then, that her rival
may know by pictured warnings what reward she may
expect for her mad daring, she weaves in the four
corners of the web four scenes of contest, each clear
with its own colours, and in miniature design.   One
corner shows Thracian Rhodope and Haemus, now
huge, bleak mountains, but once audacious mortals
who dared assume the names of the most high gods.
A second corner shows the wretched fate of the
Pygmaean queen, whom Juno conquered in a strife,
then changed into a crane, and bade her war upon
those whom once she ruled.   Again she pictures
how Antigone once dared to set herself against the
consort of mighty Jove, and how Queen Juno changed
her into a bird; Ilium availed her nothing, nor
Laomedon, her father; nay, she is clothed in white
feathers, and claps her rattling bill, a stork.   The
remaining corner shows Cinyras bereft of his
daughters; there, embracing the marble temple-
steps, once their limbs, he lies on the stone, and seems
to weep.   The goddess then wove around her work a
border of peaceful olive-wreath.   This was the end;
and so, with her own tree, her task was done.

Arachne pictures Europa cheated by the disguise
of the bull: a real bull and real waves you would
think them.   The maid seems to be looking back
upon the land she has left, calling on her companions,
and, fearful of the touch of the leaping waves, to be
drawing back her timid feet.   She wrought Asterie,
held by the struggling eagle; she wrought Leda,

fecit olorinis Ledam recubare sub alis;
addidit, ut satyri celatus imagine pulchram   110
Iuppiter inplerit gemino Nycteida fetu,
Amphitryon fuerit, cum te, Tirynthia, cepit,
aureus ut Danaen, Asopida luserit ignis,
Mnemosynen pastor, varius Deoida serpens.
te quoque mutatum torvo, Neptune, iuvenco   115
virgine in Aeolia posuit; tu visus Enipeus
gignis Aloidas, aries Bisaltida fallis,
et te flava comas frugum mitissima mater
sensit equum, sensit volucrem crinita colubris
mater equi volucris, sensit delphina Melantho: 120
omnibus his faciemque suam faciemque locorum
reddidit. est illic agrestis imagine Phoebus,
utque modo accipitris pennas, modo terga leonis
gesserit, ut pastor Macareida luserit Issen,
Liber ut Erigonen falsa deceperit uva,   125
ut Saturnus equo geminum Chirona crearit.
ultima pars telae, tenui circumdata limbo,
nexilibus flores hederis habet intertextos.
  Non illud Pallas, non illud carpere Livor
possit opus: doluit successu flava virago   130
et rupit pictas, caelestia crimina, vestes,
utque Cytoriaco radium de monte tenebat,
ter quater Idmoniae frontem percussit Arachnes.
non tulit infelix laqueoque animosa ligavit
guttura: pendentem Pallas miserata levavit   135
atque ita "vive quidem, pende tamen, inproba" dixit,
"lexque eadem poenae, ne sis secura futuri,
dicta tuo generi serisque nepotibus esto!"
post ea discedens sucis Hecateidos herbae

beneath the swan's wings. She added how, in a satyr's image hidden, Jove filled lovely Antiope with twin offspring; how he was Amphitryon when he cheated thee, Alcmena; how in a golden shower he tricked Danaë; Aegina, as a flame; Mnemosyne, as a shepherd; Deo's daughter, as a spotted snake. Thee also, Neptune, she pictured, changed to a grim bull with the Aeolian maiden; now as Enipeus thou dost beget the Aloidae, as a ram deceivedst Bisaltis. The golden-haired mother of corn, most gentle, knew thee as a horse; the snake-haired mother of the winged horse knew thee as a winged bird; Melantho knew thee as a dolphin. To all these Arachne gave their own shapes and appropriate surroundings. Here is Phoebus like a countryman; and she shows how he wore now a hawk's feathers, now a lion's skin; how as a shepherd he tricked Macareus' daughter, Isse; how Bacchus deceived Erigone with the false bunch of grapes; how Saturn in a horse's shape begot the centaur, Chiron. The edge of the web with its narrow border is filled with flowers and clinging ivy intertwined.

Not Pallas, nor Envy himself, could find a flaw in that work. The golden-haired goddess was indignant at her success, and rent the embroidered web with its heavenly crimes; and, as she held a shuttle of Cytorian boxwood, thrice and again she struck Idmonian Arachne's head. The wretched girl could not endure it, and put a noose about her bold neck. As she hung, Pallas lifted her in pity, and said: "Live on, indeed, wicked girl, but hang thou still; and let this same doom of punishment (that thou mayst fear for future times as well) be declared upon thy race, even to remote posterity." So saying, as she turned to go she sprinkled her with

sparsit: et extemplo tristi medicamine tactae   140
defluxere comae, cum quis et naris et aures,
fitque caput minimum; toto quoque corpore parva est:
in latere exiles digiti pro cruribus haerent,
cetera venter habet, de quo tamen illa remittit
stamen et antiquas exercet aranea telas.   145
   Lydia tota fremit, Phrygiaeque per oppida facti
rumor it et magnum sermonibus occupat orbem.
ante suos Niobe thalamos cognoverat illam,
tum cum Maeoniam virgo Sipylumque colebat;
nec tamen admonita est poena popularis Arachnes,   150
cedere caelitibus verbisque minoribus uti.
multa dabant animos; sed enim nec coniugis artes
nec genus amborum magnique potentia regni
sic placuere illi, quamvis ea cuncta placerent,
ut sua progenies; et felicissima matrum   155
dicta foret Niobe, si non sibi visa fuisset.
nam sata Tiresia venturi praescia Manto
per medias fuerat divino concita motu
vaticinata vias: " Ismenides, ite frequentes
et date Latonae Latonigenisque duobus   160
cum prece tura pia lauroque innectite crinem:
ore meo Latona iubet." paretur, et omnes
Thebaides iussis sua tempora frondibus ornant
turaque dant sanctis et verba precantia flammis.
   Ecce venit comitum Niobe celeberrima turba   165
vestibus intexto Phrygiis spectabilis auro
et, quantum ira sinit, formosa; movensque decoro
cum capite inmissos umerum per utrumque capillos

the juices of Hecate's herb; and forthwith her hair, touched by the poison, fell off, and with it both nose and ears; and the head shrank up; her whole body also was small; the slender fingers clung to her side as legs; the rest was belly. Still from this she ever spins a thread; and now, as a spider, she exercises her old-time weaver-art.

All Lydia is in a tumult; the story spreads throughout the towns of Phrygia and fills the whole world with talk. Now Niobe, before her marriage, had known Arachne, when, as a girl, she dwelt in Maeonia, near Mount Sipylus. And yet she did not take warning by her countrywoman's fate to give place to the gods and speak them reverently. Many things gave her pride; but in truth neither her husband's art nor the high birth of both and their royal power and state so pleased her, although all those did please, as her children did. And Niobe would have been called most blessed of mothers, had she not seemed so to herself. For Manto, daughter of Tiresias, whose eyes could see what was to come, had fared through the streets of Thebes inspired by divine impulse, and proclaiming to all she met: "Women of Thebes, go throng Latona's temple, and give to her and to her children twain incense and pious prayer, wreathing your hair with laurel. By my mouth Latona speaks." They obey; all the Theban women deck their temples with laurel wreaths and burn incense in the altar flames, with words of prayer.

But lo! comes Niobe, thronged about with a numerous following, a notable figure in Phrygian robes wrought with threads of gold, and beautiful as far as anger suffered her to be; and tossing her shapely head with the hair falling on either shoulder, she halts and, drawn up to her full

constitit, utque oculos circumtulit alta superbos,
" quis furor auditos " inquit " praeponere visis 170
caelestes? aut cur colitur Latona per aras,
numen adhuc sine ture meum est? mihi Tantalus
    auctor,
cui licuit soli superorum tangere mensas;
Pleiadum soror est genetrix mea; maximus Atlas
est avus, aetherium qui fert cervicibus axem; 175
Iuppiter alter avus; socero quoque glorior illo.
me gentes metuunt Phrygiae, me regia Cadmi
sub domina est, fidibusque mei commissa mariti
moenia cum populis a meque viroque reguntur.
in quamcumque domus adverti lumina partem, 180
inmensae spectantur opes; accedit eodem
digna dea facies; huc natas adice septem
et totidem iuvenes et mox generosque nurusque!
quaerite nunc, habeat quam nostra superbia causam,
nescio quoque audete satam Titanida Coeo 185
Latonam praeferre mihi, cui maxima quondam
exiguam sedem pariturae terra negavit!
nec caelo nec humo nec aquis dea vestra recepta est:
exsul erat mundi, donec miserata vagantem
' hospita tu terris erras, ego ' dixit ' in undis ' 190
instabilemque locum Delos dedit. illa duorum
facta parens: uteri pars haec est septima nostri.
sum felix (quis enim neget hoc?) felixque manebo
(hoc quoque quis dubitet?): tutam me copia fecit.
maior sum quam cui possit Fortuna nocere, 195
multaque ut eripiat, multo mihi plura relinquet.

height, casts her haughty eyes around and cries:
" What madness this, to prefer gods whom you have
only heard of to those whom you have seen? Or
why is Latona worshipped at these altars, while my
divinity still waits for incense? I have Tantalus
to my father, the only mortal ever allowed to touch
the table of the gods; my mother is a sister of the
Pleiades; most mighty Atlas is one grandfather,
who supports the vault of heaven on his shoulders;
my other grandsire is Jove himself, and I boast him
as my father-in-law as well. The Phrygian nations
hold me in reverent fear. I am queen of Cadmus'
royal house, and the walls of Thebes, erected by the
magic of my husband's lyre, together with its people,
acknowledge me and him as their rulers. Wherever
I turn my eyes in the palace I see great stores of
wealth. Besides, I have beauty worthy of a goddess;
add to all this that I have seven daughters and as
many sons, and soon shall have sons- and daughters-
in-law. Ask now what cause I have for pride; and
then presume to prefer to me the Titaness, Latona,
daughter of Coeus, whoever he may be—Latona, to
whom the broad earth once refused a tiny spot for
bringing forth her children. Neither heaven nor
earth nor sea was open for this goddess of yours; she
was outlawed from the universe, until Delos, pitying
the wanderer, said to her: ' You are a vagrant on
the land; I, on the sea,' and gave her a place that
stood never still. And there she bore two children,
the seventh part only of my offspring. Surely I am
happy. Who can deny it? And happy I shall remain.
This also who can doubt? My very abundance has
made me safe. I am too great for Fortune to harm;
though she should take many from me, still many
more will she leave to me. My blessings have

excessere metum mea iam bona.   fingite demi
huic aliquid populo natorum posse meorum:
non tamen ad numerum redigar spoliata duorum,
Latonae turbam, qua quantum distat ab orba?   200
ite—satis pro re sacri—laurumque capillis
ponite!" deponunt et sacra infecta relinquunt,
quodque licet, tacito venerantur murmure numen.

Indignata dea est summoque in vertice Cynthi
talibus est dictis gemina cum prole locuta: 205
" en ego vestra parens, vobis animosa creatis,
et nisi Iunoni nulli cessura dearum,
an dea sim, dubitor perque omnia saecula cultis
arceor, o nati, nisi vos succurritis, aris.
nec dolor hic solus; diro convicia facto   210
Tantalis adiecit vosque est postponere natis
ausa suis et me, quod in ipsam reccidat, orbam
dixit et exhibuit linguam scelerata paternam."
adiectura preces erat his Latona relatis:
" desine!" Phoebus ait, " poenae mora longa
    querella est!"   215
dixit idem Phoebe, celerique per aera lapsu
contigerant tecti Cadmeida nubibus arcem.

Planus erat lateque patens prope moenia campus,
adsiduis pulsatus equis, ubi turba rotarum
duraque mollierat subiectas ungula glaebas.   220
pars ibi de septem genitis Amphione fortes
conscendunt in equos Tyrioque rubentia suco
terga premunt auroque graves moderantur habenas.
e quibus Ismenus, qui matri sarcina quondam

302

banished fear. Even suppose that some part of this tribe of children could be taken from me, not even so despoiled would I be reduced to the number of two, Latona's throng, with which how far is she from childlessness? Away with you, you have sacrificed quite enough, and take off those laurels from your hair." They take off the wreaths and leave the sacrifice unfinished; but, as they may, they still worship the goddess with unspoken words.

The goddess was angry, and on the top of Cynthus she thus addressed Apollo and Diana: " Lo, I, your mother, proud of your birth and willing to yield place to no goddess save Juno only, I have had my divinity called in question; and through all coming ages I shall be denied worship at the altar, unless you, my children, come to my aid. Nor is this my only cause for resentment. This daughter of Tantalus has added insult to her injuries: she has dared to prefer her own children to you, and has called me childless—may that fall on her head!—and by her impious speech has displayed her father's unbridled tongue." To this story of her wrongs Latona would have added prayers; but here Phoebus cried: " Have done! a long complaint is but delay of punishment! " Phoebe said the same. Then, swiftly gliding through the air, they alighted on Cadmus' citadel, covered in clouds.

There was a broad and level plain near the walls, beaten by the constant tread of horses, where a host of wheels and the hard hoof had levelled the clods beneath them. There some of Amphion's seven sons mounted their strong horses, sitting firm on their backs bright with Tyrian purple, and guided them with rich gold-mounted bridles. While one of these, Ismenus, who was his mother's first-born son,

prima suae fuerat, dum certum flectit in orbem   225
quadripedis cursus spumantiaque ora coercet,
" ei mihi! " conclamat medioque in pectore fixa
tela gerit frenisque manu moriente remissis
in latus a dextro paulatim defluit armo.
proximus audito sonitu per inane pharetrae   230
frena dabat Sipylus, veluti cum praescius imbris
nube fugit visa pendentiaque undique rector
carbasa deducit, ne qua levis effluat aura :
frena tamen dantem non evitabile telum
consequitur, summaque tremens cervice sagitta   235
haesit, et exstabat nudum de gutture ferrum ;
ille, ut erat, pronus per crura admissa iubasque
volvitur et calido tellurem sanguine foedat.
Phaedimus infelix et aviti nominis heres
Tantalus, ut solito finem inposuere labori,   240
transierant ad opus nitidae iuvenale palaestrae ;
et iam contulerant arto luctantia nexu
pectora pectoribus, cum tento concita nervo,
sicut erant iuncti, traiecit utrumque sagitta.
ingemuere simul, simul incurvata dolore   245
membra solo posuere, simul suprema iacentes
lumina versarunt, animam simul exhalarunt.
adspicit Alphenor laniataque pectora plangens
advolat, ut gelidos conplexibus adlevet artus,
inque pio cadit officio ; nam Delius illi   250
intima fatifero rupit praecordia ferro.
quod simul eductum est, pars et pulmonis in hamis
eruta cumque anima cruor est effusus in auras.
at non intonsum simplex Damasicthona vulnus

304

was guiding his charger's course round the curving track and pulling hard on the foaming bit, "Ah me!" he cried, and, with an arrow fixed in his breast, he dropped the reins from his dying hands and slowly sank sidewise down to the earth over his horse's right shoulder. Next, hearing through the void air the sound of the rattling quiver, Sipylus gave full rein; as when a shipmaster, conscious of an approaching storm, flees at the sight of a cloud and crowds on all sail that he may catch each passing breeze. He gave full rein, and as he gave it the arrow that none may escape overtook him, and the shaft stuck quivering in his neck; while the iron point showed from his throat in front. He, leaning forward, as he was, pitched over the galloping horse's mane and legs, and stained the ground with his warm blood. Unhappy Phaedimus and Tantalus, who bore his grandsire's name, when they had finished their wonted task had passed to the youthful exercise of the shining wrestling-match. And now they were straining together, breast to breast, in close embrace, when an arrow, sped from the drawn bow, pierced them both just as they stood clasped together. They groaned together; together they fell writhing in pain to the ground; together as they lay they moved their dying eyes; together they breathed their last. Alphenor saw them die, and beating his breast in agony, he ran to lift up their cold bodies in his arms; and in this pious duty he fell; for Apollo pierced him through the midriff with death-dealing steel. When this was removed, a piece of his lungs was drawn out sticking to the barbs, and his life-blood came rushing forth into the air. But one wound was not all that pierced youthful Damasichthon. He was struck where the

adficit : ictus erat, qua crus esse incipit et qua   255
mollia nervosus facit internodia poples.
dumque manu temptat trahere exitiabile telum,
altera per iugulum pennis tenus acta sagitta est.
expulit hanc sanguis seque eiaculatus in altum
emicat et longe terebrata prosilit aura.   260
ultimus Ilioneus non profectura precando
bracchia sustulerat "di" que "o communiter omnes,"
dixerat ignarus non omnes esse rogandos
" parcite! "   motus erat, cum iam revocabile telum
non fuit, arcitenens; minimo tamen occidit ille   265
vulnere, non alte percusso corde sagitta.
   Fama mali populique dolor lacrimaeque suorum
tam subitae matrem certam fecere ruinae,
mirantem potuisse irascentemque, quod ausi
hoc essent superi, quod tantum iuris haberent;   270
nam pater Amphion ferro per pectus adacto
finierat moriens pariter cum luce dolorem.
heu! quantum haec Niobe Niobe distabat ab illa,
quae modo Latois populum submoverat aris
et mediam tulerat gressus resupina per urbem   275
invidiosa suis; at nunc miseranda vel hosti!
corporibus gelidis incumbit et ordine nullo
oscula dispensat natos suprema per omnes;
a quibus ad caelum liventia bracchia tollens
" pascere, crudelis, nostro, Latona, dolore,   280
pascere " ait " satiaque meo tua pectora luctu!
[corque ferum satia! " dixit. " per funera septem]
efferor: exsulta victrixque inimica triumpha!
cur autem victrix? miserae mihi plura supersunt,
quam tibi felici; post tot quoque funera vinco!"   285

lower leg just begins, and where the sinews of the
hough give a soft spot; and while he was trying to
draw out the fatal shaft with his hand, a second
arrow was driven clear to the feathers through his
throat. The blood drove it forth and gushing out
spurted high in air in a long, slender stream.
Ilioneus was the last; stretching out his arms in
prayer doomed to be vain, he cried: " Oh, spare me,
all ye gods," not knowing that he need not pray to
them all. The archer-god was moved to pity, but
too late to recall his shaft. Still the youth fell
smitten by a slight wound only, since the arrow did
not deeply pierce his heart.

Rumour of the trouble, the people's grief, and the
tears of her own friends informed the mother of this
sudden disaster, amazed that it could have happened,
and angry because the gods had dared so far, that
they should have such power; for the father, Am-
phion, had already driven a dagger through his heart,
and so in dying had ended his grief and life together.
Alas, how different now was this Niobe from that
Niobe who had but now driven the people from
Latona's altar, and had walked proudly through the
city streets, enviable then to her friends, but now
one for even her enemies to pity. She threw her-
self upon the cold bodies of her sons, wildly giving
the last kisses to them all. From them she lifted
her bruised arms to high heaven and cried: " Feed
now upon my grief, cruel Latona, feed and glut your
heart on my sorrow. [Yes, glut your bloodthirsty
heart! By the deaths of my seven sons] I am
destroyed. Exult, and triumph in your hateful
victory. But why victory? In my misery I still
have more than you in your felicity. After so many
deaths, I triumph still! "

OVID

Dixerat, et sonuit contento nervus ab arcu;
qui praeter Nioben unam conterruit omnes:
illa malo est audax. stabant cum vestibus atris
ante toros fratrum demisso crine sorores;
e quibus una trahens haerentia viscere tela   290
inposito fratri moribunda relanguit ore;
altera solari miseram conata parentem
conticuit subito duplicataque vulnere caeco est.
[oraque compressit, nisi postquam spiritus ibat]
haec frustra fugiens collabitur, illa sorori   295
inmoritur; latet haec, illam trepidare videres.
sexque datis leto diversaque vulnera passis
ultima restabat; quam toto corpore mater,
tota veste tegens " unam minimamque relinque!
de multis minimam posco " clamavit " et unam." 300
dumque rogat, pro qua rogat, occidit: orba resedit
exanimes inter natos natasque virumque
deriguitque malis; nullos movet aura capillos,
in vultu color est sine sanguine, lumina maestis
stant inmota genis, nihil est in imagine vivum.   305
ipsa quoque interius cum duro lingua palato
congelat, et venae desistunt posse moveri;
nec flecti cervix nec bracchia reddere motus
nec pes ire potest; intra quoque viscera saxum est.
flet tamen et validi circumdata turbine venti   310
in patriam rapta est: ibi fixa cacumine montis
liquitur, et lacrimas etiam nunc marmora manant.
    Tum vero cuncti manifestam numinis iram
femina virque timent cultuque inpensius omnes

She spoke, and the taut bowstring twanged, which
terrified all save Niobe alone; misery made her bold.
The sisters were standing about their brothers' biers,
with loosened hair and robed in black. One of these,
while drawing out the shaft fixed in a brother's
vitals, sank down with her face upon him, fainting
and dying. A second, attempting to console her
grieving mother, ceased suddenly, and was bent in
agony by an unseen wound. [She closed her lips till
her dying breath had passed.] One fell while trying
in vain to flee. Another died upon her sister; one
hid, and one stood trembling in full view. And
now six had suffered various wounds and died; the
last remained. The mother, covering her with her
crouching body and her sheltering robes, cried out:
" Oh, leave me one, the littlest! Of all my many
children, the littlest I beg you spare—just one! "
And even while she prayed, she for whom she
prayed fell dead. Now does the childless mother
sit down amid the lifeless bodies of her sons, her
daughters, and her husband, in stony grief. Her
hair stirs not in the breeze; her face is pale and
bloodless, and her eyes are fixed and staring in her
sad face. There is nothing alive in the picture.
Her very tongue is silent, frozen to her mouth's roof,
and her veins can move no longer; her neck cannot
bend nor her arms move nor her feet go. Within
also her vitals are stone. But still she weeps; and,
caught up in a strong, whirling wind, she is rapt away
to her own native land. There, set on a mountain's
peak, she weeps; and even to this day tears trickle
from the marble.

Then truly do all men and women fear the wrath
of the goddess so openly displayed; and all more
zealously than ever worship the dread divinity of

magna gemelliparae venerantur numina divae; 315
utque fit, a facto propiore priora renarrant.
e quibus unus ait: " Lyciae quoque fertilis agris
non inpune deam veteres sprevere coloni.
res obscura quidem est ignobilitate virorum,
mira tamen: vidi praesens stagnumque locumque
prodigio notum.   nam me iam grandior aevo 321
inpatiensque viae genitor deducere lectos
iusserat inde boves gentisque illius eunti
ipse ducem dederat, cum quo dum pascua lustro,
ecce lacu medio sacrorum nigra favilla 325
ara vetus stabat tremulis circumdata cannis.
restitit et pavido ' faveas mihi! ' murmure dixit
dux meus, et simili ' faveas! ' ego murmure dixi.
Naiadum Faunine foret tamen ara rogabam
indigenaene, dei, cum talia rettulit hospes: 330
' non hac, o iuvenis, montanum numen in ara est;
illa suam vocat hanc, cui quondam regia coniunx
orbem interdixit, quam vix erratica Delos
orantem accepit tum, cum levis insula nabat;
illic incumbens cum Palladis arbore palmae 335
edidit invita geminos Latona noverca.
hinc quoque Iunonem fugisse puerpera fertur
inque suo portasse sinu, duo numina, natos.
iamque Chimaeriferae, cum sol gravis ureret arva,
finibus in Lyciae longo dea fessa labore 340

the twin gods' mother. And, as usual, stirred by the later, they tell over former tales. Then one of them begins: " So also in the fertile fields of Lycia, peasants of olden time scorned the goddess and suffered for it. The story is little known because of the humble estate of the men concerned, but it is remarkable. I myself saw the pool and the place made famous by the wonder. For my father, who at that time was getting on in years and too weak to travel far, had bidden me go and drive down from that country some choice steers which were grazing there, and had given me a man of that nation to serve as guide. While I fared through the grassy glades with him, there, in the midst of a lake, an ancient altar was standing, black with the fires of many sacrifices, surrounded with shivering reeds. My guide halted and said with awe-struck whisper: ' Be merciful to me!' and in like whisper I said: ' Be merciful!' Then I asked my guide whether this was an altar to the Naiads, or Faunus, or some deity of the place, and he replied: ' No, young man; no mountain deity dwells in this altar. She claims its worship, whom the queen of heaven once shut out from all the world, whom wandering Delos would scarce accept at her prayer, when it was an island, lightly floating on the sea. There, reclining on the palm and Pallas' tree,[1] in spite of their step-mother, she brought forth her twin babes. Even thence the new-made mother is said to have fled from Juno, carrying in her bosom her infant children, both divine. And now, having reached the borders of Lycia, home of the Chimaera, when the hot sun beat fiercely upon the fields, the goddess, weary of her long struggle, was faint by reason of the

---

[1] *i.e.* the olive.

sidereo siccata sitim collegit ab aestu,
uberaque ebiberant avidi lactantia nati.
forte lacum mediocris aquae prospexit in imis
vallibus; agrestes illic fruticosa legebant
vimina cum iuncis gratamque paludibus ulvam; 345
accessit positoque genu Titania terram
pressit, ut hauriret gelidos potura liquores.
rustica turba vetat; dea sic adfata vetantis:
"quid prohibetis aquis? usus communis aquarum est.
nec solem proprium natura nec aera fecit 350
nec tenues undas: ad publica munera veni;
quae tamen ut detis, supplex peto. non ego nostros
abluere hic artus lassataque membra parabam,
sed relevare sitim. caret os umore loquentis,
et fauces arent, vixque est via vocis in illis. 355
haustus aquae mihi nectar erit, vitamque fatebor
accepisse simul: vitam dederitis in unda.
hi quoque vos moveant, qui nostro bracchia tendunt
parva sinu," et casu tendebant bracchia nati.
quem non blanda deae potuissent verba movere?
hi tamen orantem perstant prohibere minasque, 361
ni procul abscedat, conviciaque insuper addunt.
nec satis est, ipsos etiam pedibusque manuque
turbavere lacus imoque e gurgite mollem
huc illuc limum saltu movere maligno. 365
distulit ira sitim; neque enim iam filia Coei
supplicat indignis nec dicere sustinet ultra
verba minora dea tollensque ad sidera palmas
"aeternum stagno" dixit "vivatis in isto!"

sun's heat and parched with thirst; and the hungry children had drained her breasts dry of milk. She chanced to see a lake of no great size down in a deep vale; some rustics were there gathering bushy osiers, with fine swamp-grass and rushes of the marsh. Latona came to the water's edge and kneeled on the ground to quench her thirst with a cooling draught. But the rustic rabble would not let her drink. Then she besought them: "Why do you deny me water? The enjoyment of water is a common right. Nature has not made the sun private to any, nor the air, nor soft water. This common right I seek; and yet I beg you to give it to me as a favour. I was not preparing to bathe my limbs or my weary body here in your pool, but only to quench my thirst. Even as I speak, my mouth is dry of moisture, my throat is parched, and my voice can scarce find utterance. A drink of water will be nectar to me, and I shall confess that I have received life with it; yes, life you will be giving me if you let me drink. These children too, let them touch your hearts, who from my bosom stretch out their little arms." And it chanced that the children did stretch out their arms. Who would not have been touched by the goddess' gentle words? Yet for all her prayers they persisted in denying with threats if she did not go away; they even added insulting words. Not content with that, they soiled the pool itself with their feet and hands, and stirred up the soft mud from the bottom, leaping about, all for pure meanness. Then wrath postponed thirst; for Coeus' daughter could neither humble herself longer to those unruly fellows, nor could she endure to speak with less power than a goddess; but stretching up her hands to heaven, she cried: "Live then for ever

eveniunt optata deae : iuvat esse sub undis   370
et modo tota cava submergere membra palude,
nunc proferre caput, summo modo gurgite nare,
saepe super ripam stagni consistere, saepe
in gelidos resilire lacus, sed nunc quoque turpes
litibus exercent linguas pulsoque pudore,   375
quamvis sint sub aqua, sub aqua maledicere temptant.
vox quoque iam rauca est, inflataque colla tumescunt,
ipsaque dilatant patulos convicia rictus ;
terga caput tangunt, colla intercepta videntur,
spina viret, venter, pars maxima corporis, albet,   380
limosoque novae saliunt in gurgite ranae.' "

    Sic ubi nescio quis Lycia de gente virorum
rettulit exitium, satyri reminiscitur alter,
quem Tritoniaca Latous harundine victum
adfecit poena.   " quid me mihi detrahis ? " inquit ;
" a! piget, a! non est " clamabat " tibia tanti." 386
clamanti cutis est summos direpta per artus,
nec quicquam nisi vulnus erat ; cruor undique manat,
detectique patent nervi, trepidaeque sine ulla
pelle micant venae ; salientia viscera possis   390
et perlucentes numerare in pectore fibras.
illum ruricolae, silvarum numina, fauni
et satyri fratres et tunc quoque carus Olympus
et nymphae flerunt, et quisquis montibus illis
lanigerosque greges armentaque bucera pavit.   395
fertilis inmaduit madefactaque terra caducas
concepit lacrimas ac venis perbibit imis ;
quas ubi fecit aquam, vacuas emisit in auras.

in that pool." It fell out as the goddess prayed. It is their delight to live in water; now to plunge their bodies quite beneath the enveloping pool, now to thrust forth their heads, now to swim upon the surface. Often they sit upon the sedgy bank and often leap back into the cool lake. But even now, as of old, they exercise their foul tongues in quarrel, and all shameless, though they may be under water, even under the water they try to utter maledictions. Now also their voices are hoarse, their inflated throats swell up, and their constant quarrelling distends their wide jaws; their shoulders meet their heads, the necks seem to have disappeared. Their backs are green; their bellies, the largest part of the body, are white; and as new-made frogs they leap in the muddy pool.' "

Then, when this unknown story-teller had told the destruction of the Lycian peasants, another recalled the satyr whom the son of Latona had conquered in a contest on Pallas' reed, and punished. "Why do you tear me from myself?" he cried. "Oh, I repent! Oh, a flute is not worth such price!" As he screams, his skin is stripped off the surface of his body, and he is all one wound: blood flows down on every side, the sinews lie bare, his veins throb and quiver with no skin to cover them: you could count the entrails as they palpitate, and the vitals showing clearly in his breast. The country people, the sylvan deities, fauns and his brother satyrs, and Olympus, whom even then he still loved, the nymphs, all wept for him, and every shepherd who fed his woolly sheep or horned kine on those mountains. The fruitful earth was soaked, and soaking caught those tears and drank them deep into her veins. Changing these then to water, she sent them forth into the free air. Thence the stream

OVID

inde petens rapidus ripis declivibus aequor
Marsya nomen habet, Phrygiae liquidissimus amnis.

Talibus extemplo redit ad praesentia dictis   401
vulgus et exstinctum cum stirpe Amphiona luget;
mater in invidia est: hanc tunc quoque dicitur unus
flesse Pelops umeroque, suas a pectore postquam
deduxit vestes, ebur ostendisse sinistro.   405
concolor hic umerus nascendi tempore dextro
corporeusque fuit; manibus mox caesa paternis
membra ferunt iunxisse deos, aliisque repertis,
qui locus est iuguli medius summique lacerti,
defuit: inpositum est non conparentis in usum   410
partis ebur, factoque Pelops fuit integer illo.

Finitimi proceres coeunt, urbesque propinquae
oravere suos ire ad solacia reges,
Argosque et Sparte Pelopeiadesque Mycenae
et nondum torvae Calydon invisa Dianae   415
Orchomenosque ferax et nobilis aere Corinthus
Messeneque ferox Patraeque humilesque Cleonae
et Nelea Pylos neque adhuc Pittheia Troezen,
quaeque urbes aliae bimari clauduntur ab Isthmo
exteriusque sitae bimari spectantur ab Isthmo;   420
credere quis posset? solae cessastis Athenae.
obstitit officio bellum, subvectaque ponto
barbara Mopsopios terrebant agmina muros.

Threicius Tereus haec auxiliaribus armis
fuderat et clarum vincendo nomen habebat;   425

within its sloping banks ran down quickly to the sea, and had the name of Marsyas, the clearest river in all Phrygia.

Straightway the company turns from such old tales to the present, and mourns Amphion dead with his children. They all blame the mother; but even then one man, her brother Pelops, is said to have wept for her, and, drawing aside his garment from his breast, to have revealed the ivory patch on the left shoulder. This at the time of his birth had been of the same colour as his right, and of flesh. But later, when his father had cut him in pieces, they say that the gods joined the parts together again; they found all the others, but one part was lacking where the neck and upper arm unite. A piece of ivory was made to take the place of the part which could not be found; and so Pelops was made whole again.

Now all the neighbouring princes assembled, and the near-by cities urged their kings to go and offer sympathy: Argos and Sparta and Peloponnesian Mycenae; Calydon, which had not yet incurred Diana's wrath; fertile Orchomenos and Corinth, famed for works of bronze; warlike Messene, Patrae, and low-lying Cleonae; Nelean Pylos and Troezen, not yet ruled by Pittheus; and all the other cities which are shut off by the Isthmus between its two seas, and those which are outside visible from the Isthmus between its two seas.[1] But of all cities—who could believe it?—you, Athens, alone did nothing. War hindered this friendly service, and barbaric hordes from oversea held the walls of Mopsopia[2] in alarm. Now Tereus of Thrace had put these to flight with his relieving troops, and by the victory had a great name. And

[1] That is, the Peloponnese and Northern Greece.
[2] Athens, from King Mopsopius.

quem sibi Pandion opibusque virisque potentem
et genus a magno ducentem forte Gradivo
conubio Procnes iunxit; non pronuba Iuno,
non Hymenaeus adest, non illi Gratia lecto:
Eumenides tenuere faces de funere raptas,   430
Eumenides stravere torum, tectoque profanus
incubuit bubo thalamique in culmine sedit.
hac ave coniuncti Procne Tereusque, parentes
hac ave sunt facti; gratata est scilicet illis
Thracia, disque ipsi grates egere; diemque,   435
quaque data est claro Pandione nata tyranno
quaque erat ortus Itys, festum iussere vocari:
usque adeo latet utilitas.

             Jam tempora Titan
quinque per autumnos repetiti duxerat anni,
cum blandita viro Procne " si gratia " dixit   440
" ulla mea est, vel me visendae mitte sorori,
vel soror huc veniat: redituram tempore parvo
promittes socero; magni mihi muneris instar
germanam vidisse dabis." iubet ille carinas
in freta deduci veloque et remige portus   445
Cecropios intrat Piraeaque litora tangit.
ut primum soceri data copia, dextera dextrae
iungitur, et fausto committitur omine sermo.
coeperat, adventus causam, mandata referre
coniugis et celeres missae spondere recursus: 450
ecce venit magno dives Philomela paratu,
divitior forma; quales audire solemus
naidas et dryadas mediis incedere silvis,

since he was strong in wealth and in men, and traced his descent, as it happened, from Gradivus, Pandion, king of Athens, allied him to himself by wedding him to Procne. But neither Juno, bridal goddess, nor Hymen, nor the Graces were present at that wedding. The Furies lighted them with torches stolen from a funeral; the Furies spread the couch, and the uncanny screech-owl brooded and sat on the roof of their chamber. Under this omen were Procne and Tereus wedded; under this omen was their child conceived. Thrace, indeed, rejoiced with them, and they themselves gave thanks to the gods; both the day on which Pandion's daughter was married to their illustrious king, and that day on which Itys was born, they made a festival: even so is our true advantage hidden.

Now Titan through five autumnal seasons had brought round the revolving years, when Procne coaxingly to her husband said: " If I have found any favour in your sight, either send me to visit my sister or let my sister come to me. You will promise my father that after a brief stay she shall return. If you give me a chance to see my sister you will confer on me a precious boon." Tereus accordingly bade them launch his ship, and plying oar and sail, he entered the Cecropian harbour and came to land on the shore of Piraeus. As soon as he came into the presence of his father-in-law they joined right hands, and the talk began with good wishes for their health. He had begun to tell of his wife's request, which was the cause of his coming, and to promise a speedy return should the sister be sent home with him, when lo! Philomela entered, attired in rich apparel, but richer still in beauty; such as we are wont to hear the naiads described, and dryads when they move about

si modo des illis cultus similesque paratus.
non secus exarsit conspecta virgine Tereus,   455
quam si quis canis ignem supponat aristis
aut frondem positasque cremet faenilibus herbas.
digna quidem facies; sed et hunc innata libido
exstimulat, pronumque genus regionibus illis
in Venerem est: flagrat vitio gentisque suoque.   460
impetus est illi comitum corrumpere curam
nutricisque fidem nec non ingentibus ipsam
sollicitare datis totumque inpendere regnum
aut rapere et saevo raptam defendere bello;
et nihil est, quod non effreno captus amore   465
ausit, nec capiunt inclusas pectora flammas.
iamque moras male fert cupidoque revertitur ore
ad mandata Procnes et agit sua vota sub illa.
facundum faciebat amor, quotiensque rogabat
ulterius iusto, Procnen ita velle ferebat.   470
addidit et lacrimas, tamquam mandasset et illas.
pro superi, quantum mortalia pectora caecae
noctis habent! ipso sceleris molimine Tereus
creditur esse pius laudemque a crimine sumit.
quid, quod idem Philomela cupit, patriosque lacertis
blanda tenens umeros, ut eat visura sororem,   476
perque suam contraque suam petit ipsa salutem.
spectat eam Tereus praecontrectatque videndo
osculaque et collo circumdata bracchia cernens
omnia pro stimulis facibusque ciboque furoris   480
accipit, et quotiens amplectitur illa parentem,
esse parens vellet: neque enim minus inpius esset.

in the deep woods, if only one should give to them refinement and apparel like hers. The moment he saw the maiden Tereus was inflamed with love, quick as if one should set fire to ripe grain, or dry leaves, or hay stored away in the mow. Her beauty, indeed, was worth it; but in his case his own passionate nature pricked him on, and, besides, the men of his clime are quick to love: his own fire and his nation's burnt in him. His impulse was to corrupt her attendants care and her nurse's faithfulness, and even by rich gifts to tempt the girl herself, even at the cost of all his kingdom; or else to ravish her and to defend his act by bloody war. There was nothing which he would not do or dare, smitten by this mad passion. His heart could scarce contain the fires that burnt in it. Now, impatient of delay, he eagerly repeated Procne's request, pleading his own cause under her name. Love made him eloquent, and as often as he asked more urgently than he should, he would say that Procne wished it so. He even added tears to his entreaties, as though she had bidden him to do this too. Ye gods, what blind night rules in the hearts of men! In the very act of pushing on his shameful plan Tereus gets credit for a kind heart and wins praise from wickedness. Ay, more— Philomela herself has the same wish; winding her arms about her father's neck, she coaxes him to let her visit her sister; by her own welfare (yes, and against it, too) she urges her prayer. Tereus gazes at her, and as he looks feels her already in his arms; as he sees her kisses and her arms about her father's neck, all this goads him on, food and fuel for his passion; and whenever she embraces her father he wishes that he were in the father's place—indeed, if he were, his intent would be no

vincitur ambarum genitor prece: gaudet agitque
illa patri grates et successisse duabus
id putat infelix, quod erit lugubre duabus.   485
    Iam labor exiguus Phoebo restabat, equique
pulsabant pedibus spatium declivis Olympi:
regales epulae mensis et Bacchus in auro
ponitur; hinc placido dant turgida corpora somno.
at rex Odrysius, quamvis secessit, in illa   490
aestuat et repetens faciem motusque manusque
qualia vult fingit quae nondum vidit et ignes
ipse suos nutrit cura removente soporem.
lux erat, et generi dextram conplexus euntis
Pandion comitem lacrimis commendat obortis: 495
" hanc ego, care gener, quoniam pia causa coegit,
et voluere ambae (voluisti tu quoque, Tereu)
do tibi perque fidem cognataque pectora supplex,
per superos oro, patrio ut tuearis amore
et mihi sollicitae lenimen dulce senectae   500
quam primum (omnis erit nobis mora longa) remittas;
tu quoque quam primum (satis est procul esse
        sororem),
si pietas ulla est, ad me, Philomela, redito! "
mandabat pariterque suae dabat oscula natae,
et lacrimae mites inter mandata cadebant;   505
utque fide pignus dextras utriusque poposcit
inter seque datas iunxit natamque nepotemque
absentes pro se memori rogat ore salutent;
supremumque vale pleno singultibus ore
vix dixit timuitque suae praesagia mentis.   510

less impious. The father yields to the prayers of both. The girl is filled with joy; she thanks her father and, poor unhappy wretch, she deems that success for both sisters which is to prove a woeful happening for them both.

Now Phoebus' toils were almost done and his horses were pacing down the western sky. A royal feast was spread, wine in cups of gold. Then they surrender their sated bodies to peaceful slumber. But although the Thracian king retired, his heart seethes with thoughts of her. Recalling her look, her movement, her hands, he pictures at will what he has not yet seen, and feeds his own fires, his thoughts preventing sleep. Morning came; and Pandion, wringing his son-in-law's hand as he was departing, consigned his daughter to him with many tears and said: "Dear son, since a natural plea has won me, and both my daughters have wished it, and you also have wished it, my Tereus, I give her to your keeping; and by your honour and the ties that bind us, by the gods, I pray you guard her with a father's love, and as soon as possible—it will seem a long time in any case to me—send back to me this sweet solace of my tedious years. And do you, my Philomela, if you love me, come back to me as soon as possible; it is enough that your sister is so far away." Thus he made his last requests and kissed his child good-bye, and gentle tears fell as he spoke the words; and he asked both their right hands as pledge of their promise, and joined them together and begged that they would remember to greet for him his daughter and her son. His voice broke with sobs, he could hardly say farewell, as he feared the forebodings of his mind.

Ut semel inposita est pictae Philomela carinae,
admotumque fretum remis tellusque repulsa est,
" vicimus! " exclamat, " mecum mea vota feruntur! "
exsultatque et vix animo sua gaudia differt
barbarus et nusquam lumen detorquet ab illa,   515
non aliter quam cum pedibus praedator obuncis
deposuit nido leporem Iovis ales in alto;
nulla fuga est capto, spectat sua praemia raptor.
    Iamque iter effectum, iamque in sua litora fessis
puppibus exierant, cum rex Pandione natam   520
in stabula alta trahit, silvis obscura vetustis,
atque ibi pallentem trepidamque et cuncta timentem
et iam cum lacrimis, ubi sit germana, rogantem
includit fassusque nefas et virginem et unam
vi superat frustra clamato saepe parente,   525
saepe sorore sua, magnis super omnia divis.
illa tremit velut agna pavens, quae saucia cani
ore excussa lupi nondum sibi tuta videtur,
utque columba suo madefactis sanguine plumis
horret adhuc avidosque timet, quibus haeserat, ungues.
mox ubi mens rediit, passos laniata capillos,   531
lugenti similis caesis plangore lacertis
intendens palmas " o diris barbare factis,
o crudelis " ait, " nec te mandata parentis
cum lacrimis movere piis nec cura sororis   535
nec mea virginitas nec coniugialia iura?
omnia turbasti; paelex ego facta sororis,
tu geminus coniunx, hostis mihi debita Procne!
324

As soon as Philomela was safely embarked upon
the painted ship and the sea was churned beneath
the oars and the land was left behind, Tereus ex-
claimed: " I have won! in my ship I carry the ful-
filment of my prayers!" The barbarous fellow
triumphs, he can scarce postpone his joys, and never
turns his eyes from her, as when the ravenous bird
of Jove has dropped in his high eyrie some hare
caught in his hooked talons; the captive has no chance
to escape, the captor gloats over his prize.

And now they were at the end of their journey,
now, leaving the travel-worn ship, they had landed on
their own shores; when the king dragged off Pandion's
daughter to a hut deep hidden in the ancient woods;
and there, pale and trembling and all fear, begging
with tears to know where her sister was, he shut her
up. Then, openly confessing his horrid purpose, he
violated her, just a weak girl and all alone, vainly
calling, often on her father, often on her sister, but
most of all upon the great gods. She trembled like
a frightened lamb, which, torn and cast aside by a
grey wolf, cannot yet believe that it is safe; and
like a dove which, with its own blood all smeared
over its plumage, still palpitates with fright, still
fears those greedy claws that have pierced it. Soon,
when her senses came back, she dragged at her
loosened hair, and like one in mourning, beating and
tearing her arms, with outstretched hands she cried:
" Oh, what a horrible thing you have done, bar-
barous, cruel wretch! Do you care nothing for my
father's injunctions, his affectionate tears, my sister's
love, my own virginity, the bonds of wedlock? You
have confused all natural relations: I have become a
concubine, my sister's rival; you, a husband to both.
Now Procne must be my enemy. Why do you not

325

OVID

quin animam hanc, ne quod facinus tibi, perfide, restet,
eripis? atque utinam fecisses ante nefandos   540
concubitus: vacuas habuissem criminis umbras.
si tamen haec superi cernunt, si numina divum
sunt aliquid, si non perierunt omnia mecum,
quandocumque mihi poenas dabis! ipsa pudore
proiecto tua facta loquar: si copia detur,   545
in populos veniam; si silvis clausa tenebor,
inplebo silvas et conscia saxa movebo;
audiet haec aether et si deus ullus in illo est!"

    Talibus ira feri postquam commota tyranni
nec minor hac metus est, causa stimulatus utraque,
quo fuit accinctus, vagina liberat ensem   551
arreptamque coma fixis post terga lacertis
vincla pati cogit; iugulum Philomela parabat
spemque suae mortis viso conceperat ense:
ille indignantem et nomen patris usque vocantem
luctantemque loqui conprensam forcipe linguam 556
abstulit ense fero.   radix micat ultima linguae,
ipsa iacet terraeque tremens inmurmurat atrae,
utque salire solet mutilatae cauda colubrae,
palpitat et moriens dominae vestigia quaerit.   560
hoc quoque post facinus (vix ausim credere) fertur
saepe sua lacerum repetisse libidine corpus.

    Sustinet ad Procnen post talia facta reverti;
coniuge quae viso germanam quaerit, at ille
326

take my life, that no crime may be left undone, you traitor? Aye, would that you had killed me before you wronged me so. Then would my shade have been innocent and clean. If those who dwell on high see these things, nay, if there are any gods at all, if all things have not perished with me, sooner or later you shall pay dearly for this deed. I will myself cast shame aside and proclaim what you have done. If I should have the chance, I would go where people throng and tell it; if I am kept shut up in these woods, I will fill the woods with my story and move the very rocks to pity. The air of heaven shall hear it, and, if there is any god in heaven, he shall hear it too."

The savage tyrant's wrath was aroused by these words, and his fear no less. Pricked on by both these spurs, he drew his sword which was hanging by his side in its sheath, caught her by the hair, and twisting her arms behind her back, he bound them fast. At sight of the sword Philomela gladly offered her throat to the stroke, filled with the eager hope of death. But he seized her tongue with pincers, as it protested against the outrage, calling ever on the name of her father and struggling to speak, and cut it off with his merciless blade. The mangled root quivers, while the severed tongue lies palpitating on the dark earth, faintly murmuring; and, as the severed tail of a mangled snake is wont to writhe, it twitches convulsively, and with its last dying movement it seeks its mistress's feet. Even after this horrid deed—one would scarce believe it—the monarch is said to have worked his lustful will again and again upon the poor mangled form.

With such crimes upon his soul he had the face to return to Procne's presence. She on seeing him

dat gemitus fictos commentaque funera narrat,   565
et lacrimae fecere fidem.   velamina Procne
deripit ex umeris auro fulgentia lato
induiturque atras vestes et inane sepulcrum
constituit falsisque piacula manibus infert
et luget non sic lugendae fata sororis.   570
   Signa deus bis sex acto lustraverat anno;
quid faciat Philomela? fugam custodia claudit,
structa rigent solido stabulorum moenia saxo,
os mutum facti caret indice.   grande doloris
ingenium est, miserisque venit sollertia rebus: 575
stamina barbarica suspendit callida tela
purpureasque notas filis intexuit albis,
indicium sceleris; perfectaque tradidit uni,
utque ferat dominae, gestu rogat; illa rogata
pertulit ad Procnen nec scit, quid tradat in illis.   580
evolvit vestes saevi matrona tyranni
germanaeque suae fatum miserabile legit
et (mirum potuisse) silet: dolor ora repressit,
verbaque quaerenti satis indignantia linguae
defuerunt, nec flere vacat, sed fasque nefasque   585
confusura ruit poenaeque in imagine tota est.
   Tempus erat, quo sacra solent trieterica Bacchi
Sithoniae celebrare nurus: (nox conscia sacris,
nocte sonat Rhodope tinnitibus aeris acuti)
nocte sua est egressa domo regina deique   590
ritibus instruitur furialiaque accipit arma;

at once asked where her sister was. He groaned in pretended grief and told a made-up story of death; his tears gave credence to the tale. Then Procne tore from her shoulders the robe gleaming with a broad golden border and put on black weeds; she built also a cenotaph in honour of her sister, brought pious offerings to her imagined spirit, and mourned her sister's fate, not meet so to be mourned.

Now through the twelve signs, a whole year's journey, has the sun-god passed. And what shall Philomela do? A guard prevents her flight; stout walls of solid stone fence in the hut; speechless lips can give no token of her wrongs. But grief has sharp wits, and in trouble cunning comes. She hangs a Thracian web on her loom, and skilfully weaving purple signs on a white background, she thus tells the story of her wrongs. This web, when completed, she gives to her one attendant and begs her with gestures to carry it to the queen. The old woman, as she was bid, takes the web to Procne, not knowing what she bears in it. The savage tyrant's wife unrolls the cloth, reads the pitiable fate of her sister, and (a miracle that she could!) says not a word. Grief chokes the words that rise to her lips, and her questing tongue can find no words strong enough to express her outraged feelings. Here is no room for tears, but she hurries on to confound right and wrong, her whole soul bent on the thought of vengeance.

It was the time when the Thracian matrons were wont to celebrate the biennial festival of Bacchus. Night was in their secret; by night Mount Rhodope would resound with the shrill clash of brazen cymbals; so by night the queen goes forth from her house, equips herself for the rites of the god and

vite caput tegitur, lateri cervina sinistro
vellera dependent, umero levis incubat hasta.
concita per silvas turba comitante suarum
terribilis Procne furiisque agitata doloris, 595
Bacche, tuas simulat: venit ad stabula avia tandem
exululatque euhoeque sonat portasque refringit
germanamque rapit raptaeque insignia Bacchi
induit et vultus hederarum frondibus abdit
attonitamque trahens intra sua moenia ducit. 600
    Ut sensit tetigisse domum Philomela nefandam,
horruit infelix totoque expalluit ore;
nacta locum Procne sacrorum pignora demit
oraque develat miserae pudibunda sororis
amplexumque petit; sed non attollere contra 605
sustinet haec oculos paelex sibi visa sororis
deiectoque in humum vultu iurare volenti
testarique deos, per vim sibi dedecus illud
inlatum, pro voce manus fuit. ardet et iram
non capit ipsa suam Procne fletumque sororis 610
corripiens "non est lacrimis hoc" inquit "agendum,
sed ferro, sed si quid habes, quod vincere ferrum
possit. in omne nefas ego me, germana, paravi:
aut ego, cum facibus regalia tecta cremabo,
artificem mediis inmittam Terea flammis, 615
aut linguam atque oculos et quae tibi membra
        pudorem
abstulerunt ferro rapiam, aut per vulnera mille
sontem animam expellam! magnum quodcumque
        paravi;
quid sit, adhuc dubito."

dons the array of frenzy; her head was wreathed with
trailing vines, a deer-skin hung from her left side, a
light spear rested on her shoulder. Swift she goes
through the woods with an attendant throng of her
companions, and driven on by the madness of grief,
Procne, terrific in her rage, mimics thy madness,
O Bacchus! She comes to the secluded lodge at last,
shrieks aloud and cries "Euhoe!" breaks down the
doors, seizes her sister, arrays her in the trappings of
a Bacchante, hides her face with ivy-leaves, and,
dragging her along in amazement, leads her within
her own walls.

When Philomela perceived that she had entered
that accursed house the poor girl shook with horror
and grew pale as death. Procne found a place, and
took off the trappings of the Bacchic rites and,
uncovering the shame-blanched face of her wretched
sister, folded her in her arms. But Philomela could
not lift her eyes to her sister, feeling herself to have
wronged her. And, with her face turned to the
ground, longing to swear and call all the gods to
witness that that shame had been forced upon her,
she made her hand serve for voice. But Procne was
all on fire, could not contain her own wrath, and chid-
ing her sister's weeping, she said: "This is no time for
tears, but for the sword, for something stronger than
the sword, if you have such a thing. I am prepared
for any crime, my sister; either to fire this palace
with a torch, and to cast Tereus, the author of our
wrongs, into the flaming ruins, or to cut out his
tongue and his eyes, to cut off the parts which
brought shame to you, and drive his guilty soul out
through a thousand wounds. I am prepared for some
great deed; but what it shall be I am still in doubt."

                  Peragit dum talia Procne,
ad matrem veniebat Itys; quid possit, ab illo   620
admonita est oculisque tuens inmitibus " a! quam
es similis patri! " dixit nec plura locuta
triste parat facinus tacitaque exaestuat ira.
ut tamen accessit natus matrique salutem
attulit et parvis adduxit colla lacertis   625
mixtaque blanditiis puerilibus oscula iunxit,
mota quidem est genetrix, infractaque constitit ira
invitique oculi lacrimis maduere coactis;
sed simul ex nimia mentem pietate labare
sensit, ab hoc iterum est ad vultus versa sororis   630
inque vicem spectans ambos " cur admovet " inquit
" alter blanditias, rapta silet altera lingua?
quam vocat hic matrem, cur non vocat illa sororem?
cui sis nupta, vide, Pandione nata, marito!
degeneras! scelus est pietas in coniuge Tereo."   635
nec mora, traxit Ityn, veluti Gangetica cervae
lactentem fetum per silvas tigris opacas,
utque domus altae partem tenuere remotam,
tendentemque manus et iam sua fata videntem
et " mater! mater! " clamantem et colla petentem
ense ferit Procne, lateri qua pectus adhaeret,   641
nec vultum vertit. satis illi ad fata vel unum
vulnus erat: iugulum ferro Philomela resolvit,
vivaque adhuc animaeque aliquid retinentia membra
dilaniant. pars inde cavis exsultat aenis,   645
pars veribus stridunt; manant penetralia tabo.
  His adhibet coniunx ignarum Terea mensis
et patrii moris sacrum mentita, quod uni

While Procne was thus speaking Itys came into his mother's presence. His coming suggested what she could do, and regarding him with pitiless eyes, she said: "Ah, how like your father you are!" Saying no more, she began to plan a terrible deed and boiled with inward rage. But when the boy came up to her and greeted his mother, put his little arms around her neck and kissed her in his winsome, boyish way, her mother-heart was touched, her wrath fell away, and her eyes, though all unwilling, were wet with tears that flowed in spite of her. But when she perceived that her purpose was wavering through excess of mother-love, she turned again from her son to her sister; and gazing at both in turn, she said: "Why is one able to make soft, pretty speeches, while her ravished tongue dooms the other to silence? Since he calls me mother, why does she not call me sister? See the kind of man you have married, daughter of Pandion! You are unworthy of your father! Faithfulness to such a husband as Tereus is a crime." Without more words she dragged Itys away, as a tigress drags a suckling fawn through the dark woods on Ganges' banks. And when they reached a remote part of the great house, while the boy stretched out pleading hands as he saw his fate, and screamed, "Mother! mother!" and sought to throw his arms around her neck, Procne smote him with a knife between breast and side—and with no change of face. This one stroke sufficed to slay the lad; but Philomela cut the throat also, and they cut up the body still warm and quivering with life. Part bubbles in brazen kettles, part sputters on spits; while the whole room drips with gore.

This is the feast to which the wife invites Tereus, little knowing what it is. She pretends that it is a

OVID

fas sit adire viro, comites famulosque removit.
ipse sedens solio Tereus sublimis avito   650
vescitur inque suam sua viscera congerit alvum,
tantaque nox animi est, " Ityn huc accersite! " dixit.
dissimulare nequit crudelia gaudia Procne
iamque suae cupiens exsistere nuntia cladis   654
" intus habes, quem poscis " ait : circumspicit ille
atque, ubi sit, quaerit; quaerenti iterumque vocanti,
sicut erat sparsis furiali caede capillis,
prosiluit Ityosque caput Philomela cruentum
misit in ora patris nec tempore maluit ullo
posse loqui et meritis testavi gaudia dictis.   660
Thracius ingenti mensas clamore repellit
vipereasque ciet Stygia de valle sorores
et modo, si posset, reserato pectore diras
egerere inde dapes semesaque viscera gestit,
flet modo seque vocat bustum miserabile nati,   665
nunc sequitur nudo genitas Pandione ferro.
corpora Cecropidum pennis pendere putares :
pendebant pennis.   quarum petit altera silvas,
altera tecta subit, neque adhuc de pectore caedis
excessere notae, signataque sanguine pluma est. 670
ille dolore suo poenaeque cupidine velox
vertitur in volucrem, cui stant in vertice cristae.
prominet inmodicum pro longa cuspide rostrum;
nomen epops volucri, facies armata videtur.
334

sacred feast after their ancestral fashion, of which only a husband may partake, and removes all attendants and slaves. So Tereus, sitting alone in his high ancestral banquet-chair, begins the feast and gorges himself with flesh of his own flesh. And in the utter blindness of his understanding he cries: " Go, call me Itys hither! " Procne cannot hide her cruel joy, and eager to be the messenger of her bloody news, she says: "You have, within, him whom you want." He looks about and asks where the boy is. And then, as he asks and calls again for his son, just as she was, with streaming hair, and all stained with her mad deed of blood, Philomela springs forward and hurls the gory head of Itys straight into his father's face; nor was there ever any time when she longed more to be able to speak, and to express her joy in fitting words. Then the Thracian king overturns the table with a great cry and invokes the snaky sisters from the Stygian pit. Now, if he could, he would gladly lay open his breast and take thence the horrid feast and half-consumed flesh of his son; now he weeps bitterly and calls himself his son's most wretched tomb; then with drawn sword he pursues the two daughters of Pandion. As they fly from him you would think that the bodies of the two Athenians were poised on wings: they were poised on wings! One flies to the woods, the other rises to the roof. And even now their breasts have not lost the marks of their murderous deed, their feathers are stained with blood. Tereus, swift in pursuit because of his grief and eager desire for vengeance, is himself changed into a bird. Upon his head a stiff crest appears, and a huge beak stands forth instead of his long sword. He is the hoopoë, with the look of one armed for war.

OVID

    Hic dolor ante diem longaeque extrema senectae
tempora Tartareas Pandiona misit ad umbras.   676
sceptra loci rerumque capit moderamen Erectheus,
iustitia dubium validisne potentior armis.
quattuor ille quidem iuvenes totidemque crearat
femineae sortis, sed erat par forma duarum.   680
e quibus Aeolides Cephalus te coniuge felix,
Procri, fuit; Boreae Tereus Thracesque nocebant,
dilectaque diu caruit deus Orithyia,
dum rogat et precibus mavult quam viribus uti;
ast ubi blanditiis agitur nihil, horridus ira,   685
quae solita est illi nimiumque domestica vento,
" et merito! " dixit; " quid enim mea tela reliqui,
saevitiam et vires iramque animosque minaces,
admovique preces, quarum me dedecet usus?
apta mihi vis est: vi tristia nubila pello,   690
vi freta concutio nodosaque robora verto
induroque nives et terras grandine pulso;
idem ego, cum fratres caelo sum nactus aperto
(nam mihi campus is est), tanto molimine luctor,
ut medius nostris concursibus insonet aether   695
exsiliantque cavis elisi nubibus ignes;
idem ego, cum subii convexa foramina terrae
supposuique ferox imis mea terga cavernis,
sollicito manes totumque tremoribus orbem.
hac ope debueram thalamos petiisse, socerque   700
non orandus erat mihi sed faciendus Erectheus.''

336

This woe shortened the days of old Pandion and sent him down to the shades of Tartarus before old age came to its full term. His sceptre and the state's control fell to Erechtheus, equally famed for justice and for prowess in arms. Four sons were born to him and four daughters also. Of these daughters two were of equal beauty, of whom thou, Procris, didst make happy in wedlock Cephalus, the grandson of Aeolus. Boreas was not favoured because of Tereus and the Thracians [1]; and so the god was long kept from his beloved Orithyia, while he wooed and preferred to use prayers rather than force. But when he could accomplish nothing by soothing words, rough with anger, which was the north-wind's usual and more natural mood, he said: " I have deserved it! For why have I given up my own weapons, fierceness and force, rage and threatening moods, and had recourse to prayers, which do not at all become me? Force is my fit instrument. By force I drive on the gloomy clouds, by force I shake the sea, I overturn gnarled oaks, pack hard the snow, and pelt the earth with hail. So also when I meet my brother in the open sky—for that is my battle-ground—I struggle with them so fiercely that the mid-heavens thunder with our meeting and fires leap bursting out of the hollow clouds. So also when I have entered the vaulted hollows of the earth, and have set my strong back beneath her lowest caverns, I fright the ghosts and the whole world, too, by my heavings. By this means I should have sought my wife. I should not have begged Erechtheus to be my father-in-law, but made him to be so." With

---

[1] Since the home of Boreas was in the north, he was included in the hatred felt at Athens for Tereus and the Thracians.

haec Boreas aut his non inferiora locutus
excussit pennas, quarum iactatibus omnis
adflata est tellus latumque perhorruit aequor,
pulvereamque trahens per summa cacumina pallam
verrit humum pavidamque metu caligine tectus   706
Orithyian amans fulvis amplectitur alis.
dum volat, arserunt agitati fortius ignes,
nec prius aerii cursus suppressit habenas,
quam Ciconum tenuit populos et moenia raptor. 710
illic et gelidi coniunx Actaea tyranni
et genetrix facta est, partus enixa gemellos,
cetera qui matris, pennas genitoris haberent.
non tamen has una memorant cum corpore natas,
barbaque dum rutilis aberat subnixa capillis,   715
inplumes Calaisque puer Zetesque fuerunt;
mox pariter pennae ritu coepere volucrum
cingere utrumque latus, pariter flavescere malae.
ergo ubi concessit tempus puerile iuventae,
vellera cum Minyis nitido radiantia villo   720
per mare non notum prima petiere carina.

these words or others no less boisterous, Boreas shook
his wings, whose mighty flutterings sent a blast over
all the earth, and ruffled the broad ocean.   And
trailing along his dusty mantle over the mountain-
tops, he swept the land; and wrapped in darkness,
the lover embraced with his tawny wings his Orithyia,
who was trembling sore with fear   As he flew his
own flames were fanned and burned stronger.   Nor
did the robber check his airy flight until he came to
the people and the city of the Cicones.   There did the
Athenian girl become the bride of the cold monarch,
and mother, when she brought forth twins sons, who
had all else of their mother, but their father's wings.
Yet these wings, they say, were not born with their
bodies; while the beard was not yet to be seen
beneath their yellow locks, both Calais and Zetes
were wingless, but soon and at the same time wings
began to spring out on either side after the fashion
of birds, and the cheeks began to grow tawny.   So
these two youths, when boyhood was passed and
they had grown to man's estate, went with the
Minyans over an unknown sea in that first ship to
seek the bright gleaming fleece of gold.

BOOK VII

1–158	*Medea and Jason*
159–293	*The Rejuvenation of Aeson*
294–349	*The Punishment of Pelias*
350–403	*The Flight of Medea*
404–452	*Theseus and Aegeus*
453–500	*Minos, Aeacus*
501–613	*The Plague at Aegina*
614–660	*The Myrmidons*
661–865	*Cephalus and Procris*

LIBER VII

Iamqve fretum Minyae Pagasaea puppe secabant,
perpetuaque trahens inopem sub nocte senectam
Phineus visus erat, iuvenesque Aquilone creati
virgineas volucres miseri senis ore fugarant,
multaque perpessi claro sub Iasone tandem   5
contigerant rapidas limosi Phasidos undas.
dumque adeunt regem Phrixeaque vellera poscunt
lexque datur Minyis magnorum horrenda laborum,
concipit interea validos Aeetias ignes
et luctata diu, postquam ratione furorem   10
vincere non poterat, " frustra, Medea, repugnas:
nescio quis deus obstat," ait, "mirumque, nisi hoc est,
aut aliquid certe simile huic, quod amare vocatur.
nam cur iussa patris nimium mihi dura videntur?
sunt quoque dura nimis! cur, quem modo denique vidi,
ne pereat, timeo?   quae tanti causa timoris?   16
excute virgineo conceptas pectore flammas,
si potes, infelix! si possem, sanior essem!
sed trahit invitam nova vis, aliudque cupido,
mens aliud suadet: video meliora proboque,   20
deteriora sequor.   quid in hospite, regia virgo,

BOOK VII

AND now the Minyans were plowing the deep
in their Thessalian ship. They had seen Phineus,
spending his last days helpless in perpetual night;
and the sons of Boreas had driven the harpies from
the presence of the unhappy king. Having ex-
perienced many adventures under their illustrious
leader Jason, they reached at last the swift waters
of muddy Phasis. There, while they were approach-
ing the king and demanding the fleece that Phrixus
had given to him, while the dreadful condition with
its great tasks was being proposed to the Minyans,
meanwhile the daughter of King Aeëtes conceived an
overpowering passion. Long she fought against it,
and when by reason she could not rid her of her
madness she cried: " In vain, Medea, do you fight.
Some god or other is opposing you; I wonder if
this is not what is called love, or at least something
like this. For why do the mandates of my father seem
too harsh? They certainly are too harsh. Why do
I fear lest he perish whom I have but now seen for
the first time? What is the cause of all this fear?
Come, thrust from your maiden breast these flames
that you feel, if you can, unhappy girl. Ah, if I could,
I should be more myself. But some strange power
draws me on against my will. Desire persuades
me one way, reason another. I see the better and
approve it, but I follow the worse. Why do you, a

343

ureris et thalamos alieni concipis orbis?
haec quoque terra potest, quod ames, dare. vivat an ille
occidat, in dis est.   vivat tamen! idque precari
vel sine amore licet: quid enim commisit Iason?   25
quem, nisi crudelem, non tangat Iasonis aetas
et genus et virtus?   quem non, ut cetera desint,
ore movere potest? certe mea pectora movit.
at nisi opem tulero, taurorum adflabitur ore
concurretque suae segeti, tellure creatis   30
hostibus, aut avido dabitur fera praeda draconi.
hoc ego si patiar, tum me de tigride natam,
tum ferrum et scopulos gestare in corde fatebor!
cur non et specto pereuntem oculosque videndo
conscelero? cur non tauros exhortor in illum   35
terrigenasque feros insopitumque draconem?
di meliora velint! quamquam non ista precanda,
sed facienda mihi.—prodamne ego regna parentis,
atque ope nescio quis servabitur advena nostra,
ut per me sospes sine me det lintea ventis   40
virque sit alterius, poenae Medea relinquar?
si facere hoc aliamve potest praeponere nobis,
occidat ingratus! sed non is vultus in illo,
non ea nobilitas animo est, ea gratia formae,
ut timeam fraudem meritique oblivia nostri.   45
et dabit ante fidem, cogamque in foedera testes
esse deos. quid tuta times? accingere et omnem
pelle moram: tibi se semper debebit Iason,
te face sollemni iunget sibi perque Pelasgas
344

royal maiden, burn for a stranger, and think upon
marriage with a foreign world? This land also can
give you something to love. Whether he live or die
is in the lap of the gods. Yet may he live! This I
may pray for even without loving him. For what
has Jason done? Who that is not heartless would
not be moved by Jason's youth, his noble birth, his
manhood? Who, though the rest were lacking, would
not be touched by his beauty? Certainly he has
touched my heart. But unless I help him he will be
breathed on by the bulls' fiery breath, and he will
have to meet an enemy of his own sowing sprung
from the earth, or he will be given as prey like any
wild beast to the greedy dragon. If I permit this,
then shall I confess that I am the child of a tigress
and that I have iron and stone in my heart.
But why can I not look on as he dies, and why is such
a sight defilement for my eyes? Why do I not urge
on the bulls against him, and the fierce earth-born
warriors, and the sleepless dragon? Heaven forefend!
and yet that is not matter for my prayers, but for my
deeds. Shall I then betray my father's throne? and
shall an unknown stranger be preserved by my aid,
that, when saved by me, he may sail off without me,
and become another's husband, while I, Medea, am
left for punishment? If he can do that, if he can prefer
another woman to me, let him perish, ungrateful man.
But no: his look, his loftiness of soul, his grace of form
are not such that I need fear deceit or forgetfulness
of my service. And he shall give me his pledge
beforehand, and I will compel the gods to be wit-
nesses of our troth. Why do you fear when all is
safe? Now for action, and away with all delay!
Jason shall always owe himself to you, he shall join
you to himself in solemn wedlock. Then you shall

servatrix urbes matrum celebrabere turba.   50
ergo ego germanam fratremque patremque deosque
et natale solum ventis ablata relinquam?
nempe pater saevus, nempe est mea barbara tellus,
frater adhuc infans; stant mecum vota sororis,
maximus intra me deus est! non magna relinquam,
magna sequar: titulum servatae pubis Achivae   56
notitiamque soli melioris et oppida, quorum
hic quoque fama viget, cultusque artesque locorum,
quemque ego cum rebus, quas totus possidet orbis,
Aesoniden mutasse velim, quo coniuge felix   60
et dis cara ferar et vertice sidera tangam.
quid, quod nescio qui mediis concurrere in undis
dicuntur montes ratibusque inimica Charybdis
nunc sorbere fretum, nunc reddere, cinctaque saevis
Scylla rapax canibus Siculo latrare profundo?   65
nempe tenens, quod amo, gremioque in Iasonis
          haerens
per freta longa ferar; nihil illum amplexa verebor
aut, siquid metuam, metuam de coniuge solo.—
coniugiumne putas speciosaque nomina culpae
inponis, Medea, tuae?—quin adspice, quantum   70
adgrediare nefas, et, dum licet, effuge crimen!"
dixit, et ante oculos rectum pietasque pudorque
constiterant, et victa dabat iam terga Cupido.

    Ibat ad antiquas Hecates Perseidos aras,
quas nemus umbrosum secretaque silva tegebat,   75
et iam fortis erat, pulsusque recesserat ardor,
cum videt Aesoniden exstinctaque flamma reluxit.

be hailed as his deliverer through the cities of
Greece by throngs of women. And shall I then
sail away and leave my sister here, my brother,
father, gods, and native land? Indeed my father is a
stern man, indeed my native land is barbarous, my
brother is still a child, my sister's goodwill is on my
side; and the greatest god is within me! I shall
not be leaving great things, but going to great
things: the title of saviour of the Achaean youth,
acquaintance with a better land, cities, whose fame
is mighty even here, the culture and arts of civilized
countries, and the man I would not give in exchange
for all that the wide world holds—the son of Aeson;
with him as my husband I shall be called the beloved
of heaven, and with my head shall touch the stars.
But what of certain mountains, which, they say, come
clashing together in mid-sea; and Charybdis, the
sailor's dread, who now sucks in and again spews
forth the waves; and greedy Scylla, girt about with
savage dogs, baying in the Sicilian seas? Nay, holding
that which I love, and resting in Jason's arms, I
shall fare over the long reaches of the sea; in his safe
embrace I shall fear nothing; or if I fear at all, I
shall fear for my husband only. But do you deem it
marriage, Medea, and do you give fair-seeming names
to your fault? Nay, rather, look ahead and see how
great a wickedness you are approaching and flee it
while you may." She spoke, and before her eyes
stood righteousness, filial affection, and modesty; and
love, defeated, was now on the point of flight.

She took her way to an ancient altar of Hecate,
the daughter of Perse, hidden in the deep shades of
a forest. And now she was strong of purpose and
the flames of her vanquished passion had died down;
when she saw the son of Aeson and the dying flame

347

erubuere genae, totoque recanduit ore,
utque solet ventis alimenta adsumere, quaeque
parva sub inducta latuit scintilla favilla   80
crescere et in veteres agitata resurgere vires,
sic iam lenis amor, iam quem languere putares,
ut vidit iuvenem, specie praesentis inarsit.
et casu solito formosior Aesone natus
illa luce fuit: posses ignoscere amanti.   85
spectat et in vultu veluti tum denique viso
lumina fixa tenet nec se mortalia demens
ora videre putat nec se declinat ab illo;
ut vero coepitque loqui dextramque prehendit
hospes et auxilium submissa voce rogavit   90
promisitque torum, lacrimis ait illa profusis:
" quid faciam, video: nec me ignorantia veri
decipiet, sed amor, servabere munere nostro,
servatus promissa dato! " per sacra triformis
ille deae lucoque foret quod numen in illo   95
perque patrem soceri cernentem cuncta futuri
eventusque suos et tanta pericula iurat:
creditus accepit cantatas protinus herbas
edidicitque usum laetusque in tecta recessit.

   Postera depulerat stellas Aurora micantes: 100
conveniunt populi sacrum Mavortis in arvum
consistuntque iugis; medio rex ipse resedit
agmine purpureus sceptroque insignis eburno.
ecce adamanteis Vulcanum naribus efflant
aeripedes tauri, tactaeque vaporibus herbae   105
ardent, utque solent pleni resonare camini,

leaped up again. Her cheeks grew red, then all her
face became pale again; and as a tiny spark, which
has lain hidden beneath the ashes, is fed by a breath
of wind, then grows and regains its former strength
as it is fanned to life; so now her smouldering love,
which you would have thought all but dying, at sight
of the young hero standing before her blazed up again.
It chanced that the son of Aeson was more beautiful
than usual that day: you could pardon her for loving
him. She gazed upon him and held her eyes fixed
on his face as if she had never seen him before; and
in her infatuation she thought the face she gazed on
more than mortal, nor could she turn herself away
from him. But when the stranger began to speak,
grasped her right hand, and in low tones asked for
her aid and promised marriage in return, she burst
into tears and said: " I see what I am about to do,
nor shall ignorance of the truth be my undoing, but
love itself. You shall be preserved by my assistance;
but when preserved, fulfil your promise." He swore
he would be true by the sacred rites of the threefold
goddess, by whatever divinity might be in that
grove, by the all-beholding father of his father-in-
law who was to be, by his own successes and his
mighty perils. She believed; and straight he re-
ceived the magic herbs and learnt their use, then
withdrew full of joy into his lodging.

The next dawn had put to flight the twinkling
stars. Then the throngs gathered into the sacred
field of Mars and took their stand on the heights.
In the midst of the company sat the king himself,
clad in purple, and conspicuous with his ivory sceptre.
—See! here come the brazen-footed bulls, breathing
fire from nostrils of adamant. The very grass shrivels
up at the touch of their hot breath. And as full furnaces

aut ubi terrena silices fornace soluti
concipiunt ignem liquidarum adspergine aquarum,
pectora sic intus clausas volventia flammas
gutturaque usta sonant; tamen illis Aesone natus
obvius it.   vertere truces venientis ad ora   111
terribiles vultus praefixaque cornua ferro
pulvereumque solum pede pulsavere bisulco
fumificisque locum mugitibus inpleverunt.
deriguere metu Minyae; subit ille nec ignes   115
sentit anhelatos (tantum medicamina possunt!)
pendulaque audaci mulcet palearia dextra
suppositosque iugo pondus grave cogit aratri
ducere et insuetum ferro proscindere campum:
mirantur Colchi, Minyae clamoribus augent   120
adiciuntque animos.   galea tum sumit aena
vipereos dentes et aratos spargit in agros.
semina mollit humus valido praetincta veneno,
et crescunt fiuntque sati nova corpora dentes,
utque hominis speciem materna sumit in alvo   125
perque suos intus numeros conponitur infans
nec nisi maturus communes exit in auras,
sic, ubi visceribus gravidae telluris imago
effecta est hominis, feto consurgit in arvo,
quodque magis mirum est, simul edita concutit arma.
quos ubi viderunt praeacutae cuspidis hastas   131
in caput Haemonii iuvenis torquere parantis,
demisere metu vultumque animumque Pelasgi;
ipsa quoque extimuit, quae tutum fecerat illum.
utque peti vidit iuvenem tot ab hostibus unum,   135

are wont to roar, or as limestones burned in the lime-
kiln hiss and grow hot when water is poured upon
them; so did the bulls' chests and parched throats
rumble with the fires pent up within. Nevertheless
the son of Aeson went forward to meet them. As he
came towards them the fierce beasts turned upon him
terrible faces and sharp horns tipped with iron, pawed
the dusty earth with their cloven feet, and filled the
place with their fiery bellowings. The Minyans
were stark with fear; he went up to the bulls, not
feeling their hot breath at all, so great is the power
of charmed drugs; and stroking their hanging dew-
laps with fearless hand, he placed the yoke on their
necks and made them draw the heavy plow and cut
through the field that had never felt steel before.
The Colchians are amazed; but the Minyans shouted
aloud and increased their hero's courage. Next he
took from a brazen helmet the serpent's teeth and
sowed them broadcast in the plowed field. The
earth softened these seeds steeped in virulent
poison and the teeth swelled up and took on new
forms. And just as in its mother's body an infant
gradually assumes human form, and is perfected
within through all its parts, and does not come forth
to the common air until it is fully formed; so,
when the forms of men had been completed in the
womb of the pregnant earth, they rose up on the
teeming soil and, what is yet more wonderful, each
clashed weapons that had been brought forth with
him. When the Greeks saw them preparing to
hurl sharp-pointed spears at the head of the
Thessalian hero, their faces fell with fear and their
hearts failed them. She also, who had safeguarded
him, was sore afraid; and when she saw him, one
man, attacked by so many foes, she grew pale, and

OVID

palluit et subito sine sanguine frigida sedit,
neve parum valeant a se data gramina, carmen
auxiliare canit secretasque advocat artes.
ille gravem medios silicem iaculatus in hostes
a se depulsum Martem convertit in ipsos: 140
terrigenae pereunt per mutua vulnera fratres
civilique cadunt acie. gratantur Achivi
victoremque tenent avidisque amplexibus haerent.
tu quoque victorem conplecti, barbara, velles:
obstitit incepto pudor, at conplexa fuisses, [1]
sed te, ne faceres, tenuit reverentia famae.
quod licet, adfectu tacito laetaris agisque
carminibus grates et dis auctoribus horum.

Pervigilem superest herbis sopire draconem,
qui crista linguisque tribus praesignis et uncis 150
dentibus horrendus custos erat arboris aureae.
hunc postquam sparsit Lethaei gramine suci
verbaque ter dixit placidos facientia somnos,
quae mare turbatum, quae concita flumina sistunt,
somnus in ignotos oculos sibi venit, et auro 155
heros Aesonius potitur spolioque superbus
muneris auctorem secum, spolia altera, portans
victor Iolciacos tetigit cum coniuge portus.

Haemoniae matres pro gnatis dona receptis
grandaevique ferunt patres congestaque flamma 160
tura liquefaciunt, inductaque cornibus aurum
victima vota cadit, sed abest gratantibus Aeson

[1] *Line 145 bracketed by Ehwald.*

352

sat there suddenly cold and bloodless. And, lest the
charmed herbs which she had given him should not
be strong enough, she chanted a spell to help them
and called in her secret arts. But he hurled a heavy
rock into the midst of his enemies and so turned
their fury away from him upon themselves. The
earth-born brethren perished by each other's
wounds and fell fighting in internecine strife. Then
did the Greeks congratulate the victorious youth,
catching him in their arms and clinging to him in
eager embraces. You also, barbarian maiden, would
gladly have embraced the victor; your modesty stood
in the way. Still, you would have embraced him;
but respect for common talk held you back. What
was allowed you did, gazing on him with silent joy
and thanking your spells and the gods who gave them.

There remained the task of putting to sleep the ever-
watchful dragon with magic herbs. This creature,
distinguished by a crest, a three-forked tongue and
hooked fangs, was the awful guardian of the golden
tree. After Jason had sprinkled upon him the
Lethaean juice of a certain herb and thrice had
recited the words that bring peaceful slumber, which
stay the swollen sea and swift-flowing rivers, then
sleep came to those eyes which had never known
sleep before, and the heroic son of Aeson gained the
golden fleece. Proud of this spoil and bearing with
him the giver of his prize, another spoil, the victor
and his wife in due time reached the harbour of
Iolchos.

The Thessalian mothers and aged fathers bring
gifts in honour of their sons' safe return, and burn
incense heaped on the altar flames, and the victim
with gilded horns which they have vowed is slain.
But Aeson is absent from the rejoicing throng, being

OVID

iam propior leto fessusque senilibus annis,
cum sic Aesonides: " o cui debere salutem
confiteor, coniunx, quamquam mihi cuncta dedisti
excessitque fidem meritorum summa tuorum,   166
si tamen hoc possunt (quid enim non carmina
    possunt?)
deme meis annis et demptos adde parenti! "
nec tenuit lacrimas: mota est pietate rogantis,
dissimilemque animum subiit Aeeta relictus;   170
nec tamen adfectus talis confessa " quod " inquit
"excidit ore tuo, coniunx, scelus? ergo ego cuiquam
posse tuae videor spatium transcribere vitae?
nec sinat hoc Hecate, nec tu petis aequa; sed isto,
quod petis, experiar maius dare munus, Iason.   175
arte mea soceri longum temptabimus aevum,
non annis revocare tuis, modo diva triformis
adiuvet et praesens ingentibus adnuat ausis."

Tres aberant noctes, ut cornua tota coirent
efficerentque orbem; postquam plenissima fulsit   180
ac solida terras spectavit imagine luna,
egreditur tectis vestes induta recinctas,
nuda pedem, nudos umeris infusa capillos,
fertque vagos mediae per muta silentia noctis
incomitata gradus: homines volucresque ferasque   185
solverat alta quies, nullo cum murmure saepes,[1]
inmotaeque silent frondes, silet umidus aer,
sidera sola micant: ad quae sua bracchia tendens
ter se convertit, ter sumptis flumine crinem
inroravit aquis ternisque ululatibus ora   190

---

[1] *Bergk, led by an extra line in some MSS. would read:*
    solverat alta quies; nullo cum murmure serpens
    sopiti similis < per gramina labitur amnis >.

now near death and heavy with the weight of years.
Then says the son of Aeson: " O wife, to whom I freely
own my deliverance is due, although you have already
given me all, and the sum of your benefits has ex-
ceeded all my hopes; still, if your spells can do this
—and what can they not do?—take some portion
from my own years of life and give this to my father."
And he could not restrain his tears. Medea was moved
by the petitioner's filial love, and the thought of
Aeëtes deserted came into her mind, how different
from Jason's! Still, not confessing such feelings, she
replied: " What impious words have fallen from your
lips, my husband? Can I then transfer to any man,
think you, a portion of your life? Neither would
Hecate permit this, nor is your request right. But a
greater boon than what you ask, my Jason, will I try
to give. By my art and not your years I will try
to renew your father's long span of life, if only
the three-formed goddess will help me and grant
her present aid in this great deed which I dare
attempt."

There were yet three nights before the horns of
the moon would meet and make the round orb.
When the moon shone at her fullest and looked
down upon the earth with unbroken shape, Medea
went forth from her house clad in flowing robes,
barefoot, her hair unadorned and streaming down
her shoulders; and all alone she wandered out into
the deep stillness of midnight. Men, birds, and
beasts were sunk in profound repose; there was no
sound in the hedgerow; the leaves hung mute and
motionless; the dewy air was still. Only the stars
twinkled. Stretching up her arms to these, she
turned thrice about, thrice sprinkled water caught
up from a flowing stream upon her head and thrice

solvit et in dura submisso poplite terra
" Nox " ait " arcanis fidissima, quaeque diurnis
aurea cum luna succeditis ignibus astra,
tuque, triceps Hecate, quae coeptis conscia nostris
adiutrixque venis cantusque artisque magorum,   195
quaeque magos, Tellus, pollentibus instruis herbis,
auraeque et venti montesque amnesque lacusque,
dique omnes nemorum, dique omnes noctis adeste,
quorum ope, cum volui, ripis mirantibus amnes
in fontes rediere suos, concussaque sisto,   200
stantia concutio cantu freta, nubila pello
nubilaque induco, ventos abigoque vocoque,
vipereas rumpo verbis et carmine fauces,
vivaque saxa sua convulsaque robora terra
et silvas moveo iubeoque tremescere montis   205
et mugire solum manesque exire sepulcris!
te quoque, Luna, traho, quamvis Temesaea labores
aera tuos minuant; currus quoque carmine nostro
pallet avi, pallet nostris Aurora venenis!
vos mihi taurorum flammas hebetastis et unco   210
inpatiens oneris collum pressistis aratro,
vos serpentigenis in se fera bella dedistis
custodemque rudem somni sopistis et aurum
vindice decepto Graias misistis in urbes:
nunc opus est sucis, per quos renovata senectus   215
in florem redeat primosque recolligat annos,
356

gave tongue in wailing cries. Then she kneeled
down upon the hard earth and prayed: " O Night,
faithful preserver of mysteries, and ye bright stars,
whose golden beams with the moon succeed the fires
of day; thou three-formed Hecate, who knowest our
undertakings and comest to the aid of the spells
and arts of magicians; and thou, O Earth, who
dost provide the magicians with thy potent herbs;
ye breezes and winds, ye mountains and streams and
pools; all ye gods of the groves, all ye gods of the
night: be with me now. With your help when I
have willed it, the streams have run back to their
fountain-heads, while the banks wondered; I lay
the swollen, and stir up the calm seas by my spell;
I drive the clouds and bring on the clouds; the
winds I dispel and summon; I break the jaws of
serpents with my incantations; living rocks and oaks
I root up from their own soil; I move the forests, I
bid the mountains shake, the earth to rumble and
the ghosts to come forth from their tombs. Thee
also, Luna, do I draw from the sky, though the
clanging bronze of Temesa strive to aid thy throes [1];
even the chariot of the Sun, my grandsire, pales at
my song; Aurora pales at my poisons. You dulled
the bulls' flames at my command; you pressed under
the curved plow those necks which had endured no
weight. You turned the savage onslaught of the
serpent-born band against themselves; you lulled
the watcher who knew no sleep, and beguiling the
defender sent the golden prize back to the cities of
Greece. Now I have need of juices by whose aid
old age may be renewed and may turn back to the
bloom of youth and regain its early years. And you

[1] At an eclipse it was usual to make a noise in order to
frighten away the malignant influence.

et dabitis.   neque enim micuerunt sidera frustra,
nec frustra volucrum tractus cervice draconum
currus adest."   aderat demissus ab aethere currus.
quo simul adscendit frenataque colla draconum   220
permulsit manibusque leves agitavit habenas,
sublimis rapitur subiectaque Thessala Tempe
despicit et certis regionibus adplicat angues:
et quas Ossa tulit, quas altum Pelion herbas,
Othrysque Pindusque et Pindo maior Olympus,   225
perspicit et placitas partim radice revellit,
partim succidit curvamine falcis aenae.
multa quoque Apidani placuerunt gramina ripis,
multa quoque Amphrysi, neque eras inmunis, Enipeu;
nec non Peneos nec non Spercheides undae   230
contribuere aliquid iuncosaque litora Boebes;
carpsit et Euboica vivax Anthedone gramen,
nondum mutato vulgatum corpore Glauci.

   Et iam nona dies curru pennisque draconum
nonaque nox omnes lustrantem viderat agros,   235
cum rediit; neque erant tacti nisi odore dracones,
et tamen annosae pellem posuere senectae.
constitit adveniens citra limenque foresque
et tantum caelo tegitur refugitque viriles
contactus, statuitque aras de caespite binas,   240
dexteriore Hecates, ast laeva parte Iuventae.
has ubi verbenis silvaque incinxit agresti,
haud procul egesta scrobibus tellure duabus
sacra facit cultrosque in guttura velleris atri
conicit et patulas perfundit sanguine fossas;   245

will give them; for not in vain have the stars gleamed in reply, not in vain is my car at hand, drawn by winged dragons." There was the car, sent down from the sky. When she had mounted therein and stroked the bridled necks of the dragon team, shaking the light reins with her hands she was whirled aloft. She looked down on Thessalian Tempe lying·below, and turned her dragons towards regions that she knew. All the herbs that Ossa bore, and high Pelion, Othrys and Pindus and Olympus, greater than Pindus, she surveyed: and those that pleased her, some she plucked up by the roots and some she cut off with the curved blade of a bronze pruning-hook. Many grasses also she chose from the banks of the Apidanus, many from Amphrysus. Nor were you, Enipeus, left without toll; Peneus also, and Spercheus gave something, and the reedy banks of Boebe. From Euboean Anthedon she culled a grass that gives long life, a herb not yet made famous by the change which it produced in Glaucus' body.

And now nine days and nine nights had seen her traversing all lands, drawn in her car by her winged dragons, when she returned. The dragons had not been touched save by the odour of the herbs, and yet they sloughed off their skins of many long years. As she came Medea stopped this side of the threshold and the door; covered by the sky alone, she avoided her husband's embrace, and built two turf altars, one on the right to Hecate and one on the left to Youth. She wreathed these with boughs from the wild wood, then hard by she dug two ditches in the earth and performed her rites; plunging her knife into the throat of a black sheep, she drenched the open ditches with his blood. Next she poured upon

tum super invergens liquidi carchesia mellis
alteraque invergens tepidi carchesia lactis,
verba simul fudit terrenaque numina civit
umbrarumque rogat rapta cum coniuge regem,
ne properent artus anima fraudare senili.   250
    Quos ubi placavit precibusque et murmure longo,
Aesonis effetum proferri corpus ad auras
iussit et in plenos resolutum carmine somnos
exanimi similem stratis porrexit in herbis.
hinc procul Aesoniden,procul hinc iubet ire ministros
et monet arcanis oculos removere profanos.   256
diffugiunt iussi; passis Medea capillis
bacchantum ritu flagrantis circuit aras
multifidasque faces in fossa sanguinis atra
tinguit et infectas geminis accendit in aris   260
terque senem flamma, ter aqua, ter sulphure lustrat.
    Interea validum posito medicamen aeno
fervet et exsultat spumisque tumentibus albet.
illic Haemonia radices valle resectas
seminaque floresque et sucos incoquit atros;   265
adicit extremo lapides Oriente petitos
et quas Oceani refluum mare lavit harenas;
addit et exceptas luna pernocte pruinas
et strigis infamis ipsis cum carnibus alas
inque virum soliti vultus mutare ferinos   270
ambigui prosecta lupi; nec defuit illis
squamea Cinyphii tenuis membrana chelydri
vivacisque iecur cervi; quibus insuper addit
ova caputque novem cornicis saecula passae.
his et mille aliis postquam sine nomine rebus   275

it bowls of liquid honey, and again bowls of milk still warm, while at the same time she uttered her incantations, called up the deities of the earth, and prayed the king of the shades with his stolen bride not to be in haste to rob the old man's body of the breath of life.

When she had appeased all these divinities by long, low-muttered prayers, she bade her people bring out under the open sky old Aeson's worn-out body; and having buried him in a deep slumber by her spells, like one dead she stretched him out on a bed of herbs. Far hence she bade Jason go, far hence all the attendants, and warned them not to look with profane eyes upon her secret rites. They retired as she had bidden. Medea, with streaming hair after the fashion of the Bacchantes, moved round the blazing altars, and dipping many-cleft sticks in the dark pools of blood, she lit the gory sticks at the altar flames. Thrice she purified the old man with fire, thrice with water, thrice with sulphur.

Meanwhile the strong potion in the bronze pot is boiling, leaping and frothing white with the swelling foam. In this pot she boils roots cut in a Thessalian vale, together with seeds, flowers, and black juices. She adds to these ingredients pebbles sought for in the farthest Orient and sands which the ebbing tide of Ocean laves. She adds hoar frost gathered under the full moon, the wings of the uncanny screech-owl with the flesh as well, and the entrails of a werewolf which has the power of changing its wild-beast features into a man's. There also in the pot is the scaly skin of a slender Cinyphian water-snake, the liver of a long-lived stag, to which she adds also eggs and the head of a crow nine generations old. When with these and a thousand other nameless things the barbarian

propositum instruxit mortali barbara maius,
arenti ramo iampridem mitis olivae
omnia confudit summisque inmiscuit ima.
ecce vetus calido versatus stipes aeno
fit viridis primo nec longo tempore frondes   280
induit et subito gravidis oneratur olivis:
at quacumque cavo spumas eiecit aeno
ignis et in terram guttae cecidere calentes,
vernat humus, floresque et mollia pabula surgunt.
quae simul ac vidit, stricto Medea recludit   285
ense senis iugulum veteremque exire cruorem
passa replet sucis; quos postquam conbibit Aeson
aut ore acceptos aut vulnere, barba comaeque
canitie posita nigrum rapuere colorem,
pulsa fugit macies, abeunt pallorque situsque,   290
adiectoque cavae supplentur corpore rugae,
membraque luxuriant: Aeson miratur et olim
ante quater denos hunc se reminiscitur annos.

    Viderat ex alto tanti miracula monstri
Liber et admonitus, iuvenes nutricibus annos   295
posse suis reddi, capit hoc a Colchide munus.

    Neve doli cessent, odium cum coniuge falsum
Phasias adsimulat Peliaeque ad limina supplex
confugit; atque illam, quoniam gravis ipse senecta est,
excipiunt natae; quas tempore callida parvo   300
Colchis amicitiae mendacis imagine cepit,
dumque refert inter meritorum maxima demptos
Aesonis esse situs atque hac in parte moratur,
spes est virginibus Pelia subiecta creatis,

woman had prepared her more than mortal
plan, she stirred it all up with a branch of the
fruitful olive long since dry and well mixed the
top and bottom together. And lo, the old dry
stick, when moved about in the hot broth, grew
green at first, in a short time put forth leaves,
and then suddenly was loaded with teeming
olives. And wherever the froth bubbled over
from the hollow pot, and the hot drops fell upon
the ground, the earth grew green and flowers and
soft grass sprang up. When she saw this, Medea
unsheathed her knife and cut the old man's throat;
then, letting the old blood all run out, she filled his
veins with her brew. When Aeson had drunk this
in part through his lips and part through the wound,
his beard and hair lost their hoary grey and quickly
became black again; his leanness vanished, away
went the pallor and the look of neglect, the deep
wrinkles were filled out with new flesh, his limbs had
the strength of youth. Aeson was filled with wonder,
and remembered that this was he forty years ago.

Now Bacchus had witnessed this marvel from his
station in the sky, and learning from this that his
own nurses might be restored to their youthful years,
he obtained this boon from the Colchian woman.

That malice might have its turn, the Phasian
woman feigned a quarrel with her husband, and fled
as a suppliant to the house of Pelias. There, since
the king himself was heavy with years, his daughters
gave her hospitable reception. These girls the crafty
Colchian in a short time won over by a false show of
friendliness; and while she was relating among the
most remarkable of her achievements the rejuvena-
tion of Aeson, dwelling particularly on that, the
daughters of Pelias were induced to hope that by

arte suum parili revirescere posse parentem,   305
idque petunt pretiumque iubent sine fine pacisci.
illa brevi spatio silet et dubitare videtur
suspenditque animos ficta gravitate rogantum.
mox ubi pollicita est, " quo sit fiducia maior
muneris huius " ait, "qui vestri maximus aevo est 310
dux gregis inter oves, agnus medicamine fiet."
protinus innumeris effetus laniger annis
attrahitur flexo circum cava tempora cornu;
cuius ut Haemonio marcentia guttura cultro
fodit et exiguo maculavit sanguine ferrum,   315
membra simul pecudis validosque venefica sucos
mergit in aere cavo: minuunt ea corporis artus
cornuaque exurunt nec non cum cornibus annos,
et tener auditur medio balatus aeno:
nec mora, balatum mirantibus exsilit agnus   320
lascivitque fuga lactantiaque ubera quaerit.

    Obstipuere satae Pelia, promissaque postquam
exhibuere fidem, tum vero inpensius instant.
ter iuga Phoebus equis in Hibero flumine mersis
dempserat et quarta radiantia nocte micabant   325
sidera, cum rapido fallax Aeetias igni
imponit purum laticem et sine viribus herbas.
iamque neci similis resoluto corpore regem
et cum rege suo custodes somnus habebat,
quem dederant cantus magicaeque potentia linguae;
intrarant iussae cum Colchide limina natae   331

skill like this their own father might be made young
again. And they beg this boon, bidding her name
the price, no matter how great. She made no reply
for a little while and seemed to hesitate, keeping the
minds of her suppliants in suspense by feigned deep
meditation. When she had at length given her
promise, she said to them: " That you may have the
greater confidence in this boon, the oldest leader of
the flock among your sheep shall become a lamb
again by my drugs." Straightway a woolly ram,
worn out with untold years, was brought forward,
his great horns curving round his hollow temples.
When the witch cut his scrawny throat with her
Thessalian knife, barely staining the weapon with his
scanty blood, she plunged his carcass into a kettle of
bronze, throwing in at the same time juices of great
potency. These made his body shrink, burnt away
his horns, and with his horns, his years. And now a
thin bleating was heard from within the pot; and,
even while they were wondering at the sound, out
jumped a lamb and ran frisking away to find some
udder to give him milk.

Pelias' daughters looked on in amazement; and now
that these promises had been performed, they urged
their request still more eagerly than before. Three
times had Phoebus unyoked his steeds after their
plunge in Ebro's stream, and on the fourth night the
stars were shining bright in the sky, when the trea-
cherous daughter of Aeëtes set some clear water over
a hot fire and put therein herbs of no potency. And
now a death-like sleep held the king, his body all
relaxed, and with the king his guards, sleep which
incantations and the potency of magic words had
given. The king's daughters, as they were bid,
entered his chamber with the Colchian and stood

OVID

ambierantque torum: "quid nunc dubitatis inertes?
stringite" ait "gladios veteremque haurite cruorem,
ut repleam vacuas iuvenali sanguine venas!
in manibus vestris vita est aetasque parentis: 335
si pietas ulla est nec spes agitatis inanis,
officium praestate patri telisque senectam
exigite, et saniem coniecto emittite ferro!"
his, ut quaeque pia est, hortatibus inpia prima est
et, ne sit scelerata, facit scelus: haud tamen ictus 340
ulla suos spectare potest, oculosque reflectunt,
caecaque dant saevis aversae vulnera dextris.
ille cruore fluens, cubito tamen adlevat artus,
semilacerque toro temptat consurgere, et inter
tot medius gladios pallentia bracchia tendens   345
"quid facitis, gnatae? quid vos in fata parentis
armat?" ait: cecidere illis animique manusque;
plura locuturo cum verbis guttura Colchis
abstulit et calidis laniatum mersit in undis.

Quod nisi pennatis serpentibus isset in auras,   350
non exempta foret poenae: fugit alta superque
Pelion umbrosum, Philyreia tecta, superque
Othryn et eventu veteris loca nota Cerambi:
hic ope nympharum sublatus in aera pennis,
cum gravis infuso tellus foret obruta ponto,   355
Deucalioneas effugit inobrutus undas.
Aeoliam Pitanen a laeva parte relinquit
factaque de saxo longi simulacra draconis
Idaeumque nemus, quo nati furta, iuvencum,
occuluit Liber falsi sub imagine cervi,   360

366

around his bed. " Why do you hesitate now, you
laggards? " Medea said. " Come, draw your swords,
and let out his old blood that I may refill his empty
veins with young blood again. In your own hands
rests your father's life and youth. If you have any
filial love, and if the hopes are not vain that you are
cherishing, come, do your duty by your father; drive
out age at your weapon's point; let out his enfeebled
blood with the stroke of the steel." Spurred on by
these words, as each was filial she became first in
the unfilial act, and that she might not be wicked did
the wicked deed. Nevertheless, none could bear to
see her own blows; they turned their eyes away; and
so with averted faces they blindly struck with cruel
hands. The old man, streaming with blood, still
raised himself on his elbow and half mangled tried
to get up from his bed; and with all those swords
round him, he stretched out his pale arms and cried:
" What are you doing, my daughters? What arms
you to your father's death? " Their courage left
them, their hands fell. When he would have spoken
further, the Colchian cut his throat and plunged his
mangled body into the boiling water.

But had she not gone away through the air drawn
by her winged dragons, she would not have escaped
punishment. High up she sped over shady Pelion,
the home of Chiron, over Othrys and the regions
made famous by the adventure of old Cerambus.
(He, by the aid of the nymphs borne up into the air
on wings, at the time when the heavy earth had sunk
beneath the overwhelming sea, escaped Deucalion's
flood undrowned.) Aeolian Pitane she passed by on
the left, with its huge serpent image made of stone;
and Ida's grove, where Bacchus, to conceal his son's
theft, changed the bullock into the seeming form of

quaque pater Corythi parva tumulatus harena est,
et quos Maera novo latratu terruit agros,
Eurypylique urbem, qua Coae cornua matres
gesserunt tum, cum discederet Herculis agmen,
Phoebeamque Rhodon et Ialysios Telchinas,   365
quorum oculos ipso vitiantes omnia visu
Iuppiter exosus fraternis subdidit undis;
transit et antiquae Cartheia moenia Ceae,
qua pater Alcidamas placidam de corpore natae
miraturus erat nasci potuisse columbam.   370
inde lacus Hyries videt et Cycneia Tempe,
quae subitus celebravit olor: nam Phylius illic
imperio pueri volucrisque ferumque leonem
tradiderat domitos; taurum quoque vincere iussus
vicerat et spreto totiens iratus amore   375
praemia poscenti taurum suprema negabat;
ille indignatus " cupies dare " dixit et alto
desiluit saxo; cuncti cecidisse putabant:
factus olor niveis pendebat in aere pennis;
at genetrix Hyrie, servati nescia, flendo   380
delicuit stagnumque suo de nomine fecit.
adiacet his Pleuron, in qua trepidantibus alis
Ophias effugit natorum vulnera Combe;
inde Calaureae Letoidos adspicit arva
in volucrem versi cum coniuge conscia regis.   385
dextera Cyllene est, in qua cum matre Menephron
concubiturus erat saevarum more ferarum;
Cephison procul hinc deflentem fata nepotis

a stag; where the father of Corythus lay buried beneath a small mound of sand; where Maera spread terror through the fields by her strange barking; over the city of Eurypylus where the women of Cos wore horns what time the band of Hercules withdrew; over Rhodes, beloved of Phoebus; and the Telchines of Ialysus whose eyes, blighting all things by their very glance, Jupiter in scorn and hatred plunged beneath his brother's waves. She passed also the walls of ancient Carthaea on the island of Cea, where father Alcidamas was sometime to marvel that a peaceful dove could have sprung from his daughter's body. Next Hyrie's lake she saw, and Tempe, which Cycnus' sudden change into a swan made famous. For there Phylius, at the command of a boy, had tamed and brought him wild birds and a savage lion; being commanded to tame a wild bull also, he had tamed him, but angry that so often his love was spurned, he withheld the last gift of the bull from the boy who asked it; whereupon the boy in anger said, "You will wish you had given it," and leaped forthwith from a cliff. They all thought that he had fallen; but changed to a swan he remained floating in the air on snowy wings. But Hyrie, his mother, ignorant of the safety of her son, melted away in tears and became a pool of the same name. Near these regions lies Pleuron, where Combe, the daughter of Ophius, escaped death at the hands of her sons on fluttering wings. After that, she sees the fertile island of Calaurea, sacred to Latona, the island that saw the king and his wife both changed into birds. On her right lies Cyllene, which Menephron was doomed to defile with incest after the wild beasts' fashion. Far off from here she looks down on the Cephisus, bewailing the fate of his

respicit in tumidam phocen ab Apolline versi
Eumelique domum lugentis in aere natum.   390
    Tandem vipereis Ephyren Pirenida pennis
contigit: hic aevo veteres mortalia primo
corpora vulgarunt pluvialibus edita fungis.
sed postquam Colchis arsit nova nupta venenis
flagrantemque domum regis mare vidit utrumque, 395
sanguine natorum perfunditur inpius ensis,
ultaque se male mater Iasonis effugit arma.
hinc Titaniacis ablata draconibus intrat
Palladias arces, quae te, iustissima Phene,
teque, senex Peripha, pariter videre volantes   400
innixamque novis neptem Polypemonis alis.
excipit hanc Aegeus facto damnandus in uno,
nec satis hospitium est, thalami quoque foedere iungit.
    Iamque aderat Theseus, proles ignara parenti,
qui virtute sua bimarem pacaverat Isthmon: 405
huius in exitium miscet Medea, quod olim
attulerat secum Scythicis aconiton ab oris.
illud Echidnaeae memorant e dentibus ortum
esse canis: specus est tenebroso caecus hiatu,
est via declivis, per quam Tirynthius heros   410
restantem contraque diem radiosque micantes
obliquantem oculos nexis adamante catenis
Cerberon abstraxit, rabida qui concitus ira
inplevit pariter ternis latratibus auras
et sparsit virides spumis albentibus agros;   415

grandson changed by Apollo into a plump sea-calf; and upon the home of Eumelus, who lamented that his son now dwelt in air.

At length, upborne by the snaky wings, she reached Corinth of the sacred spring. Here, according to ancient tradition, in the earliest times men's bodies sprang from mushrooms. But after the new wife had been burnt by the Colchian witchcraft, and the two seas had seen the king's palace aflame, she stained her impious sword in the blood of her sons; and then, after this horrid vengeance, the mother fled Jason's sword. Borne hence by her dragons sprung from Titans' blood, she entered the citadel of Pallas, which beheld you, most righteous Phene, and you, old Periphas, flying side by side, and the grand-daughter [1] of Polypemon upborne by new-sprung wings. Aegeus received her, that one deed enough to doom him; but he was not content with hospitality: he made her his wife as well.

And now came Theseus, a son that his father knew not; who by his manly prowess had established peace on the Isthmus between its two seas. Bent on his destruction, Medea mixed in a cup a poison which she had brought long ago from the Scythian shores. This poison, they say, came from the mouth of the Echidnean dog. There is a cavern with a dark, yawning throat and a way down-sloping, along which Hercules, the hero of Tiryns, dragged Cerberus with chains wrought of adamant, while the great dog fought and turned away his eyes from the bright light of day. He, goaded on to mad frenzy, filled all the air with his threefold howls, and sprinkled the green fields with white foam. Men think that these flecks of foam grew; and,

[1] Alcyone.

has concresse putant nactasque alimenta feracis
fecundique soli vires cepisse nocendi;
quae quia nascuntur dura vivacia caute,
agrestes aconita vocant.   ea coniugis astu
ipse parens Aegeus nato porrexit ut hosti.   420
sumpserat ignara Theseus data pocula dextra,
cum pater in capulo gladii cognovit eburno
signa sui generis facinusque excussit ab ore.
effugit illa necem nebulis per carmina motis;

   At genitor, quamquam laetatur sospite nato,   425
attonitus tamen est, ingens discrimine parvo
committi potuisse nefas: fovet ignibus aras
muneribusque deos inplet, feriuntque secures
colla torosa boum vinctorum cornua vittis.
nullus Erecthidis fertur celebratior illo   430
inluxisse dies: agitant convivia patres
et medium vulgus nec non et carmina vino
ingenium faciente canunt: " te, maxime Theseu,
mirata est Marathon Cretaei sanguine tauri,
quodque suis securus arat Cromyona colonus,   435
munus opusque tuum est; tellus Epidauria per te
clavigeram vidit Vulcani occumbere prolem,
vidit et inmitem Cephisias ora Procrusten,
Cercyonis letum vidit Cerealis Eleusin.
occidit ille Sinis magnis male viribus usus,   440
qui poterat curvare trabes et agebat ab alto
ad terram late sparsuras corpora pinus.
tutus ad Alcathoen, Lelegeia moenia, limes
conposito Scirone patet, sparsisque latronis

drawing nourishment from the rich, rank soil, they
gained power to hurt; and because they spring up
and flourish on hard rocks, the country folk call
them aconite.[1] This poison, through the treachery
of his wife, father Aegeus himself presented to his
son as though to a stranger. Theseus had taken and
raised the cup in his unwitting hand, when the father
recognized the tokens of his own family on the ivory
hilt of the sword which Theseus wore, and he dashed
the vile thing from his lips. But Medea escaped
death in a dark whirlwind her witch songs raised.

But the father, though he rejoiced at his son's
deliverance, was still horror-struck that so monstrous
an iniquity could have been so nearly done. He
kindled fires upon the altars, made generous gifts
to the gods; his axes struck at the brawny necks of
bulls with ribbons about their horns. It is said that
no day ever dawned for the Athenians more glad
than that. The elders and the common folk made
merry together. Together they sang their songs,
with wit inspired by wine: " You, O most mighty
Theseus, Marathon extols for the blood of the Cretan
bull; and that the farmer of Cromyon may till his
fields without fear of the sow is your gift and your
deed. Through you the land of Epidaurus saw Vul-
can's club-wielding son [2] laid low; the banks of Cephi-
sus saw the merciless Procrustes slain; Eleusis, the
town of Ceres, beheld Cercyon's death. By your hand
fell that Sinis of great strength turned to evil uses,
who could bend the trunks of trees, and force down
to earth the pine-tops to shoot men's bodies far out
through the air. A way lies safe and open now to
Alcathoë and the Lelegeïan walls, now that Sciron is
no more. To this robber's scattered bones both land

[1] *i.e.* " growing without soil." [2] Periphetes.

373

terra negat sedem, sedem negat ossibus unda; 445
quae iactata diu fertur durasse vetustas
in scopulos: scopulis nomen Scironis inhaeret.
si titulos annosque tuos numerare velimus,
facta prement annos.   pro te, fortissime, vota
publica suscipimus, Bacchi tibi sumimus haustus." 450
consonat adsensu populi precibusque faventum
regia, nec tota tristis locus ullus in urbe est.
    Nec tamen (usque adeo nulla est sincera voluptas,
sollicitumque aliquid laetis intervenit) Aegeus
gaudia percepit nato secura recepto: 455
bella parat Minos; qui quamquam milite, quamquam
classe valet, patria tamen est firmissimus ira
Androgeique necem iustis ulciscitur armis.
ante tamen bello vires adquirit amicas,
quaque potens habitus volucri freta classe pererrat:
hinc Anaphen sibi iungit et Astypaleia regna, 461
(promissis Anaphen, regna Astypaleia bello);
hinc humilem Myconon cretosaque rura Cimoli
florentemque thymo Syron planamque Seriphon
marmoreamque Paron, quamque inpia prodidit Arne
Siphnon et accepto, quod avara poposcerat, auro 466
mutata est in avem, quae nunc quoque diligit aurum,
nigra pedes, nigris velata monedula pennis.
    At non Oliaros Didymeque et Tenos et Andros
et Gyaros nitidaeque ferax Peparethos olivae 470
Cnosiacas iuvere rates; latere inde sinistro
Oenopiam Minos petit, Aeacideia regna:
Oenopiam veteres adpellavere, sed ipse
Aeacus Aeginam genetricis nomine dixit.

374

and sea denied a resting-place; but, long tossed
about, it is said that in time they hardened into
cliffs; and the cliffs still bear the name of Sciron.
If we should wish to count your praises and your
years, your deeds would exceed your years. For
you, brave hero, we give public thanks and prayers,
to you we drain our cups of wine." The palace
resounds with the applause of the people and the
prayers of the happy revellers; nowhere in the whole
city is there any place for gloom.

And yet—so true it is that there is no pleasure
unalloyed, and some care always comes to mar our
joys—Aegeus' rejoicing over his son's return was not
unmixed with care. Minos was threatening war.
Strong in men and ships, he was yet most strong in
fatherly resentment and with just arms was seeking
to avenge the death of his son Androgeos. But first
he sought for friendly aid for his warfare; and he
scoured the sea in the swift fleet in which his chief
strength lay. He joined to his cause Anaphe and
Astypalaea, the first by promises, the second by
threats of war; the low-lying Myconus and the
chalky fields of Cimolus; Syros covered with wild
thyme, level Seriphos, Paros of the marble cliffs, and
Siphnos, which impious Arne betrayed, and having
received the gold which she in her greed had de-
manded, was changed into a bird which even now
delights in gold, a black-footed, black-winged
daw.

But Oliaros and Didyme, Tenos, Andros, Gyaros
and Peparethos, rich in glossy olives, gave no aid to
the Cretan fleet. Sailing thence to the left, Minos
sought Oenopia, the realm of the Aeacidae. Men of
old time had called the place Oenopia; but Aeacus
himself styled it Aegina by his mother's name. At

turba ruit tantaeque virum cognoscere famae   475
expetit; occurrunt illi Telamonque minorque
quam Telamon Peleus et proles tertia Phocus;
ipse quoque egreditur tardus gravitate senili
Aeacus et, quae sit veniendi causa, requirit.
admonitus patrii luctus suspirat et illi   480
dicta refert rector populorum talia centum:
" arma iuves oro pro gnato sumpta piaeque
pars sis militiae; tumulo solacia posco."
huic Asopiades " petis inrita " dixit " et urbi
non facienda meae; neque enim coniunctior ulla 485
Cecropidis est hac tellus: ea foedera nobis."
tristis abit "stabunt" que "tibi tua foedera magno"
dixit et utilius bellum putat esse minari
quam gerere atque suas ibi praeconsumere vires.
classis ab Oenopiis etiamnum Lyctia muris   490
spectari poterat, cum pleno concita velo
Attica puppis adest in portusque intrat amicos,
quae Cephalum patriaeque simul mandata ferebat.
Aeacidae longo iuvenes post tempore visum
agnovere tamen Cephalum dextrasque dedere   495
inque patris duxere domum: spectabilis heros
et veteris retinens etiamnum pignora formae
ingreditur ramumque tenens popularis olivae
a dextra laevaque duos aetate minores
maior habet, Clyton et Buten, Pallante creatos.   500
    Postquam congressus primi sua verba tulerunt,
Cecropidae Cephalus peragit mandata rogatque
auxilium foedusque refert et iura parentum,
imperiumque peti totius Achaidos addit.

his approach a rabble rushed forth, eager to see and
know so famous a man. Him Telamon met, and
Peleus, younger than Telamon, and Phocus, third in
age. Aeacus himself came also, slow with the weight
of years, and asked him what was the cause of his
coming. Reminded of his fatherly grief, the ruler
of a hundred cities sighed and thus made answer:
" I beg you aid the arms which for my son's sake I
have taken up; and be a part of my pious warfare.
Repose for the dead I ask." To him Aeacus replied:
" You ask in vain that which my city cannot give;
for no land is more closely linked to the Athenians
than this: so strong are the treaties between us."
The other, disappointed, turned away saying: "Your
treaty shall cost you dear "; for he thought it were
better to threaten war than to wage it and to waste
his strength there untimely. Still the Cretan fleet
could be seen from the Oenopian walls, when,
driven on under full sail, an Attic ship arrived and
entered the friendly port, bringing Cephalus and
his country's greetings. The men of the house of
Aeacus, though it was long since they had seen
Cephalus, yet knew him, grasped his hand, and
brought him into their father's house. The hero
advanced, the centre of all eyes, retaining even yet
the traces of his old beauty and charm, bearing a
branch of his country's olive, and, himself the elder,
flanked on right and left by two of lesser age, Clytos
and Butes, sons of Pallas.

After they had exchanged greetings, Cephalus
delivered the message of the Athenian king, asking
for aid and quoting the ancestral league and treaty
between their two nations. He added that not
alone Athens but the sovereignty over all Greece
was Minos' aim. When thus his eloquence had com-

sic ubi mandatam iuvit facundia causam,   505
Aeacus, in capulo sceptri nitente sinistra,
" ne petite auxilium, sed sumite " dixit, " Athenae,
nec dubie vires, quas haec habet insula, vestras
ducite, et (o maneat rerum status iste mearum!)
robora non desunt; superat mihi miles et hoc est,   510
gratia dis, felix et inexcusabile tempus."
" immo ita sit " Cephalus, " crescat tua civibus opto
urbs " ait; " adveniens equidem modo gaudia cepi,
cum tam pulchra mihi, tam par aetate iuventus
obvia processit; multos tamen inde requiro,   515
quos quondam vidi vestra prius urbe receptus."
Aeacus ingemuit tristique ita voce locutus:
" flebile principium melior fortuna secuta est;
hanc utinam possem vobis memorare sine illo!
ordine nunc repetam, neu longa ambage morer vos,
ossa cinisque iacent, memori quos mente requiris, 521
et quota pars illi rerum periere mearum!
dira lues ira populis Iunonis iniquae
incidit exosae dictas a paelice terras.
dum visum mortale malum tantaeque latebat   525
causa nocens cladis, pugnatum est arte medendi:
exitium superabat opem, quae victa iacebat.
principio caelum spissa caligine terras
pressit et ignavos inclusit nubibus aestus;
dumque quater iunctis explevit cornibus orbem 530
Luna, quater plenum tenuata retexuit orbem,
letiferis calidi spirarunt aestibus austri.
constat et in fontis vitium venisse lacusque,
miliaque incultos serpentum multa per agros
errasse atque suis fluvios temerasse venenis.   535

mended his cause, Aeacus, his left hand resting on the
sceptre's hilt, exclaimed : " Ask not our aid, but take
it, Athens; boldly count your own the forces which
this island holds, and (could only this state of my
fortunes continue!) strength is not lacking; I have
soldiers enough and, thanks to the gods, the present
moment is propitious and permits no excuse." " May
it prove even so," said Cephalus, " and may your
city multiply in men.   In truth, as I came hither, I
was rejoiced to meet youth so fair, so matched in age.
And yet I miss many among them whom I saw before
when last I visited your city."   Aeacus groaned and
with sad voice thus replied : " It was an unhappy be-
ginning, but better fortune followed.   Would that I
could tell you the last without the first!   Now I will
take each in turn; and, not to delay you with long
circumlocution, they are but bones and dust whom
with kindly interest you ask for.   And oh, how large
a part of all my kingdom perished with them!   A dire
pestilence came on my people through angry Juno's
wrath, who hated us for that our land was called by
her rival's name.   So long as the scourge seemed of
mortal origin and the cause of the terrible plague
was still unknown, we fought against it with the
physician's art.   But the power of destruction ex-
ceeded our resources, which were completely baffled.
At first heaven rested down upon the earth in thick
blackness, and held the sluggish heat confined in the
clouds.   And while the moon four times waxed to a
full orb with horns complete, and four times waned
from that full orb, hot south winds blew on us with
pestilential breath.   Consistently with this, the bale-
ful infection reached our springs and pools ; thousands
of serpents crawled over our deserted fields and defiled

strage canum primo volucrumque oviumque boumque
inque feris subiti deprensa potentia morbi.
concidere infelix validos miratur arator
inter opus tauros medioque recumbere sulco;
lanigeris gregibus balatus dantibus aegros   540
sponte sua lanaeque cadunt et corpora tabent;
acer equus quondam magnaeque in pulvere famae
degenerat palmas veterumque oblitus honorum
ad praesepe gemit leto moriturus inerti.
non aper irasci meminit, non fidere cursu   545
cerva nec armentis incurrere fortibus ursi.
omnia languor habet: silvisque agrisque viisque
corpora foeda iacent, vitiantur odoribus aurae.
mira loquar: non illa canes avidaeque volucres,
non cani tetigere lupi; dilapsa liquescunt   550
adflatuque nocent et agunt contagia late.

  " Pervenit ad miseros damno graviore colonos
pestis et in magnae dominatur moenibus urbis.
viscera torrentur primo, flammaeque latentis'
indicium rubor est et ductus anhelitus; igni   555
aspera lingua tumet, tepidisque arentia ventis
ora patent, auraeque graves captantur hiatu.
non stratum, non ulla pati velamina possunt,
nuda sed in terra ponunt praecordia, nec fit
corpus humo gelidum, sed humus de corpore fervet.
nec moderator adest, inque ipsos saeva medentes   561
erumpit clades, obsuntque auctoribus artes;
quo propior quisque est servitque fidelius aegro,
in partem leti citius venit, utque salutis

our rivers with their poison. At first the swift power
of the disease was confined to the destruction of dogs
and birds, sheep and cattle, or among the wild beasts.
The luckless plowman marvels to see his strong bulls
fall in the midst of their task and sink down in the
furrow. The woolly flocks bleat feebly while their
wool falls off of itself and their bodies pine away.
The horse, once of high courage and of great renown
on the race-course, has now lost his victorious spirit
and, forgetting his former glory, groans in his
stall, doomed to an inglorious death. The boar
forgets his rage, the hind to trust his fleetness, the
bears to attack the stronger herds. Lethargy holds
all. In woods and fields and roads foul carcasses
lie; and the air is defiled by the stench. And,
strange to say, neither dogs nor ravenous birds nor
grey wolves did touch them. The bodies lie rotting
on the ground, blast with their stench, and spread the
contagion far and near.

"At last, now grown stronger, the pestilence attacks
the wretched countrymen, and lords it within the great
city's walls. As the first symptoms, the vitals are burnt
up, and a sign of the lurking fire is a red flush and
panting, feverish breath. The tongue is rough and
swollen with fever; the lips stand apart, parched with
hot respiration, and catch gasping at the heavy air.
The stricken can endure no bed, no covering of any kind,
but throw themselves naked face down on the ground;
but their bodies gain no coolness from the ground;
rather is the ground heated by their bodies. No one
can control the pest, but it fiercely breaks out upon the
very physicians, and their arts do but injure those who
use them. The nearer one is to the sick and the more
faithfully he serves them, the more quickly is he him-
self stricken unto death. And as the hope of life

spes abiit finemque vident in funere morbi,   565
indulgent animis et nulla, quid utile, cura est:
utile enim nihil est.   passim positoque pudore
fontibus et fluviis puteisque capacibus haerent,
nec sitis est exstincta prius quam vita bibendo.
inde graves multi nequeunt consurgere et ipsis   570
inmoriuntur aquis, aliquis tamen haurit et illas;
tantaque sunt miseris invisi taedia lecti,
prosiliunt aut, si prohibent consistere vires,
corpora devolvunt in humum fugiuntque penates
quisque suos, sua cuique domus funesta videtur, 575
et quia causa latet, locus est in crimine; partim
semianimes errare viis, dum stare valebant,
adspiceres, flentes alios terraque iacentes
lassaque versantes supremo lumina motu;
membraque pendentis tendunt ad sidera caeli,   580
hic illic, ubi mors deprenderat, exhalantęs.
    " Quid mihi tunc animi fuit? an, quod debuit esse,
ut vitam odissem et cuperem pars esse meorum?
quo se cumque acies oculorum flexerat, illic
vulgus erat stratum, veluti cum putria motis   585
poma cadunt ramis agitataque ilice glandes.
templa vides contra gradibus sublimia longis:
Iuppiter illa tenet.   quis non altaribus illis
inrita tura dedit?   quotiens pro coniuge coniunx,
pro gnato genitor dum verba precantia dicit,   590
non exoratis animam finivit in aris,
inque manu turis pars inconsumpta reperta est!
admoti quotiens templis, dum vota sacerdos
concipit et fundit durum inter cornua vinum,

deserts them and they see the end of their malady
only in death, they indulge their desires, and they
have no care for what is best—for nothing is best.
Everywhere, shameless they lie, in fountain-basins, in
streams and roomy wells; nor by drinking is their
thirst quenched so long as life remains. Many of
these are too weak to rise, and die in the very water;
and yet others drink even that water. To many poor
wretches so great is the irksomeness of their hateful
beds that they jump out, or, if they have not strength
enough to stand, they roll out on the ground. They
flee from their own homes: for each man's home
seems a place of death to him. Since the cause of the
disease is hidden, the place itself is held to blame.
You might have seen some wandering half dead along
the ways while they could keep on their feet, others
lying on the ground and weeping bitterly, turning
their dull eyes upward with a last weak effort, and
stretching out their arms to the sky that hung over
them like a pall—here, there, wherever death has
caught them, breathing out their lives.

" What were my feelings then? Was it not natural
that I should hate life and long to be with my friends?
Wherever I turned my eyes there was a confused heap
of dead, as mellow apples fall when the boughs are
shaken, and acorns from the wind-tossed oak. You
see a temple yonder, raised on high, approached by a
long flight of steps. It is sacred to Jupiter. Who
did not bear his fruitless offerings to those altars?
How often a husband for his wife's sake, a father for
his son, while still uttering his prayer, has died before
the implacable altars, and in his hand a portion of
the incense was unused! How often the sacrificial
bulls brought to the temples, while yet the priest
was praying and pouring pure wine between their

haud exspectato ceciderunt vulnere tauri!   595
ipse ego sacra Iovi pro me patriaque tribusque
cum facerem natis, mugitus victima diros
edidit et subito conlapsa sine ictibus ullis
exiguo tinxit subiectos sanguine cultros.
exta quoque aegra notas veri monitusque deorum 600
perdiderant: tristes penetrant ad viscera morbi.
ante sacros vidi proiecta cadavera postes,
ante ipsas, quo mors foret invidiosior, aras.
pars animam laqueo claudunt mortisque timorem
morte fugant ultroque vocant venientia fata.   605
corpora missa neci nullis de more feruntur
funeribus (neque enim capiebant funera portae):
aut inhumata premunt terras aut dantur in altos
indotata rogos; et iam reverentia nulla est,
deque rogis pugnant alienisque ignibus ardent.   610
qui lacriment, desunt, indefletaeque vagantur
natorumque patrumque animae iuvenumque senum-
    que,
nec locus in tumulos, nec sufficit arbor in ignes.
    Attonitus tanto miserarum turbine rerum,
'Iuppiter o!' dixi, 'si te non falsa loquuntur   615
dicta sub amplexus Aeginae Asopidos isse,
nec te, magne pater, nostri pudet esse parentem,
aut mihi redde meos aut me quoque conde sepulcro!'
ille notam fulgore dedit tonitruque secundo.
'accipio sintque ista precor felicia mentis   620
signa tuae!' dixi, 'quod das mihi, pigneror omen.'
forte fuit iuxta patulis rarissima ramis
sacra Iovi quercus de semine Dodonaeo;

horns, have fallen without waiting for the stroke!
While I myself was sacrificing to Jove on my own
behalf and for my country and my three sons, the
victim uttered dreadful bellowings and, suddenly
falling without any stroke of mine, it barely stained
the knife with its scanty blood; the diseased entrails
also had lost the marks of truth and the warnings of
the gods: for to the very vitals does the grim pest go.
Before the temple doors I saw the corpses cast away,
nay, before the very altars, that their death might be
even more odious. Some hung themselves, driving
away the fear of death by death and going out to
meet their approaching fate. The dead bodies were
not borne out to burial in the accustomed way; for
the gates would not accommodate so many funerals.
They either lie on the ground unburied, or else they
are piled high on funeral pyres without honours. And
by this time there is no reverence for the dead; men
fight for pyres, and with stolen flames they burn.
There are none left to mourn the dead. Unwept
they go wandering out, the souls of children and of
parents, and of both young and old. There was no
more space for graves, nor wood for fires.

" Dazed by such an overwhelming flood of woe, I
cried to Jove: ' O Jove, if it is not falsely said that
thou didst love Aegina, daughter of Asopus, and if thou,
great father, art not ashamed to be our father, either
give me back my people or consign me also to the tomb.'
He gave a sign with lightning and a peal of thunder
in assent. ' I accept the sign,' I said, ' and may those
tokens of thy mind towards us be happy signs. The
omen which thou givest me I take as pledge.' It
chanced there was an oak near by with branches un-
usually widespread, sacred to Jove and of Dodona's
stock. Here we spied a swarm of grain-gathering

hic nos frugilegas adspeximus agmine longo
grande onus exiguo formicas ore gerentes   625
rugosoque suum servantes cortice callem;
dum numerum miror, ' totidem, pater optime,' dixi,
' tu mihi da cives et inania moenia supple! '
intremuit ramisque sonum sine flamine motis
alta dedit quercus: pavido mihi membra timore 630
horruerant, stabantque comae; tamen oscula terrae
roboribusque dedi, nec me sperare fatebar;
sperabam tamen atque animo mea vota fovebam.
nox subit, et curis exercita corpora somnus
occupat: ante oculos eadem mihi quercus adesse 635
et ramis totidem totidemque animalia ramis
ferre suis visa est pariterque tremescere motu
graniferumque agmen subiectis spargere in arvis;
crescere desubito et maius maiusque videri
ac se tollere humo rectoque adsistere trunco   640
et maciem numerumque pedum nigrumque colorem
ponere et humanam membris inducere formam.
somnus abit: damno vigilans mea visa querorque
in superis opis esse nihil; at in aedibus ingens 644
murmur erat, vocesque hominum exaudire videbar
iam mihi desuetas; dum suspicor has quoque somni
esse, venit Telamon properus foribusque reclusis
' speque fideque, pater ', dixit ' maiora videbis:
egredere! ' egredior, qualesque in imagine somni
visus eram vidisse viros, ex ordine tales   650
adspicio noscoque: adeunt regemque salutant.
vota Iovi solvo populisque recentibus urbem
partior et vacuos priscis cultoribus agros,

ants in a long column, bearing heavy loads with their tiny mouths, and keeping their own path along the wrinkled bark. Wondering at their numbers, I said: ' O most excellent father, grant thou me just as many subjects, and fill my empty walls.' The lofty oak trembled and moved its branches, rustling in the windless air. My limbs were horror-smit with quaking fear and my hair stood on end. Yet I kissed the earth and the oak-tree; nor did I own my hopes to myself, and yet I did hope and I cherished my desires within my mind. Night came and sleep claimed our care-worn bodies. Before my eyes the same oak-tree seemed to stand, with just as many branches and with just as many creatures on its branches, to shake with the same motion, and to scatter the grain-bearing column on the ground below. These seemed suddenly to grow larger and ever larger, to raise themselves from the ground and stand with form erect, to throw off their leanness, their many feet, their back colour, and to take on human limbs and a human form. Then sleep departed. Once awake I thought lightly of my vision, bewailing that there was no help in the gods. But there was a great confused noise in the palace, and I seemed to hear the voices of men to which I was long unused. And while I half believed that this also was a trick of sleep, Telamon came running and, throwing open the door, exclaimed: ' O father, more than you believed or hoped for shall you see. Come out! " I went without, and there just such men as I had seen in my dream I now saw and recognized with my waking eyes. They approached and greeted me as king. I gave thanks to Jove, and to my new subjects I portioned out my city and my fields, forsaken by their former occupants; and I called them

OVID

Myrmidonasque voco nec origine nomina fraudo.
corpora vidisti; mores, quos ante gerebant,   655
nunc quoque habent: parcum genus est patiensque
   laborum
quaesitique tenax et quod quaesita reservet.
hi te ad bella pares annis animisque sequentur,
cum primum qui te feliciter attulit eurus "
(eurus enim attulerat) "fuerit mutatus in austrum." 660
   Talibus atque aliis longum sermonibus illi
inplevere diem; lucis pars ultima mensae
est data, nox somnis. iubar aureus extulerat Sol,
flabat adhuc eurus redituraque vela tenebat:
ad Cephalum Pallante sati, cui grandior aetas,   665
ad regem Cephalus simul et Pallante creati
conveniunt, sed adhuc regem sopor altus habebat.
excipit Aeacides illos in limine Phocus;
nam Telamon fraterque viros ad bella legebant.
Phocus in interius spatium pulchrosque recessus 670
Cecropidas ducit, cum quis simul ipse resedit.
adspicit Aeoliden ignota ex arbore factum
ferre manu iaculum, cuius fuit aurea cuspis.
pauca prius mediis sermonibus ille locutus
" sum nemorum studiosus " ait " caedisque ferinae;
qua tamen e silva teneas hastile recisum,   676
iamdudum dubito: certe si fraxinus esset,
fulva colore foret; si cornus, nodus inesset.
unde sit, ignoro, sed non formosius isto
viderunt oculi telum iaculabile nostri."   680
excipit Actaeis e fratribus alter et " usum
388

Myrmidons,[1] nor did I cheat the name of its origin.
You have seen their bodies; the habits which they
had before they still keep, a thrifty race, inured to
toil, keen in pursuit of gain and keeping what they
get. These men will follow you to the wars well
matched in years and courage, as soon as the east
wind which brought you so fortunately hither "—for
the east wind it was that brought him—" shall have
changed to the south."

With such and other talk they filled the lingering
day. The last hours of the day were given to feasting,
the night to sleep. When the golden sun had shown
his light, the east wind was still blowing and kept
the sails from the homeward voyage. The sons of
Pallas came to Cephalus, who was the older, and
Cephalus with the sons of Pallas went together to
the king. But deep sleep still held the king. Phocus,
son of Aeacus, received them at the threshold; for
Telamon and his brother were marshalling the men
for war. Into the inner court and beautiful apart-
ments Phocus conducted the Athenians, and there
they sat them down together. There Phocus noticed
that Cephalus carried in his hand a javelin with a
golden head, and a shaft made of some strange wood.
After some talk, he said abruptly: "I am devoted to
the woods and the hunting of wild beasts. Still, I
have for some time been wondering from what wood
that weapon you hold is made. Surely if it were
of ash it would be of deep yellow hue; if it were of
cornel-wood there would be knots upon it. What
wood it is made of I cannot tell; but my eyes have
never seen a javelin for throwing more beautiful
than that." And one of the Athenian brothers
replied: "You will admire the weapon's use more

---

[1] Fancifully derived from μύρμηξ, an ant.

maiorem specie mirabere " dixit " in isto.
consequitur, quodcumque petit, fortunaque missum
non regit, et revolat nullo referente cruentum."
tum vero iuvenis Nereius omnia quaerit,   685
cur sit et unde datum, quis tanti muneris auctor.
quae petit, ille refert, sed enim narrare pudori est,
qua tulerit mercede; silet tactusque dolore
coniugis amissae lacrimis ita fatur obortis:
" hoc me, nate dea, (quis possit credere?) telum 690
flere facit facietque diu, si vivere nobis
fata diu dederint; hoc me cum coniuge cara
perdidit: hoc utinam caruissem munere semper!
  " Procris erat, si forte magis pervenit ad aures
Orithyia tuas, raptae soror Orithyiae,   695
si faciem moresque velis conferre duarum,
dignior ipsa rapi! pater hanc mihi iunxit Erectheus,
hanc mihi iunxit amor: felix dicebar eramque;
non ita dis visum est, aut nunc quoque forsitan essem.
alter agebatur post sacra iugalia mensis,   700
cum me cornigeris tendentem retia cervis
vertice de summo semper florentis Hymetti
lutea mane videt pulsis Aurora tenebris
invitumque rapit. liceat mihi vera referre
pace deae: quod sit roseo spectabilis ore,   705
quod teneat lucis, teneat confinia noctis,
nectareis quod alatur aquis, ego Procrin amabam;
pectore Procris erat, Procris mihi semper in ore.
sacra tori coitusque novos thalamosque recentes
primaque deserti referebam foedera lecti: 710

than its beauty; it goes straight to any mark, and chance does not guide its flight; and it flies back, all bloody, with no hand to bring it." Then indeed young Phocus was eager to know why it was so, and whence it came, who was the giver of so wonderful a gift. Cephalus told what the youth asked, but he was ashamed to tell at what price he gained it. He was silent; then, touched with grief for his lost wife, he burst into tears and said: " It is this weapon makes me weep, thou son of a goddess—who could believe it?—and long will it make me weep if the fates shall give me long life. This destroyed me and my dear wife together. And oh, that I had never had it! My wife was Procris, or, if by more likely chance the name of Orithyia has come to your ears, the sister of the ravished Orithyia. If you should compare the form and bearing of the two, Procris herself is the more worthy to be ravished away. It is she that her father, Erechtheus, joined to me; it is she that love joined to me. I was called happy, and happy I was. But the gods decreed it otherwise, or, perchance, I should be happy still. It was in the second month after our marriage rites. I was spreading my nets to catch the antlered deer, when from the top of ever-blooming Hymettus the golden goddess of the dawn, having put the shades to flight, beheld me and carried me away, against my will: may the goddess pardon me for telling the simple truth; but as truly as she shines with the blush of roses on her face, as truly as she holds the portals of the day and night, and drinks the juices of nectar, it was Procris I loved; Procris was in my heart, Procris was ever on my lips. I kept talking of my wedding and its fresh joys of love and the first union of my now deserted couch. The

mota dea est et ' siste tuas, ingrate, querellas;
Procrin habe!' dixit, 'quod si mea provida mens est,
non habuisse voles.'   meque illi irata remisit.
cum redeo mecumque deae memorata retracto,
esse metus coepit, ne iura iugalia coniunx   715
non bene servasset: facies aetasque iubebat
credere adulterium, prohibebant credere mores;
sed tamen afueram, sed et haec erat, unde redibam,
criminis exemplum, sed cuncta timemus amantes.
quaerere, quod doleam, statuo donisque pudicam   720
sollicitare fidem; favet huic Aurora timori
inmutatque meam (videor sensisse) figuram.
Palladias ineo non cognoscendus Athenas
ingrediorque domum; culpa domus ipsa carebat
castaque signa dabat dominoque erat anxia rapto:
vix aditus per mille dolos ad Erecthida factus.   726
ut vidi, obstipui meditataque paene reliqui
temptamenta fide; male me, quin vera faterer,
continui, male, quin, et oportuit, oscula ferrem.
tristis erat (sed nulla tamen formosior illa   730
esse potest tristi) desiderioque dolebat
coniugis abrepti: tu collige, qualis in illa,
Phoce, decor fuerit, quam sic dolor ipse decebat!
quid referam, quotiens temptamina nostra pudici
reppulerint mores, quotiens ' ego ' dixerit ' uni 735
servor; ubicumque est, uni mea gaudia servo.'
cui non ista fide satis experientia sano
magna foret? non sum contentus et in mea pugno

goddess was provoked and exclaimed: ' Cease your complaints, ungrateful boy; keep your Procris! but, if my mind can foresee at all, you will come to wish that you had never had her '; and in a rage she sent me back to her. As I was going home, and turned over in my mind the goddess' warning, I began to fear that my wife herself had not kept her marriage vows. Her beauty and her youth made me fear unfaithfulness; but her character forbade that fear. Still, I had been absent long, and she from whom I was returning was herself an example of unfaithfulness; and besides, we lovers fear every-thing. I decided to make a cause for grievance and to tempt her chaste faith by gifts. Aurora helped me in this jealous undertaking and changed my form; (I seemed to feel the change). And so, unrecognizable I entered Athens, Pallas' sacred city, and went into my house. The household itself was blameless, showed no sign of aught amiss, was only anxious for its lost lord. With much difficulty and by a thousand wiles I gained the presence of Erechtheus' daughter; and when I looked upon her my heart failed me and I almost abandoned the test of her fidelity which I had planned. I scarce kept from confessing the truth, from kissing her as was her due. She was sad; but no woman could be more beautiful than was she in her sadness. She was all grief with longing for the husband who had been torn away from her. Imagine, Phocus, how beautiful she was, how that grief itself became her. Why should I tell how often her chastity repelled my temptations? To every plea she said: ' I keep myself for one alone. Wherever he is I keep my love for one.' What husband in his senses would not have found that test of her fidelity enough. But I was not content and strove on to my own undoing

OVID

vulnera, dum census dare me pro nocte loquendo
muneraque augendo tandem dubitare coegi.   740
exclamo male victor: ' adest, mala, fictus adulter!
verus eram coniunx! me, perfida, teste teneris.'
illa nihil; tacito tantummodo victa pudore
insidiosa malo cum coniuge limina fugit;
offensaque mei genus omne perosa virorum   745
montibus errabat, studiis operata Dianae.
tum mihi deserto violentior ignis ad ossa
pervenit: orabam veniam et peccasse fatebar
et potuisse datis simili succumbere culpae
me quoque muneribus, si munera tanta darentur. 750
haec mihi confesso, laesum prius ulta pudorem,
redditur et dulces concorditer exigit annos;
dat mihi praeterea, tamquam se parva dedisset
dona, canem munus; quem cum sua traderet illi
Cynthia, ' currendo superabit ' dixerat ' omnes.' 755
dat simul et iaculum, manibus quod, cernis, habemus.
muneris alterius quae sit fortuna, requiris?
accipe mirandum: novitate movebere facti!

   " Carmina Laiades non intellecta priorum
solverat ingeniis, et praecipitata iacebat   760
inmemor ambagum vates obscura suarum:
protinus Aoniis inmittitur altera Thebis   763
[scilicet alma Themis nec talia linquit inulta!]   762
pestis, et exitio multi pecorumque suoque
rurigenae pavere feram; vicina iuventus   765
394

until by promising to give a fortune for her favour and by adding to my offer I finally forced her to hesitate. Then, victor to my sorrow, I exclaimed: 'False one, he that is here is a feigned adulterer! I was really your husband! By my own witness, traitress, you are detected!' She, not a word. Only in silence, overwhelmed with shame, she fled her treacherous husband and his house. In hate for me, loathing the whole race of men, she wandered over the mountains, devoted to Diana's pursuits. Then in my loneliness the fire of love burned more fiercely, penetrating to the marrow. I craved pardon, owned that I had sinned, confessed that I too might have yielded in the same way under the temptation of gifts, if so great gifts were offered to me. When I had made this confession and she had sufficiently avenged her outraged feelings, she came back to me and we spent sweet years together in harmony. She gave me beside, as though she had given but small gifts in herself, a wonderful hound which her own Cynthia had given, and said as she gave: 'He will surpass all other hounds in speed.' She gave me a javelin also, this one which, as you see, I hold in my hands. Would you know the story of both gifts? Hear the wonderful story: you will be moved by the strangeness of the deed.

" Oedipus, the son of Laïus, had solved the riddle which had been inscrutable to the understanding of all before; fallen headlong she lay, the dark prophet, forgetful of her own riddle. Straightway a second monster was sent against Aonian Thebes [and surely kind Themis does not let such things go unpunished!] and many country dwellers were in terror of the fierce creature, fearing both for their own and their flocks' destruction. We, the neighbouring youths,

venimus et latos indagine cinximus agros.
illa levi velox superabat retia saltu
summaque transibat postarum lina plagarum:
copula detrahitur canibus, quas illa sequentes
effugit et coetum non segnior alite ludit.   770
poscor et ipse meum consensu Laelapa magno
(muneris hoc nomen): iamdudum vincula pugnat
exuere ipse sibi colloque morantia tendit.
vix bene missus erat, nec iam poteramus, ubi esset,
scire; pedum calidus vestigia pulvis habebat,   775
ipse oculis ereptus erat: non ocior illo
hasta nec excussae contorto verbere glandes
nec Gortyniaco calamus levis exit ab arcu.
collis apex medii subiectis inminet arvis:
tollor eo capioque novi spectacula cursus,   780
quo modo deprendi, modo se subducere ab ipso
vulnere visa fera est; nec limite callida recto
in spatiumque fugit, sed decipit ora sequentis
et redit in gyrum, ne sit suus inpetus hosti:
inminet hic sequiturque parem similisque tenenti
non tenet et vanos exercet in aera morsus.   786
ad iaculi vertebar opem; quod dextera librat
dum mea, dum digitos amentis addere tempto,
lumina deflexi.   revocataque rursus eodem
rettuleram: medio (mirum) duo marmora campo
adspicio; fugere hoc, illud captare putares.   791
scilicet invictos ambo certamine cursus
esse deus voluit, si quis deus adfuit illis."

came and encircled the broad fields with our hunting-nets. But that swift beast leaped over the nets, over the very tops of the toils which we had spread. Then we let slip our hounds from the leash; but she escaped their pursuit and mocked the whole pack with speed like any bird. Then all the hunters called upon me for my Laelaps (that is the name of the hound my wife had given me). Long since he had been struggling to get loose from the leash and straining his neck against the strap that held him. Scarce was he well released when we could not tell where he was. The warm dust kept the imprint of his feet, he himself had quite disappeared from sight. No spear is swifter than he, nor leaden bullets thrown by a whirled sling, or the light reed shot from a Gortynian bow. There was a high hill near by, whose top overlooked the surrounding plain. Thither I climbed and gained a view of that strange chase, in which the beast seemed now to be caught and now to slip from the dog's very teeth. Nor does the cunning creature flee in a straight course off into the distance, but it eludes the pursuer's jaws and wheels sharply round, so that its enemy may lose his spring. The dog presses him hard, follows him step for step, and, while he seems to hold him, does not hold, and snaps at the empty air. I turned to my javelin's aid. As my right hand was balancing it, while I was fitting my fingers into the loop, I turned my eyes aside for a single moment; and when I turned them back again to the same spot—oh, wonderful! I saw two marble images in the plain; the one you would think was fleeing, the other catching at the prey. Doubtless some god must have willed, if there was any god with them, that both should be unconquered in their race." Thus far he spoke and fell silent.

hactenus, et tacuit; "iaculo quod crimen in ipso est?"
Phocus ait; iaculi sic crimina reddidit ille: 795
  " Gaudia principium nostri sunt, Phoce, doloris:
illa prius referam.   iuvat o meminisse beati
temporis, Aeacide, quo primos rite per annos
coniuge eram felix, felix erat illa marito.
mutua cura duos et amor socialis habebat,   800
nec Iovis illa meo thalamos praeferret amori,
nec me quae caperet, non si Venus ipsa veniret,
ulla erat; aequales urebant pectora flammae.
sole fere radiis feriente cacumina primis
venatum in silvas iuvenaliter ire solebam   805
nec mecum famuli nec equi nec naribus acres
ire canes nec lina sequi nodosa solebant:
tutus eram iaculo; sed cum satiata ferinae
dextera caedis erat, repetebam frigus et umbras
et quae de gelidis exibat vallibus aura: 810
aura petebatur medio mihi lenis in aestu,
auram exspectabam, requies erat illa labori.
' aura ' (recordor enim), ' venias ' cantare solebam,
' meque iuves intresque sinus, gratissima, nostros,
utque facis, relevare velis, quibus urimur, aestus! '
forsitan addiderim (sic me mea fata trahebant),   816
blanditias plures et ' tu mihi magna voluptas '
dicere sim solitus, ' tu me reficisque fovesque,
tu facis, ut silvas, ut amem loca sola: meoque
spiritus iste tuus semper captatur ab ore.'   820
vocibus ambiguis deceptam praebuit aurem
nescio quis nomenque aurae tam saepe vocatum

" But what charge have you to bring against the javelin itself? " asked Phocus. The other thus told what charge he had against the javelin:

" My joys, Phocus, were the beginning of my woe. These I will describe first. Oh, what a joy it is, son of Aeacus, to remember the blessed time when during those first years I was happy in my wife, as I should be, and she was happy in her husband. Mutual cares and mutual love bound us together. Not Jove's love would she have preferred to mine; nor was there any woman who could lure me away from her, no, not if Venus herself should come. An equal passion burned in both our two hearts. In the early morning, when the sun's first rays touched the tops of the hills, with a young man's eagerness I used to go hunting in the woods. Nor did I take attendants with me, or horses or keen-scented dogs or knotted nets. I was safe with my javelin. But when my hand had had its fill of slaughter of wild creatures, I would come back to the cool shade and the breeze that came forth from the cool valleys. I wooed the breeze, blowing gently on me in my heat; the breeze I waited for. She was my labour's rest. ' Come, Aura,' I remember I used to cry, ' come soothe me; come into my breast, most welcome one, and, as indeed you do, relieve the heat with which I burn.' Perhaps I would add, for so my fates drew me on, more endearments, and say: ' Thou art my greatest joy; thou dost refresh and comfort me; thou makest me to love the woods and solitary places. It is ever my joy to feel thy breath upon my face.' Some one overhearing these words was deceived by their double meaning; and, thinking that the word ' Aura ' so often on my lips was a nymph's name, was convinced that I was in love with

esse putat nymphae: nympham mihi credit amari.
criminis extemplo ficti temerarius index
Procrin adit linguaque refert audita susurra.   825
credula res amor est: subito conlapsa dolore,
ut mihi narratur, cecidit; longoque refecta
tempore se miseram, se fati dixit iniqui
deque fide questa est et crimine concita vano,
quod nihil est, metuit, metuit sine corpore nomen   830
et dolet infelix veluti de paelice vera.
saepe tamen dubitat speratque miserrima falli
indiciique fidem negat et, nisi viderit ipsa,
damnatura sui non est delicta mariti.
postera depulerant Aurorae lumina noctem: 835
egredior silvamque peto victorque per herbas
' aura, veni ' dixi ' nostroque medere labori! '
et subito gemitus inter mea verba videbar
nescio quos audisse; ' veni' tamen 'optima!' dicens
fronde levem rursus strepitum faciente caduca   840
sum ratus esse feram telumque volatile misi:
Procris erat medioque tenens in pectore vulnus
' ei mihi ' conclamat! vox est ubi cognita fidae
coniugis, ad vocem praeceps amensque cucurri.   844
semianimem et sparsas foedantem sanguine vestes
et sua (me miserum!) de vulnere dona trahentem
invenio corpusque meo mihi carius ulnis
mollibus attollo scissaque a pectore veste
vulnera saeva ligo conorque inhibere cruorem
neu me morte sua sceleratum deserat, oro.   850

400

some nymph.   Straightway the rash tell-tale went
to Procris with the story of my supposed unfaithful-
ness and reported in whispers what he had heard.
A credulous thing is love.   Smitten with sudden
pain (as I heard the story), she fell down in a swoon.
Reviving at last, she called herself wretched, victim
of cruel fate; complained of my unfaithfulness,
and, excited by an empty charge, she feared a
mere nothing, feared an empty name and grieved,
poor girl, as over a real rival.   And yet she would
often doubt and hope in her depth of misery that
she was mistaken; she rejected as untrue the story
she had heard, and, unless she saw it with her own
eyes, would not think her husband guilty of such
sin.   The next morning, when the early dawn had
banished night, I left the house and sought the
woods; there, successful, as I lay on the grass, I
cried: ' Come, Aura, come and soothe my toil '—
and suddenly, while I was speaking, I thought I
heard a groan.   Yet ' Come, dearest,' I cried again,
and as the fallen leaves made a slight rustling sound,
I thought it was some beast and hurled my javelin
at the place.   It was Procris, and, clutching at the
wound in her breast, she cried, ' Oh, woe is me.'
When I recognized the voice of my faithful wife,
I rushed headlong towards the sound, beside myself
with horror.   There I found her dying, her dis-
ordered garments stained with blood, and oh, the pity!
trying to draw the very weapon she had given me
from her wounded breast.   With loving arms I raised
her body, dearer to me than my own, tore open the
garment from her breast and bound up the cruel
wound, and tried to staunch the blood, praying
that she would not leave me stained with her
death.   She, though strength failed her, with a

viribus illa carens et iam moribunda coegit
haec se pauca loqui : ' per nostri foedera lecti
perque deos supplex oro superosque meosque,
per si quid merui de te bene perque manentem
nunc quoque, cum pereo, causam mihi mortis amorem,
ne thalamis Auram patiare innubere nostris !'   856
dixit, et errorem tum denique nominis esse
et sensi et docui.   sed quid docuisse iuvabat ?
labitur, et parvae fugiunt cum sanguine vires,
dumque aliquid spectare potest, me spectat et in me
infelicem animam nostroque exhalat in ore ;   861
sed vultu meliore mori secura videtur."

    Flentibus haec lacrimans heros memorabat, et ecce
Aeacus ingreditur duplici cum prole novoque
milite ; quem Cephalus cum fortibus accipit armis. 865

dying effort forced herself to say these few words:
' By the union of our love, by the gods above and
my own gods, by all that I have done for you, and by
the love that still I bear you in my dying hour, the
cause of my own death, I beg you, do not let this
Aura take my place.' And then I knew at last that
it was a mistake in the name, and I told her the
truth. But what availed then the telling? She fell
back in my arms and her last faint strength fled with
her blood. So long as she could look at anything
she looked at me and breathed out her unhappy
spirit on my lips. But she seemed to die content
and with a happy look upon her face."

This story the hero told with many tears. And
now Aeacus came in with his two sons and his new
levied band of soldiers, which Cephalus received with
their valiant arms.

BOOK VIII

1–151	*Scylla and Nisus*
152–182	*The Minotaur, Ariadne*
183–235	*Daedalus and Icarus*
236–259	*Perdix*
260–546	*Meleager and the Calydonian Boar*
547–610	*Achelous and Perimele*
611–724	*Philemon and Baucis*
725–884	*Erysichthon*

LIBER VIII

Iᴀᴍ nitidum retegente diem noctisque fugante
tempora Lucifero cadit Eurus, et umida surgunt
nubila: dant placidi cursum redeuntibus Austri
Aeacidis Cephaloque; quibus feliciter acti
ante exspectatum portus tenuere petitos.   5
interea Minos Lelegeia litora vastat
praetemptatque sui vires Mavortis in urbe
Alcathoi, quam Nisus habet, cui splendidus ostro
inter honoratos medioque in vertice canos
crinis inhaerebat, magni fiducia regni.   10
    Sexta resurgebant orientis cornua lunae,
et pendebat adhuc belli fortuna, diuque
inter utrumque volat dubiis Victoria pennis.
regia turris erat vocalibus addita muris,
in quibus auratam proles Letoia fertur   15
deposuisse lyram: saxo sonus eius inhaesit.
saepe illuc solita est ascendere filia Nisi
et petere exiguo resonantia saxa lapillo,
tum cum pax esset; bello quoque saepe solebat
spectare ex illa rigidi certamina Martis,   20
iamque mora belli procerum quoque nomina norat
armaque equosque habitusque Cydoneasque
        pharetras;

BOOK VIII

Now when Lucifer had banished night and ushered
in the shining day, the east wind fell and moist
clouds arose. The peaceful south wind offered a
safe return to Cephalus and the mustered troops of
Aeacus, and, speeding their voyage, brought them,
sooner than they had hoped, to their desired haven.
Meanwhile King Minos was laying waste the coast
of Megara, and was trying his martial strength
against the city of Alcathoüs,[1] where Nisus reigned.
This Nisus had growing on his head, amidst his locks
of honoured grey, a brilliant purple lock on whose
preservation rested the safety of his throne.

Six times had the new moon shown her horns,
and still the fate of war hung in the balance; so long
did Victory hover on doubtful wings between the
two. There was a royal tower reared on the tuneful
walls where Latona's son was said to have laid down
his golden lyre, whose music still lingered in the
stones. Often to this tower the daughter of King
Nisus used to climb and set the rocks resounding
with a pebble, in the day when peace was. Also
after the war began she would often look out from
this place upon the rough martial combats. And
now, as the war dragged on, she had come to know
even the names of the warring chieftains, their arms,
their horses, their dress, their Cretan quivers. And

---

[1] i.e. Megara.

OVID

noverat ante alios faciem ducis Europaei,
plus etiam, quam nosse sat est: hac iudice Minos,
seu caput abdiderat cristata casside pennis,   25
in galea formosus erat; seu sumpserat aere
fulgentem clipeum, clipeum sumpsisse decebat;
torserat adductis hastilia lenta lacertis:
laudabat virgo iunctam cum viribus artem;
inposito calamo patulos sinuaverat arcus: 30
sic Phoebum sumptis iurabat stare sagittis;
cum vero faciem dempto nudaverat aere
purpureusque albi stratis insignia pictis
terga premebat equi spumantiaque ora regebat,
vix sua, vix sanae virgo Niseia compos   35
mentis erat: felix iaculum, quod tangeret ille,
quaeque manu premeret, felicia frena vocabat.
impetus est illi, liceat modo, ferre per agmen
virgineos hostile gradus, est impetus illi
turribus e summis in Cnosia mittere corpus   40
castra vel aeratas hosti recludere portas,
vel siquid Minos aliud velit.   utque sedebat
candida Dictaei spectans tentoria regis,   .
" laeter," ait " doleamne geri lacrimabile bellum,
in dubio est; doleo, quod Minos hostis amanti est. 45
sed nisi bella forent, numquam mihi cognitus esset!
me tamen accepta poterat deponere bellum
obside: me comitem, me pacis pignus haberet.
si quae te peperit, talis, pulcherrime regum,
qualis es ipse, fuit, merito deus arsit in illa.   50
o ego ter felix, si pennis lapsa per auras
Cnosiaci possem castris insistere regis
fassaque me flammasque meas, qua dote, rogarem,

408

above all others did she know the face of their
leader, Europa's son, yes, better than she should.
If he had hidden his head in a crested casque, Minos
in a helmet was lovely to her eyes: or if he carried his
shining golden shield, the shield became him well.
Did he hurl his tough spear with tense muscles, the
girl admired the strength and the skill he showed.
Did he bend the wide-curving bow with arrow fitted
to the string, thus she would swear that Phoebus
stood with arrows in his hand. But when unhelmed
he showed his face, when clad in purple he bestrode
his milk-white steed gorgeous with broidered trap-
pings, and managed the foaming bit, then was Nisus'
daughter hardly her own, hardly mistress of a sane
mind. Happy the javelin which he touched and
happy the reins which he held in his hand, she
thought. She longed, were it but allowed, to speed
her maiden steps through the foemen's line; she
longed to leap down from her lofty tower into the
Cretan camp, to open the city's bronze-bound gates to
the enemy, to do any other thing which Minos might
desire. And, as she sat gazing at the white tents of
the Cretan king, she said: "Whether I should rejoice
or grieve at this woeful war, I cannot tell. I grieve
because Minos is the foe of her who loves him; but
if there were no war, he would never have been
known to me. Suppose he had me as a hostage, then
he could give up the war; I should be in his com-
pany, should be a pledge of peace. If she who bore
you, O loveliest of sovereigns, was such as you are,
good reason was it that the god burned for her. Oh,
thrice happy should I be, if only I might fly through
the air and stand within the camp of the Cretan king,
and confess my love, and ask what dower he would
wish to be paid for me. Only let him not ask my

vellet emi, tantum patrias ne posceret arces!
nam pereant potius sperata cubilia, quam sim   55
proditione potens!—quamvis saepe utile vinci
victoris placidi fecit clementia multis.
iusta gerit certe pro nato bella perempto:
et causaque valet causamque tuentibus armis.
at, puto, vincemur; qui si manet exitus urbem,   60
cur suus haec illi reseret mea moenia Mavors
et non noster amor?   melius sine caede moraque
inpensaque sui poterit superare cruoris.
non metuam certe, ne quis tua pectora, Minos,
vulneret inprudens: quis enim tam durus, ut in te   65
derigere inmitem non inscius audeat hastam?
coepta placent, et stat sententia tradere mecum
dotalem patriam finemque inponere bello;
verum velle parum est!   aditus custodia servat,
claustraque portarum genitor tenet: hunc ego solum
infelix timeo, solus mea vota moratur.   71
di facerent, sine patre forem!   sibi quisque profecto
est deus: ignavis precibus Fortuna repugnat.
altera iamdudum succensa cupidine tanto
perdere gauderet, quodcumque obstaret amori.   75
et cur ulla foret me fortior?   ire per ignes
et gladios ausim; nec in hoc tamen ignibus ullis
aut gladiis opus est, opus est mihi crine paterno.
illa mihi est auro pretiosior, illa beatam
purpura me votique mei factura potentem.''   80
    Talia dicenti curarum maxima nutrix
nox intervenit, tenebrisque audacia crevit.
prima quies aderat, qua curis fessa diurnis

country's citadel. For may all my hopes of wedlock perish ere I gain it by treachery. And yet oft-times many have found it good to be overcome, when an appeased victor has been merciful. Surely he wages a just war for his murdered son; and he is strong both in his cause and in the arms that defend his cause. No doubt we shall be conquered. And if that doom awaits our city, why shall his warrior hand unbar these walls of ours, and not my love? Far better will it be without massacre and suspense and the cost of his own blood for him to conquer. In that case truly I should not fear lest someone should pierce your breast unwittingly, dear Minos; for, if not unwitting, who so cruel that he could bring himself to throw his pitiless spear at you? I like the plan, and I am resolved to give myself up with my country as my dowry, and so to end the war. But merely to will is not enough. A watch guards the entry; my father holds the keys of the city gates. Him only do I fear, unhappy! Only he delays the wish of my heart. Would to God I had no father! But surely everyone is his own god; Fortune resists half-hearted prayers. Another girl in my place, fired with so great a love, would long since have destroyed, and that with joy, whatever stood in the way of her love. And why should another be braver than I? Through fire and sword would I dare go. And yet here there is no need of fire or sword. I need but my father's lock of hair. That is to me more precious than gold; that purple lock will make me blest, will give me my heart's desire."

While she thus spoke night came on, most potent healer of our cares; and with the darkness her boldness grew. The first rest had come, when sleep

pectora somnus habet: thalamos taciturna paternos
intrat et (heu facinus!) fatali nata parentem   85
crine suum spoliat praedaque potita nefanda
per medios hostes (meriti fiducia tanta est)   88
pervenit ad regem; quem sic adfata paventem est:
" suasit amor facinus: proles ego regia Nisi   90
Scylla tibi trado patriaeque meosque penates;
praemia nulla peto nisi te: cape pignus amoris
purpureum crinem nec me nunc tradere crinem,
sed patrium tibi crede caput! " scelerataque dextra
munera porrexit; Minos porrecta refugit   95
turbatusque novi respondit imagine facti:
" di te summoveant, o nostri infamia saecli,
orbe suo, tellusque tibi pontusque negetur!
certe ego non patiar Iovis incunabula, Creten,
qui meus est orbis, tantum contingere monstrum."100
   Dixit, et ut leges captis iustissimus auctor
hostibus inposuit, classis retinacula solvi
iussit et aeratas impelli remige puppes.
Scylla freto postquam deductas nare carinas
nec praestare ducem sceleris sibi praemia vidit,   105
consumptis precibus violentam transit in iram
intendensque manus passis furibunda capillis
" quo fugis " exclamat " meritorum auctore relicta,
o patriae praelate meae, praelate parenti?
quo fugis, inmitis, cuius victoria nostrum   110
et scelus et meritum est? nec te data munera, nec te
noster amor movit, nec quod spes omnis in unum

holds the heart weary with the cares of day: the daughter steals silently into her father's chamber, and—oh, the horrid crime!—she despoils him of the fateful lock of hair. With this cursed prize, through the midst of her foes, so sure is she of a welcome for her deed, she goes straight to the king; and thus she addresses him, startled at her presence: "Love has led me to this deed. I, Scylla, daughter of King Nisus, do here deliver to your hands my country and my house. I ask no reward save only you. Take as the pledge of my love this purple lock, and know that I am giving to you not a lock, but my father's life." And in her sin-stained hand she held out the prize to him. Minos recoiled from the proffered gift, and, in horror at the sight of so unnatural an act, he replied: "May the gods banish you from their world, O foul disgrace of our age! May both land and sea be denied to you! Be sure that I shall not permit so vile a monster to set foot on Crete, my world, the cradle of Jove's infancy."

He spoke; and when this most upright lawgiver had imposed laws upon his conquered foes, he bade loose the hawsers of the fleet, and the rowers to speed the bronze-bound ships. When Scylla saw that the ships were launched and afloat, and that the king refused her the reward of her sin, having prayed until she could pray no more, she became violently enraged, and stretching out her hands, with streaming hair and mad with passion, she exclaimed: "Whither do you flee, abandoning the giver of your success, O you whom I put before my fatherland, before my father? Whither do you flee, you cruel man, whose victory is my sin, 'tis true, but is my merit also? Does not the gift I gave move you, do not my love and

te mea congesta est? nam quo deserta revertar?
in patriam? superata iacet! sed finge manere:
proditione mea clausa est mihi! patris ad ora?   115
quem tibi donavi? cives odere merentem,
finitimi exemplum metuunt: exponimur orbae
terrarum, nobis ut Crete sola pateret.
hac quoque si prohibes et nos, ingrate, relinquis,
non genetrix Europa tibi est, sed inhospita Syrtis,   120
Armeniae tigres austroque agitata Charybdis.
Nec Iove tu natus, nec mater imagine tauri
ducta tua est: generis falsa est ea fabula! verus,
[et ferus et captus nullius amore iuvencae]
qui te progenuit, taurus fuit. exige poenas,   125
Nise pater! gaudete malis, modo prodita, nostris,
moenia! nam, fateor, merui et sum digna perire.
sed tamen ex illis aliquis, quos impia laesi,
me perimat! cur, qui vicisti crimine nostro,
insequeris crimen? scelus hoc patriaeque patrique est,
officium tibi sit! te vere coniuge digna est,   131
quae torvum ligno decepit adultera taurum
discordemque utero fetum tulit. ecquid ad aures
perveniunt mea dicta tuas, an inania venti
verba ferunt idemque tuas, ingrate, carinas?   135
iam iam Pasiphaen non est mirabile taurum
praeposuisse tibi: tu plus feritatis habebas.
me miseram! properare iubet! divulsaque remis
unda sonat, mecumque simul mea terra recedit.

all my hopes built on you alone? Deserted, whither shall I go? Back to my fatherland? It lies overthrown. But suppose it still remained: it is closed to me by my treachery. To my father's presence? him whom I betrayed to you? My countrymen hate me, and with just cause; the neighbouring peoples fear my example. I am banished from all the world, that Crete alone might be open to me. And if you forbid me Crete as well, and, O ungrateful, leave me here, Europa is not your mother, but the inhospitable Syrtis, the Armenian tigress and storm-tossed Charybdis. You are no son of Jove, nor was your mother tricked by the false semblance of a bull. That story of your birth is a lie: it was a real bull that begot you [a fierce, wild thing that loved no heifer]. Inflict my punishment, O Nisus, my father! Rejoice in my woes, O ye walls that I have but now betrayed! For I confess I have merited your hate and I deserve to die. But let some one of those whom I have foully injured slay me. Why should you, who have triumphed through my sin, punish my sin? Let this act which was a crime against my country and my father be but a service in your eyes. She is a true mate [1] for you who with unnatural passion deceived the savage bull by that shape of wood and bore a hybrid offspring in her womb. Does my voice reach your ears? Or do the same winds blow away my words to emptiness that fill your sails, you ingrate? Now, now I do not wonder that Pasiphaë preferred the bull to you, for you were a more savage beast than he. Alas for me! He orders his men to haste away! and the waves resound as the oars dash into them, and I and my land are both fading from his sight. But it

---

[1] Pasiphaë, the wife of Minos and mother of the Minotaur.

nil agis, o frustra meritorum oblite meorum :   140
insequar invitum puppimque amplexa recurvam
per freta longa trahar." Vix dixerat, insilit undis
consequiturque rates faciente cupidine vires
Cnosiacaeque haeret comes invidiosa carinae.
quam pater ut vidit (nam iam pendebat in aura   145
et modo factus erat fulvis haliaeetus alis),
ibat, ut haerentem rostro laceraret adunco ;
illa metu puppim dimisit, et aura cadentem
sustinuisse levis, ne tangeret aequora, visa est.
pluma subit palmis : in avem mutata vocatur   150
Ciris et a tonso est hoc nomen adepta capillo.

    Vota Iovi Minos taurorum corpora centum
solvit, ut egressus ratibus Curetida terram
contigit, et spoliis decorata est regia fixis.
creverat obprobrium generis, foedumque patebat 155
matris adulterium monstri novitate biformis ;
destinat hunc Minos thalamo removere pudorem
multiplicique domo caecisque includere tectis.
Daedalus ingenio fabrae celeberrimus artis
ponit opus turbatque notas et lumina flexum   160
ducit in errorem variarum ambage viarum.
non secus ac liquidus Phrygiis Maeandros in arvis
ludit et ambiguo lapsu refluitque fluitque
occurrensque sibi venturas aspicit undas
et nunc ad fontes, nunc ad mare versus apertum 165
incertas exercet aquas : ita Daedalus implet

is in vain; you have forgotten my deserts in vain; I shall follow you against your will, and clinging to the curving stern, I shall be drawn over the long reaches of the sea." Scarce had she spoken when she leaped into the water, swam after the ship, her passion giving strength, and clung, hateful and unwelcome, to the Cretan boat. When her father saw her—for he was hovering in the air, having but now been changed into an osprey with tawny wings—he came on that he might tear her, as she clung there, with his hooked beak. In terror she let go her hold upon the boat, and as she fell the light air seemed to hold her up and keep her from touching the water. Her hands sprout feathers: changed to a bird, she is called Ciris, and takes this name from the shorn lock of hair.[1]

Minos duly paid his vows to Jove, a hundred bulls, when he disembarked upon the Cretan strand; and he hung up his spoils of war to adorn his palace. But now his family's disgrace had grown big, and the queen's foul adultery was revealed to all by her strange hybrid monster-child. Minos planned to remove this shame from his house and to hide it away in a labyrinthine enclosure with blind passages. Daedalus, a man famous for his skill in the builder's art, planned and performed the work. He confused the usual passages and deceived the eye by a conflicting maze of divers winding paths. Just as the watery Maeander plays in the Phrygian fields, flows back and forth in doubtful course and, turning back on itself, beholds its own waves coming on their way, and sends its uncertain waters now towards their source and now towards the open sea: so Daedalus made those innumerable winding passages, and was

[1] Cīris, as if from κείρω, "I cut."

innumeras errore vias vixque ipse reverti
ad limen potuit: tanta est fallacia tecti.
   Quo postquam geminam tauri iuvenisque figuram
clausit, et Actaeo bis pastum sanguine monstrum 170
tertia sors annis domuit repetita novenis,
utque ope virginea nullis iterata priorum
ianua difficilis filo est inventa relecto,
protinus Aegides rapta Minoide Diam
vela dedit comitemque suam crudelis in illo   175
litore destituit; desertae et multa querenti
amplexus et opem Liber tulit, utque perenni
sidere clara foret, sumptam de fronte coronam
inmisit caelo: tenues volat illa per auras
dumque volat, gemmae nitidos vertuntur in ignes 180
consistuntque loco specie remanente coronae,
qui medius Nixique genu est Anguemque tenentis.
   Daedalus interea Creten longumque perosus
exilium tactusque loci natalis amore
clausus erat pelago.   " terras licet " inquit " et undas
obstruat: et caelum certe patet; ibimus illac: 186
omnia possideat, non possidet aera Minos."
dixit et ignotas animum dimittit in artes
naturamque novat.   nam ponit in ordine pennas
a minima coeptas, longam breviore sequenti,   190
ut clivo crevisse putes: sic rustica quondam
fistula disparibus paulatim surgit avenis;
tum lino medias et ceris alligat imas
atque ita conpositas parvo curvamine flectit,
418

himself scarce able to find his way back to the place of entry, so deceptive was the enclosure he had built.

In this labyrinth Minos shut up the monster of the bull-man form and twice he fed him on Athenian blood; but the third tribute, demanded after each nine years, brought the creature's overthrow. And when, by the virgin Ariadne's help, the difficult entrance, which no former adventurer had ever reached again, was found by winding up the thread, straightway the son of Aegeus, taking Minos' daughter, spread his sails for Dia; and on that shore he cruelly abandoned his companion. To her, deserted and bewailing bitterly, Bacchus brought love and help. And, that she might shine among the deathless stars, he sent the crown she wore up to the skies. Through the thin air it flew; and as it flew its gems were changed to gleaming fires and, still keeping the appearance of a crown, it took its place between the Kneeler[1] and the Serpent-holder.[2]

Meanwhile Daedalus, hating Crete and his long exile, and longing to see his native land, was shut in by the sea. " Though he may block escape by land and water," he said, " yet the sky is open, and by that way will I go. Though Minos rules over all, he does not rule the air." So saying, he sets his mind at work upon unknown arts, and changes the laws of nature. For he lays feathers in order, beginning at the smallest, short next to long, so that you would think they had grown upon a slope. Just so the old-fashioned rustic pan-pipes with their unequal reeds rise one above another. Then he fastened the feathers together with twine and wax at the middle and bottom; and, thus arranged, he bent them with a gentle curve, so that they looked like

---

[1] The constellation of Hercules.   [2] Ophiuchus.

ut veras imitetur aves.　puer Icarus una　　　195
stabat et, ignarus sua se tractare pericla,
ore renidenti modo, quas vaga moverat aura,
captabat plumas, flavam modo pollice ceram
mollibat lusuque suo mirabile patris
impediebat opus.　postquam manus ultima coepto 200
inposita est, geminas opifex libravit in alas
ipse suum corpus motaque pependit in aura;
instruit et natum " medio "que " ut limite curras,
Icare," ait " moneo, ne, si demissior ibis,
unda gravet pennas, si celsior, ignis adurat:　　205
inter utrumque vola.　nec te spectare Booten
aut Helicen iubeo strictumque Orionis ensem:
me duce carpe viam! " pariter praecepta volandi
tradit et ignotas umeris accommodat alas.
inter opus monitusque genae maduere seniles,　210
et patriae tremuere manus; dedit oscula nato
non iterum repetenda suo pennisque levatus
ante volat comitique timet, velut ales, ab alto
quae teneram prolem produxit in aera nido,
hortaturque sequi damnosasque erudit artes　　215
et movet ipse suas et nati respicit alas.
hos aliquis tremula dum captat harundine pisces,
aut pastor baculo stivave innixus arator
vidit et obstipuit, quique aethera carpere possent,
credidit esse deos.　et iam Iunonia laeva　　220
parte Samos (fuerant Delosque Parosque relictae)
dextra Lebinthos erat fecundaque melle Calymne,
cum puer audaci coepit gaudere volatu

real birds' wings. His son, Icarus, was standing by
and, little knowing that he was handling his own
peril, with gleeful face would now catch at the
feathers which some passing breeze had blown about,
now mould the yellow wax with his thumb, and by his
sport would hinder his father's wondrous task. When
now the finishing touches had been put upon the
work, the master workman himself balanced his body
on two wings and hung poised on the beaten air. He
taught his son also and said: " I warn you, Icarus,
to fly in a middle course, lest, if you go too low, the
water may weight your wings; if you go too high,
the fire may burn them. Fly between the two.
And I bid you not to shape your course by Boötes or
Helice or the drawn sword of Orion, but fly where
I shall lead." At the same time he tells him the
rules of flight and fits the strange wings on his boy's
shoulders. While he works and talks the old man's
cheeks are wet with tears, and his fatherly hands
tremble. He kissed his son, which he was destined
never again to do, and rising on his wings, he flew on
ahead, fearing for his companion, just like a bird which
has led forth her fledglings from the high nest into the
unsubstantial air. He encourages the boy to follow,
instructs him in the fatal art of flight, himself flap-
ping his wings and looking back on his son. Now
some fisherman spies them, angling for fish with his
flexible rod, or a shepherd, leaning upon his crook,
or a plowman, on his plow-handles—spies them
and stands stupefied, and believes them to be
gods that they could fly through the air. And now
Juno's sacred Samos had been passed on the left, and
Delos and Paros; Lebinthos was on the right and
Calymne, rich in honey, when the boy began to
rejoice in his bold flight and, deserting his leader,

deseruitque ducem caelique cupidine tractus
altius egit iter. rapidi vicinia solis   225
mollit odoratas, pennarum vincula, ceras;
tabuerant cerae: nudos quatit ille lacertos,
remigioque carens non ullas percipit auras,
oraque caerulea patrium clamantia nomen
excipiuntur aqua, quae nomen traxit ab illo.   230
at pater infelix, nec iam pater, " Icare," dixit,
" Icare," dixit " ubi es? qua te regione requiram? "
" Icare " dicebat: pennas aspexit in undis
devovitque suas artes corpusque sepulcro
condidit, et tellus a nomine dicta sepulti.   235
    Hunc miseri tumulo ponentem corpora nati
garrula limoso prospexit ab elice perdix
et plausit pennis testataque gaudia cantu est,
unica tunc volucris nec visa prioribus annis,
factaque nuper avis longum tibi, Daedale, crimen. 240
namque huic tradiderat, fatorum ignara, docendam
progeniem germana suam, natalibus actis
bis puerum senis, animi ad praecepta capacis;
ille etiam medio spinas in pisce notatas
traxit in exemplum ferroque incidit acuto   245
perpetuos dentes et serrae repperit usum;
primus et ex uno duo ferrea bracchia nodo
vinxit, ut aequali spatio distantibus illis
altera pars staret, pars altera duceret orbem.
Daedalus invidit sacraque ex arce Minervae   250
praecipitem misit, lapsum mentitus; at illum,
quae favet ingeniis, excepit Pallas avemque
reddidit et medio velavit in aere pennis,

led by a desire for the open sky, directed his course
to a greater height. The scorching rays of the nearer
sun softened the fragrant wax which held his wings.
The wax melted; his arms were bare as he beat them
up and down, but, lacking wings, they took no hold
on the air. His lips, calling to the last upon his
father's name, were drowned in the dark blue sea,
which took its name from him. But the unhappy
father, now no longer father, called: "Icarus, Icarus,
where are you? In what place shall I seek you?
Icarus," he called again; and then he spied the
wings floating on the deep, and cursed his skill.
He buried the body in a tomb, and the land was
called from the name of the buried boy.

As he was consigning the body of his ill-fated son
to the tomb, a chattering partridge looked out from
a muddy ditch and clapped her wings uttering a
joyful note. She was at that time a strange bird,
of a kind never seen before, and but lately made a
bird; a lasting reproach to you, Daedalus. For the
man's sister, ignorant of the fates, had sent him
her son to be trained, a lad of teachable mind, who
had now passed his twelfth birthday. This boy,
moreover, observed the backbone of a fish and,
taking it as a model, cut a row of teeth in a thin
strip of iron and thus invented the saw. He also
was the first to bind two arms of iron together
at a joint, so that, while the arms kept the same
distance apart, one might stand still while the other
should trace a circle. Daedalus envied the lad and
thrust him down headlong from the sacred citadel of
Minerva, with a lying tale that the boy had fallen.
But Pallas, who favours the quick of wit, caught him
up and made him a bird, and clothed him with
feathers in mid-air. His old quickness of wit passed

sed vigor ingenii quondam velocis in alas
inque pedes abiit; nomen, quod et ante, remansit.
non tamen haec alte volucris sua corpora tollit,   256
nec facit in ramis altoque cacumine nidos:
propter humum volitat ponitque in saepibus ova
antiquique memor metuit sublimia casus.

Iamque fatigatum tellus Aetnaea tenebat   260
Daedalon, et sumptis pro supplice Cocalus armis
mitis habebatur; iam lamentabile Athenae
pendere desierant Thesea laude tributum:
templa coronantur, bellatricemque Minervam
cum Iove disque vocant aliis, quos sanguine voto   265
muneribusque datis et acerris turis honorant;
sparserat Argolicas nomen vaga fama per urbes
Theseos, et populi, quos dives Achaia cepit,
huius opem magnis inploravere periclis,
huius opem Calydon, quamvis Meleagron haberet,
sollicita supplex petiit prece: causa petendi   271
sus erat, infestae famulus vindexque Dianae.
Oenea namque ferunt pleni successibus anni
primitias frugum Cereri, sua vina Lyaeo,
Palladios flavae latices libasse Minervae;   275
coeptus ab agricolis superos pervenit ad omnes
ambitiosus honor: solas sine ture relictas
praeteritae cessasse ferunt Latoidos aras.
tangit et ira deos. " at non inpune feremus,
quaeque inhonoratae, non et dicemur inultae "   280
inquit, et Olenios ultorem spreta per agros

into his wings and legs, but he kept the name which
he had before. Still the bird does not lift her body
high in flight nor build her nest on trees or on high
points of rock; but she flutters along near the ground
and lays her eggs in hedgerows; and, remembering
that old fall, she is ever fearful of lofty places.

Now the land of Aetna received the weary Dae-
dalus, where King Cocalus took up arms in the sup-
pliant's defence and was esteemed most kind.[1] Now
also Athens, thanks to Theseus, had ceased to pay
her doleful tribute. The temple is wreathed with
flowers, the people call on Minerva, goddess of
battles, with Jove and the other gods, whom they
worship with sacrificial blood, with gifts and burning
incense. Quick-flying fame had spread the name of
Theseus through all the towns of Greece, and all
the peoples of rich Achaia prayed his help in their
own great perils. Suppliant Calydon sought his help
with anxious prayers, although she had her Meleager.
The cause of seeking was a monster boar, the
servant and avenger of outraged Diana. For they
say that Oeneus, king of Calydon, in thanksgiving
for a bounteous harvest-time, paid the first-fruits
of the grain to Ceres, paid his wine to Bacchus,
and her own flowing oil to golden-haired Minerva.
Beginning with the rural deities, the honour they
craved was paid to all the gods of heaven; only
Diana's altar was passed by (they say) and left with-
out its incense. Anger also can move the gods. "But
we shall not bear this without vengeance," she said;
"and though unhonoured, it shall not be said that
we are unavenged." And the scorned goddess sent
over the fields of Aetolia an avenging boar, as great as

[1] This phrase has no point, and there seems to be something
wrong with the text.

OVID

misit aprum, quanto maiores herbida tauros
non habet Epiros, sed habent Sicula arva minores:
sanguine et igne micant oculi, riget horrida cervix,
et setae similes rigidis hastilibus horrent: [1]   285
fervida cum rauco latos stridore per armos   287
spuma fluit, dentes aequantur dentibus Indis,
fulmen ab ore venit, frondes afflatibus ardent.
is modo crescentes segetes proculcat in herba,   290
nunc matura metit fleturi vota coloni
et Cererem in spicis intercipit: area frustra
et frustra exspectant promissas horrea messes.
sternuntur gravidi longo cum palmite fetus
bacaque cum ramis semper frondentis olivae.   295
saevit et in pecudes: non has pastorve canisve,
non armenta truces possunt defendere tauri.
diffugiunt populi nec se nisi moenibus urbis
esse putant tutos, donec Meleagros et una
lecta manus iuvenum coiere cupidine laudis: 300
Tyndaridae gemini, praestantes caestibus alter,
alter equo, primaeque ratis molitor Iason,
et cum Pirithoo, felix concordia, Theseus,
et duo Thestiadae prolesque Aphareia, Lynceus
et velox Idas, et iam non femina Caeneus,   305
Leucippusque ferox iaculoque insignis Acastus
Hippothousque Dryasque et cretus Amyntore Phoenix
Actoridaeque pares et missus ab Elide Phyleus.
nec Telamon aberat magnique creator Achillis
cumque Pheretiade et Hyanteo Iolao   310

---

[1] *Ehwald omits, as well as line 286:*
    stantque velut vallum, velut alta hastilia setae.

the bulls which feed on grassy Epirus, and greater than those of Sicily. His eyes glowed with blood and fire; his neck was stiff and bristly; his bristles stood up like lines of stiff spear-shafts; amidst deep, hoarse grunts the hot foam flecked his broad shoulders; his tusks were long as the Indian elephant's, lightning flashed from his mouth, the herbage shrivelled beneath his breath. Now he trampled down the young corn in the blade, and now he laid waste the full-grown crops of some farmer who was doomed to mourn, and cut off the ripe grain in the ear. In vain the threshing-floor, in vain the granary awaited the promised harvests. The heavy bunches of grapes with their trailing vines were cast down, and berry and branch of the olive whose leaf never withers. He vents his rage on the cattle, too. Neither herdsmen nor dogs can protect them, nor can the fierce bulls defend their herds. The people flee in all directions, nor do they count themselves safe until protected by a city's walls. Then at last Meleager and a picked band of youths assembled, fired with the love of glory: the twin sons of Leda, wife of Tyndarus, one famous for boxing, the other for horsemanship; Jason, the first ship's builder; Theseus and Pirithoüs, inseparable friends; the two sons of Thestius;[1] Lynceus and swift-footed Idas, sons of Aphareus; Caeneus,[2] no longer a woman; warlike Leucippus and Acastus, famed for his javelin; Hippothoüs and Dryas; Phoenix, the son of Amyntor; Actor's two sons[3] and Elean Phyleus. Telamon was also there, and the father of great Achilles; and, along with the son of Pheres[4] and Boeotian Iolaüs,

---

[1] Plexippus and Toxeus, brothers of Althaea, the mother of Meleager.
[2] See XII. 189 ff. [3] Eurytus and Cleatus. [4] Admetus.

inpiger Eurytion et cursu invictus Echion
Naryciusque Lelex Panopeusque Hyleusque feroxque
Hippasus et primis etiamnum Nestor in annis,
et quos Hippocoon antiquis misit Amyclis,
Penelopaeque socer cum Parrhasio Ancaeo,   315
Ampycidesque sagax et adhuc a coniuge tutus
Oeclides nemorisque decus Tegeaea Lycaei:
rasilis huic summam mordebat fibula vestem,
crinis erat simplex, nodum conlectus in unum,
ex umero pendens resonabat eburnea laevo   320
telorum custos, arcum quoque laeva tenebat;
talis erat cultu, facies, quam dicere vere
virgineam in puero, puerilem in virgine possis.
hanc pariter vidit, pariter Calydonius heros
optavit renuente deo flammasque latentes   325
hausit et " o felix, siquem dignabitur " inquit
" ista virum ! "· nec plura sinit tempusque pudorque
dicere: maius opus magni certaminis urguet.

  Silva frequens trabibus, quam nulla ceciderat aetas,
incipit a plano devexaque prospicit arva: 330
quo postquam venere viri, pars retia tendunt,
vincula pars adimunt canibus, pars pressa sequuntur
signa pedum, cupiuntque suum reperire periclum.
concava vallis erat, quo se demittere rivi
adsuerant pluvialis aquae; tenet ima lacunae   335
lenta salix ulvaeque leves iuncique palustres
viminaque et longa parvae sub harundine cannae:
428

were Eurytion, quick in action, and Echion, of un-
conquered speed; Locrian Lelex, Panopeus, Hyleus
and Hippasus, keen for the fray; Nestor, then in
the prime of his years; and those whom Hippocoön
sent from ancient Amyclae; the father-in-law of
Penelope,[1] and Arcadian Ancaeus; Ampycus' pro-
phetic son,[2] and the son [3] of Oecleus, who had not
yet been ruined by his wife; and Atalanta of Tegea,
the pride of the Arcadian woods. A polished buckle
clasped her robe at the neck; her hair, plainly dressed,
was caught up in one knot. From her left shoulder
hung an ivory quiver, resounding as she moved, with
its shafts, and her left hand held a bow. Such was
she in dress. As for her face, it was one which you
could truly say was maidenly for a boy or boyish
for a maiden. As soon as his eyes fell on her, the
Calydonian hero straightway longed for her (but
God forbade); he felt the flames of love steal
through his heart; and " O happy man," he said,
" if ever that maiden shall deem any man worthy to
be hers." Neither the occasion nor his own modesty
permitted him more words; the greater task of the
mighty conflict urged him to action.

There was a dense forest, that past ages had never
touched with the axe, rising from the plain and look-
ing out on the downward-sloping fields. When the
heroes came to this, some stretched the hunting-nets,
some slipped the leashes from the dogs, some fol-
lowed the well-marked trail as they longed to come
at their dangerous enemy. There was a deep dell,
where the rain-water from above drained down; the
lowest part of this marshy spot was covered with a
growth of pliant willows, sedge-grass and swamp-
rushes, osiers and tall bulrushes, with an under-

---

[1] Laërtes.   [2] Mopsus.   [3] Amphiaraüs.

OVID

hinc aper excitus medios violentus in hostes
fertur, ut excussis elisi nubibus ignes.
sternitur incursu nemus, et propulsa fragorem   340
silva dat : exclamant iuvenes praetentaque forti
tela tenent dextra lato vibrantia ferro.
ille ruit spargitque canes, ut quisque furenti
obstat, et obliquo latrantes dissipat ictu.
cuspis Echionio primum contorta lacerto   345
vana fuit truncoque dedit leve vulnus acerno ;
proxima, si nimiis mittentis viribus usa
non foret, in tergo visa est haesura petito :
longius it ; auctor teli Pagasaeus Iason.
" Phoebe," ait Ampycides, " si te coluique coloque,
da mihi, quod petitur, certo contingere telo ! "   351
qua potuit, precibus deus adnuit : ictus ab illo est,
sed sine vulnere aper : ferrum Diana volanti
abstulerat iaculo ; lignum sine acumine venit.
ira feri mota est, nec fulmine lenius arsit :   355
emicat ex oculis, spirat quoque pectore flamma,
utque volat moles adducto concita nervo,
cum petit aut muros aut plenas milite turres,
in iuvenes certo sic impete vulnificus sus
fertur et Hippalmon Pelagonaque, dextra tuentes   360
cornua, prosternit : socii rapuere iacentes ;
at non letiferos effugit Enaesimus ictus
Hippocoonte satus : trepidantem et terga parantem
vertere succiso liquerunt poplite nervi.

430

growth of small reeds. From this covert the boar
was roused and launched himself with a mad rush
against his foes, like lightning struck out from the
clashing clouds. The grove is laid low by his on-
rush, and the trees crash as he knocks against them.
The heroes raise a halloo and with unflinching hands
hold their spears poised with the broad iron heads
well forward. The boar comes rushing on, scatters
the dogs one after another as they strive to stop his
mad rush, and thrusts off the baying pack with his
deadly sidelong stroke. The first spear, thrown by
Echion's arm, missed its aim and struck glancing on
the trunk of a maple-tree. The next, if it had not
been thrown with too much force, seemed sure of
transfixing the back where it was aimed. It went
too far. Jason of Pagasae was the marksman. Then
Mopsus cried: "O Phoebus, if I have ever worshipped
and do still worship thee, grant me with unerring spear
to reach my mark." So far as possible the god heard
his prayer. His spear did strike the boar, but with-
out injury; for Diana had wrenched the iron point
from the javelin as it sped, and pointless the wooden
shaft struck home. But the beast's savage anger
was roused, and it burned hotter than the lightning.
Fire gleamed from his eyes, seemed to breathe from
his throat. And, as a huge rock, shot from a catapult
sling, flies through the air against walls or turrets
filled with soldiery; so with irresistible and death-
dealing force the beast rushed on the youths, and
overbore Hippalmus and Pelagon, who were stationed
on the extreme right. Their comrades caught them
up as they lay. But Enaesimus, the son of Hippo-
coön, did not escape the boar's fatal stroke. As he
in fear was just turning to run he was hamstrung
and his muscles gave way beneath him. Pylian

forsitan et Pylius citra Troiana perisset   365
tempora, sed sumpto posita conamine ab hasta
arboris insiluit, quae stabat proxima, ramis
despexitque, loco tutus, quem fugerat, hostem.
dentibus ille ferox in querno stipite tritis
inminet exitio fidensque recentibus armis   370
Eurytidae magni rostro femur hausit adunco.
at gemini, nondum caelestia sidera, fratres,
ambo conspicui, nive candidioribus ambo
vectabantur equis, ambo vibrata per auras
hastarum tremulo quatiebant spicula motu.   375
vulnera fecissent, nisi saetiger inter opacas
nec iaculis isset nec equo loca pervia silvas.
persequitur Telamon studioque incautus eundi
pronus ab arborea cecidit radice retentus.
dum levat hunc Peleus, celerem Tegeaea sagittam
inposuit nervo sinuatoque expulit arcu: 381
fixa sub aure feri summum destrinxit harundo
corpus et exiguo rubefecit sanguine saetas;
nec tamen illa sui successu laetior ictus
quam Meleagros erat: primus vidisse putatur   385
et primus sociis visum ostendisse cruorem
et " meritum " dixisse " feres virtutis honorem."
erubuere viri seque exhortantur et addunt
cum clamore animos iaciuntque sine ordine tela:
turba nocet iactis et, quos petit, impedit ictus.   390
ecce furens contra sua fata bipennifer Arcas

Nestor came near perishing before he ever went to
the Trojan War; but, putting forth all his strength,
he leaped by his spear-pole into the branches of a
tree which stood near by, and from this place of
safety he looked down upon the foe he had escaped.
The raging beast whetted his tusks on an oak-tree's
trunk; and, threatening destruction and emboldened
by his freshly sharpened tusks, ripped up the thigh
of the mighty Hippasus with one sweeping blow.
But now the twin brothers,[1] not yet set in the starry
heavens, came riding up, both conspicuous among the
rest, both on horses whiter than snow, both poising
their spears, which they threw quivering through the
air.   And they would have struck the boar had not
the bristly monster taken refuge in the dense woods,
whither neither spear nor horse could follow him.
Telamon did attempt to follow, and in his eagerness,
careless where he went, he fell prone on the ground,
caught by a projecting root.   While Peleus was
helping him to rise, Atalanta notched a swift arrow
on the cord and sent it speeding from her bent bow.
The arrow just grazed the top of the boar's back and
remained stuck beneath his ear, staining the bristles
with a trickle of blood.   Nor did she show more joy
over the success of her own stroke than Meleager.
He was the first to see the blood, the first to point it
out to his companions, and to say: " Due honour
shall your brave deed receive."   The men, flushed
with shame, spurred each other on, gaining courage
as they cried out, hurling their spears in disorder.
The mass of missiles made them of no effect, and
kept them from striking as they were meant to do.
Then Ancaeus, the Arcadian, armed with a two-
headed axe raging to meet his fate, cried out:

---

[1] Castor and Pollux.

OVID

" discite, femineis quid tela virilia praestent,
o iuvenes, operique meo concedite! " dixit.
" ipsa suis licet hunc Latonia protegat armis,
invita tamen hunc perimet mea dextra Diana."   395
talia magniloquo tumidus memoraverat ore
ancipitemque manu tollens utraque securim
institerat digitis pronos suspensus in ictus:
occupat audentem, quaque est via proxima leto,
summa ferus geminos derexit ad inguina dentes. 400
concidit Ancaeus glomerataque sanguine multo
viscera lapsa fluunt: madefacta est terra cruore.
ibat in adversum proles Ixionis hostem
Pirithous valida quatiens venabula dextra;
cui "procul" Aegides "o me mihi carior" inquit   405
" pars animae consiste meae! licet eminus esse
fortibus: Ancaeo nocuit temeraria virtus."
dixit et aerata torsit grave cuspide cornum;
quo bene librato votique potente futuro
obstitit aesculea frondosus ab arbore ramus.   410
misit et Aesonides iaculum: quod casus ab illo
vertit in inmeriti fatum latrantis et inter
ilia coniectum tellure per ilia fixum est.
at manus Oenidae variat, missisque duabus
hasta prior terra, medio stetit altera tergo.   415
nec mora, dum saevit, dum corpora versat in orbem
stridentemque novo spumam cum sanguine fundit,
vulneris auctor adest hostemque inritat ad iram
splendidaque adversos venabula condit in armos.
434

" Learn now, O youths, how far a man's weapons surpass a girl's; and leave this task to me. Though Latona's daughter herself shield this boar with her own arrows, in spite of Diana shall my good right arm destroy him." So, swollen with pride and with boastful lips, he spoke: and, lifting in both hands his two-edged axe, he stood on tiptoe, poised for a downward blow. The boar anticipated his bold enemy, and, as the nearest point for death, he fiercely struck at the upper part of the groins with his two tusks. Ancaeus fell; his entrails poured out amid streams of blood and the ground was soaked with gore. Then Ixion's son, Pirithoüs, advanced against the foe, brandishing a hunting-spear in his strong right hand. To him Theseus cried out in alarm: " Keep away, O dearer to me than my own self, my soul's other half; it is no shame for brave men to fight at long range. Ancaeus' rash valour has proved his bane." He spoke and hurled his own heavy shaft with its sharp bronze point. Though this was well aimed and seemed sure to reach the mark, a leafy branch of an oak-tree turned it aside. Then the son of Aeson hurled his javelin, which chance caused to swerve from its aim and fatally wound an innocent dog, passing clear through his flanks and pinning him to the ground. But the hand of Meleager had a different fortune: he threw two spears, the first of which stood in the earth, but the second stuck squarely in the middle of the creature's back. Straightway, while the boar rages and whirls round and round, spouting forth foam and fresh blood in a hissing stream, the giver of the wound presses his advantage, pricks his enemy on to madness, and at last plunges his gleaming hunting-spear right through the shoulder. The others vent their joy by wild

gaudia testantur socii clamore secundo   420
victricemque petunt dextrae coniungere dextram
inmanemque ferum multa tellure iacentem
mirantes spectant neque adhuc contingere tutum
esse putant, sed tela tamen sua quisque cruentat.
   Ipse pede inposito caput exitiabile pressit   425
atque ita " sume mei spolium, Nonacria, iuris,"
dixit " et in partem veniat mea gloria tecum."
protinus exuvias rigidis horrentia saetis
terga dat et magnis insignia dentibus ora.
illi laetitiae est cum munere muneris auctor;   430
invidere alii, totoque erat agmine murmur.
e quibus ingenti tendentes bracchia voce
" pone age nec titulos intercipe, femina, nostros,"
Thestiadae clamant, " nec te fiducia formae
decipiat, ne sit longe tibi captus amore   435
auctor," et huic adimunt munus, ius muneris illi.
non tulit et tumida frendens Mavortius ira
" discite, raptores alieni " dixit " honoris,
facta minis quantum distent," hausitque nefando
pectora Plexippi nil tale timentia ferro.   440
Toxea, quid faciat, dubium pariterque volentem
ulcisci fratrem fraternaque fata timentem
haud patitur dubitare diu calidumque priori
caede recalfecit consorti sanguine telum.
   Dona deum templis nato victore ferebat,   445
cum videt exstinctos fratres Althaea referri.
quae plangore dato maestis clamoribus urbem
436

shouts of applause and crowd around to press the victor's hand. They gaze in wonder at the huge beast lying stretched out over so much ground, and still think it hardly safe to touch him. But each dips his spear in the blood.

Then Meleager, standing with his foot upon that death-dealing head, spoke thus to Atalanta: " Take thou the prize that is of my right, O fair Arcadian, and let my glory be shared with thee." And therewith he presented her with the spoils: the skin with its bristling spikes, and the head remarkable for its huge tusks. She rejoiced in the gift and no less in the giver; but the others begrudged it, and an angry murmur rose through the whole company. Then two, the sons of Thestius, stretching out their arms, cried with a loud voice: " Let be, girl, and do not usurp our honours. And be not deceived by trusting in your beauty, lest this lovesick giver be far from helping you." And they took from her the gift, and from him the right of giving. This was more than that son of Mars could bear, and, gnashing his teeth with rage, he cried: " Learn then, you that plunder another's rights, the difference between deeds and threats," and plunged his impious steel deep in Plexippus' heart, who was taken off his guard. Then, as Toxeus stood hesitating what to do, wishing to avenge his brother, but at the same time fearing to share his brother's fate, Meleager gave him scant time to hesitate, but, while his spear was still warm with its first victim's slaughter, he warmed it again in his comrade's blood.

Althaea in the temple of the gods was offering thanksgiving for her son's victory, when she saw the corpses of her brothers carried in. She beat her breast and filled the city with woeful lamentation,

inplet et auratis mutavit vestibus atras;
at simul est auctor necis editus, excidit omnis
luctus et a lacrimis in poenae versus amorem est. 450
    Stipes erat, quem, cum partus enixa iaceret
Thestias, in flammam triplices posuere sorores
staminaque inpresso fatalia pollice nentes
" tempora " dixerunt " eadem lignoque tibique,
o modo nate, damus."   quo postquam carmine dicto
excessere deae, flagrantem mater ab igne   456
eripuit ramum sparsitque liquentibus undis.
ille diu fuerat penetralibus abditus imis
servatusque tuos, iuvenis, servaverat annos.
protulit hunc genetrix taedasque et fragmina poni
imperat et positis inimicos admovet ignes.   461
tum conata quater flammis inponere ramum
coepta quater tenuit: pugnat materque sororque,
et diversa trahunt unum duo nomina pectus.
saepe metu sceleris pallebant ora futuri,   465
saepe suum fervens oculis dabat ira ruborem,
et modo nescio quid similis crudele minanti
vultus erat, modo quem misereri credere posses;
cumque ferus lacrimas animi siccaverat ardor,
inveniebantur lacrimae tamen, utque carina,   470
quam ventus ventoque rapit contrarius aestus,
vim geminam sentit paretque incerta duobus,
Thestias haud aliter dubiis affectibus errat
inque vices ponit positamque resuscitat iram.
incipit esse tamen melior germana parente   475
et consanguineas ut sanguine leniat umbras,
inpietate pia est.   nam postquam pestifer ignis

and changed her gold-spangled robes for black. But when she learned who was their murderer, her grief all fell away and was changed from tears to the passion for vengeance.

There was a billet of wood which, when the daughter of Thestius lay in childbirth, the three sisters threw into the fire and, spinning the threads of life with firm-pressed thumb, they sang: " An equal span of life we give to thee and to this wood, O babe new-born." When the three goddesses had sung this prophecy and vanished, the mother snatched the blazing brand from the fire, and quenched it in water. Long had it lain hidden away in a secret place and, guarded safe, had safeguarded your life, O youth. And now the mother brought out this billet and bade her servants make a heap of pine-knots and fine kindling, and lit the pile with cruel flame. Then four times she made to throw the billet in the flames and four times she held her hand. Mother and sister strove in her, and the two names tore one heart this way and that. Often her cheeks grew pale with fear of the impious thing she planned; as often blazing wrath gave its own colour to her eyes. Now she looked like one threatening some cruel deed, and now you would think her pitiful. And when the fierce anger of her heart had dried up her tears, still tears would come again. And as a ship, driven by the wind, and against the wind by the tide, feels the double force and yields uncertainly to both, so Thestius' daughter wavered betwixt opposing passions; now quenched her wrath and now fanned it again. At last the sister in her overcomes the mother, and, that she may appease with blood the shades of her blood-kin, she is pious in impiety. For when the devouring flames grow hot, she cries: " Be that

OVID

convaluit, " rogus iste cremet mea viscera " dixit,
utque manu dira lignum fatale tenebat,
ante sepulcrales infelix adstitit aras   480
" poenarum " que " deae triplices, furialibus," inquit
" Eumenides, sacris vultus advertite vestros!
ulciscor facioque nefas; mors morte pianda est,
in scelus addendum scelus est, in funera funus :
per coacervatos pereat domus inpia luctus!   485
an felix Oeneus nato victore fruetur,
Thestius orbus erit?   melius lugebitis ambo.
vos modo, fraterni manes animaeque recentes,
officium sentite meum magnoque paratas
accipite inferias, uteri mala pignora nostri!   490
ei mihi! quo rapior? fratres, ignoscite matri!
deficiunt ad coepta manus : meruisse fatemur
illum, cur pereat; mortis mihi displicet auctor.
ergo inpune feret vivusque et victor et ipso
successu tumidus regnum Calydonis habebit,   495
vos cinis exiguus gelidaeque iacebitis umbrae?
haud equidem patiar : pereat sceleratus et ille
spemque patris regnumque trahat patriaeque ruinam!
mens ubi materna est? ubi sunt pia iura parentum
et quos sustinui bis mensum quinque labores?   500
o utinam primis arsisses ignibus infans,
idque ego passa forem! vixisti munere nostro;
nunc merito moriere tuo!   cape praemia facti
bisque datam, primum partu, mox stipite rapto,
redde animam vel me fraternis adde sepulcris!   505
et cupio et nequeo. quid agam? modo vulnera fratrum
ante oculos mihi sunt et tantae caedis imago,

the funeral pyre of my own flesh." And, as she held the fateful billet in her relentless hand and stood, unhappy wretch, before the sepulchral fires, she said: "O ye triple goddesses of vengeance, Eumenides, behold these fearful rites. I avenge and I do a wicked deed: death must be atoned by death; to crime must crime be added, death to death. Through woes on woes heaped up let this accursed house go on to ruin! Shall happy Oeneus rejoice in his victorious son and Thestius be childless? 'Twill be better for you both to grieve. Only do you, my brothers' manes, fresh-made ghosts, appreciate my service, and accept the sacrifice I offer at so heavy cost, the baleful tribute of my womb. Ah me, whither am I hurrying? Brothers, forgive a mother's heart! My hands refuse to finish what they began. I confess that he deserves to die; but that I should be the agent of his death, I cannot bear. And shall he go scathless then? Shall he live, victorious and puffed up with his own success, and lord it in Calydon, while you are naught but a handful of ashes, shivering ghosts? I will not suffer it. Let the wretch die and take with him his father's hopes, his kingdom and his ruined fatherland! Where is my mother-love? Where are parents' pious cares? Where are those pangs which ten long months I bore? O that you had perished in your infancy by those first fires, and I had suffered it! You lived by my gift; now you shall die by your own desert; pay the price of your deed. Give back the life I twice gave you, once at your birth, once when I saved the brand; or else add me to my brothers' pyre. I both desire to act, and cannot. Oh, what shall I do? Now I can see only my brothers' wounds, the sight of that deed of blood: and now

nunc animum pietas maternaque nomina frangunt.
me miseram! male vincetis, sed vincite, fratres,
dummodo, quae dedero vobis, solacia vosque   510
ipsa sequar!" dixit dextraque aversa trementi
funereum torrem medios coniecit in ignes:
aut dedit aut visus gemitus est ipse dedisse
stipes, ut invitis conreptus ab ignibus arsit.

Inscius atque absens flamma Meleagros ab illa 515
uritur et caecis torreri viscera sentit
ignibus ac magnos superat virtute dolores.
quod tamen ignavo cadat et sine sanguine leto,
maeret et Ancaei felicia vulnera dicit
grandaevumque patrem fratresque piasque sorores
cum gemitu sociamque tori vocat ore supremo,   521
forsitan et matrem.   crescunt ignisque dolorque
languescuntque iterum; simul est exstinctus uterque,
inque leves abiit paulatim spiritus auras
paulatim cana prunam velante favilla.   525

Alta iacet Calydon: lugent iuvenesque senesque,
vulgusque proceresque gemunt, scissaeque capillos
planguntur matres Calydonides Eueninae;
pulvere canitiem genitor vultusque seniles
foedat humi fusus spatiosumque increpat aevum. 530
nam de matre manus diri sibi conscia facti
exegit poenas acto per viscera ferro.
non mihi si centum deus ora sonantia linguis
ingeniumque capax totumque Helicona dedisset,
tristia persequerer miserarum fata sororum.   535
inmemores decoris liventia pectora tundunt,
dumque manet corpus, corpus refoventque foventque,

love and the name of mother break me down. Woe is my, my brothers! It is ill that you should win, but win you shall; only let me have the solace that I grant to you, and let me follow you!" She spoke, and turning away her face, with trembling hand she threw the fatal billet into the flames. The brand either gave or seemed to give a groan as it was caught and consumed by the unwilling fire.

Unconscious, far away, Meleager burns with those flames; he feels his vitals scorching with hidden fire, and o'ercomes the great pain with fortitude. But yet he grieves that he must die a cowardly and bloodless death, and he calls Ancaeus happy for the wounds he suffered. With groans of pain he calls with his dying breath on his aged father, his brothers and loving sisters and his wife, perchance also upon his mother. The fire and his pains increase, and then die down. Both fire and pain go out together; his spirit gradually slips away into the thin air as white ashes gradually overspread the glowing coals.

Lofty Calydon is brought low. Young men and old, chieftains and commons, lament and groan; and the Calydonian women, dwellers by Euenus' stream, tear their hair and beat their breasts. The father, prone on the ground, defiles his white hair and his aged head with dust, and laments that he has lived too long. For the mother, now knowing her awful deed, has punished herself, driving a dagger through her heart. Not if some god had given me a hundred mouths each with its tongue, a master's genius, and all Helicon's inspiration, could I describe the piteous plight of those poor sisters. Careless of decency, they beat and bruise their breasts; and, while their brother's corpse remains, they caress that corpse over and

oscula dant ipsi, posito dant oscula lecto.
post cinerem cineres haustos ad pectora pressant
adfusaeque iacent tumulo signataque saxo   540
nomina conplexae lacrimas in nomina fundunt.
quas Parthaoniae tandem Latonia clade
exsatiata domus praeter Gorgenque nurumque
nobilis Alcmenae natis in corpore pennis
adlevat et longas per bracchia porrigit alas   545
corneaque ora facit versasque per aera mittit.
    Interea Theseus sociati parte laboris
functus Erectheas Tritonidos ibat ad arces.
clausit iter fecitque moras Achelous eunti
imbre tumens: " succede meis," ait " inclite, tectis,
Cecropide, nec te committe rapacibus undis: 551
ferre trabes solidas obliquaque volvere magno
murmure saxa solent.   vidi contermina ripae
cum gregibus stabula alta trahi; nec fortibus illic
profuit armentis nec equis velocibus esse.   555
multa quoque hic torrens nivibus de monte solutis
corpora turbineo iuvenalia vertice mersit.
tutior est requies, solito dum flumina currant
limite, dum tenues capiat suus alveus undas."
adnuit Aegides "utar," que "Acheloe, domoque   560
consilioque tuo " respondit; et usus utroque est.
pumice multicavo nec levibus atria tophis
structa subit: molli tellus erat umida musco,
444

over, kiss him and kiss the bier as it stands before them. And, when he is ashes, they gather the ashes and press them to their hearts, throw themselves on his tomb in abandonment of grief and, clasping the stone on which his name has been carved, they drench the name with their tears. At length Diana, satisfied with the destruction of Parthaon's house, made feathers spring on their bodies—all save Gorge and great Alcmena's daughter-in-law[1]—stretched out long wings over their arms, gave them a horny beak, and sent them transfigured into the air.[2]

Meanwhile Theseus, having done his part in the confederate task, was on his way back to Tritonia's city where Erechtheus ruled. But Acheloüs, swollen with rain, blocked his way and delayed his journey. "Enter my house, illustrious hero of Athens," said the river-god, "and do not entrust yourself to my greedy waters. The current is wont to sweep down solid trunks of trees and huge boulders in zig-zag course with crash and roar. I have seen great stables that stood near by the bank swept away, cattle and all, and in that current neither strength availed the ox nor speed the horse. Many a strong man also has been overwhelmed in its whirling pools when swollen by melting snows from the mountain-sides. It is safer for you to rest until the waters shall run within their accustomed bounds, until its own bed shall hold the slender stream." The son of Aegeus replied: "I will use both your house, Acheloüs, and your advice." And he did use them both. He entered the river-god's dark dwelling, built of porous pumice and rough tufa; the floor was damp with soft

---

[1] Deianira, the wife of Hercules.
[2] These birds were called *Meleagrides*, guinea-hens.

summa lacunabant alterno murice conchae.
iamque duas lucis partes Hyperione menso   565
discubuere toris Theseus comitesque laborum,
hac Ixionides, illa Troezenius heros
parte Lelex, raris iam sparsus tempora canis,
quosque alios parili fuerat dignatus honore
Amnis Acarnanum, laetissimus hospite tanto.   570
protinus adpositas nudae vestigia nymphae
instruxere epulis mensas dapibusque remotis
in gemma posuere merum.   tum maximus heros,
aequora prospiciens oculis subiecta, " quis " inquit
" ille locus? " (digitoque ostendit) " et insula
     nomen   575
quod gerit illa, doce, quamquam non una videtur! "
Amnis ad haec " non est " inquit " quod cernitis
     unum:
quinque iacent terrae; spatium discrimina fallit.
quoque minus spretae factum mirere Dianae,
naides hae fuerant, quae cum bis quinque iuvencos
mactassent rurisque deos ad sacra vocassent,   581
inmemores nostri festas duxere choreas.
intumui, quantusque feror, cum plurimus umquam,
tantus eram, pariterque animis inmanis et undis
a silvis silvas et ab arvis arva revelli   585
cumque loco nymphas, memores tum denique nostri,
in freta provolvi. fluctus nosterque marisque
continuam diduxit humum partesque resolvit
in totidem, mediis quot cernis Echinadas undis.
ut tamen ipse vides, procul, en procul una recessit
insula, grata mihi; Perimelen navita dicit: 591

moss, conchs and purple-shells panelled the ceiling.
Now had the blazing sun traversed two-thirds of his
daily course, when Theseus and his comrades of the
chase disposed themselves upon the couches. Ixion's
son [1] lay here, and there Lelex, the hero of Troezen,
took his place, his temples already sprinkled with
grey; and others who had been deemed worthy of
equal honour by the Acarnanian river-god, who was
filled with joy in his noble guest. Without delay
barefoot nymphs set the feast upon the tables, and
then when the food had been removed, they set out
the wine in jewelled cups. Then the noble hero,
looking forth upon the wide water spread before his
eyes, pointed with his finger and said: " What place
is that? Tell me the name which that island bears.
And yet it seems not to be one island." The river-
god replied: " No, what you see is not one island.
There are five islands lying there together; but the
distance hides their divisions. And, that you may
wonder the less at what Diana did when she
was slighted, those islands once were nymphs,
who, when they had slaughtered ten bullocks
and had invited all the other rural gods to their
sacred feast, forgot me as they led the festal dance.
I swelled with rage, as full as when my flood flows
at the fullest; and so, terrible in wrath, terrible in
flood, I tore forests from forests, fields from fields;
and with the place they stood on, I swept the nymphs
away, who at last remembered me then, into the sea.
There my flood and the sea, united, cleft the undivided
ground into as many parts as now you see the
Echinades yonder amid the waves. But, as you
yourself see, away, look, far away beyond the others
is one island that I love: the sailors call it Perimele.

[1] Pirithoüs.

OVID

huic ego virgineum dilectae nomen ademi;
quod pater Hippodamas aegre tulit inque profun-
    dum
propulit e scopulo periturae corpora natae.
excepi nantemque ferens 'o proxima mundi
regna vagae ' dixi ' sortite, Tridentifer, undae,   596
adfer opem, mersaeque, precor, feritate paterna 601
da, Neptune, locum, vel sit locus ipsa licebit! '
dum loquor, amplexa est artus nova terra natantes 609
et gravis increvit mutatis insula membris."   610
    Amnis ab his tacuit.   factum mirabile cunctos
moverat: inridet credentes, utque deorum
spretor erat mentisque ferox, Ixione natus
" ficta refers nimiumque putas, Acheloe, potentes
esse deos," dixit " si dant adimuntque figuras." 615
obstipuere omnes nec talia dicta probarunt,
ante omnesque Lelex animo maturus et aevo,
sic ait: " inmensa est finemque potentia caeli
non habet, et quicquid superi voluere, peractum est;
quoque minus dubites, tiliae contermina quercus 620
collibus est Phrygiis modico circumdata muro;
ipse locum vidi; nam me Pelopeia Pittheus
misit in arva suo quondam regnata parenti.
haud procul hinc stagnum est, tellus habitabilis olim,
nunc celebres mergis fulicisque palustribus undae;
Iuppiter huc specie mortali cumque parente   626
venit Atlantiades positis caducifer alis.
mille domos adiere locum requiemque petentes,
mille domos clausere serae; tamen una recepit,

448

She was beloved by me, and from her I took the name
of maiden. Her father, Hippodamas, was enraged
with this, and he hurled his daughter to her death
down from a high cliff into the deep. I caught her,
and supporting her as she swam, I cried: ' O thou
god of the trident, to whom the lot gave the kingdom
next to the world, even the wandering waves, bring
aid, and to one drowned by a father's cruelty, I pray,
give a place, O Neptune, or else let her become
a place herself.' While I prayed a new land em-
braced her floating form and a solid island grew
from her transformed shape."

With these words the river was silent. The story
of the miracle had moved the hearts of all. But one
mocked at their credulity, a scoffer at the gods, one
reckless in spirit, Ixion's son, Pirithoüs. " These are
but fairy-tales you tell, Acheloüs," he said, " and
you concede too much power to the gods, if they
give and take away the forms of things." All the
rest were shocked and disapproved such words, and
especially Lelex, ripe both in mind and years, who
replied: " The power of heaven is indeed immeasur-
able and has no bounds; and whatever the gods
decree is done. And, that you may believe it, there
stand in the Phrygian hill-country an oak and a
linden-tree side by side, surrounded by a low wall.
I have myself seen the spot; for Pittheus sent me to
Phrygia, where his father once ruled. Not far from
the place I speak of is a marsh, once a habitable land,
but now water, the haunt of divers and coots. Hither
came Jupiter in the guise of a mortal, and with his
father came Atlas' grandson, he that bears the
caduceus, his wings laid aside. To a thousand
homes they came, seeking a place for rest; a thousand
homes were barred against them. Still one house

OVID

parva quidem, stipulis et canna tecta palustri,   630
sed pia Baucis anus parilique aetate Philemon
illa sunt annis iuncti iuvenalibus, illa
consenuere casa paupertatemque fatendo
effecere levem nec iniqua mente ferendo;
nec refert, dominos illic famulosne requiras: 635
tota domus duo sunt, idem parentque iubentque.
ergo ubi caelicolae parvos tetigere penates
summissoque humiles intrarunt vertice postes,
membra senex posito iussit relevare sedili;
cui superiniecit textum rude sedula Baucis   640
inque foco tepidum cinerem dimovit et ignes
suscitat hesternos foliisque et cortice sicco
nutrit et ad flammas anima producit anili
multifidasque faces ramaliaque arida tecto
detulit et minuit parvoque admovit aeno,   645
quodque suus coniunx riguo conlegerat horto,
truncat holus foliis; furca levat ille bicorni
sordida terga suis nigro pendentia tigno
servatoque diu resecat de tergore partem
exiguam sectamque domat ferventibus undis.   650
interea medias fallunt sermonibus horas [1]
concutiuntque torum de molli fluminis ulva   655
inpositum lecto sponda pedibusque salignis.
vestibus hunc velant, quas non nisi tempore festo
sternere consuerant, sed et haec vilisque vetusque
vestis erat, lecto non indignanda saligno.
adcubuere dei.   mensam succincta tremensque   660

[1] *The following lines are omitted by Ehwald:*

> sentirique moram prohibent.   erat alveus illic   652
> fagineus, dura clavo suspensus ab ansa:
> is tepidis impletur aquis artusque fovendos
> accipit, in medio torus est de mollibus ulvis.   655ᵃ

received them, humble indeed, thatched with straw and reeds from the marsh; but pious old Baucis and Philemon, of equal age, were in that cottage wedded in their youth, and in that cottage had grown old together; there they made their poverty light by owning it, and by bearing it in a contended spirit. It was of no use to ask for masters or for servants in that house; they two were the whole household, together they served and ruled. And so when the heavenly ones came to this humble home and, stooping, entered in at the lowly door, the old man set out a bench and bade them rest their limbs, while over this bench busy Baucis threw a rough covering. Then she raked aside the warm ashes on the hearth and fanned yesterday's coals to life, which she fed with leaves and dry bark, blowing them into flame with the breath of her old body. Then she took down from the roof some fine-split wood and dry twigs, broke them up and placed them under the little copper kettle. And she took the cabbage which her husband had brought in from the well-watered garden and lopped off the outside leaves. Meanwhile the old man with a forked stick reached down a chine of smoked bacon, which was hanging from a blackened beam and, cutting off a little piece of the long-cherished pork, he put it to cook in the boiling water. Meanwhile they beguiled the intervening time with their talk and smoothed out a mattress of soft sedge-grass placed on a couch with frame and feet of willow. They threw drapery over this, which they were not accustomed to bring out except on festal days; but even this was a cheap thing and well-worn, a very good match for the willow couch. The gods reclined. The old woman, with her skirts tucked up, with trembling hands set out the table.

ponit anus, mensae sed erat pes tertius inpar:
testa parem fecit; quae postquam subdita clivum
sustulit, aequatam mentae tersere virentes.
ponitur hic bicolor sincerae baca Minervae
conditaque in liquida corna autumnalia faece   665
intibaque et radix et lactis massa coacti
ovaque non acri leviter versata favilla,
omnia fictilibus.   post haec caelatus eodem
sistitur argento crater fabricataque fago
pocula, qua cava sunt, flaventibus inlita ceris;   670
parva mora est, epulasque foci misere calentes,
nec longae rursus referuntur vina senectae
dantque locum mensis paulum seducta secundis:
hic nux, hic mixta est rugosis carica palmis
prunaque et in patulis redolentia mala canistris   675
et de purpureis conlectae vitibus uvae,
candidus in medio favus est; super omnia vultus
accessere boni nec iners pauperque voluntas.
   " Interea totiens haustum cratera repleri
sponte sua per seque vident succrescere vina: 680
attoniti novitate pavent manibusque supinis
concipiunt Baucisque preces timidusque Philemon
et veniam dapibus nullisque paratibus orant.
unicus anser erat, minimae custodia villae:
quem dis hospitibus domini mactare parabant;   685
ille celer penna tardos aetate fatigat
eluditque diu tandemque est visus ad ipsos
confugisse deos: superi vetuere necari

But one of its three legs was too short; so she propped it up with a potsherd. When this had levelled the slope, she wiped it, thus levelled, with green mint. Next she placed on the board some olives, green and ripe, truthful Minerva's berries, and some autumnal cornel-cherries pickled in the lees of wine; endives and radishes, cream cheese and eggs, lightly roasted in the warm ashes, all served in earthen dishes. After these viands, an embossed mixing-bowl of the same costly ware was set on together with cups of beechwood coated on the inside with yellow wax. A moment and the hearth sent its steaming viands on, and wine of no great age was brought out, which was then pushed aside to give a small space for the second course. Here were nuts and figs, with dried dates, plums and fragrant apples in broad baskets, and purple grapes just picked from the vines; in the centre of the table was a comb of clear white honey. Besides all this, pleasant faces were at the board and lively and abounding goodwill.

"Meanwhile they saw that the mixing-bowl, as often as it was drained, kept filling of its own accord, and that the wine welled up of itself. The two old people saw this strange sight with amaze and fear, and with upturned hands they both uttered a prayer, Baucis and the trembling old Philemon, and they craved indulgence for their fare and meagre entertainment. They had one goose, the guardian of their tiny estate; and him the hosts were preparing to kill for their divine guests. But the goose was swift of wing, and quite wore the slow old people out in their efforts to catch him. He eluded their grasp for a long time, and finally seemed to flee for refuge to the gods themselves. Then the gods told them not

' di ' que ' sumus, meritasque luet vicinia poenas
inpia ' dixerunt; ' vobis inmunibus huius   690
esse mali dabitur; modo vestra relinquite tecta
ac nostros comitate gradus et in ardua montis
ite simul! ' parent ambo baculisque levati
nituntur longo vestigia ponere clivo.
tantum aberant summo, quantum semel ire sagitta 695
missa potest: flexere oculos et mersa palude
cetera prospiciunt, tantum sua tecta manere,
dumque ea mirantur, dum deflent fata suorum,
illa vetus dominis etiam casa parva duobus
vertitur in templum: furcas subiere columnae, 700
stramina flavescunt aurataque tecta videntur
caelataeque fores adopertaque marmore tellus.
talia tum placido Saturnius edidit ore:
' dicite, iuste senex et femina coniuge iusto
digna, quid optetis.' cum Baucide pauca locutus 705
iudicium superis aperit commune Philemon:
' esse sacerdotes delubraque vestra tueri
poscimus, et quoniam concordes egimus annos,
auferat hora duos eadem, nec coniugis umquam
busta meae videam, neu sim tumulandus ab illa.' 710
vota fides sequitur: templi tutela fuere,
donec vita data est; annis aevoque soluti
ante gradus sacros cum starent forte locique
narrarent casus, frondere Philemona Baucis,
Baucida conspexit senior frondere Philemon. 715
iamque super geminos crescente cacumine vultus
mutua, dum licuit, reddebant dicta ' vale ' que
  o coniunx ' dixere simul, simul abdita texit

to kill the goose. 'We are gods,' they said, 'and this wicked neighbourhood shall be punished as it deserves; but to you shall be given exemption from this punishment. Leave now your dwelling and come with us to that tall mountain yonder.' They both obeyed and, propped on their staves, they struggled up the long slope. When they were a bowshot distant from the top, they looked back and saw the whole country-side covered with water, only their own house remaining. And, while they wondered at this, while they wept for the fate of their neighbours, that old house of theirs, which had been small even for its two occupants, was changed into a temple. Marble columns took the place of the forked wooden supports; the straw grew yellow and became a golden roof; there were gates richly carved, a marble pavement covered the ground. Then calmly the son of Saturn spoke: 'Now ask of us, thou good old man, and thou wife, worthy of thy good husband, any boon you will.' When he had spoken a word with Baucis, Philemon announced their joint decision to the gods: 'We ask that we may be your priests, and guard your temple; and, since we have spent our lives in constant company, we pray that the same hour may bring death to both of us—that I may never see my wife's tomb, nor be buried by her.' Their request was granted. They had the care of the temple as long as they lived. And at last, when, spent with extreme old age, they chanced to stand before the sacred edifice talking of old times, Baucis saw Philemon putting forth leaves, Philemon saw Baucis; and as the tree-top formed over their two faces, while still they could they cried with the same words: 'Farewell, dear mate,' just as the bark closed over and hid

ora frutex: ostendit adhuc Thyneius illic
incola de gemino vicinos corpore truncos.   720
haec mihi non vani (neque erat, cur fallere vellent)
narravere senes; equidem pendentia vidi
serta super ramos ponensque recentia dixi
' cura deum di sint, et, qui coluere, colantur.'

Desierat, cunctosque et res et moverat auctor,   725
Thesea praecipue; quem facta audire volentem
mira deum innixus cubito Calydonius amnis
talibus adloquitur: " sunt, o fortissime, quorum
forma semel mota est et in hoc renovamine mansit;
sunt, quibus in plures ius est transire figuras,   730
ut tibi, conplexi terram maris incola, Proteu.
nam modo te iuvenem, modo te videre leonem,
nunc violentus aper, nunc, quem tetigisse timerent,
anguis eras, modo te faciebant cornua taurum;
saepe lapis poteras, arbor quoque saepe videri,   735
interdum, faciem liquidarum imitatus aquarum,
flumen eras, interdum undis contrarius ignis.

" Nec minus Autolyci coniunx, Erysicthone nata,
iuris habet: pater huius erat, qui numina divum
sperneret et nullos aris adoleret odores;   740
ille etiam Cereale nemus violasse securi
dicitur et lucos ferro temerasse vetustos.
stabat in his ingens annoso robore quercus,
una nemus; vittae mediam memoresque tabellae
sertaque cingebant, voti argumenta potentum.   745

456

their lips. Even to this day the Bithynian peasant in that region points out two trees standing close together, and growing from one double trunk. These things were told me by staid old men who could have had no reason to deceive. With my own eyes I saw votive wreaths hanging from the boughs, and placing fresh wreaths there myself, I said: 'Let those beloved of the gods be gods; let those who have worshipped be worshipped.'"

Lelex made an end: both the tale and the teller had moved them all; Theseus especially. When he would hear more of the wonderful doings of the gods, the Calydonian river-god, propped upon his elbow, thus addressed him: "Some there are, bravest of heroes, whose form has been once changed and remained in its new state. To others the power is given to assume many forms, as to thee, Proteus, dweller in the earth-embracing sea. For now men saw thee as a youth, now as a lion; now thou wast a raging boar, now a serpent whom men would fear to touch; now horns made thee a bull; often thou couldst appear as a stone, often, again, a tree; sometimes, assuming the form of flowing water, thou wast a stream, and sometimes a flame, the water's enemy.

"No less power had the wife of Autolycus, Erysichthon's daughter. This Erysichthon was a man who scorned the gods and burnt no sacrifice on their altars. He, so the story goes, once violated the sacred grove of Ceres with the axe and profaned those ancient trees with steel. There stood among these a mighty oak with strength matured by centuries of growth, itself a grove. Round about it hung woollen fillets, votive tablets, and wreaths of flowers, witnesses of granted prayers. Often beneath

OVID

saepe sub hac dryades festas duxere choreas,
saepe etiam manibus nexis ex ordine trunci
circuiere modum, mensuraque roboris ulnas
quinque ter inplebat, nec non et cetera tantum
silva sub hac, silva quantum fuit herba sub omni. 750
non tamen idcirco ferrum Triopeius illa
abstinuit famulosque iubet succidere sacrum
robur, et ut iussos cunctari vidit, ab uno
edidit haec rapta sceleratus verba securi:
' non dilecta deae solum, sed et ipsa licebit   755
sit dea, iam tanget frondente cacumine terram.'
dixit, et obliquos dum telum librat in ictus,
contremuit gemitumque dedit Deoia quercus,
et pariter frondes, pariter pallescere glandes
coepere ac longi pallorem ducere rami.   760
cuius ut in trunco fecit manus inpia vulnus,
haud aliter fluxit discusso cortice sanguis,
quam solet, ante aras ingens ubi victima taurus
concidit, abrupta cruor e cervice profundi.
obstipuere omnes, aliquisque ex omnibus audet
deterrere nefas saevamque inhibere bipennem: 766
aspicit hunc ' mentis' que ' piae cape praemia!' dixit
Thessalus inque virum convertit ab arbore ferrum
detruncatque caput repetitaque robora caedit,
redditus e medio sonus est cum robore talis: 770
' nympha sub hoc ego sum Cereri gratissima ligno,
quae tibi factorum poenas instare tuorum
vaticinor moriens, nostri solacia leti.'
persequitur scelus ille suum, labefactaque tandem
ictibus innumeris adductaque funibus arbor   775
corruit et multam prostravit pondere silvam.

this tree dryads held their festival dances; often
with hand linked to hand in line they would encircle
the great tree whose mighty girth was full fifteen
ells. It towered as high above other trees as they
were higher than the grass that grew beneath. Yet
not for this did Triopas' son [1] withhold his axe, as
he bade his slaves cut down the sacred oak. But
when he saw that they shrank back, the wretch
snatched an axe from one of them and said: ' Though
this be not only the tree that the goddess loves, but
even the goddess herself, now shall its leafy top touch
the ground.' He spoke; and while he poised his
axe for the slanting stroke, the oak of Deo [2] trembled
and gave forth a groan; at the same time its leaves
and its acorns grew pale, its long branches took on a
pallid hue. But when that impious stroke cut into
the trunk, blood came streaming forth from the
severed bark, even as when a huge sacrificial bull has
fallen at the altar, and from his smitten neck the
blood pours forth. All were astonied, and one,
bolder than the rest, tried to stop his wicked deed
and stay his cruel axe. But the Thessalian looked at
him and said: ' Take that to pay you for your pious
thought! ' and, turning the axe from the tree against
the man, lopped off his head. Then, as he struck
the oak blow after blow, from within the tree a voice
was heard: ' I, a nymph most dear to Ceres, dwell
within this wood, and I prophesy with my dying
breath, and find my death's solace in it, that punish-
ment is at hand for what you do.' But he accom-
plished his crime; and at length the tree, weakened
by countless blows and drawn down by ropes, fell and
with its weight laid low a wide stretch of woods
around.

[1] Erysichthon. [2] *i.e.* Ceres.

459

OVID

"Attonitae dryades damno nemorumque suoque,
omnes germanae, Cererem cum vestibus atris
maerentes adeunt poenamque Erysicthonis orant.
adnuit his capitisque sui pulcherrima motu   780
concussit gravidis oneratos messibus agros,
moliturque genus poenae miserabile, si non
ille suis esset nulli miserabilis actis,
pestifera lacerare Fame: quae quatenus ipsi
non adeunda deae est (neque enim Cereremque
          Famemque   785
fata coire sinunt), montani numinis unam
talibus agrestem conpellat oreada dictis:
' est locus extremis Scythiae glacialis in oris,
triste solum, sterilis, sine fruge, sine arbore tellus;
Frigus iners illic habitant Pallorque Tremorque   790
et ieiuna Fames: ea se in praecordia condat
sacrilegi scelerata, iube, nec copia rerum
vincat eam superetque meas certamine vires,
neve viae spatium te terreat, accipe currus,
accipe, quos frenis alte moderere, dracones!'   795
et dedit; illa dato subvecta per aera curru
devenit in Scythiam: rigidique cacumine montis
(Caucason appellant) serpentum colla levavit
quaesitamque Famem lapidoso vidit in agro
unguibus et raras vellentem dentibus herbas.   800
hirtus erat crinis, cava lumina, pallor in ore,
labra incana situ, scabrae rubigine fauces,
dura cutis, per quam spectari viscera possent;
ossa sub incurvis exstabant arida lumbis,
ventris erat pro ventre locus; pendere putares   805
pectus et a spinae tantummodo crate teneri.

" All the dryad sisters were stupefied at their own
and their forest's loss and, mourning, clad in
black robes, they went to Ceres and prayed her to
punish Erysichthon. The beautiful goddess con-
sented, and with a nod of her head shook the fields
heavy with ripening grain. She planned in her
mind a punishment that might make men pity (but
that no man could pity him for such deeds), to rack
him with dreadful Famine. But, since the goddess
herself could not go to her (for the fates do not
permit Ceres and Famine to come together), she
summoned one of the mountain deities, a rustic
oread, and thus addressed her: ' There is a place
on the farthest border of icy Scythia, a gloomy
and barren soil, a land without corn, without trees.
Sluggish Cold dwells there and Pallor, Fear, and
gaunt Famine. So, bid Famine hide herself in the
sinful stomach of that impious wretch. Let no
abundance satisfy her, and let her overcome my
utmost power to feed. And, that the vast journey
may not daunt you, take my chariot and my winged
dragons and guide them aloft.' And she gave the
reins into her hands. The nymph, borne through
the air in her borrowed chariot, came to Scythia, and
on a bleak mountain-top which men call Caucasus,
unyoked her dragon steeds. Seeking out Famine, she
saw her in a stony field, plucking with nails and
teeth at the scanty herbage. Her hair hung in matted
locks, her eyes were sunken, her face ghastly pale; her
lips were wan and foul, her throat rough with scurf;
her skin was hard and dry so that the entrails could
be seen through it; her skinny hip-bones bulged
out beneath her hollow loins, and her belly was but
a belly's place; her breast seemed to be hanging free
and just to be held by the framework of the spine;

auxerat articulos macies, genuumque tumebat
orbis, et inmodico prodibant tubere tali.
   " Hanc procul ut vidit, (neque enim est accedere
      iuxta
ausa) refert mandata deae paulumque morata,   810
quamquam aberat longe, quamquam modo venerat
      illuc,
visa tamen sensisse famem est, retroque dracones
egit in Haemoniam versis sublimis habenis.
   " Dicta Fames Cereris, quamvis contraria semper
illius est operi, peragit perque aera vento   815
ad iussam delata domum est, et protinus intrat
sacrilegi thalamos altoque sopore solutum
(noctis enim tempus) geminis amplectitur ulnis,
seque viro inspirat, faucesque et pectus et ora
adflat et in vacuis spargit ieiunia venis;   820
functaque mandato fecundum deserit orbem
inque domos inopes adsueta revertitur antra.
   " Lenis adhuc Somnus placidis Erysicthona pennis
mulcebat: petit ille dapes sub imagine somni,
oraque vana movet dentemque in dente fatigat, 825
exercetque cibo delusum guttur inani
proque epulis tenues nequiquam devorat auras;
ut vero est expulsa quies, furit ardor edendi
perque avidas fauces incensaque viscera regnat.
nec mora; quod pontus, quod terra, quod educat aer,
poscit et adpositis queritur ieiunia mensis   831
inque epulis epulas quaerit; quodque urbibus esse,
quodque satis poterat populo, non sufficit uni,
plusque cupit, quo plura suam demittit in alvum.
utque fretum recipit de tota flumina terra   835

her thinness made her joints seem large, her knees were swollen, and her ankles were great bulging lumps.

"When the nymph saw her in the distance (for she did not dare approach her), she delivered to her the goddess' commands. And, though she tarried but a little while, though she kept far from her and had but now arrived, still she seemed to feel the famine. Then, mounting high in air, she turned her course and drove the dragons back to Thessaly.

"Famine did the bidding of Ceres, although their tasks are ever opposite, and flew through the air on the wings of the wind to the appointed mansion. Straight she entered the chamber of the impious king, who was sunk in deep slumber (for it was night); there she wrapped her skinny arms about him and filled him with herself, breathing upon his throat and breast and lips; and in his hollow veins she planted hunger. When her duty was done, she left the fertile world, and returned to the homes of want and her familiar caverns.

"Still gentle Sleep, hovering on peaceful wings, soothes Erysichthon. And in his sleep he dreams of feasting, champs his jaws on nothing, wearies tooth upon tooth, cheats his gullet with fancied food; for his banquet is nothing but empty air. But when he awakes, a wild craving for food lords it in his ravenous jaws and in his burning stomach. Straightway he calls for all that sea and land and air can furnish; with loaded tables before him, he complains still of hunger; in the midst of feasts seeks other feasts. What would be enough for whole cities, enough for a whole nation, is not enough for one. The more he sends down into his maw the more he wants. And as the ocean receives the streams from a whole land

nec satiatur aquis peregrinosque ebibit amnes,
utque rapax ignis non umquam alimenta recusat
innumerasque trabes cremat et, quo copia maior
est data, plura petit turbaque voracior ipsa est:
sic epulas omnes Erysicthonis ora profani   840
accipiunt poscuntque simul. cibus omnis in illo
causa cibi est, semperque locus fit inanis edendo.
  " Iamque fame patrias altique voragine ventris
attenuarat opes, sed inattenuata manebat
tum quoque dira fames, inplacataeque vigebat   845
flamma gulae.   tandem, demisso in viscera censu,
filia restabat, non illo digna parente.
hanc quoque vendit inops: dominum generosa recusat
et vicina suas tendens super aequora palmas
' eripe me domino, qui raptae praemia nobis   850
virginitatis habes! ' ait: haec Neptunus habebat;
qui prece non spreta, quamvis modo visa sequenti
esset ero, formamque novat vultumque virilem
induit et cultus piscem capientibus aptos.
hanc dominus spectans ' o qui pendentia parvo   855
aera cibo celas, moderator harundinis,' inquit
' sic mare conpositum, sic sit tibi piscis in unda
credulus et nullos, nisi fixus, sentiat hamos:
quae modo cum vili turbatis veste capillis   859
litore in hoc steterat (nam stantem in litore vidi),
dic, ubi sit: neque enim vestigia longius exstant.'
illa dei munus bene cedere sensit et a se
se quaeri gaudens his est resecuta rogantem:
' quisquis es, ignoscas; in nullam lumina partem

464

and is not filled with his waters, but swallows up the streams that come to it from afar; and as the all-devouring fire never refuses fuel, but burns countless logs, seeks ever more as more is given it, and is more greedy by reason of the quantity: so do the lips of impious Erysichthon receive all those banquets, and ask for more. All food in him is but the cause of food, and ever does he become empty by eating.

"And now famine and his belly's deep abyss had exhausted his ancestral stores; but even then ravenous Famine remained unexhausted and his raging greed was still unappeased. At last, when all his fortunes had been swallowed up, there remained only his daughter, worthy of a better father. Penniless, he sold even her. The high-spirited girl refused a master, and stretching out her hands over the neighbouring waves, she cried: 'Save me from slavery, O thou who hast already stolen my virginity.' This Neptune had taken; he did not refuse her prayer; and though her master following her had seen her but now, the god changed her form, gave her the features of a man and garments proper to a fisherman. Her master, looking at this person, said: 'Ho, you who conceal the dangling hook in a little bait, you that handle the rod; so may the sea be calm, so be the fish trustful in the wave for your catching, and feel no hook until you strike: where is she, tell me, who but now stood on this shore with mean garments and disordered hair, for I saw her standing upon the shore, and her tracks go no farther!' She perceived by this that the god's gift was working well, and, delighted that one asked her of herself, answered his question in these words: 'Whoever you are, excuse me, sir; I have not taken my eyes from this pool to look in any direction. I

gurgite ab hoc flexi studioque operatus inhaesi,   865
quoque minus dubites, sic has deus aequoris artes
adiuvet, ut nemo iamdudum litore in isto,
me tamen excepto, nec femina constitit ulla.'
credidit et verso dominus pede pressit harenam
elususque abiit : illi sua reddita forma est.   870
ast ubi habere suam transformia corpora sensit,
saepe pater dominis Triopeida tradit, at illa
nunc equa, nunc ales, modo bos, modo cervus abibat
praebebatque avido non iusta alimenta parenti.
vis tamen illa mali postquam consumpserat omnem
materiam derantque gravi nova pabula morbo,   876
ipse suos artus lacerans divellere morsu
coepit et infelix minuendo corpus alebat.—
  " Quid moror externis ? etiam mihi nempe novandi
    est
corporis, o iuvenis, numero finita, potestas.   880
nam modo, qui nunc sum, videor, modo flector in
    anguem,
armenti modo dux vires in cornua sumo,—
cornua, dum potui. nunc pars caret altera telo
frontis, ut ipse vides." gemitus sunt verba secuti.

have been altogether bent on my fishing. And that you may believe me, so may the god of the sea assist this art of mine, as it is true that for a long time back no man has stood upon this shore except myself, and no woman, either.' Her master believed, and turning upon the sands, he left the spot, completely deceived. Then her former shape was given back to her. But when her father perceived that his daughter had the power to change her form, he sold her often and to many masters. But now in the form of a mare, now bird, now cow, now deer, away she went, and so found food, though not fairly, for her greedy father. At last, when the strength of the plague had consumed all these provisions, and his grievous malady needed more food, the wretched man began to tear his limbs and rend them apart with his teeth and, by consuming his own body, fed himself.

" But why do I dwell on tales of others? I myself, young sirs, have often changed my form; but my power is limited in its range. For sometimes I appear as you see me now; sometimes I change to a serpent; again I am leader of a herd and put my strength into my horns—horns, I say, so long as I could. But now one of the weapons of my forehead is gone, as you yourself can see." He ended with a groan.